PRAISE FOR THE #1 *NEW YORK TIMES* AND *USA TODAY* BESTSELLING
THRONE OF GLASS SERIES

THE ASSASSIN'S BLADE

"Action-packed . . . What a ride!" —*BOOKLIST*

THRONE OF GLASS

"A thrilling read." —*PUBLISHERS WEEKLY*, STARRED REVIEW

CROWN OF MIDNIGHT

"An epic fantasy readers will immerse themselves in
and never want to leave." —*KIRKUS REVIEWS*, STARRED REVIEW

HEIR OF FIRE

"Celaena is as much an epic hero as Frodo or Jon Snow!"
—*NEW YORK TIMES* BESTSELLING AUTHOR TAMORA PIERCE

QUEEN OF SHADOWS

"Packed . . . with brooding glances, simmering sexual tension, twisty plot
turns, lush world building, and snarky banter." —*BOOKLIST*

EMPIRE OF STORMS

"Tightly plotted, delightful escapism." —*KIRKUS REVIEWS*

TOWER OF DAWN

"Turns a corner from
psychological fa

KINGDO

"A worthy finale to one o

BOOKS BY SARAH J. MAAS

THE THRONE OF GLASS SERIES

The Assassin's Blade
Throne of Glass
Crown of Midnight
Heir of Fire
Queen of Shadows
Empire of Storms
Tower of Dawn
Kingdom of Ash

•

The Throne of Glass Colouring Book

THE COURT OF THORNS AND ROSES SERIES

A Court of Thorns and Roses
A Court of Mist and Fury
A Court of Wings and Ruin
A Court of Frost and Starlight
A Court of Silver Flames

•

A Court of Thorns and Roses Colouring Book

THE CRESCENT CITY SERIES

House of Earth and Blood
House of Sky and Breath

SARAH J. MAAS

THRONE OF GLASS

BLOOMSBURY PUBLISHING
LONDON • OXFORD • NEW YORK • NEW DELHI • SYDNEY

BLOOMSBURY PUBLISHING
Bloomsbury Publishing Plc
50 Bedford Square, London WC1B 3DP, UK
29 Earlsfort Terrace, Dublin 2, Ireland

BLOOMSBURY, BLOOMSBURY PUBLISHING and the Diana logo are trademarks of Bloomsbury Publishing Plc

First published in Great Britain 2012
This edition published 2023

Map by Virginia Allyn

A catalogue record for this book is available from the British Library

ISBN: PB: 978-1-5266-3529-7; HB: 978-1-6397-3094-0;
eBook: 978-1-4088-3234-9; ePDF: 978-1-5266-3445-0

2 4 6 8 10 9 7 5 3 1

Typeset by Westchester Publishing Services
Printed and bound in Great Britain by CPI Group (UK) Ltd, Croydon CR0 4YY

To find out more about our authors and books visit www.bloomsbury.com and sign up for our newsletters, including news about Sarah J. Maas.

To all my readers from FictionPress—
for being with me at the beginning and staying long after the end.
Thank you for everything.

Erilea
N
Amaroth
The Frozen Wastes
Ruins of Morla
Jungle of Morla
The Western Wastes
Briarcliff
The Witch Kingdom
Bogdano Jungle
The Deserted Land
The Singing Sands
The Red Desert
Yurpa
Gulf of Oro
Oasis of Barg
Silent Assassins
Roll
Xandria
The Cleaver
The Black Dunes
Volcano Flows
The Black Sands of Roth

Terrasen
North Sea
Wolf Tribe
Staghorn Mountains
Allsbrook
Rosamel
Orynth
Suria
Perranth Mountains
Florine River
Anascaul Mountains
Eldrys
Perranth
Ilium
Ruhnn Mountains
Endovier Salt Mines
Meah
Adarlan
The Omega
Oakwald Forest
Great Ocean
The Ferian Gap
The Northern Fang
Mountains of Ararat
The Silver Lake
Rifthold
White Fang Mountains
Anielle
Avery River
To Wendlyn
Acanthus River
Fenharrow
Morath
Bellhaven
Melisande
Dead Islands
nnish
Skull's Bay
The Dead End
Calaculla
Eyllwe
Leriba
Grasslands of Eyllwe
Banjali
Stone Marshes
To the Southern Continent
The Narrow Sea

1

After a year of slavery in the Salt Mines of Endovier, Celaena Sardothien was accustomed to being escorted everywhere in shackles and at sword-point. Most of the thousands of slaves in Endovier received similar treatment—though an extra half-dozen guards always walked Celaena to and from the mines. That was expected by Adarlan's most notorious assassin. What she did not usually expect, however, was a hooded man in black at her side—as there was now.

He gripped her arm as he led her through the shining building in which most of Endovier's officials and overseers were housed. They strode down corridors, up flights of stairs, and around and around until she hadn't the slightest chance of finding her way out again.

At least, that was her escort's intention, because she hadn't failed to notice when they went up and down the same staircase within a matter of minutes. Nor had she missed when they zigzagged between levels, even though the building was a standard grid of hallways and stairwells.

As if she'd lose her bearings that easily. She might have been insulted if he wasn't trying so hard.

They entered a particularly long hallway, silent save for their footsteps. Though the man grasping her arm was tall and fit, she could see nothing of the features concealed beneath his hood. Another tactic meant to confuse and intimidate her. The black clothes were probably a part of it, too. His head shifted in her direction, and Celaena flashed him a grin. He looked forward again, his iron grip tightening.

It was flattering, she supposed, even if she *didn't* know what was happening, or why he'd been waiting for her outside the mine shaft. After a day of cleaving rock salt from the innards of the mountain, finding him standing there with six guards hadn't improved her mood.

But her ears had pricked when he'd introduced himself to her overseer as Chaol Westfall, Captain of the Royal Guard, and suddenly, the sky loomed, the mountains pushed from behind, and even the earth swelled toward her knees. She hadn't tasted fear in a while—hadn't *let* herself taste fear. When she awoke every morning, she repeated the same words: *I will not be afraid.* For a year, those words had meant the difference between breaking and bending; they had kept her from shattering in the darkness of the mines. Not that she'd let the captain know any of that.

Celaena examined the gloved hand holding her arm. The dark leather almost matched the dirt on her skin.

She adjusted her torn and filthy tunic with her free hand and held in her sigh. Entering the mines before sunrise and departing after dusk, she rarely glimpsed the sun. She was frightfully pale beneath the dirt. It was true that she had been attractive once, beautiful even, but—well, it didn't matter now, did it?

They turned down another hallway, and she studied the stranger's finely crafted sword. Its shimmering pommel was shaped like an eagle midflight. Noticing her stare, his gloved hand descended to rest upon its golden head. Another smile tugged at the corners of her lips.

"You're a long way from Rifthold, Captain," she said, clearing her throat. "Did you come with the army I heard thumping around earlier?" She peered into the darkness beneath his hood but saw nothing. Still, she felt his eyes upon her face, judging, weighing, testing. She stared right back. The Captain of the Royal Guard would be an interesting opponent. Maybe even worthy of some effort on her part.

Finally, the man raised his sword hand, and the folds of his cloak fell to conceal the blade. As his cloak shifted, she spied the gold wyvern embroidered on his tunic. The royal seal.

"What do you care for the armies of Adarlan?" he replied. How lovely it was to hear a voice like her own—cool and articulate—even if he was a nasty brute!

"Nothing," she said, shrugging. He let out a low growl of annoyance.

Oh, it'd be nice to see his blood spill across the marble. She'd lost her temper once before—once, when her first overseer chose the wrong day to push her too hard. She still remembered the feeling of embedding the pickax into his gut, and the stickiness of his blood on her hands and face. She could disarm two of these guards in a heartbeat. Would the captain fare better than her late overseer? Contemplating the potential outcomes, she grinned at him again.

"Don't you look at me like that," he warned, and his hand drifted back toward his sword. Celaena hid her smirk this time. They passed a series of wooden doors that she'd seen a few minutes ago. If she wanted to escape, she simply had to turn left at the next hallway and take the stairs down three flights. The only thing all the intended disorientation had accomplished was to familiarize her with the building. Idiots.

"Where are we going again?" she said sweetly, brushing a strand of her matted hair from her face. When he didn't reply, she clenched her jaw.

The halls echoed too loudly for her to attack him without alerting the whole building. She hadn't seen where he'd put the key to her irons, and the six guards who trailed them would be nuisances. Not to mention the shackles.

They entered a hallway hung with iron chandeliers. Outside the windows lining the wall, night had fallen; lanterns kindled so bright they offered few shadows to hide in.

From the courtyard, she could hear the other slaves shuffling toward the wooden building where they slept. The moans of agony amongst the clank of chains made a chorus as familiar as the dreary work songs they sang all day. The occasional solo of the whip added to the symphony of brutality Adarlan had created for its greatest criminals, poorest citizens, and latest conquests.

While some of the prisoners were people accused of attempting to practice magic—not that they *could*, given that magic had vanished from the kingdom—these days, more and more rebels arrived at Endovier. Most were from Eyllwe, one of the last countries still fighting Adarlan's rule. But when she pestered them for news, many just stared at her with empty eyes. Already broken. She shuddered to consider what they'd endured at the hands of Adarlan's forces. Some days, she wondered if they would have been better off dying on the butchering blocks instead. And if she might have been better off dying that night she'd been betrayed and captured, too.

But she had other things to think about as they continued their walk. Was she finally to be hanged? Sickness coiled in her stomach. She *was* important enough to warrant an execution from the Captain of the Royal Guard himself. But why bring her inside this building first?

At last, they stopped before a set of red-and-gold glass doors so thick that she couldn't see through them. Captain Westfall jerked his chin at the two guards standing on either side of the doors, and they stomped their spears in greeting.

The captain's grip tightened until it hurt. He yanked Celaena closer, but her feet seemed made of lead and she pulled against him. "You'd rather stay in the mines?" he asked, sounding faintly amused.

"Perhaps if I were told what this was all about, I wouldn't feel so inclined to resist."

"You'll find out soon enough." Her palms became sweaty. Yes, she was going to die. It had come at last.

The doors groaned open to reveal a throne room. A glass chandelier shaped like a grapevine occupied most of the ceiling, spitting seeds of diamond fire onto the windows along the far side of the room. Compared to the bleakness outside those windows, the opulence felt like a slap to the face. A reminder of how much they profited from her labor.

"In here," the Captain of the Guard growled, and shoved her with his free hand, finally releasing her. Celaena stumbled, her calloused feet slipping on the smooth floor as she straightened herself. She looked back to see another six guards appear.

Fourteen guards, plus the captain. The gold royal emblem embroidered on the breast of black uniforms. These were members of the Royal Family's personal guard: ruthless, lightning-swift soldiers trained from birth to protect and kill. She swallowed tightly.

Lightheaded and immensely heavy all at once, Celaena faced the room. On an ornate redwood throne sat a handsome young man. Her heart stopped as everyone bowed.

She was standing in front of the Crown Prince of Adarlan.

2

"Your Highness," said the Captain of the Guard. He straightened from a low bow and removed his hood, revealing close-cropped chestnut hair. The hood had definitely been meant to intimidate her into submission during their walk. As if that sort of trick could work on *her.* Despite her irritation, she blinked at the sight of his face. He was so young!

Captain Westfall was not excessively handsome, but she couldn't help finding the ruggedness of his face and the clarity of his golden-brown eyes rather appealing. She cocked her head, now keenly aware of her wretched dirtiness.

"This is she?" the Crown Prince of Adarlan asked, and Celaena's head whipped around as the captain nodded. Both of them stared at her, waiting for her to bow. When she remained upright, Chaol shifted on his feet, and the prince glanced at his captain before lifting his chin a bit higher.

Bow to him indeed! If she were bound for the gallows, she would most certainly *not* spend the last moments of her life in groveling submission.

Thundering steps issued from behind her, and someone grabbed her by the neck. Celaena only glimpsed crimson cheeks and a sandy mustache before being thrown to the icy marble floor. Pain slammed through her face, light splintering her vision. Her arms ached as her bound hands kept her joints from properly aligning. Though she tried to stop them, tears of pain welled.

"*That* is the proper way to greet your future king," a red-faced man snapped at Celaena.

The assassin hissed, baring her teeth as she twisted her head to look at the kneeling bastard. He was almost as large as her overseer, clothed in reds and oranges that matched his thinning hair. His obsidian eyes glittered as his grip tightened on her neck. If she could move her right arm just a few inches, she could throw him off balance and grab his sword . . . The shackles dug into her stomach, and fizzing, boiling rage turned her face scarlet.

After a too-long moment, the Crown Prince spoke. "I don't quite comprehend why you'd force someone to bow when the purpose of the gesture is to display allegiance and respect." His words were coated with glorious boredom.

Celaena tried to pivot a free eye to the prince, but could only see a pair of black leather boots against the white floor.

"It's clear that *you* respect me, Duke Perrington, but it's a bit unnecessary to put such effort into forcing *Celaena Sardothien* to have the same opinion. You and I know very well she has no love for my family. So perhaps your intent is to humiliate her." He paused, and she could have sworn his eyes fell on her face. "But I think she's had enough of that." He stopped for another moment, then asked: "Don't you have a meeting with Endovier's treasurer? I wouldn't want you to be late, especially when you came all this way to meet with him."

Understanding the dismissal, her tormentor grunted and released her. Celaena peeled her cheek from the marble but lay on the floor until he stood and left. If she managed to escape, perhaps she'd hunt down this Duke Perrington fellow and return the warmth of his greeting.

As she rose, she frowned at the imprint of grit she left behind on the otherwise spotless floor, and at the clank of her shackles echoing through the silent room. But she'd been trained to be an assassin since the age of eight, since the day the King of the Assassins found her half-dead on the banks of a frozen river and brought her to his keep. She wouldn't be humiliated by anything, least of all being dirty. Gathering her pride, she tossed her long braid behind a shoulder and lifted her head. Her eyes met those of the prince.

Dorian Havilliard smiled at her. It was a polished smile, and reeked of court-trained charm. Sprawled across the throne, he had his chin propped by a hand, his golden crown glinting in the soft light. On his black doublet, an emblazoned gold rendering of the royal wyvern occupied the entirety of the chest. His red cloak fell gracefully around him and his throne.

Yet there was something in his eyes, strikingly blue—the color of the waters of the southern countries—and the way they contrasted with his raven-black hair that made her pause. He was achingly handsome, and couldn't have been older than twenty.

Princes are not supposed to be handsome! They're sniveling, stupid, repulsive creatures! This one . . . this . . . How unfair of him to be royal and *beautiful.*

She shifted on her feet as he frowned, surveying her in turn. "I thought I asked you to clean her," he said to Captain Westfall, who stepped forward. She'd forgotten there was anyone else in the room. She looked at her rags and stained skin, and she couldn't suppress the twinge of shame. What a miserable state for a girl of former beauty!

At a passing glance, one might think her eyes blue or gray, perhaps even green, depending on the color of her clothing. Up close, though, these warring hues were offset by the brilliant ring of gold around her pupils. But it was her golden hair that caught the attention of most, hair that still maintained a glimmer of its glory. In short, Celaena Sardothien was blessed with a handful of attractive features that compensated for the majority of average ones; and, by early adolescence, she'd discovered that with the help of cosmetics, these average features could easily match the extraordinary assets.

But now, standing before Dorian Havilliard as little more than a gutter rat! Her face warmed as Captain Westfall spoke. "I didn't want to keep you waiting."

The Crown Prince shook his head when Chaol reached for her. "Don't bother with the bath just yet. I can see her potential." The prince straightened, keeping his attention on Celaena. "I don't believe that we've ever had the pleasure of an introduction. But, as you probably know, I'm Dorian Havilliard, Crown Prince of Adarlan, perhaps now Crown Prince of most of Erilea."

She ignored the surge and crash of bitter emotions that awoke with the name.

"And *you're* Celaena Sardothien, Adarlan's greatest assassin. Perhaps the greatest assassin in all of Erilea." He studied her tensed body before he raised his dark, well-groomed brows. "You seem a little young." He rested his elbows on his thighs. "I've heard some rather fascinating stories about you. How do you find Endovier after living in such excess in Rifthold?"

Arrogant ass.

"I couldn't be happier," she crooned as her jagged nails cut into her palms.

"After a year, you seem to be more or less alive. I wonder how that's possible when the average life expectancy in these mines is a month."

"Quite a mystery, I'm sure." She batted her eyelashes and readjusted her shackles as if they were lace gloves.

The Crown Prince turned to his captain. "She has somewhat of a tongue, doesn't she? And she doesn't sound like a member of the rabble."

"I should hope not!" Celaena interjected.

"Your Highness," Chaol Westfall snapped at her.

"What?" Celaena asked.

"You will address him as 'Your Highness.'"

Celaena gave him a mocking smile, and then returned her attention to the prince.

Dorian Havilliard, to her surprise, laughed. "You do *know* that you're now a slave, don't you? Has your sentence taught you nothing?"

Had her arms been unshackled, she would have crossed them. "I don't see how working in a mine can teach anything beyond how to use a pickax."

"And you never tried to escape?"

A slow, wicked smile spread across her lips. "Once."

The prince's brows rose, and he turned to Captain Westfall. "I wasn't told that."

Celaena glanced over her shoulder at Chaol, who gave his prince an apologetic look. "The Chief Overseer informed me this afternoon that there was *one* incident. Three months—"

"Four months," she interrupted.

"Four months," Chaol said, "after Sardothien arrived, she attempted to flee."

She waited for the rest of the story, but he was clearly finished. "That's not even the best part!"

"There's a 'best part'?" the Crown Prince said, face caught between a wince and a smile.

Chaol glared at her before speaking. "There's no hope of escaping from Endovier. Your father made sure that each of Endovier's sentries could shoot a squirrel from two hundred paces away. To attempt to flee is suicide."

"But you're alive," the prince said to her.

Celaena's smile faded as the memory struck her. "Yes."

"What happened?" Dorian asked.

Her eyes turned cold and hard. "I snapped."

"That's all you have to offer as an explanation for what you did?" Captain Westfall demanded. "She killed her overseer and twenty-three sentries before they caught her. She was a *finger's tip* from the wall before the guards knocked her unconscious."

"So?" Dorian said.

Celaena seethed. "So? Do you know how far the wall is from the mines?" He gave her a blank look. She closed her eyes and sighed dramatically. "From my shaft, it was three hundred sixty-three feet. I had someone measure."

"So?" Dorian repeated.

"Captain Westfall, how far do slaves make it from the mines when they try to escape?"

"Three feet," he muttered. "Endovier sentries usually shoot a man down before he's moved three feet."

The Crown Prince's silence was not her desired effect. "You knew it was suicide," he said at last, the amusement gone.

Perhaps it had been a bad idea for her to bring up the wall. "Yes," she said.

"But they didn't kill you."

"Your father ordered that I was to be kept alive for as long as possible—to endure the misery that Endovier gives in abundance." A chill that had nothing to do with the temperature went through her. "I never intended to escape." The pity in his eyes made her want to hit him.

"Do you bear many scars?" asked the prince. She shrugged and he smiled, forcing the mood to lift as he stepped from the dais. "Turn around, and let me view your back." Celaena frowned, but obeyed as he walked to her, Chaol stepping closer. "I can't make them out clearly through all this dirt," the prince said, inspecting what skin showed through the scraps of her shirt. She scowled, and scowled even more when he said, "And what a terrible stench, too!"

"When one doesn't have access to a bath and perfume, I suppose one cannot smell as finely as you, *Your Highness*."

The Crown Prince clicked his tongue and circled her slowly. Chaol—and all the guards—watched them with hands on their swords. As they should. In less than a second, she could get her arms over the prince's head and have her shackles crushing his windpipe. It might be worth it just to see the expression on Chaol's face. But the prince went on, oblivious to how dangerously close he stood to her. Perhaps she should be insulted. "From what I can see," he said, "there are three large scars—and perhaps some smaller ones. Not as awful as I expected, but . . . well, the dresses can cover it, I suppose."

"Dresses?" He was standing so near that she could see the fine thread detail on his jacket, and smelled not perfume, but horses and iron.

Dorian grinned. "What remarkable eyes you have! And how angry you are!"

Coming within strangling distance of the Crown Prince of Adarlan, son of the man who sentenced her to a slow, miserable death, her self-control balanced on a fragile edge—dancing along a cliff.

"I demand to know," she began, but the Captain of the Guard pulled her back from the prince with spine-snapping force. "I wasn't going to kill him, you buffoon."

"Watch your mouth before I throw you back in the mines," the brown-eyed captain said.

"Oh, I don't think you'd do that."

"And why is that?" Chaol replied.

Dorian strode to his throne and sat down, his sapphire eyes bright.

She looked from one man to another and squared her shoulders. "Because there's something you want from me, something you want badly enough to come here yourselves. I'm not an idiot, though I was foolish enough to be captured, and I can see that this is some sort of secret business. Why else would you leave the capital and venture this far? You've been testing me all this time to see if I am physically and mentally sound. Well, I know that I'm still sane, and that I'm not broken, despite what the incident at the wall might suggest. So I demand to be told why you're here, and what services you wish of me, if I'm not destined for the gallows."

The men exchanged glances. Dorian steepled his fingers. "I have a proposition for you."

Her chest tightened. Never, not in her most fanciful dreams, had she imagined that the opportunity to speak with Dorian Havilliard would arise. She could kill him so easily, tear that grin from his face . . . She could destroy the king as he had destroyed her . . .

But perhaps his proposition could lead to escape. If she got beyond the wall, she could make it. Run and run and disappear into the mountains and live in solitude in the dark green of the wild, with a pine-needle carpet and a blanket of stars overhead. She could do it. She just needed to clear the wall. She had come so close before . . .

"I'm listening," was all she said.

3

The prince's eyes shone with amusement at her brashness but lingered a bit too long on her body. Celaena could have raked her nails down his face for staring at her like that, yet the fact that he'd even bother to *look* when she was in such a filthy state . . . A slow smile spread across her face.

The prince crossed his long legs. "Leave us," he ordered the guards. "Chaol, stay where you are."

Celaena stepped closer as the guards shuffled out, shutting the door. Foolish, foolish move. But Chaol's face remained unreadable. He couldn't honestly believe he'd contain her if she tried to escape! She straightened her spine. What were they planning that would make them so irresponsible?

The prince chuckled. "Don't you think it's risky to be so bold with me when your freedom is on the line?"

Of all the things he could have said, *that* was what she had least expected. "My freedom?" At the sound of the word, she saw a land of pine and snow, of sun-bleached cliffs and white-capped seas, a land where light was swallowed in the velvety green of bumps and hollows—a land that she had forgotten.

"Yes, your freedom. So, I highly suggest, *Miss* Sardothien, that you get your arrogance in check before you end up back in the mines." The prince uncrossed his legs. "Though perhaps your attitude will be useful. I'm not going to pretend that my father's empire was built on trust and understanding. But you already know that." Her fingers curled as she waited for him to continue. His eyes met hers, probing, intent. "My father has gotten it into his head that he needs a Champion."

It took a delicious moment for her to understand.

Celaena tipped back her head and laughed. "Your father wants *me* to be his Champion? What—don't tell me that he's managed to eliminate every noble soul out there! Surely there's *one* chivalrous knight, one lord of steadfast heart and courage."

"Mind your mouth," Chaol warned from beside her.

"What about you, hmm?" she said, raising her brows at the captain. Oh, it was too funny! *Her*—the King's Champion! "Our beloved king finds you lacking?"

The captain put a hand on his sword. "If you'd be quiet, you'd hear the rest of what His Highness has to tell you."

She faced the prince. "Well?"

Dorian leaned back in his throne. "My father needs someone to aid the empire—someone to help him maneuver around difficult people."

"You mean he needs a lackey for his dirty work."

"If you want to put it that bluntly, then, yes," the prince said. "His *Champion* would keep his opponents quiet."

"As quiet as the grave," she said sweetly.

A smile tugged on Dorian's lips, but he kept his face straight. "Yes."

To work for the King of Adarlan as his loyal servant. She raised her chin. To kill *for* him—to be a fang in the mouth of the beast that had already consumed half of Erilea . . . "And if I accept?"

"Then, after six years, he'll grant you your freedom."

"Six years!" But the word "freedom" echoed through her once more.

"If you decline," Dorian said, anticipating her next question, "you'll remain in Endovier." His sapphire eyes became hard, and she swallowed. *And die here* was what he didn't need to add.

Six years as the king's crooked dagger . . . or a lifetime in Endovier.

"However," the prince said, "there's a catch." She kept her face neutral as he toyed with a ring on his finger. "The position isn't being offered to you. Yet. My father thought to have a bit of fun. He's hosting a competition. He invited twenty-three members of his council to each sponsor a would-be Champion to train in the glass castle and ultimately compete in a duel. Were you to win," he said with a half smile, "you'd *officially* be Adarlan's Assassin."

She didn't return his smile. "Who, exactly, are my competitors?"

Seeing her expression, the prince's grin faded. "Thieves and assassins and warriors from across Erilea." She opened her mouth, but he cut her off. "If you win, and prove yourself both skilled and trustworthy, my father has *sworn* to grant you your freedom. *And*, while you're his Champion, you'll receive a considerable salary."

She barely heard his last few words. A competition! Against some nobody men from the-gods-knew-where! And assassins! "What other assassins?" she demanded.

"None that I've heard of. None as famous as *you*. And that reminds me—you won't be competing as Celaena Sardothien."

"What?"

"You'll compete under an alias. I don't suppose you heard about what happened after your trial."

"News is rather hard to come by when you're slaving in a mine."

Dorian chuckled, shaking his head. "No one knows that Celaena

Sardothien is just a young woman—they all thought you were far older."

"What?" she asked again, her face flushing. "How is that possible?" She should be proud that she'd kept it hidden from most of the world, but . . .

"You kept your identity a secret all the years you were running around killing everyone. After your trial, my father thought it would be . . . wise not to inform Erilea who you are. He wants to keep it that way. What would our enemies say if they knew we'd all been petrified of a girl?"

"So I'm slaving in this miserable place for a name and title that don't even belong to me? Who does everyone *think* Adarlan's Assassin really is?"

"I don't know, nor do I entirely care. But I *do* know that you were the best, and that people still whisper when they mention your name." He fixed her with a stare. "If you're willing to fight for me, to be *my* Champion during the months the competition will go on, I'll see to it that my father frees you after *five* years."

Though he tried to conceal it, she could see the tension in his body. He wanted her to say yes. Needed her to say yes so badly he was willing to bargain with her. Her eyes began glittering. "What do you mean, '*were* the best'?"

"You've been in Endovier for a year. Who knows what you're still capable of?"

"I'm capable of quite a lot, thank you," she said, picking at her jagged nails. She tried not to cringe at all the dirt beneath them. When was the last time her hands had been clean?

"That remains to be seen," Dorian said. "You'll be told the details of the competition when we arrive in Rifthold."

"Despite the amount of *fun* you nobles will have betting on us, this competition seems unnecessary. Why not just hire me already?"

"As I just said, you must prove yourself worthy."

She put a hand on her hip, and her chains rattled loudly through the room. "Well, I think being Adarlan's Assassin exceeds any sort of proof you might need."

"Yes," Chaol said, his bronze eyes flashing. "It proves that you're a criminal, and that we shouldn't immediately trust you with the king's private business."

"I give my solemn oa—"

"I doubt that the king would take the word of *Adarlan's Assassin* as bond."

"Yes, but I don't see why I have to go through the training and the competition. I mean, I'm bound to be a bit . . . out of shape, but . . . what else do you expect when I have to make do with rocks and pickaxes in this place?" She gave Chaol a spiteful glance.

Dorian frowned. "So, you won't take the offer?"

"Of course I'm going to take the offer," she snapped. Her wrists chafed against her shackles badly enough that her eyes watered. "I'll be your absurd Champion if you agree to free me in three years, not five."

"Four."

"Fine," she said. "It's a bargain. I might be trading one form of slavery for another, but I'm not a fool."

She could win back her freedom. *Freedom.* She felt the cold air of the wide-open world, the breeze that swept from the mountains and carried her away. She could live far from Rifthold, the capital that had once been her realm.

"Hopefully you're right," Dorian replied. "And hopefully, you'll live up to your reputation. I anticipate winning, and I won't be pleased if you make me look foolish."

"And what if I lose?"

The gleam vanished from his eyes as he said: "You'll be sent back here, to serve out the remainder of your sentence."

Celaena's lovely visions exploded like dust from a slammed book. "Then I might as well leap from the window. A year in this place has worn me through—imagine what will happen if I return. I'd be dead by my second year." She tossed her head. "Your offer seems fair enough."

"Fair enough indeed," Dorian said, and waved a hand at Chaol. "Take her to her rooms and clean her up." He fixed her with a stare. "We depart for Rifthold in the morning. Don't disappoint me, Sardothien."

It was nonsense, of course. How difficult could it be to outshine, outsmart, and then obliterate her competitors? She didn't smile, for she knew that if she did, it would open her to a realm of hope that had long been closed. But still, she felt like seizing the prince and dancing. She tried to think of music, tried to think of a celebratory tune, but could only recall a solitary line from the mournful bellowing of the Eyllwe work songs, deep and slow like honey poured from a jar: "*And go home at last . . .*"

She didn't notice when Captain Westfall led her away, nor did she notice when they walked down hall after hall.

Yes, she would go—to Rifthold, to anywhere, even through the Gates of the Wyrd and into Hell itself, if it meant freedom.

After all, you aren't Adarlan's Assassin for nothing.

4

When Celaena finally collapsed onto a bed after her meeting in the throne room, she couldn't fall asleep, despite the exhaustion in every inch of her body. After being roughly bathed by brutish servants, the wounds on her back throbbed and her face felt like it had been scrubbed to the bone. Shifting to lie on her side to ease the pain in her dressed and bound back, she ran her hand down the mattress, and blinked at the freeness of movement. Before she'd gotten into the bath, Chaol had removed her shackles. She'd felt everything—the reverberations of the key turning in the lock of her irons, then again as they loosened and fell to the floor. She could still feel the ghost chains hovering just above her skin. Looking up at the ceiling, she rotated her raw, burning joints and gave a sigh of contentment.

But it was too strange to lie on a mattress, to have silk caress her skin and a pillow cradle her cheek. She had forgotten what food other than soggy oats and hard bread tasted like, what a clean body and clothes could do to a person. Now it was utterly foreign.

Though her dinner hadn't been *that* wonderful. Not only was the roast chicken unimpressive, but after a few forkfuls, she'd dashed into the bathroom to deposit the contents of her stomach. She wanted to *eat*, to put a hand to a swollen belly, to wish that she'd never eaten a morsel and swear that she'd never eat again. She'd eat well in Rifthold, wouldn't she? And, more importantly, her stomach would adjust.

She'd wasted away to nothing. Beneath her nightgown, her ribs reached out from inside of her, showing bones where flesh and meat should have been. And her breasts! Once well-formed, they were now no larger than they'd been in the midst of puberty. A lump clogged her throat, which she promptly swallowed down. The softness of the mattress smothered her, and she shifted again, lying on her back, despite the pain it gave her.

Her face hadn't been much better when she glimpsed it in the washroom mirror. It was haggard: her cheekbones were sharp, her jaw pronounced, and her eyes slightly, but ever so disturbingly, sunken in. She took steadying breaths, savoring the hope. She'd eat. A lot. And exercise. She could be healthy again. Imagining outrageous feasts and regaining her former glory, she finally fell asleep.

When Chaol came to fetch her the next morning, he found her sleeping on the floor, wrapped in a blanket. "Sardothien," he said. She made a mumbling noise, burying her face farther into the pillow. "Why are you sleeping on the ground?" She opened an eye. Of course, he didn't mention how different she looked now that she was *clean*.

She didn't bother concealing herself with the blanket as she stood. The yards of fabric they called a nightgown covered her enough. "The bed was uncomfortable," she said simply, but quickly forgot the captain as she beheld the sunlight.

Pure, fresh, warm sunlight. Sunlight that she could bask in day after day if she got her freedom, sunlight to drown out the endless dark of the mines. It leaked in through the heavy drapes, smearing itself across the room in thick lines. Gingerly, Celaena stretched out a hand.

Her hand was pale, almost skeletal, but there was something about it, something beyond the bruises and cuts and scars, that seemed beautiful and new in the morning light.

She ran to the window and nearly ripped the curtains from their hangings as she opened them to the gray mountains and bleakness of Endovier. The guards positioned beneath the window didn't glance upward, and she gaped at the bluish-gray sky, at the clouds slipping on their shoes and shuffling toward the horizon.

I will not be afraid. For the first time in a while, the words felt true.

Her lips peeled into a smile. The captain raised an eyebrow, but said nothing.

She was cheerful—jubilant, really—and her mood improved when the servants coiled her braided hair onto the back of her head and dressed her in a surprisingly fine riding habit that concealed her miserably thin form. She loved clothes—loved the feeling of silk, of velvet, of satin, of suede and chiffon—and was fascinated by the grace of seams, the intricate perfection of an embossed surface. And when she won this ridiculous competition, when she was free . . . she could buy all the clothes she wanted.

She laughed when Chaol, irked at how Celaena stood in front of the mirror for five minutes, admiring herself, half-dragged her out of the room. The budding sky made her want to dance and skip down the halls before they entered the main yard. However, she faltered as she beheld the mounds of bone-colored rock at the far end of the compound, and the small figures going in and out of the many mouthlike holes cut into the mountains.

Work had already begun for the day, work that would continue without her when she left them all to this miserable fate. Her stomach clenching, Celaena averted her eyes from the prisoners, keeping up with the captain as they headed to a caravan of horses near the towering wall.

Yapping filled the air, and three black dogs sprinted from the center of the caravan to greet them. They were each sleek as arrows—undoubtedly from the Crown Prince's kennels. She knelt on one knee, her bound wounds protesting as she cupped their heads and stroked their smooth hair. They licked her fingers and face, their tails slashing the ground like whips.

A pair of ebony boots stopped before her, and the dogs immediately calmed and sat. Celaena lifted her gaze to find the sapphire eyes of the Crown Prince of Adarlan studying her face. He smiled slightly. "How unusual for them to notice you," he said, scratching one of the dogs behind the ears. "Did you give them food?"

She shook her head as the captain stepped behind her, so close that his knees grazed the folds of her forest-green velvet cape. It would take all of two movements to disarm him.

"Are you fond of dogs?" asked the prince. She nodded. Why was it already so hot? "Am I going to be blessed with the pleasure of hearing your voice, or have you resolved to be silent for the duration of our journey?"

"I'm afraid your questions didn't merit a verbal response."

Dorian bowed low. "Then I apologize, my lady! How terrible it must be to condescend to answer! Next time, I'll try to think of something more stimulating to say." With that, he turned on his heel and strode away, his dogs trailing after him.

She scowled as she stood. Her frown deepened when she discovered the Captain of the Guard smirking as they walked into the fray of the readying company. However, the unbearable urge to splatter someone across a wall lessened when they brought her a piebald mare to ride.

She mounted. The sky came closer, and it stretched forever above her, away and away to distant lands she'd never heard of. Celaena gripped the saddle horn. She was truly leaving Endovier. All those hopeless months, those freezing nights . . . gone now. She breathed in deeply. She knew—she just *knew*—that if she tried hard enough, she could fly from her saddle. That is, until she felt iron clamp around her arms.

It was Chaol, fastening her bandaged wrists into shackles. A long chain led to his horse, where it disappeared beneath the saddlebags. He mounted his black stallion, and she considered leaping from her horse and using the chain to hang him from the nearest tree.

It was a rather large company, twenty all together. Behind two imperial flag-bearing guards rode the prince and Duke Perrington. Then came a band of six royal guards, dull and bland as porridge. But still trained to protect him—from *her*. She clanked her chains against her saddle and flicked her eyes to Chaol. He didn't react.

The sun rose higher. After one last inspection of their supplies, they left. With most of the slaves working the mines, and only a few toiling inside the ramshackle refining sheds, the giant yard was almost deserted. The wall suddenly loomed, and her blood throbbed in her veins. The last time she'd been this close to the wall . . .

The crack of the whip sounded, followed by a scream. Celaena looked over her shoulder, past the guards and the supplies wagon, to the near-empty yard. None of these slaves would ever leave here—even when they died. Each week, they dug new mass graves behind the refining sheds. And each week, those graves filled up.

She became all too aware of the three long scars down her back. Even if she won her freedom . . . even if she lived in peace in the countryside . . . those scars would always remind her of what she'd endured. And that even if she was free, others were not.

Celaena faced forward, pushing those thoughts from her mind as they entered the passage through the wall. The interior was thick, almost smoky, and damp. The sounds of the horses echoed like rolling thunder.

The iron gates opened, and she glimpsed the wicked name of the mine before it split in two and swung wide. Within a few heartbeats, the gates groaned shut behind them. She was out.

She shifted her hands in their shackles, watching the chain sway and clank between her and the Captain of the Guard. It was attached to his saddle, which was cinched around his horse, which, when they stopped, could be subtly unbridled, just enough so that with a fierce tug from her end, the chain would rip the saddle off the beast, he'd tumble to the ground, and she would—

She sensed Captain Westfall's attention. He stared at her beneath lowered brows, his lips tightly pursed, and she shrugged as she dropped the chain.

As the morning wore on, the sky became a crisp blue with hardly a cloud. Taking the forest road, they swiftly passed from the mountainous wasteland of Endovier and into fairer country.

By midmorning they were within Oakwald Forest, the wood that surrounded Endovier and served as a continental divide between the "civilized" countries of the East and the uncharted lands of the West. Legends were still told of the strange and deadly people who dwelt there—the cruel and bloodthirsty descendents of the fallen Witch Kingdom. Celaena had once met a young woman from that cursed land, and though she'd turned out to be both cruel and bloodthirsty, she was still just a human. And had still bled like one.

After hours of silence, Celaena turned to Chaol. "Rumor has it that once the king is finished with his war against Wendlyn, he'll begin colonizing the West." She said it casually, but hoped he'd confirm or deny. The more she knew of the king's current position and maneuverings, the better. The captain surveyed her up and down, frowned, and then looked away. "I agree," she said, sighing loudly. "The fate of those empty, wide plains and those miserable mountain regions seems dull to me as well."

His jaw tightened as he clamped his teeth.

"Do you intend to ignore me forever?"

Captain Westfall's brows rose. "I didn't know I was ignoring you."

She pursed her lips, checking her irritation. She wouldn't give him the satisfaction. "How old are you?"

"Twenty-two."

"So young!" She batted her eyelashes, watching him for some kind of response. "It only took a few years to climb the ranks?"

He nodded. "And how old are *you*?"

"Eighteen." But he said nothing. "I know," she continued. "It *is* impressive that I accomplished so much at such an early age."

"Crime isn't an accomplishment, Sardothien."

"Yes, but becoming the world's most famous assassin is!" He didn't respond. "You might ask me how I did it."

"Did what?" he said tightly.

"Became so talented and famous so quickly."

"I don't want to hear about it."

Those weren't the words she'd wanted to hear.

"You're not very kind," she said through her teeth. If she were going to get under his skin, she'd have to push a lot harder.

"You're a criminal. I'm Captain of the Royal Guard. I'm not obligated to bestow any kindness or conversation upon you. Be grateful we don't keep you locked up in the wagon."

"Yes, well, I'd wager that you're rather unpleasant to talk to even when you're *bestowing* kindness upon others." When he failed to respond again, Celaena couldn't help but feel a bit foolish. A few minutes passed. "Are you and the Crown Prince close friends?"

"My personal life is none of your concern."

She clicked her tongue. "How wellborn are you?"

"Well enough." His chin lifted almost imperceptibly higher.

"Duke?"

"No."

"Lord?" He didn't reply, and she smiled slowly. "Lord Chaol Westfall." She fanned herself with a hand. "How the court ladies must *fawn* over you!"

"Don't call me that. I'm not given the title of lord," he said quietly.

"You have an older brother?"

"No."

"Then why don't you bear the title?" Again, no response. She knew she should stop prying, but she couldn't help it. "A scandal? A deprived birthright? In what sort of messy intrigue are you involved?"

His lips squeezed together so tightly they turned white.

She leaned toward him. "Do you find that—"

"Shall I gag you, or are you capable of being silent without my assistance?" He stared ahead at the Crown Prince, his face blank again.

She tried not to laugh when he grimaced as she began speaking again. "Are you married?"

"No."

She picked at her nails. "I'm not married, either." His nostrils flared. "How old were you when you became Captain of the Guard?"

He gripped the reins of his horse. "Twenty."

The party halted in a clearing and the soldiers dismounted. She faced Chaol, who swung a leg over his horse. "Why have we stopped?"

Chaol unhooked the chain from his saddle and gave it a firm yank, motioning for her to dismount. "Lunch," he said.

5

Celaena brushed a stray wisp of hair from her face and allowed herself to be led into the clearing. If she wanted to break free, she'd have to go through Chaol first. Had they been alone, she might have attempted it, though the chains would make it difficult; but with an entourage of royal guards trained to kill without hesitation . . .

Chaol remained close beside her while a fire was kindled and food prepared from the boxes and sacks of supplies. The soldiers rolled logs to make small circles, where they sat while their companions stirred and fried. The Crown Prince's dogs, who had dutifully trotted along-side their master, approached the assassin with wagging tails and lay at her feet. At least someone was glad for her company.

Hungry by the time a plate was finally laid in her lap, Celaena became a bit more than irritated when the captain did not immediately remove her irons. After giving her a long warning look, he unlocked her chains and clamped them onto her ankles. She only rolled her eyes as she raised a small portion of meat to her lips. She chewed slowly.

The last thing she needed was to be sick in front of them. While the soldiers talked amongst themselves, Celaena took in their surroundings. She and Chaol sat with five soldiers. The Crown Prince, of course, sat with Perrington on their own two logs, far from her. While Dorian had been all arrogance and amusement the previous night, his features were grave as he spoke to the duke. His entire body seemed tensed, and she didn't fail to notice the way he clenched his jaw when Perrington spoke. Whatever their relationship was, it wasn't cordial.

Midbite, Celaena tore her focus from the prince to study the trees. The forest had gone silent. The ebony hounds' ears were erect, though they didn't seem to be bothered by the stillness. Even the soldiers quieted. Her heart skipped a beat. The forest was different here.

The leaves dangled like jewels—tiny droplets of ruby, pearl, topaz, amethyst, emerald, and garnet; and a carpet of such riches coated the forest floor around them. Despite the ravages of conquest, this part of Oakwald Forest remained untouched. It still echoed with the remnants of the power that had once given these trees such unnatural beauty.

She'd been only eight when Arobynn Hamel, her mentor and the King of the Assassins, found her half-submerged on the banks of a frozen river and brought her to his keep on the border between Adarlan and Terrasen. While training her to be his finest and most loyal assassin, Arobynn had never allowed her to return home to Terrasen. But she still remembered the beauty of the world before the King of Adarlan had ordered so much of it burned. Now there was nothing left for her there, nor would there ever be. Arobynn had never said it aloud, but if she'd refused his offer to train her, he would have handed her to those who would have killed her. Or worse. She'd been newly orphaned, and even at eight, she knew that a life with Arobynn, with a new name that no one would recognize but someday everyone would fear, was a chance to start over. To escape the fate that led her to leap into the icy river that night ten years ago.

"Damned forest," said an olive-skinned soldier in their circle. A soldier beside him chuckled. "The sooner it's burned, the better, I say." The other soldiers nodded, and Celaena stiffened. "It's full of hate," said another.

"Did you expect anything else?" she interrupted. Chaol's hand darted to his sword as the soldiers turned to her, some of them sneering. "This isn't just any forest." She beckoned with her fork to the woods. "It's Brannon's forest."

"My father used to tell me stories about it being full of faeries," a soldier said. "They're all gone now." One took a bite from an apple, and said: "Along with those damned wretched Fae." Another said: "We got rid of them, didn't we?"

"I'd watch your tongues," Celaena snapped. "King Brannon was Fae, and Oakwald is still his. I wouldn't be surprised if some of the trees remember him."

The soldiers laughed. "They'd have to be two thousand years old, them trees!" said one.

"Fae are immortal," she said.

"Trees ain't."

Bristling, Celaena shook her head and took another small forkful of food.

"What do you know about this forest?" Chaol quietly asked her. Was he mocking her? The soldiers sat forward, poised to laugh. But the captain's golden-brown eyes held mere curiosity.

She swallowed her meat. "Before Adarlan began its conquest, this forest was cloaked in magic," she said softly, but not meekly.

He waited for her to continue, but she had said enough. "And?" he prodded.

"And that's all I know," she said, meeting his gaze. Disappointed at the lack of anything to mock, the soldiers returned to their meals.

She had lied, and Chaol knew it. She knew plenty about this forest, knew that the denizens of this place had once been faeries: gnomes, sprites, nymphs, goblins, more names than anyone could count or remember. All ruled by their larger, human-like cousins, the immortal Fae—the original inhabitants and settlers of the continent, and the oldest beings in Erilea.

With the growing corruption of Adarlan and the king's campaign to hunt them down and execute them, the faeries and Fae fled, seeking shelter in the wild, untouched places of the world. The King of Adarlan had outlawed it all—magic, Fae, faeries—and removed any trace so thoroughly that even those who had magic in their blood almost believed it had never really existed, Celaena herself being one of them. The king had claimed that magic was an affront to the Goddess and her gods—that to wield it was to impertinently imitate their power. But even though the king had banned magic, most knew the truth: within a month of his proclamation, magic had completely and utterly disappeared of its own accord. Perhaps it had realized what horrors were coming.

She could still smell the fires that had raged throughout her eighth and ninth years—the smoke of burning books chock-full of ancient, irreplaceable knowledge, the screams of gifted seers and healers as they'd been consumed by the flames, the storefronts and sacred places shattered and desecrated and erased from history. Many of the magic-users who hadn't been burned wound up prisoners in Endovier—and most didn't survive long there. It had been a while since she'd contemplated the gifts she'd lost, though the memory of her abilities haunted her dreams. Despite the carnage, perhaps it *was* good that magic had vanished. It was far too dangerous for any sane person to wield; her gifts might have destroyed her by this point.

The smoking fire burned her eyes as she took another bite. She'd never forget the stories about Oakwald Forest, legends of dark, terrible glens and deep, still pools, and caves full of light and heavenly singing. But they were now only stories and nothing more. To speak of them was to invite trouble.

She looked at the sunlight filtering through the canopy, how the trees swayed in the wind with their long, bony arms around each other. She suppressed a shiver.

Lunch, thankfully, was over quickly. Her chains were transferred to her wrists again, and the horses were refreshed and reloaded. Celaena's legs had become so stiff that Chaol was forced to help her onto her horse. It was painful to ride, and her nose also suffered a blow as the continual stench of horse sweat and excrement floated to the back of the entourage.

They traveled for the remainder of the day, and the assassin sat in silence as she watched the forest pass, the tightness in her chest not easing until they'd left that shimmering glen far behind. Her body ached by the time they stopped for the night. She didn't bother to speak at dinner, nor to care when her small tent was erected, guards posted outside, and she was allowed to sleep, still shackled to one of them. She didn't dream, but when she awoke, she couldn't believe her eyes.

Small white flowers lay at the foot of her cot, and many infant-sized footprints led in and out of the tent. Before someone could enter and notice, Celaena swept a foot over the tracks, destroying any trace, and stuffed the flowers into a nearby satchel.

Though no one mentioned another word about faeries, as they traveled onward, Celaena continually scanned the soldiers' faces for any indication that they'd seen something strange. She spent a good portion of the following day with sweaty palms and a racing heartbeat, and kept one eye fixed on the passing woods.

6

For the next two weeks, they traveled down through the continent, the nights becoming colder, the days shorter. Icy rain kept them company for four days, during which time Celaena was so miserably cold that she contemplated throwing herself into a ravine, hopefully dragging Chaol with her.

Everything was wet and half-frozen, and while she could bear sodden hair, she couldn't withstand the agony of wet shoes. She had little sensation in her toes. Each night, she wrapped them in whatever spare, dry clothing she could find. She felt as though she were in a state of partial decay, and with each gust of frigid, stinging wind, she wondered when her skin would rip from her bones. But, as it was autumn weather, the rain suddenly disappeared, and cloudless, brilliant skies once more stretched over them.

Celaena was half-asleep on her horse when the Crown Prince pulled out of line and came trotting toward them, his dark hair bouncing. His red cape rose and fell in a crimson wave. Above his unadorned white shirt was a fine cobalt-blue jerkin trimmed with gold. She would have snorted, but he *did* look rather good in his knee-high brown boots. And his leather belt *did* go nicely—even though the hunting knife seemed a bit too bejeweled. He pulled up alongside Chaol. "Come," he said to the captain, and jerked his head at the steep, grassy hill that the company was starting to ascend.

"Where?" the captain asked, jangling Celaena's chain for Dorian to notice. Wherever he went, she went.

"Come see the view," Dorian clarified. "Bring that one, I suppose." Celaena bristled. "That one"! As if she were a piece of baggage!

Chaol moved them out of line, giving her chain a fierce tug. She grasped the reins as they advanced into a gallop, the tangy smell of horsehair creeping into her nostrils. They rode quickly up the steep hill, the horse jerking and surging beneath her. Celaena tried not to wince as she slid backward in the saddle. If she fell, she'd die of humiliation. But the setting sun emerged from the trees behind them, and her breath caught in her throat as a spire, then three, then six more appeared, piercing the sky.

Atop the hill, Celaena stared at the crowning achievement of Adarlan. The glass castle of Rifthold.

It was gargantuan, a vertical city of shimmering, crystalline towers and bridges, chambers and turrets, domed ballrooms and long, endless hallways. It had been built above the original stone castle, and cost a kingdom's wealth to construct.

She thought of the first time she'd seen it, eight years ago, cold and still, frozen like the earth beneath her fat pony. Even then, she found the castle tasteless, a waste of resources and talent, its towers reaching into the sky like clawed fingers. She remembered the powder-blue cloak that she kept touching, the weight of her fresh curls, the scratch of her stockings against the saddle, how she'd worried about the spot of mud on her red velvet shoes, and how she kept on thinking about that man—the man she'd killed three days earlier.

"One more tower and the whole thing will collapse," the Crown Prince said from his spot on the other side of Chaol. The sounds of their approaching party filled the air. "We've still got a few miles left, and I'd rather navigate these foothills in the daylight. We'll camp here tonight."

"I wonder what your father will think of her," Chaol said.

"Oh, he'll be fine—until she opens her mouth. Then the bellowing and the blustering will begin, and I'll regret wasting the past two months tracking her down. But—well, I think my father has more important matters to worry over." With that, the prince moved off.

Celaena couldn't keep her eyes from the castle. She felt so small, even from far away. She'd forgotten how dwarfing the building was.

The soldiers scurried about, lighting fires and raising tents. "You look as if you're facing the gallows, not your freedom," the captain said beside her.

She wound and unwound a strap of leather rein around a finger. "It's odd to see it."

"The city?"

"The city, the castle, the slums, the river." The shadow of the castle grew across the city like a hulking beast. "I still don't entirely know how it happened."

"How you were captured?"

She nodded. "Despite your visions of a perfect world under an empire, your rulers and politicians are quick to destroy each other. So are assassins, I suppose."

"You believe one of your kind betrayed you?"

"Everyone knew I received the best hires and could demand any payment." She scanned the twisting city streets and the winding glimmer of the river. "Were I gone, a vacancy would arise from which they could profit. It might have been one; it might have been many."

“You shouldn’t expect to find honor amongst such company.”

“I didn’t say that I did. I never trusted most of them, and I knew they hated me.” She had her suspicions, of course. And the one that seemed most likely was a truth she wasn’t yet ready to face—not now, not ever.

“Endovier must have been terrible,” Chaol said. Nothing malicious or mocking lay beneath his words. Did she dare call it sympathy?

“Yes,” she said slowly. “It was.” He gave her a look that asked for more. Well, what did she care if she told him? “When I arrived, they cut my hair, gave me rags, and put a pickax in my hand as if I knew what to do with it. They chained me to the others, and I endured my whippings with the rest of them. But the overseers had been instructed to treat me with extra care, and took the liberty of rubbing salt into my wounds—salt *I* mined—and whipped me often enough so that some of the gashes never really closed. It was through the kindness of a few prisoners from Eyllwe that my wounds didn’t become infected. Every night, one of them stayed up the hours it took to clean my back.”

Chaol didn’t reply, and only glanced at her before dismounting. Had she been a fool to tell him something so personal? He didn’t speak to her again that day, except to bark commands.

Celaena awoke with a gasp, a hand on her throat, cold sweat sliding down her back and pooling in the hollow between her mouth and chin. She’d had the nightmare before—that she was lying in one of those mass graves in Endovier. And when she tried to pull herself from the tangle of rotting limbs, she’d been dragged down into a pile twenty bodies deep. And then no one noticed that she was still screaming when they buried her alive.

Nauseated, Celaena wrapped her arms around her knees. She breathed—in and out, in and out—and tilted her head, her sharp kneecaps pushing against her cheekbone. Due to the unseasonably warm weather, they'd foregone sleeping in tents—which gave her an unparalleled view of the capital. The illuminated castle rose from the sleeping city like a mound of ice and steam. There was something greenish about it, and it seemed to pulse.

By this time tomorrow, she'd be confined within those walls. But tonight—tonight it was so quiet, like the calm before a storm.

She imagined that the whole world was asleep, enchanted by the sea-green light of the castle. Time came and went, mountains rising and falling, vines creeping over the slumbering city, concealing it with layers of thorns and leaves. She was the only one awake.

She pulled her cloak around her. She would win. She'd win, and serve the king, and then vanish into nothing, and think no more of castles or kings or assassins. She didn't wish to reign over this city again. Magic was dead, the Fae were banished or executed, and she would never again have anything to do with the rise and fall of kingdoms.

She wasn't fated for anything. Not anymore.

A hand upon his sword, Dorian Havilliard watched the assassin from his spot on the other side of the sleeping company. There was something sad about her—sitting so still with her legs against her chest, the moonlight coloring her hair silver. No bold, swaggering expressions strutted across her face as the glow of the castle rippled in her eyes.

He found her beautiful, if a bit strange and sour. It was something in the way that her eyes sparked when she looked at something lovely in the landscape. He couldn't understand it.

She stared at the castle unflinchingly, her form silhouetted against the blazing brightness that sat on the edge of the Avery River. Clouds gathered above them and she raised her head. Through a clearing in the swirling mass, a cluster of stars could be seen. He couldn't help thinking that they gazed down at her.

No, he had to remember she was an assassin with the blessing of a pretty face and sharp wits. She washed her hands with blood, and was just as likely to slit his throat as offer him a kind word. And she was his Champion. She was here to fight for him—and for her freedom. And nothing more. He lay down, his hand still upon his sword, and fell asleep.

Still, the image haunted his dreams throughout the night: a lovely girl gazing at the stars, and the stars who gazed back.

7

Trumpeters signaled their arrival as they passed through the looming alabaster walls of Rifthold. Crimson flags depicting gold wyverns flapped in the wind above the capital city, the cobblestone streets were cleared of traffic, and Celaena, unchained, dressed, painted, and seated in front of Chaol, frowned as the odor of the city met her nose.

Beneath the smell of spices and horses lay a foundation of filth, blood, and spoiled milk. The air held a hint of the salty waters of the Avery—different from the salt of Endovier. This brought with it warships from every ocean in Erilea, merchant vessels crammed with goods and slaves, and fishing boats with half-rotted, scale-covered flesh that people somehow managed to eat. From bearded peddlers to servant girls carrying armfuls of hatboxes, everyone paused as the flag-bearers trotted proudly ahead, and Dorian Havilliard waved.

They followed the Crown Prince, who, like Chaol, was swathed in a red cape, pinned over the left breast with a brooch fashioned after the royal seal. The prince wore a golden crown upon his neat hair, and she had to concede that he looked rather regal.

Young women flocked to them, waving. Dorian winked and grinned. Celaena couldn't help but notice the sharp stares from the same women when they beheld her in the prince's retinue. She knew how she appeared, seated atop a horse like some prize lady being brought to the castle. So Celaena only smiled at them, tossed her hair, and batted her eyelashes at the prince's back.

Her arm stung. "What?" she hissed at the Captain of the Guard as he pinched her.

"You look ridiculous," he said through his teeth, smiling at the crowd.

She mirrored his expression. "*They're* ridiculous."

"Be quiet and act normally." His breath was hot on her neck.

"I should jump from the horse and run," she said, waving at a young man, who gaped at what he thought was a court lady's attention. "I'd vanish in an instant."

"Yes," he said, "you'd vanish with three arrows buried in your spine."

"Such pleasant talk."

They entered the shopping district, where the crowd swelled between the trees lining the broad avenues of white stone. The glass storefronts were nearly invisible beyond the crowd, but a ravenous sort of hunger arose in her as they passed shop after shop. Each window displayed dresses and tunics, which stood proudly behind lines of sparkling jewelry and broad-rimmed hats clumped together like bouquets of flowers. Above it all, the glass castle loomed, so high she had to tilt her head back to see the uppermost towers. Why had they chosen such a long and inconvenient route? Did they really wish to parade about?

Celaena swallowed. There was a break in the buildings, and sails spread like moth's wings greeted them as they turned onto the avenue along the Avery. Ships sat docked along the pier, a mess of rope and netting with sailors calling to each other, too busy to notice the royal procession. At the sound of a whip, her head snapped to the side.

Slaves staggered down the gangplank of a merchant ship. A mix of conquered nations bound together, each of them had the hollow, raging face she'd seen so many times before. Most of the slaves were prisoners of war—rebels who survived the butchering blocks and endless lines of Adarlan's armies. Some were probably people who had been caught or accused of trying to practice magic. But others were just ordinary folk, in the wrong place at the wrong time. Now that she noticed, there were countless chained slaves working the docks, lifting and sweating, holding parasols and pouring water, eyes on the ground or the sky—never on what was before them.

She wanted to leap from her horse and run to them, or to simply scream that she wasn't a part of this prince's court, that she had no hand in bringing them here, chained and starved and beaten, that she had worked and bled with them, with their families and friends—she was not like these monsters that destroyed everything. That she had *done* something, nearly two years ago, when she had freed almost two hundred slaves from the Pirate Lord. Even that, though, wasn't enough.

The city was suddenly separate, ripped from her. People still waved and bowed, cheering and laughing, throwing flowers and other nonsense before their horses. She had difficulty breathing.

Sooner than she would have liked, the iron and glass gate of the castle appeared, latticework doors opened, and a dozen guards flanked the cobblestone path that led through the archway. Spears erect, they held rectangular shields, and their eyes were dark beneath bronze helmets. Each wore a red cape. Their armor, while tarnished, was well crafted from copper and leather.

Beyond the archway sloped a road, lined with trees of gold and silver. Glass lampposts sprouted up between the hedges bordering the path. The sounds of the city vanished as they passed under another arch, this one made of sparkling glass, and then the castle rose before them.

Chaol sighed as he dismounted in the open courtyard. Hands pulled Celaena from the saddle and set her on wobbly legs. Glass gleamed everywhere, and a hand clamped on her shoulder. Stableboys quietly and quickly led her horse away.

Chaol pulled her to his side, keeping a firm grip on her cloak as the Crown Prince approached. "Six hundred rooms, military and servant's quarters, three gardens, a game park, and stables on either side," said Dorian, staring at his home. "Who could ever need so much space?"

She managed a weak smile, a bit baffled by his sudden charm. "I don't know how you can sleep at night with only a wall of glass keeping you from death." She glanced up, but quickly lowered her focus to the ground. She wasn't afraid of heights, but the thought of being so high up with nothing but glass to protect her made her stomach clench.

"Then you're like me." Dorian chuckled. "Thank the gods I gave you rooms in the stone castle. I'd hate for you to be uncomfortable."

Deciding that scowling at him wouldn't be the wisest decision, Celaena looked instead toward the massive castle gates. The doors were made of cloudy red glass, gaping at her like the mouth of a giant. But she could see the interior was made of stone, and it seemed to her that the glass castle had been dropped on top of the original building. What a ridiculous idea: a castle made of glass.

"Well," said Dorian. "You've fattened up a bit, and your skin has some color now. Welcome to my home, Celaena Sardothien." He nodded at a few passing nobles, who scraped and bowed. "The competition begins tomorrow. Captain Westfall will show you to your chambers."

She rolled her shoulders and searched for any sign of her competitors. No one else seemed to be arriving, though.

The prince nodded to another flock of cooing courtiers, and didn't look at either the assassin or the Captain of the Guard as he spoke again.

"I have to meet with my father," he said, running his gaze along the body of a particularly pretty lady. He winked at her, and she hid her face behind a lace fan as she continued her walk. Dorian nodded to Chaol. "I'll see you later tonight." Without saying a word to Celaena, he strode up the steps to the palace, his red cape blowing in the wind.

The Crown Prince lived up to his word. Her chambers were in a wing of the stone castle, and much bigger than she anticipated. They consisted of a bedroom with an attached bathing chamber and a dressing room, a small dining room, and a music and gaming room. Each room was furnished in gold and crimson, her bedroom also decorated with a giant tapestry along one wall, with couches and deep-cushioned chairs scattered in a tasteful manner. Her balcony overlooked a fountain in one of the gardens, and whichever it was, it was beautiful—never mind the guards she spotted posted beneath.

Chaol left her, and Celaena didn't wait to hear the door shut before closing herself in her bedroom. Between her murmurs of appreciation during Chaol's brief tour of her rooms, she'd counted the windows—twelve—the exits—one—and the guards posted outside her door, windows, and balcony—nine. They were each armed with a sword, knife, and crossbow, and though they'd been alert while their captain passed by, she knew a crossbow wasn't exactly a light weight to bear for hours on end.

Celaena crept to her bedroom window, pressing herself against the marble wall, and glanced down. Sure enough, the guards had already strapped the crossbows across their backs. It would waste precious seconds to grab the weapon and load it—seconds when she could take their swords, cut their throats, and vanish into the gardens. She smiled as she stepped fully in front of the window to study the garden. Its far border ended in the trees of a game park. She knew enough about the castle to know that she was on the southern side, and if she went through the game park, she'd reach a stone wall and the Avery River beyond.

Celaena opened and closed the doors of her armoire, dresser, and vanity. Of course, there weren't any weapons, not even a fire poker, but she grabbed the few bone hairpins left in the back of a dresser drawer, and some string she found in a mending basket in her giant dressing room. No needles. She knelt on the carpeted floor of the dressing room—which was void of clothes—and, one eye on the door behind her, she made quick work of the hairpins, snapping their heads off before binding them all together with the string. When she finished, she held up the object and frowned.

Well, it wasn't a knife, but clustered together like that, the jagged points of the broken pins could do some damage. She tested the tips with a finger, and winced as a shard of bone pricked her calloused skin. Yes, it would certainly hurt if she jammed it into a guard's neck. And disable him long enough for her to grab his weapons.

Celaena reentered the bedroom, yawning, and stood on the edge of the mattress to tuck the makeshift weapon into one of the folds of the partial canopy over the bed. When she'd concealed it, she glanced around the room again. Something about the dimensions seemed a little off—something with the height of the walls, but she couldn't be sure. Regardless, the canopy provided plenty of hiding places. What else could she take without them noticing? Chaol had probably had the room looked over before they arrived. She listened at the bedroom door for any signs of activity. When she was certain no one was in her chambers, she entered the foyer and strode through it to the gaming room. She beheld the billiards cues along the far wall, and the heavy colored balls stacked on the green felt table, and grinned. Chaol wasn't nearly as smart as he thought he was.

Ultimately, she left the billiards equipment, if only because it would arouse suspicion if it all disappeared, but it would be easy enough to get a stick if she needed to escape, or to use the dense balls to knock the guards unconscious. Exhausted, she returned to her bedroom and finally hoisted herself onto the enormous bed. The mattress was so soft that she sank down a few inches, and it was wide enough for three people to sleep without noticing each other. Curling on her side, Celaena's eyes grew heavier and heavier.

She slept for an hour, until a servant announced the arrival of the tailor, to outfit her with proper court attire. And thus another hour was spent being measured and pinned, and sitting through a presentation of different fabrics and colors. She hated most of them. A few caught her attention, but when she tried to recommend specific styles that flattered her, she received only the wave of a hand and a curl of the lip. She considered jabbing one of the tailor's pearl-headed pins through his eye.

She bathed, feeling almost as dirty as she had in Endovier, and was grateful for the gentle servants who attended her. Many of the wounds had scabbed or remained as thin white lines, though her back retained most of its damage. After nearly two hours of pampering—trimming her hair, shaping her nails, and scraping away the callouses on her feet and hands—Celaena grinned at the mirror in the dressing room.

Only in the capital could servants have done such fine work. She looked spectacular. Utterly and completely spectacular. She wore a dress with skirts and long sleeves of white, streaked and spotted with orchid-purple. The indigo bodice was bordered with a thin line of gold, and an ice-white cape hung from her shoulders. Her hair, half up and twisted with a fuchsia ribbon, fell in loose waves. But her smile faltered as she remembered why, exactly, she was here.

The King's Champion indeed. She looked more like the King's Lapdog.

"Beautiful," said an older, female voice, and Celaena pivoted, the yards of cumbersome fabric twisting with her. Her corset—the stupid, cursed thing—pushed on her ribs so hard that the breath was sucked from her. *This* was why she mostly preferred tunics and pants.

It was a woman, large but well contained within the gown of cobalt and peach that marked her as one of the servants of the royal household. Her face, while a bit wrinkled, was red-cheeked and finely colored. She bowed. "Philippa Spindlehead," said the woman, rising. "Your personal servant. You must be—"

"Celaena Sardothien," she said flatly.

Philippa's eyes widened. "Keep that to yourself, miss," she whispered. "I'm the only one who knows. And the guards, I suppose."

"Then what do people think about all my guards?" she asked.

Philippa approached, ignoring Celaena's glower as she adjusted the folds of the assassin's gown, fluffing them in the right places. "Oh, the other . . . *Champions* have guards outside their rooms, too. Or people just think you're another lady-friend of the prince."

"*Another?*"

Philippa smiled, but kept her eyes upon the dress. "He has a big heart, His Highness."

Celaena wasn't at all surprised. "A favorite with women?"

"It's not my place to speak about His Highness. And you should mind your tongue, too."

"I'll do as I please." She surveyed the withered face of her servant. Why send such a soft woman to serve her? She'd overpower her in a heartbeat.

"Then you'll find yourself back in those mines, poppet." Philippa put a hand on her hip. "Oh, don't scowl—you ruin your face when you look like that!" She reached to pinch Celaena's cheek, and Celaena pulled away.

"Are you mad? I'm an assassin—not some court idiot!"

Philippa clucked. "You're still a woman, and so long as you're under my charge, you'll act like one, or Wyrd help me!"

Celaena blinked, then slowly said: "You're awfully bold. I hope you don't act like this around court ladies."

"Ah. There was surely a reason why I was assigned to attend you."

"You understand what my occupation entails, don't you?"

"No disrespect, but this sort of finery is worth far more than seeing my head roll on the ground." Celaena's upper lip pulled back from her teeth as the servant turned from the room. "Don't make such a face," Philippa called over her shoulder. "It squishes that little nose of yours."

Celaena could only gape as the servant woman shuffled away.

The Crown Prince of Adarlan stared at his father unblinkingly, waiting for him to speak. Seated on his glass throne, the King of Adarlan watched him back. Sometimes Dorian forgot how little he looked like his father—it was his younger brother, Hollin, who took after the king, with his broad frame and his round, sharp-eyed face. But Dorian, tall, toned, and elegant, bore no resemblance to him. And then there was the matter of Dorian's sapphire eyes—not even his mother had his eyes. No one knew where they came from.

"She has arrived?" his father asked. His voice was hard, edged with the clash of shields and the scream of arrows. As far as greetings went, that was probably the kindest one he'd get.

"She shouldn't pose any threat or problem while she's here," Dorian said as calmly as he could. Picking Sardothien had been a gamble—a bet against his father's tolerance. He was about to see if it was worth it.

"You think like every fool she's murdered." Dorian straightened as the king continued. "She owes allegiance to none but herself, and won't balk at putting a knife through your heart."

"Which is why she'll be fully capable of winning this competition of yours." His father said nothing, and Dorian went on, his heart racing. "Come to think of it, the whole competition might be unnecessary."

"You say that because you're afraid of losing good coin." If only his father knew that he hadn't just ventured to find a champion to win gold, but also to get out—to get away from *him*, for as long as he could manage.

Dorian steeled his nerve, remembering the words he'd been brooding over for the entire journey from Endovier. "I guarantee she'll be able to fulfill her duties; we truly don't need to train her. I've told you already: it's foolish to have this competition at all."

"If you do not mind your tongue, I'll have her use you for practice."

"And then what? Have Hollin take the throne?"

"Do not doubt me, Dorian," his father challenged. "You might think this . . . *girl* can win, but you forget that Duke Perrington is sponsoring Cain. You would have been better off picking a Champion like him—forged in blood and iron on the battlefield. A true Champion."

Dorian stuffed his hands in his pockets. "Don't you find the title a little ridiculous, given that our 'Champions' are no more than criminals?"

His father rose from his throne and pointed at the map painted on the far wall of his council chamber. "I am the conqueror of this continent, and soon to be ruler of *all* Erilea. You will not question me."

Dorian, realizing how close he was to crossing a boundary between impertinence and rebellion—a boundary that he'd been very, very careful to maintain—mumbled his apologies.

"We're at war with Wendlyn," his father went on. "I have enemies all around. Who better to do my work than someone utterly grateful for being granted not only a second chance, but also wealth and the power of my name?" The king smiled when Dorian didn't reply. Dorian tried not to flinch as his father studied him. "Perrington tells me that you behaved yourself well on this trip."

"With Perrington as a watchdog, I couldn't do otherwise."

"I'll not have some peasant woman banging on the gate, wailing that you've broken her heart." Dorian's face colored, but he did not drop his father's stare. "I've toiled too hard and long to establish my empire; you will not complicate it with illegitimate heirs. Marry a proper woman, then dally as you will after you give me a grandson or two. When you are king, you will understand consequences."

"When I'm king, I won't declare control over Terrasen through thin claims of inheritance." Chaol had warned him to watch his mouth when speaking to his father, but when he spoke to him like that, as if he were a pampered idiot . . .

"Even if you offered them self-rule, those rebels would mount your head on a pike before the gates of Orynth."

"Perhaps alongside all my illegitimate heirs, if I'm so fortunate."

The king gave him a poisonous smile. "My silver-tongued son." They watched each other in silence before Dorian spoke again.

"Perhaps you should consider our difficulty in getting past Wendlyn's naval defenses to be a sign that you should stop playing at being a god."

"Playing?" The king smiled, his crooked teeth glowing yellow in the firelight. "I am not playing. And this is not a game." Dorian's shoulders stiffened. "Though she may look pleasant, she's still a witch. You are to keep your distance, understood?"

"Who? The assassin?"

"She's dangerous, boy, even if you're sponsoring her. She wants one thing and one thing only—don't think she won't use you to get it. If you court her, the consequences will not be pleasant. Not from her, and not from me."

"And if I condescend to associate with her, what would you do, father? Throw me in the mines as well?"

His father was upon him before Dorian could brace himself. The back of the king's hand connected with Dorian's cheek, and the prince staggered, but regained his countenance. His face throbbed, stinging so badly he fought to keep his eyes from watering. "Son or no son," the king snarled, "I am still your king. You will obey me, Dorian Havilliard, or you will pay. I'll have no more of your questioning."

Knowing he'd only cause more trouble for himself if he stayed, the Crown Prince of Adarlan bowed silently and left his father, eyes gleaming with barely controlled anger.

8

Celaena walked down a marble hall, her dress flowing behind in a purple and white wave. Chaol strode beside her, a hand on the eagle-shaped pommel of his sword.

"Is there anything interesting down this hall?"

"What else would you care to see? We've already seen all three gardens, the ballrooms, the historical rooms, and the nicest views offered from the stone castle. If you refuse to go into the glass castle, there's nothing else to see."

She crossed her arms. She'd managed to convince him to give her a tour under the pretense of extreme boredom—when, in fact, she'd used every moment to plot a dozen escape routes from her room. The castle was old, and most of its halls and stairwells went nowhere; escaping would require some thought. But with the competition beginning tomorrow, what else did she have to do? And what better way to prepare for a potential disaster?

"I don't understand why you refuse to enter the glass addition," he went on. "There's no difference between the interiors—you wouldn't even know that you were inside it unless someone told you or you looked out the window."

"Only an idiot would walk in a house made of glass."

"It's as sturdy as steel and stone."

"Yes, until someone just a bit too heavy enters and it comes crashing down."

"That's impossible."

The thought of standing on floors of glass made her queasy. "Is there no menagerie or library that we could see?" They passed by a set of closed doors. The sounds of lilting speech reached them, along with the gentle strumming of a harp. "What's in there?"

"The queen's court." He grabbed her arm and pulled her down the hall.

"Queen Georgina?" Didn't he have any idea what information he was giving away? Perhaps he honestly thought she wasn't a threat. She hid her scowl.

"Yes, Queen Georgina Havilliard."

"Is the young prince at home?"

"Hollin? He's at school."

"And is he as handsome as his older brother?" Celaena smirked as Chaol tensed.

It was well known that the ten-year-old prince was rotten and spoiled, inside and out, and she remembered the scandal that had erupted a few months before her capture. Hollin Havilliard, upon finding his porridge burnt, had beaten one of his servants so badly that there was no possibility of it being concealed. The woman's family had been paid off, and the young prince shipped to school in the mountains. Of course everyone knew. Queen Georgina had refused to hold court for a month.

"Hollin will grow into his lineage," Chaol grumbled. There was a bounce to her step as Celaena walked on, the court fading away behind them. They were silent for a few minutes before an explosion sounded nearby, then another.

"What is that awful noise?" Celaena said. The captain led her through a set of glass doors, and he pointed up as they entered into a garden.

"The clock tower," he said, his bronze eyes shining with amusement, as the clock finished its war cry. She'd never heard bells like that.

From the garden sprouted a tower made of inky black stone. Two gargoyles, wings spread for flight, perched on each of the four clock faces, soundlessly roaring at those beneath. "What a horrible thing," she whispered. The numbers were like war paint on the white face of the clock, the hands like swords as they slashed across the pearly surface.

"As a child, I wouldn't go near it," Chaol admitted.

"You'd see something like this before the Gates of Wyrd—not in a garden. How old is it?"

"The king had it built around Dorian's birth."

"This king?" Chaol nodded. "Why would he build such a wretched thing?"

"Come on," he said, turning as he ignored her question. "Let's go."

Celaena examined the clock for a second more. The thick, clawed finger of a gargoyle pointed at her. She could have sworn that its jaws had widened. As she made to follow Chaol, she noticed a tile on the paved pathway. "What's this?"

He stopped. "What's what?"

She pointed at the mark engraved on the slate. It was a circle with a vertical line through the middle that extended beyond the circumference. Both ends of the line were hooked, one directing downward, the other up. "What is this mark on the path here?"

He walked around until he stood beside her. "I have no idea."

Celaena examined the gargoyle again. "He's pointing at it. What does the symbol mean?"

"It means you're wasting my time," he said. "It's probably some sort of decorative sundial."

"Are there other marks?"

"If you looked, I'm sure you'd find them." She allowed herself to be dragged from the garden, away from the shadow of the clock tower and into the marble halls of the castle. Try as she might, and walk as far as they did, she couldn't shake the feeling that those bulging eyes were still upon her.

They continued past the kitchen quarters, which were a mess of shouting, clouds of flour, and surging fires. Once beyond, they entered a long hallway, empty and silent save for their footsteps. Celaena suddenly halted. "What," she breathed, "is *that*?" She pointed at the twenty-foot oak doors, her eyes widening at the dragons that grew out of either side of the stone wall. Four-legged dragons—not vicious, bipedal wyverns like those on the royal seal.

"The library." The two words were like a shot of lightning.

"The . . ." She looked at the claw-shaped iron handles. "Can we—may we go in?"

The Captain of the Guard opened the doors reluctantly, the strong muscles of his back shifting as he pushed hard against the worn oak. Compared to the sunlit hallway, the interior that stretched beyond them seemed formidably dark, but as she stepped inside, candelabras came into view, along with black-and-white marble floors, large mahogany tables with red velvet chairs, a slumbering fire, mezzanines, bridges, ladders, railings, and then books—books and books and books.

She'd entered a city made entirely of leather and paper. Celaena put a hand against her heart. Escape routes be damned. "I've never seen—how many volumes are there?"

Chaol shrugged. "The last time anyone bothered to count, it was a million. But that was two hundred years ago. I'd say maybe more than that, especially given the legends that a second library lies deep beneath, in catacombs and tunnels."

"Over a million? A million *books*?" Her heart leapt and danced, and she cracked a smile. "I'd die before I even got through half of that!"

"You like to read?"

She raised an eyebrow. "Don't you?" Not waiting for an answer, she moved farther into the library, the train of her gown sweeping across the floor. She neared a shelf and looked at the titles. She recognized none of them.

Grinning, she whirled and moved through the main floor, running a hand across the dusty books. "I didn't know assassins liked to read," Chaol called. If she were to die now, it would be in complete bliss. "You said you were from Terrasen; did you ever visit the Great Library of Orynth? They say it's twice the size of this—and that it used to hold all the knowledge of the world."

She turned from the stack she was currently studying. "Yes," she admitted. "When I was very young. Though they wouldn't let me explore—the Master Scholars were too afraid I'd ruin some valuable manuscript." She hadn't returned to the Great Library since—and wondered how many of those invaluable works had been ordered destroyed by the King of Adarlan when he outlawed magic. From the way Chaol said "used to" with a tinge of sadness, she assumed much had been lost. Though part of her savored the hope that those Master Scholars had smuggled many of the priceless books to safety—that when the royal family had been slaughtered and the King of Adarlan invaded, those stuffy old men had had the good sense to start hiding two thousand years' worth of ideas and learning.

A dead, empty space opened inside her. Needing to change the subject, she asked, "Why are none of your folk here?"

"Guards are of no use in a library." Oh, how wrong he was! Libraries were full of ideas—perhaps the most dangerous and powerful of all weapons.

She said, "I was referring to your noble companions."

He leaned against a table, a hand still on his sword. At least one of them remembered that they were alone together in the library. "Reading is a bit out of fashion, I'm afraid."

"Yes, well—more for me to read, then."

"Read? These belong to the king."

"It's a library, isn't it?"

"It's the king's property, and you aren't of noble blood. You need permission from either him or the prince."

"I highly doubt either would notice the loss of a few books."

Chaol sighed. "It's late. I'm hungry."

"So?" she said. He growled and practically dragged her from the library.

After a solitary supper, over which she contemplated all of her planned escape routes and how she might make more weapons for herself, Celaena paced through her rooms. Where were the other competitors being kept? Did they have access to books, if they wanted?

Celaena slumped into a chair. She was tired, but the sun had barely set. Instead of reading, she could perhaps use the pianoforte, but . . . well, it had been a while, and she wasn't sure she could endure the sound of her own stumbling, clumsy playing. She traced a finger over a splotch of fuchsia silk on her dress. All those books, with no one to read them.

An idea flashed, and she jumped to her feet, only to sit at the desk and grab a piece of parchment. If Captain Westfall insisted on protocol, then she'd give it to him in abundance. She dipped the glass pen in a pot of ink and held it over the paper.

How odd it felt to hold a pen! She traced the letters in the air. It was impossible that she'd forgotten how to write. Her fingers moved awkwardly as the pen touched the paper, but she carefully wrote her name, then the alphabet, three times. The letters were uneven, but she could do it. She pulled out another piece of paper and began to write.

Your Highness—

It has come to my attention that your library isn't a library, but rather a personal collection for only you and your esteemed father to enjoy. As many of your million books seem to be present and underused, I must beg you to grant me permission to borrow a few so that they might receive the attention they deserve. Since I am deprived of company and entertainment, this act of kindness is the least someone of your importance could deign to bestow upon a lowly, miserable wretch such as I.

Yours most truly,
Celaena Sardothien

Celaena beamed at her note and handed it to the nicest-looking servant she could find, with specific instructions to give it immediately to the Crown Prince. When the woman returned half an hour later with a stack of books piled in her arms, Celaena laughed as she swiped the note that crowned the column of leather.

My Most True Assassin,

Enclosed are seven books from my personal library that I have recently read and enjoyed immensely. You are, of course, free to read as many of the books in the castle library as you wish, but I command you to read these first so that we might discuss them. I promise they are not dull, for I am not one inclined to sit through pages of *nonsense and bloated speech, though perhaps you enjoy works and authors who think very highly of themselves.*

Most affectionately,
Dorian Havilliard

Celaena laughed again and took the books from the woman's arms, thanking her for her trouble. She walked into her bedroom, shutting the door with a backward kick, and dropped onto the bed, scattering the books across the crimson surface. She didn't recognize any of the titles, though one author was familiar. Choosing the book that seemed the most interesting, Celaena flipped onto her back and began to read.

Celaena awoke the next morning to the wretched booming of the clock tower. Half-asleep, she counted the chimes. Noon. She sat up. Where was Chaol? And, more importantly, what about the competition? Wasn't it supposed to have started today?

She leapt from bed and stalked through her chambers, half expecting to find him sitting in a chair, a hand upon his sword. He wasn't there. She popped her head into the hallway, but the four guards only reached for their weapons. She paced onto the balcony, the crossbows of five guards beneath clicking into position, and put her hands on her hips as she surveyed the autumn day.

The trees in the garden were gold and brown, half of the leaves already dead on the earth. Yet the day was so warm it could have passed for summer. Celaena took a seat on the rail, and waved at the guards with their crossbows aimed at her. Out across Rifthold, she could make out the sails of ships, and the wagons and people streaming through the streets. The green roofs of the city glowed emerald in the sun.

She looked again at the five guards beneath the balcony. They stared right back at her, and when they slowly lowered their crossbows, she grinned. She could knock them senseless with a few heavy books.

A sound flitted through the garden, and some of the guards glanced toward the source. Three women appeared from around a nearby hedge, clustered in conversation.

Most of the talk Celaena had overheard yesterday was immensely dull, and she didn't expect much as the women neared. They wore fine dresses, though the one in the middle—the raven-haired one—wore the finest. The red skirts were the size of a tent, and her bodice was so tightly bound that Celaena wondered if her waist were any more than sixteen inches. The other women were blondes dressed in pale blue, their matching gowns suggesting their rank as ladies-in-waiting. Celaena backed away from the ledge as they stopped at the nearby fountain.

From her place at the back of the balcony, Celaena could still see as the woman in red brushed a hand down the front of her skirts. "I should have worn my white dress," she said loudly enough for everyone in Rifthold to hear. "Dorian likes white." She adjusted a pleat in her skirt. "But I'll wager that everyone's wearing white."

"Shall we go change, milady?" asked one of the blondes.

"No," snapped the woman. "This dress is fine. Old and shabby as it is."

"But—" said the other blonde, then stopped as her mistress's head whipped around. Celaena approached the rail again and peered over. The dress hardly looked old.

"It won't take long for Dorian to ask me for a private audience." Celaena now leaned over the edge of the balcony. The guards watched the three girls, rapt for another reason entirely. "Though I worry how much Perrington's courting will interfere; but I *do* adore the man for inviting me to Rifthold. My mother must be writhing in her grave!" She paused, and then said: "I wonder who she is."

"Your mother, milady?"

"The girl the prince brought into Rifthold. I heard he traveled all over Erilea to find her, and that she rode into the city on the Captain of the Guard's horse. I've heard nothing else about her. Not even her name." The two women lagged behind their mistress and exchanged exasperated looks that informed the assassin this conversation had been held many times before. "I don't need to worry," the woman mused. "The prince's harlot won't be well-received."

His what?

The ladies in waiting stopped beneath the balcony, batting their eyelashes at the guards. "I need my pipe," the woman murmured, rubbing her temples. "I feel a headache coming on." Celaena's brows rose. "Regardless," the woman continued, striding away, "I shall have to watch my back. I might even have to—"

CRASH!

The women screamed, the guards whirled with their crossbows pointed, and Celaena looked skyward as she retreated from the rail and into the shadows of the balcony doorway. The flowerpot had missed. This time.

The woman cursed so colorfully that Celaena clamped a hand over her mouth to keep from laughing. The servants cooed, wiping mud from the woman's skirts and suede shoes. "Be quiet!" the woman hissed. The guards, wisely, didn't let their amusement show. "Be quiet and let's go!"

The women hurried off as the prince's harlot strode into her chambers and called for her servants to dress her in the finest gown they could find.

9

Celaena stood before the rosewood mirror, smiling.

She ran a hand down her gown. Sea-foam white lace bloomed from the sweeping neckline, washing upon her breast from the powder-green ocean of silk that made up the dress. A red sash covered the waist, forming an inverted peak that separated the bodice from the explosion of skirts beneath. Patterns of clear green beads were embroidered in whorls and vines across the whole of it, and bone-colored stitching stretched along the ribs. Tucked inside her bodice was the small makeshift hairpin dagger, though it poked mercilessly at her chest. She lifted her hands to touch her curled and pinned hair.

She didn't know what she planned to do now that she was dressed, especially if she'd probably have to change before the competition started, but—

Skirts rustled from the doorway, and Celaena raised her eyes in the reflection to see Philippa enter behind her. The assassin tried not to preen—and failed miserably. "It's such a pity you are who you are," Philippa said, turning Celaena to face her. "I wouldn't be surprised if you managed to ensnare some lord into marriage. Maybe even His Highness, if you were charming enough." She adjusted the green folds of Celaena's dress before kneeling down to brush the assassin's ruby-colored slippers.

"Well, it seems rumor has already suggested that. I overheard a girl saying that the Crown Prince brought me here to woo me. I thought the entire court knew about this stupid competition."

Philippa rose. "Whatever the rumors are, it'll all be forgotten in a week—just you wait. Let him find a new woman he likes and you'll vanish from the whisperings of the court." Celaena straightened as Philippa fixed a stray curl. "Oh, it's not meant as an offense, poppet. Beautiful ladies are always associated with the Crown Prince—you should be flattered that you're attractive enough to be considered his lover."

"I'd rather not be seen that way at all."

"Better than as an assassin, I'd wager."

She looked at Philippa and then laughed.

Philippa shook her head. "Your face is much more pretty when you smile. Girlish, even. Far better than that frown you always have."

"Yes," Celaena admitted, "you might be right." She made to sit down upon the mauve ottoman.

"Ah!" Philippa said, and Celaena froze, standing upright. "You'll wrinkle the fabric."

"But my feet hurt in these shoes." She frowned pitifully. "You can't intend for me to stand all day? Even through my meals?"

"Only until someone tells me how lovely you look."

"No one knows you're my servant."

"Oh, they know I've been assigned to the *lover* the prince brought to Rifthold."

Celaena chewed on her lip. *Was* it a good thing that no one knew who she truly was? What would her competition think? Perhaps a tunic and pants would have been better.

Celaena reached to move a curl that itched her cheek, and Philippa batted her hand away. "You'll ruin your hair."

The doors to her apartment slammed open, followed by an already familiar snarling and stomping about. She watched in the mirror as Chaol appeared in the doorway, panting. Philippa curtsied.

"You," he began, then stopped as Celaena faced him. His brows lowered as his eyes traveled along her body. His head cocked, and he opened his mouth as if to say something, but only shook his head and scowled. "Upstairs. Now."

She curtsied, looking up at him beneath lowered lashes. "Where, pray tell, are we going?"

"Oh, don't simper at me." He grabbed her by the arm, guiding her out of the room.

"Captain Westfall!" Philippa scolded. "She'll trip on her dress. At least let her hold her skirts."

She actually did trip on her dress, and her shoes cut into her heels quite terribly, but he would hear none of her objections as he dragged her into the hall. She smiled at the guards outside her door, and her smile burst into a grin at their exchanged approving glances. The captain's grip tightened until it hurt. "Hurry," he said. "We can't be late."

"Perhaps if you'd given me ample warning, I'd have dressed earlier and you wouldn't have to drag me!" It was hard to breathe with the corset crushing her ribs. As they hurried up a long staircase, she raised a hand to her hair to ensure that it hadn't fallen out.

"My mind was elsewhere; you were fortunate to be dressed, though I wish you'd worn something less . . . frilly to see the king."

"The king?" She was thankful that she hadn't yet eaten.

"Yes, the king. Did you think you wouldn't see him? The Crown

Prince told you the competition was to start today—this meeting will mark the official beginning. The real work begins tomorrow."

Her arms became heavy and she forgot all about her aching feet and crushed ribs. In the garden, the queer, off-kilter clock tower began chiming the hour. They reached the top of the staircase and rushed down a long hallway. She couldn't breathe.

Nauseated, she looked out the windows that lined the passage. The earth was far below—far, far below. They were in the glass addition. She didn't want to be there. She couldn't be in the glass castle. "Why didn't you tell me sooner?"

"Because he just decided to see you now. He'd originally said this evening. Hopefully, the other Champions will be later than us."

She felt like fainting. The king.

"When you enter," he said over his shoulder, "stop where I stop. Bow—low. When you raise your head, keep it high and stand straight. Don't look the king in the eye, don't answer anything without 'Your Majesty' attached, and do *not,* under any circumstances, talk back. He'll have you hanged if you don't please him."

She had a terrible headache around her left temple. Everything was sickly and frail. They were so high up, so dangerously high . . . Chaol stopped before rounding a corner. "You're pale."

She had difficulty focusing on his face as she breathed in and out, in and out. She hated corsets. She hated the king. She hated glass castles.

The days surrounding her capture and sentencing had been like a fever dream, but she could perfectly visualize her trial—the dark wood of the walls, the smoothness of the chair beneath her, the way her injuries still ached from the capture, and the terrible silence that had overtaken her body and soul. She had glanced at the king—only once. It was enough to make her reckless, to wish for any punishment that would take her far from him—even a quick death.

"Celaena." She blinked, her cheeks burning. Chaol's features softened. "He's just a man. But a man you should treat with the respect his rank demands." He began walking with her again, slower. "This meeting is only to remind you and the other Champions of why you're here, and what you're to do, and what you stand to gain. You're not on trial. You will not be tested today." They entered a long hallway, and she spied four guards posted before large glass doors at the other end. "Celaena." He stopped a few feet from the guards. His eyes were rich, molten brown.

"Yes?" Her heartbeat steadied.

"You look rather pretty today," was all he said before the doors opened and they walked forward. Celaena raised her chin as they entered the crowded room.

10

She saw the floor first. Red marble, its white veins illuminated in the light of the sun, which slowly vanished as the opaque glass doors groaned shut. Chandeliers and torches hung all around. Her eyes darted from one side of the large, crowded chamber to the next. There were no windows, just a wall of glass looking out into nothing but sky. No escape, save for the door behind her.

To her left, a fireplace occupied most of the wall, and as Chaol led her farther into the room, Celaena tried not to stare at the thing. It was monstrous, shaped like a roaring, fanged mouth, a blazing fire burning within. There was something greenish about the flame, something that made her spine straighten.

The captain stopped in the open space before the throne, and Celaena halted with him. He didn't seem to notice their ominous surroundings, or if he did, he hid it far better. She pulled her gaze forward, taking in the crowd that filled the room. Stiffly, knowing that many eyes were upon her, Celaena dropped into a low bow, her skirts whispering.

She found her legs weak when Chaol put a hand on her back to motion her to rise. He led her from the center of the room, where they took up a spot beside Dorian Havilliard. The absence of dirt and three weeks' worth of hard travel had a noticeable effect on his smooth face. He wore a red-and-gold jacket, his black hair brushed and shining. An expression of surprise crossed his features when he beheld her in her finery, but it quickly melted into a wry grin as he looked toward his father. She might have returned it, had she not been focusing so much on keeping her hands from shaking.

The king spoke at last. "Now that you've all finally bothered to arrive, perhaps we can begin."

It was a voice she had heard before, deep and raspy. It made her bones crack and splinter, made her feel the astonishing cold of a winter long since past. Her eyes only dared to venture as far as his chest. It was broad, not entirely with muscle, and seemed tightly restrained within a crimson and black tunic. A cape of white fur hung from his shoulders, and a sword was sheathed at his side. Atop its hilt perched a wyvern, open-mouthed and screaming. None that came before that broad blade lived to see another day. She knew that sword.

Nothung was its name.

"You have all been retrieved from across Erilea for the purpose of serving your country."

It was easy enough to tell the nobility from her competitors. Old and wrinkled, each nobleman wore fine clothes and decorative swords. Beside each of them stood a man—some tall and slender, some burly, some average, all of them surrounded by at least three vigilant guards.

Twenty-three men stood between her and freedom. Most of them had enough bulk to warrant a double take, but when she scanned their faces—often scarred, pockmarked, or just plain hideous—there was no spark behind their eyes, no shining kernel of cleverness. They'd been picked for muscles, not brains. Three of them were actually in chains. Were they that dangerous?

A few of them met her gaze, and she stared right back, wondering if they thought she was a competitor or just a court lady. Most of the competitors' attention jumped right over her. She gritted her teeth. The dress had been a mistake. Why had Chaol not told her about the meeting *yesterday*?

A moderately handsome black-haired young man stared at her, though, and she willed her face into neutrality while his gray eyes took her in. He was tall and lean, but not gangly, and he inclined his head to her. She studied him for a moment longer, from the way he balanced his weight to his left, to what feature he first noticed when his eyes moved on and he examined the other competitors.

One was a gargantuan man standing beside Duke Perrington, who seemed crafted of muscle and steel—and took pains to display it with his sleeveless armor. The man's arms looked capable of crushing a horse's skull. It wasn't that he was ugly—in fact, his tanned face was rather pleasant, but there was something nasty about his demeanor, about his obsidian eyes as they shifted and met her own. His large, white teeth gleamed.

The king spoke. "You are each competing for the title of my Champion—my right-hand sword in a world brimming with enemies."

A flicker of shame sparked within her. What was "Champion" but a dressed-up name for murderer? Could she actually stomach working for him? She swallowed. She had to. She had no other choice.

"Over the next thirteen weeks, you shall each dwell and compete in my home. You will train every day, and be tested once a week—a test during which one of you will be eliminated." Celaena did the calculations. There were twenty-four of them—and only thirteen weeks. As if sensing her question, the king said, "These tests will not be easy, nor will your training. Some of you might die in the process. We will add additional elimination tests as we see fit. And if you fall behind, if you fail, if you displease me, you will be packed off to whatever dark hole you came from.

"The week after Yulemas, the four remaining Champions will face each other in a duel to win the title. Until then, while my court is aware that some sort of contest is being held among my closest friends and advisors"—he waved a huge, scarred hand to encompass the room—"you will keep your business private. Any wrongdoing on your part, and I'll stake you to the front gates."

By accident, her gaze slipped onto the king's face, and she found his dark eyes staring into hers. The king smirked. Her heart threw itself backward and clung to the bars of her ribcage.

Murderer.

He should be hanging from the gallows. He had killed many more than she—people undeserving and defenseless. He'd destroyed cultures, destroyed invaluable knowledge, destroyed so much of what had once been bright and good. His people should revolt. Erilea should revolt—the way those few rebels had dared to do. Celaena struggled to maintain his gaze. She couldn't retreat.

"Is that understood?" the king asked, still staring at her.

Her head was heavy as she nodded. She had only until Yulemas to beat them all. One test a week—perhaps more.

"Speak!" the king bellowed to the room, and she tried not to flinch. "Are you not grateful for this opportunity? Do you not wish to give me your thanks and allegiance?"

She bowed her head and stared at his feet. "Thank you, Your Majesty. I am most appreciative," she murmured, the sound blending in with the words of the other Champions.

The king put a hand upon Nothung's hilt. "This should be an interesting thirteen weeks." She could feel his attention still upon her face, and she ground her teeth. "Prove trustworthy, become my Champion, and wealth and glory will be yours eternal."

Only thirteen weeks to win her freedom.

"I am to depart next week for my own purposes. I will not return until Yulemas. But don't think I won't be able to give the command to execute any of you, should I hear word of any trouble, or *accidents*." The Champions nodded once more.

"If we're finished, I'm afraid I must take my leave," interrupted Dorian from beside her, and her head snapped up at the sound of his voice—and his impertinence in interrupting his father. He bowed to his father, and nodded to the mute councilors. The king waved his son away, not even bothering to look at him. Dorian winked at Chaol before walking from the room.

"If there are no questions," the king said to the Champions and their sponsors in a tone that suggested that asking questions would only guarantee a trip to the gallows, "then you have my leave. Do not forget that you are here to honor me—and my empire. Be gone, all of you."

Celaena and Chaol didn't speak as they strode down the hallway, quickly moving from the throng of competitors and their sponsors, who lingered to speak with one another—and size each other up. With every step away from the king, steadying warmth returned. It wasn't until they rounded a corner that Chaol let out a deep breath and removed his hand from her back.

"Well, you managed to keep your mouth shut—for once," he said.

"But how convincing she was in her nodding and bowing!" said a cheerful voice. It was Dorian, leaning against a wall.

"What are you doing?" Chaol asked.

Dorian pushed off the wall. "Why, waiting for you, of course."

"We're to dine this evening," Chaol said.

"I was speaking to my Champion," Dorian said with a roguish wink. Remembering how he'd smiled at the court lady the day of their arrival, she kept her gaze ahead. The Crown Prince took up a place safely beside Chaol as they walked on. "I apologize for my father's gruffness." She stared down the hall, at the servants who bowed to Dorian. He ignored them.

"By the Wyrd!" Dorian laughed. "He's trained you well already!" He nudged Chaol with his elbow. "From the way you two are blatantly ignoring me, I'd say she could pass for your sister! Though you don't really look like each other—it would be hard to pass off someone so pretty as *your* sister."

Celaena was unable to keep a hint of a smile from her lips. Both she and the prince had grown up under strict, unforgiving fathers—well, father figure in her case. Arobynn had never replaced the father she'd lost, nor had he ever tried to. But at least Arobynn had an excuse for being equal parts tyrannical and doting. Why had the King of Adarlan let his son become anything but an identical copy of himself?

"There!" Dorian said. "A reaction—thank the gods I've amused her." He glanced behind them, making sure there was no one there, before his voice quieted. "I don't think Chaol told you our plan before the meeting—risky, on all of our parts."

"What plan?" She traced a finger along the beading on her skirts, watching it shimmer in the afternoon light.

"For your identity. Which you should keep quiet about; your competitors might know a thing or two about Adarlan's Assassin and use it against you."

Fair enough, even if it had taken them weeks to bother to fill her in. "And who, exactly, am I to be, if not a ruthless killer?"

"To everyone in this castle," Dorian said, "your name is Lillian Gordaina. Your mother is dead and your father is a wealthy merchant from Bellhaven. You are the sole heir to his fortune. However, you have a dark secret: you spend your nights as a jewel thief. I met you this summer after you tried to rob me while I was vacationing in Bellhaven, and I saw your potential then. But your father discovered your nightly fun, and removed you from the lure of the city to a town near Endovier. When my father decided to have this competition, I journeyed to find you, and brought you here as my Champion. You can fill in the gaps yourself."

She raised her brows. "Really? A *jewel thief*?"

Chaol snorted, but Dorian went on. "It's rather charming, don't you think?" When she didn't respond, the prince asked, "Do you find my home to your liking?"

"It's very fine indeed," she said dully.

"'Very fine indeed'? Maybe I should move my Champion to even *larger* chambers."

"If it pleases you."

Dorian chuckled. "I'm glad to find that seeing your competition hasn't damaged that swagger of yours. What'd you make of Cain?"

She knew whom he meant. "Perhaps you should start feeding me whatever Perrington is giving him." When Dorian continued staring at her, she rolled her eyes. "Men of his size usually aren't very fast, or very nimble. He could knock me out in one punch, probably, but he'd have to be swift enough to catch me." She gave Chaol a quick glance, daring him to challenge her claim, but Dorian answered.

"Good. I thought so. And what of the others? Any potential rivals? Some of the Champions have rather gruesome reputations."

"Everyone else looks pathetic," she lied.

The prince's smile grew. "I bet they won't expect to be trounced by a beautiful lady."

This was all a game to him, wasn't it? Before Celaena could ask, someone curtsied in the middle of their path. "Your Highness! What a surprise!" The voice was high, but smooth and calculated. It was the woman from the garden. She'd changed—she now wore a gown of white and gold that, despite herself, Celaena greatly admired. She was unfairly stunning.

And Celaena was willing to bet a fortune that this was anything *but* a surprise—the woman had probably been waiting here for a while.

"Lady Kaltain," Dorian said tersely, his body tensing.

"I've just come from Her Majesty's side," said Kaltain, putting her back to Celaena. The assassin might have bothered to care about the slight if she had any interest in courtiers. "Her Majesty wishes to see Your Highness. Of course, I informed Her Majesty that Your Highness was in a meeting and could not be—"

"Lady Kaltain," interrupted Dorian, "I'm afraid you haven't been introduced to my friend." Celaena could have sworn the young woman bristled. "Allow me to present the Lady Lillian Gordaina. Lady Lillian, meet Lady Kaltain Rompier."

Celaena curtsied, restraining the urge to keep walking; if she had to deal with too much courtly nonsense, she might be better off back in Endovier. Kaltain bowed, the gold streaks in her dress glistening in the sunlight.

"Lady Lillian is from Bellhaven—she arrived just yesterday."

The woman studied Celaena from beneath dark, shaped eyebrows. "And how long will you be staying with us?"

"Only a few years," Dorian said with a sigh.

"'Only'! Why, Your Highness! How droll! That is a very long stretch of time!" Celaena studied Kaltain's narrow, narrow waist. Was it really that small? Or could she barely breathe in her corset?

She caught a glance exchanged between the two men—exasperation, annoyance, condescension. "The Lady Lillian and Captain Westfall are very close companions," Dorian said dramatically. To Celaena's delight, Chaol blushed. "It will feel short for them, I assure you."

"And for you, Your Highness?" Kaltain said coyly. A concealed edge lingered beneath her voice.

Mischief coiled and sprang within her, but Dorian answered. "I suppose," he drawled, turning those brilliant blue eyes on Celaena, "that it *will* be difficult for Lady Lillian and I as well. Perhaps more so."

Kaltain snapped her attention to Celaena. "Wherever did you find that dress?" she purred. "It's extraordinary."

"I had it made for her," Dorian said casually, picking at his nails. The assassin and the prince glanced at each other, their blue eyes reflecting the same intent. At least they had *one* common enemy. "It *does* look extraordinary on her, doesn't it?"

Kaltain's lips pursed for a moment, but then bloomed into a full smile. "Simply stunning. Though such pale green tends to wash out women of pallid skin."

"The Lady Lillian's paleness was a source of pride for her father. It makes her rather unusual." Dorian looked to Chaol, who failed in his attempt to not appear incredulous. "Don't you agree, Captain Westfall?"

"Agree about what?" he snapped.

"How *unusual* our Lady Lillian is!"

"Shame on you, Your Highness!" Celaena chided, concealing her wicked amusement beneath a giggle. "I *pale* in comparison to Lady Kaltain's fine features."

Kaltain shook her head, but looked at Dorian as she spoke. "You are too kind."

Dorian shifted on his feet. "Well, I've dallied enough. I must attend to my mother." He bowed to Kaltain, then to Chaol. Finally, he faced Celaena. She watched with raised brows as he lifted her hand to his lips. His mouth was soft and smooth upon her skin, and the kiss sent a red-hot line of fire up through her arm that singed her cheeks. She fought against the urge to step back. Or smack him. "Until our next meeting, Lady Lillian," he said with a charming smile. She would have highly enjoyed seeing Kaltain's face, but she dipped into a curtsy.

"We must be on our way as well," Chaol said as Dorian strode off, whistling to himself, his hands in his pockets. "May we escort you anywhere?" It was an insincere offer.

"No," Kaltain said flatly, the facade falling. "I'm meeting with His Grace, Duke Perrington. I do hope we'll see more of each other, Lady Lillian," she said, watching her with a keenness that would make any assassin proud. "We must be friends, you and I."

"Of course," Celaena said. Kaltain swept past them, the skirts of her dress floating in the air around her. They resumed walking, waiting until her footsteps had vanished from their ears before speaking. "Enjoyed that, did you?" Chaol growled.

"Immensely." Celaena patted Chaol's arm as she took it in her own. "Now you must pretend that you *like* me, or else everything will be ruined."

"You and the Crown Prince share the same sense of humor, it seems."

"Perhaps he and I will become dear friends, and you will be left to rot."

"Dorian is more inclined to associate with ladies of better breeding and beauty." She whipped her head to look at him. He smiled. "How vain you are."

She glared. "I hate women like that. They're so desperate for the attention of men that they'd willingly betray and harm members of their own sex. And we claim men cannot think with their brains! At least men are direct about it."

"They say that her father is as rich as a king," Chaol said. "I suppose that's part of why Perrington is so infatuated. She arrived here in a litter bigger than most peasant huts; it was carried here from her home. A distance of almost two hundred miles."

"What debauchery."

"I pity her servants."

"I pity her father!" They chuckled, and he lifted the arm linked with hers a bit higher. She nodded to the guards outside her chambers as they stopped. She faced Chaol. "Are you eating lunch? I'm starved."

He glanced at the guards, his smile fading. "I have important work to do. Like prepare a company of men for the king to bring with him on his journey."

She opened the door, but looked at him. The tiny freckle upon his cheek moved upward as a smile spread once more.

"What?" she asked. Something smelled delicious inside her chambers, and her stomach grumbled.

Chaol shook his head. "Adarlan's Assassin," he chuckled, and began walking back down the hall. "You should rest," he called over his shoulder. "The competition *actually* begins tomorrow. And even if you're as fantastic as you claim to be, you're going to need every moment of sleep you can get."

Though she rolled her eyes and slammed the door, Celaena found herself humming throughout her meal.

11

Celaena felt as if she'd barely closed her eyes when a hand jabbed her side. She groaned, wincing as the drapes were thrown back to welcome the morning sun.

"Wake up." Not surprisingly, it was Chaol.

She shimmied beneath the blankets, pulling them over her head, but he grabbed the covers and threw them to the floor. Her nightgown was wrapped around her thighs. Celaena shivered.

"It's cold," she moaned, holding her knees to her body. She didn't care that she had only a few months to beat the other Champions—she needed *sleep*. It would have been nice if the Crown Prince had considered springing her from Endovier earlier so she could have *some* time to regain her strength; how long had he known about this competition, anyway?

"Get up." Chaol ripped the pillows from beneath her head. "Now you're wasting my time." If he noticed how much skin she was showing, he didn't react.

Grumbling, Celaena slithered to the edge of the bed, dangling a hand over the edge to touch the floor. "Fetch my slippers," she mumbled. "The floor's like ice."

He growled, but Celaena ignored him as she got to her feet. She staggered and slouched into the dining room, where an enormous breakfast lay on the table. Chaol jerked his chin toward the food. "Eat up. The competition starts in an hour."

Whatever nerves she felt, she kept them hidden from him as she gave an exaggerated sigh and collapsed into a chair with the grace of a large beast. Celaena scanned the table. Yet again, there were no knives. She stabbed her fork into a piece of sausage.

From the doorway, Chaol asked, "Why, might I ask, are you so tired?"

She gulped down the rest of the pomegranate juice and wiped her mouth on a napkin. "I was up until four reading," she said. "I sent a letter to your princeling, asking for permission to borrow books from the library. He granted my wish, and sent seven books from his *personal* library that I'm commanded to read."

Chaol shook his head in disbelief. "It isn't your place to write to the Crown Prince."

She gave him a simpering smile and took a bite of ham. "He could have ignored the letter. And besides, I'm his *Champion.* Not everyone feels obligated to be as nasty to me as you do."

"You're an assassin."

"If I say I'm a jewel thief, will you treat me with more courtesy?" She waved a hand. "Don't answer that." She spooned porridge into her mouth, found it to be bland, and scooped four heaping mounds of brown sugar into the gray mess.

Would the competitors actually be worthy opponents? Before she could start worrying, she examined his black clothes. "Don't you ever wear normal clothing?"

"Hurry up," was all he said. The competition awaited.

Suddenly not hungry, she pushed away her bowl of porridge. "I should get dressed, then." She turned her head to call for Philippa, but paused. "Just what sort of activities might I expect at the tournament today? So I can dress accordingly, of course."

"I don't know—they don't give us the details until you arrive." The captain rose and drummed the pommel of his sword before calling to a servant as Celaena walked into her bedroom. Behind her, Chaol spoke to the servant girl. "Dress her in pants and a shirt—something loose, nothing frilly or revealing, and bring a cloak." The girl disappeared into the dressing room. Celaena followed after her, unceremoniously stripping down to her underclothes and enjoying it far too much when Chaol's cheeks reddened before he turned away.

A few minutes later, Celaena frowned at herself as she hurried after the captain into the foyer. "I look ridiculous! These pants are absurd, and this shirt is awful."

"Stop whining. No one gives a damn about your clothes." He flung open the door to the hall, the guards outside instantly at attention. "Besides, you can take them off at the barracks. I'm sure everyone will be thrilled to see you in your undergarments." She swore violently under her breath, pulling her green velvet cloak tight around herself, and trailed after him.

The Captain of the Guard rushed through the castle, still freezing with the early-morning chill, and they soon entered the barracks. Guards in various states of armor saluted them. An open doorway revealed a large mess hall, where many of the guards were just sitting down to breakfast.

Finally, Chaol stopped somewhere on the ground floor. The giant rectangular room they entered was the size of the Grand Ballroom. Lined with pillars that supported a mezzanine, the floor was checkered black-and-white tile, and the floor-to-ceiling glass doors that made up one entire wall were open, the gossamer curtains blowing in the chilly breeze that drifted in from the garden. Most of the twenty-three other Champions were already scattered throughout the room, sparring with what could only be their sponsors' trainers. Everyone was carefully monitored by guards. None bothered to look at her, save for that slightly handsome young man with the gray eyes, who gave her a half smile before returning to firing arrows at a target across the room with unnerving accuracy. She lifted her chin and surveyed a rack of weapons. "You expect me to use a mace an hour after sunrise?"

Six guards appeared in the doorway behind them, joining the dozens already in the chamber, swords at the ready. "If you attempt anything foolish," Chaol said quietly, "they'll be here."

"I'm just a jewel thief, remember?" She approached the rack. Foolish, foolish decision to leave all those weapons out. Swords, swordbreakers, axes, bows, pikes, hunting daggers, maces, spears, throwing knives, wooden staves . . . While she generally preferred the stealth of a dagger, she was familiar with every weapon here. She glanced around the sparring room and hid her grimace. So were most of the competitors, it seemed. As she inspected them, she caught a movement in the corner of her vision.

Cain entered the hall, flanked by two guards and a scarred, burly man who must have been his trainer. She squared her shoulders as Cain strode straight toward her, his thick lips parting in a grin.

"Good morning," he said, his voice raspy and deep. His dark eyes snaked along her body, then found her face again. "I'd have thought you'd be running home by now."

She gave him a close-lipped smile. "The fun's just starting, isn't it?" Cain returned her smile and stalked off.

It would have been so, so easy. *So* easy to whirl and grab him by the neck and slam his face into the ground. She didn't even realize she was trembling with rage until Chaol stepped into her line of vision. "Save it for the competition," he said softly, but not weakly.

"I'm going to kill him," she breathed.

"No, you're not. If you want to shut him up, then beat him. He's just a brute from the king's army—don't waste your strength on hating him."

She rolled her eyes. "Thank you *so much* for interfering on my behalf."

"You don't need me to rescue you."

"It still would have been nice."

"You can fight your own battles." He pointed with his sword to the weapons rack. "Pick one." His eyes shone with the challenge as she untied her cloak and tossed it behind her. "Let's see if you can actually back up your swaggering."

She'd shut Cain up—in an unmarked grave for all eternity. But for now . . . Now, she'd make Chaol eat his words.

All the weapons were finely made, and glistened in the sunlight. Celaena eliminated her options one by one, seeing each weapon for what sort of damage she might do to the captain's face.

Her heart beat rapidly as she ran a finger across the blades and handles of each. She found herself torn between the hunting daggers and a lovely rapier with an ornate bell-guard. She could cut out his heart from a safe distance with that.

The sword whined as she drew it from the stand and held it in her hands. It was a good blade—strong, smooth, light. They wouldn't let her have a butter knife on her table, but they gave her access to *this*?

Why not wear him down a bit?

Chaol tossed his cape on top of hers, his toned body flexing through the dark threads of his shirt. He drew his sword. "On your guard!" He moved into defensive position, and Celaena looked at him dully.

Who do you think you are? What sort of person says "On your guard"?

"Aren't you first going to show me the *basics*?" she said quietly enough for only him to hear, her sword dangling from one hand. She rubbed the hilt, her fingers contracting on the cool surface. "I was in Endovier for a year, you realize. I could have easily forgotten."

"From the amount of killing that went on in your section of the mines, I highly doubt you've forgotten a thing."

"That was with a pickax," she said, her smile growing feral. "All I had to do was crack a man's head open or hurl the ax into his stomach." Thankfully, none of the other Champions paid them any heed. "If you consider that sort of gracelessness *equal* to swordsmanship . . . what sort of fighting do *you* do, Captain Westfall?" She put a spare hand over her heart and closed her eyes for emphasis.

With a growl, the Captain of the Guard lunged.

But she had been waiting for some time now, and her eyes flew open as soon as his boots scraped against the ground. With a turn of her arm she brought the sword into blocking position, her legs bracing for the impact as steel struck steel. The noise was strange, somehow more painful than receiving the blow, but Celaena thought little of it when he charged again and she met his weapon, parrying with ease. Her arms ached as they were shaken from their slumber, but she continued to deflect and parry.

Swordplay was like dancing—certain steps must be followed or else it would fall apart. Once she heard the beat, it all came rushing back. The other competitors faded away into shadows and sunlight.

"Good," he said through his teeth, blocking her thrust as she forced him to take a defensive stance. Her thighs burned. "Very good," he breathed. He was pretty good himself—better than good, actually. Not that she'd tell him that.

With a clang, the two swords met, and they pressed each other's blades. He was stronger, and she grunted at the force required to hold her sword against his. But, strong as he might be, he was not as quick.

She withdrew and feinted, her feet jabbing and flexing on the floor with birdlike grace. Caught off-guard, he only had time to deflect, his parry lost in his size.

She surged forward, her arm coming down again and again, twisting and turning, loving the smooth ache within her shoulder as the blade slammed against his. She was moving fast—fast like a dancer in a temple ritual, fast like a snake in the Red Desert, fast like water down the side of a mountain.

He kept up, and she allowed him to advance before reclaiming the position. He tried to catch her unawares with a blow to the face, but her anger awoke as her elbow snapped up and deflected, slamming into his fist and forcing it down.

"Something to remember when fighting me, Sardothien," he panted. The sun caught in his golden-brown eyes.

"Hmm?" she grunted, lunging to deflect his newest attack.

"I don't lose." He grinned at her, and before she could comprehend the words, something cut into her feet and—

She had the sickening feeling of falling. She gasped as her spine collided with marble, the rapier flying from her hand. Chaol pointed his blade at her heart. "I win," he breathed.

She pushed herself onto her elbows. "You had to resort to tripping me. That's hardly winning at all."

"I'm not the one with the sword at my heart."

The sound of clashing weapons and labored breathing filled the air. She flicked her eyes to the other Champions, who were all in the middle of sparring. All, of course, except Cain. He grinned broadly at her, and Celaena bared her teeth.

"You have the skills," Chaol said, "but some of your moves are still undisciplined."

She broke her stare with Cain and glared up into Chaol's face. "That's never stopped me from killing before," she spat.

Chaol chuckled at her agitation and pointed his sword at the rack, allowing her to get to her feet. "Pick another—something different. Make it interesting, too. Something that will make me sweat, please."

"You'll be sweating when I skin you alive and squish your eyeballs beneath my feet," she muttered, picking up the rapier.

"That's the spirit."

She practically threw the rapier into place, and drew the hunting knives without hesitation.

My dear old friends.

A wicked smile spread across her face.

12

Just as Celaena was about to launch herself and her knives at the captain, someone stomped a spear on the ground and called the room to attention. She faced the voice and found a stocky, balding man standing beneath the mezzanine.

"Your attention *now*," the man repeated. Celaena looked to Chaol, who nodded, taking the knives from her as they joined the twenty-three other competitors encircling the man. "I'm Theodus Brullo, Weapons Master and judge of this competition. Of course, our king's the final judge of you sorry lot, but I'll be the one determining every day if you're fit to be his Champion."

He patted his sword hilt, and Celaena had to admire the beautiful woven gold of the pommel. "I've been Weapons Master here for thirty years, and lived in this castle for twenty-five more than that. I've trained many a lord and knight—and many a would-be Champion of Adarlan. It will be *very* hard to impress me."

Beside Celaena, Chaol stood with his shoulders thrown back. It occurred to her that Brullo might have trained the captain. Given how easily Chaol had kept up with her, if Brullo had trained him, then the Weapons Master must live up to his title. She knew better than anyone not to underestimate opponents based on their appearance.

"The king's already told you all there is to know about this competition," Brullo said, holding his hands behind his back. "But I figured you lot are itching to know more about each other." He pointed a stubby finger at Cain. "You. What's your name, occupation, and where do you hail from? And be honest about it—I know none of you are bakers and candlestick makers."

Cain's insufferable grin returned. "Cain, soldier in the king's army. I hail from the White Fang Mountains." Of course he did. She'd heard tales of the brutality of the mountain folk from that region, and seen a few of them up close, seen the fierceness in their eyes. Many of them had rebelled against Adarlan—and most wound up dead. What would his fellow mountain-dwellers say if they could see him now? She gritted her teeth; what would the people of Terrasen say if they could see *her* now?

Brullo, however, either didn't know or didn't care, and didn't even give a nod before he pointed to the man to Cain's right. Celaena immediately liked him. "And you?"

A slender, tall man with thinning blond hair surveyed the circle and sneered. "Xavier Forul. Master Thief of Melisande." Master Thief! *That* man? Of course, she realized, his reed-thinness probably aided in slipping into houses. Maybe it wasn't a bluff.

One by one, the twenty-one other competitors introduced themselves. There were six more seasoned soldiers—all of them thrown out of the army for questionable behavior, which must have been truly questionable, given that Adarlan's army was notorious for ruthlessness. Then there were the three other thieves—including the dark-haired, gray-eyed Nox Owen, whom she'd actually heard of in passing, and who'd been giving her such charming smiles all morning. The three mercenaries looked ready to boil someone alive, and then there were the two shackled murderers.

As his name suggested, Bill Chastain, the Eye Eater, ate the eyes of his victims. He looked surprisingly plain, with mousy brown hair, tan skin, and average height, though Celaena had trouble not staring at his scar-flecked mouth. The other murderer was Ned Clement, who'd gone for three years under the name Scythe, for the weapon he'd used to torture and hack apart temple priestesses. It was a wonder they hadn't executed either man, though from their tanned skin, she guessed they'd spent the years since their captures toiling under the sun in Calaculla, the southern sister labor camp to Endovier.

Next came two scarred, silent men who seemed to be cronies of some far-off warlord, and then the five assassins.

She immediately forgot the names of the first four: a gangly, haughty boy; a hulking brute; a disdainful runt of a man; and a sniveling, hawk-nosed prat who claimed he had an affinity for knives. They weren't even in the Assassins Guild—not that Arobynn Hamel would ever allow them in. Membership required years of training and a more-than-impressive track record. While these four might be skilled, they lacked the refinement that Arobynn favored in his followers. She'd have to keep an eye on them, but at least they weren't the Silent Assassins from the windswept dunes of the Red Desert. Those would be worthy of her—they'd make her sweat a bit. She'd spent a month training with them one burning summer, and her muscles still ached at the memory of their grueling exercises.

The last assassin, who called himself Grave, made her pause. He was slight and short, with the kind of wicked face that made people quickly look away. He'd entered the room wearing shackles, and only had them removed when his guards—all five of them—gave him a stern warning.

Even now, they stood nearby, watching him relentlessly. As he introduced himself, Grave flashed an oily smile, revealing his brown teeth. Her disgust didn't improve when Grave ran an eye over her body. An assassin like that never stopped at just killing. Not if his victim was female. She willed herself to hold his hungry gaze.

"And you?" Brullo said, cutting into her thoughts.

"Lillian Gordaina," she said, holding her chin high. "Jewel thief from Bellhaven."

Some of the men sniggered, and she clenched her teeth. They'd stop their laughing if they knew her true name, if they knew that this "jewel thief" could skin them alive without a knife.

"Fine," Brullo said, waving a hand. "You all have five minutes to put away your weapons and catch your breath. Then we're on a mandatory run to see how fit you are. Those of you who can't run the distance go home, or back to whatever prison your sponsors found you rotting in. Your first Test is in five days; consider us merciful it's not sooner."

With that, everyone scattered, the Champions murmuring to their trainers about whatever competitor they deemed the biggest threat. Cain or Grave, most likely. Certainly not a jewel thief from Bellhaven. Chaol remained beside her, watching the Champions stride off. She hadn't spent eight years building a reputation and a year laboring in Endovier to be disregarded like *this*. "If I have to call myself a jewel thief again—"

Chaol raised his brows. "You'll do what, exactly?"

"Do you know how insulting it is to pretend to be some nobody thief from a small city in Fenharrow?"

He stared her down, quiet for a moment. "Are you *that* arrogant?" She bristled, but he went on. "It was foolish to spar with you just now. I'll admit that I hadn't realized you'd be that good. Thankfully, no one noticed. And do you want to know *why*, Lillian?" He took a step closer, his voice lowering. "Because you're some pretty little girl. Because you're a nobody jewel thief from a small city in Fenharrow. Look around." He half-turned to the other Champions. "Is anyone staring at you? Are any of them sizing *you* up? No. Because you're not real competition. Because *you* don't stand between them and whatever freedom or wealth they're looking for."

"Exactly! It's insulting!"

"It's smart, that's what it is. And you're going to keep a low profile throughout this entire competition. You're not going to excel, and you're not going to trounce those thieves and soldiers and unknown assassins. You're going to stay solidly in the middle, where no one will look your way, because you're not a threat, because they'll think that you'll be eliminated sooner or later, and they should focus their attention on getting rid of bigger, stronger, faster Champions like Cain.

"But you're going to outlast them," Chaol continued. "And when they wake up on the morning of the final duel and find that *you* are their opponent, and that *you* have beaten them, the look on their faces will make all of the insults and lack of attention worthwhile." He extended his hand to lead her outside. "So, what do you have to say about *that*, Lillian Gordaina?"

"I can look out for myself," she said lightly, taking his hand. "But I have to say that you're rather brilliant, Captain. So brilliant, actually, that I might give you one of the jewels I plan to steal from the queen tonight."

Chaol chuckled, and they strode outside to where the running contest awaited.

Her lungs burned and her legs were leaden, but she kept running, kept her position in the middle of the pack of Champions. Brullo, Chaol, and the other trainers—along with three dozen armed guards—followed them around the game park on horseback. Some of the Champions,

Grave, Ned, and Bill included, had been given long manacles. She supposed it was a privilege that Chaol hadn't locked her up, too. But to her surprise, Cain led the pack, and was nearly ten yards in front of the rest of them. How could he possibly be that fast?

The sound of crunching leaves and labored breathing filled the warm autumn air, and Celaena kept her gaze on the damp and gleaming dark hair of the thief in front of her. One step after another, one breath in, one breath out. Breathe—she had to remember to keep breathing.

Ahead, Cain turned a corner, heading north—back toward the castle. Like a flock of birds, they followed him. One step after another, never slowing down. Let them all watch Cain, let them plot against him. She didn't need to win the race to prove she was better—she was better without any kind of validation that the king could give her! She missed a breath, and her knees wobbled, but she kept upright. The run would be over soon. Soon.

She hadn't even dared to look behind her to see if any had fallen. She could feel Chaol's eyes on her, though, reminding her to keep in the middle. At least he had that much faith in her.

The trees parted, revealing the field that lay between the game park and the stables. The end of the path. Her head spun, and she would have cursed at the stitch that lanced through her side had she had any breath to do so. She had to stay in the middle. Stay in the middle.

Cain cleared the trees and raised his arms above his head in victory. He ran a few more feet, slowing his pace to cool down, and his trainer cheered for him. Celaena's only response was to keep her feet moving. Only a few yards left. The light of the open field grew brighter and brighter as it approached. Stars flashed before her eyes, swarming in her vision. She had to stay in the middle. Years of training with Arobynn Hamel had taught her the dangers of giving up too easily.

Then, she was through the trees, and the open field surrounded her in an explosion of space and grass and blue sky. The men in front of her slowed to a stop. It was all she could do to keep from sinking to her knees, but she made her legs slow, slow, slow, made her feet walk, made herself take breath after breath as the stars continued bursting before her eyes.

"Good," Brullo said, reining his horse and surveying whoever had first returned. "Get water. We've got more training after this."

Through the spots in her vision, she saw Chaol stop his horse. Her feet moved of their own accord toward him, then past, back to the woods. "Where are you going?"

"I dropped my ring back there," she lied, doing her best to look scatterbrained. "Just give me a moment to find it." Without waiting for his approval, she entered the trees to the sneers and snickers of the Champions who had overheard. From the approaching crashing noises, she knew another Champion was on his way out. She stepped into the cover of the bushes, stumbling as the world became dark and light and tilted. She had barely sunk to her knees when she vomited.

She heaved and heaved until she had nothing left inside. The straggling Champion passed by. On trembling limbs, she grappled onto a nearby tree and hauled herself upright again. She found Captain Westfall standing across the path, watching her with pursed lips.

She wiped her mouth on the back of her wrist and said nothing to him as she exited the woods.

13

It was lunchtime when Brullo released them for the day, and to say that Celaena was hungry would be a severe understatement. She was halfway through her meal, shoveling meat and bread down her throat, when the dining room door opened. "What are you doing here?" she said through a mouthful.

"What?" said the Captain of the Guard, taking a seat at the table. He'd changed his clothes and taken a bath. He pulled a platter of salmon toward him and piled it on his plate. Celaena made a disgusted face, her nose crinkling. "You don't care for salmon?"

"I hate fish. I'd rather die than eat it."

"That's surprising," he said, taking a bite.

"Why?"

"Because you smell like one."

She opened her mouth to expose the ball of bread and beef that she was chewing. He shook his head. "You might fight well, but your manners are a disgrace."

She waited for him to mention her earlier vomiting, but he didn't continue. "I can act and talk like a lady, if it pleases me."

"Then I suggest that you begin to do so." After a pause, he asked, "How are you enjoying your temporary freedom?"

"Is that a snide remark or an honest question?"

He took a bite of fish. "Whichever you like."

The window revealed the afternoon sky, slightly pale, but still lovely. "I'm enjoying it, for the most part. Especially now that I have books to read whenever you lock me in here. I don't suppose you'd understand."

"On the contrary. I might not have as much time to read as you and Dorian do, but that doesn't mean I love books any less."

She bit into an apple. It was tart, with a sweet, honey-like aftertaste. "Oh? And what books do you love?" He named a few, and she blinked. "Well, those are good choices—for the most part. What others?" she asked, and somehow, an hour flew by, carrying them on the wings of conversation. Suddenly, the clock chimed one, and he rose.

"The afternoon is yours to spend in any way that you like."

"Where are you going?"

"To rest my limbs and my lungs."

"Yes, well, hopefully you'll read something of quality before I see you again."

He sniffed the air as he walked out of her room. "Hopefully you'll take a bath before I see *you* again."

Sighing, Celaena called to her servants to draw her bath. An afternoon of reading on the balcony beckoned.

The following dawn, Celaena's bedroom door opened, and a familiar stalking gait echoed through the room. Chaol Westfall stopped short when he found the assassin dangling from the beam of the bedroom doorway, repeatedly hoisting herself up to touch her chin to the wooden bar. Sweat soaked her undershirt and ran in rivulets down her pale skin.

She'd been exercising for an hour already. Her arms quivered as she lifted herself again.

Though she might pretend to be in the middle of the pack, there was no reason to train like it. Even if every repetition made her body scream for her to stop. She wasn't *that* out of shape—after all, her pickax in the mines had been heavy. And it definitely had nothing to do with her fellow competitors walloping her at the race yesterday.

She already had an edge on them. She just needed it to be a bit sharper.

She didn't pause her exercising as she smiled at him, panting through her clenched teeth. To her surprise, he smiled back.

By that afternoon, a vicious rainstorm arrived, and Chaol permitted Celaena to walk around the castle with him after she'd finished training with the other Champions for the day. Though he spoke little, she was glad to be out of her rooms, and dressed in one of her new gowns—a lovely lilac silk dress with pale pink lace accents and pearl beading. But then they rounded a corner and nearly collided with Kaltain Rompier. The assassin would have grimaced, but she forgot all about Kaltain as her eyes fell upon her companion. It was an Eyllwe woman.

She was stunning, long and lean, each of her features perfectly formed and smooth. Her loose white dress contrasted with her creamy brown skin, and a three-plated gold torque covered much of her chest and neck. Bracelets of ivory and gold glimmered around her wrists, and her feet were sandaled beneath matching anklets. A thin circlet comprising dangling gold and jewels crowned her head. She had two male guards with her, armed to the teeth with an assortment of curved Eyllwe daggers and swords, both of them studying Chaol and Celaena closely—weighing the threat.

The Eyllwe girl was a princess.

"Captain Westfall!" Kaltain said, and curtsied. Beside her, a short man dressed in the red-and-black garb of a councilman bowed to the pair.

The Eyllwe princess stood perfectly still, her brown eyes wary as she took in Celaena and her companion. Celaena offered her a slight smile, and the princess stepped closer, her guards tensing slightly. She moved with an easy grace.

Kaltain gestured to the girl, poorly hidden distaste written across her beautiful face. "This is Her Royal Highness the Princess Nehemia Ytger of Eyllwe."

Chaol bowed low. The princess nodded, barely a dip of her chin. Celaena knew the name—she had often heard the Eyllwe slaves in Endovier boast of Nehemia's beauty and bravery. Nehemia, the Light of Eyllwe, who would save them from their plight. Nehemia, who might someday pose a threat to the King of Adarlan's rule over her home country when she ascended to the throne. Nehemia, they whispered, who smuggled information and supplies to the rebel groups hiding in Eyllwe. But what was she doing here?

"And the Lady Lillian," Kaltain added briskly.

Celaena dropped into the lowest curtsy she could give without falling and said in Eyllwe, "Welcome to Rifthold, Your Highness."

Princess Nehemia smiled slowly, and the others gaped. The councilman beamed, wiping the sweat from his brow. Why hadn't they sent Nehemia with the Crown Prince, or even Perrington? Why was the princess herded around by Kaltain Rompier?

"Thank you," the princess replied, her voice low.

"I imagine you've had a long journey," Celaena continued in Eyllwe. "Have you arrived today, Your Highness?"

Nehemia's guards exchanged glances, and Nehemia's brows rose slightly. Not too many northerners spoke their language. "Yes, and the queen sent *this* one"—Nehemia jerked her head at Kaltain—"to bring me around with that sweating worm of a man as well." The princess narrowed her eyes at the small councilman, who wrung his hands and dabbed his forehead with a handkerchief. Perhaps he knew what sort of threat Nehemia posed; but why bring her to the castle?

Celaena ran her tongue across her teeth, trying not to laugh. "He seems a bit nervous." She had to change the subject or else she'd indeed laugh. "What do you make of the castle?"

"It's the most foolish thing I've ever seen," Nehemia said, scanning the ceiling as if she could see through the stone and into the glass sections. "I'd sooner enter a castle made of sand."

Chaol watched them, somewhat disbelievingly.

"I'm afraid I haven't understood a word you've said," Kaltain interrupted. Celaena tried not to roll her eyes—she'd forgotten the woman was there.

"We," the princess said, struggling for the word in the common language, "were talking with the weather."

"*About* the weather," Kaltain corrected sharply.

"Watch your mouth," Celaena snapped before she could think.

Kaltain gave Celaena a vicious little smile. "If she's here to learn our ways, I should correct her so she doesn't sound foolish."

Here to learn their ways, or for something else entirely? The faces of the princess and her guards were unreadable.

"Your Highness," Chaol said, stepping forward, a subtle movement to keep himself between Nehemia and Celaena. "Are you having a tour of the castle?"

Nehemia chewed on the words and then looked to Celaena, brows high—as if she'd expected a translation by now. A smile tugged on the corners of Celaena's lips. No wonder the councilman was sweating so profusely. Nehemia was a force to be reckoned with. Celaena translated Chaol's question with ease.

"If you consider this structure of madness to be a castle," Nehemia replied.

Celaena turned to Chaol. "She says yes."

"I never knew so many words to mean one," Kaltain said with faux sweetness. Celaena's nails dug into her palms.

I'm going to rip your hair out.

Chaol took another step toward Nehemia—effectively blocking Celaena's path to Kaltain. Smart man. He put a hand on his chest. "Your Highness, I am the Captain of the Royal Guard. Please allow me to escort you."

Celaena translated again, and the princess nodded. "Get rid of her," she said flatly to Celaena, and then waved a hand toward Kaltain. "I don't care for her temperament."

"You're dismissed," Celaena said to Kaltain, flashing a bright smile. "The princess tires of your company."

Kaltain started. "But the queen—"

"If that is Her Highness's wish, then it will be granted," Chaol interrupted. Though his features were a mask of protocol, she could have sworn she glimpsed a glimmer of amusement in his eyes. Celaena wanted to hug him. She didn't bother to nod her farewell to Kaltain as the princess and the councilman joined them and they strode down the hall, leaving the fuming lady behind.

"Are all of your royal women like that?" the princess said to Celaena in Eyllwe.

"Like Kaltain? Unfortunately, Your Highness."

Nehemia examined the assassin, and Celaena knew she was taking in her clothes, her gait, her posture—everything Celaena herself had observed about the princess already. "But you—you're not like them. How do you know how to speak Eyllwe so well?"

"I"—Celaena thought of a lie—"studied it for several years."

"You use the intonation of the peasants. Is that taught in your books?"

"I knew an Eyllwe woman who taught it to me."

"A slave of yours?" Her tone sharpened, and Chaol flicked his eyes toward them.

"No," Celaena said hurriedly. "I don't believe in keeping slaves." Something twisted in her gut at the thought of all those slaves she'd left behind in Endovier, all those people doomed to suffer until they died. Just because she'd left Endovier didn't mean Endovier had ceased to be.

Nehemia's voice was soft. "Then you are very unlike your court companions."

Celaena could only manage a nod to the princess as they turned their attention to the hall ahead. Servants darted past, eyes wide when they beheld the princess and her guards. After a moment of silence, Celaena squared her shoulders. "Why are you in Rifthold, if I might ask?" She added: "Your Highness."

"You don't need to bother calling me that." The princess toyed with one of the gold bangles around her wrist. "I came at the request of my father, the King of Eyllwe, to learn your language and customs so I might better serve Eyllwe and my people."

Given what she'd heard of Nehemia, Celaena didn't think that was the entirety of it, but she smiled politely as she said, "How long will you remain in Rifthold?"

"Until my father sends for me again." She stopped playing with her bracelets as she frowned at the rain pounding the windows. "If I'm fortunate, I'll only be here until spring. Unless my father decides that a man from Adarlan might make me a good consort, and then I'll be here until *that* matter is settled." Seeing the annoyance in the princess's eyes, Celaena felt a shred of pity for whatever man her father chose.

A thought struck her, and Celaena tilted her head to the side. "Whom would you marry? Prince Dorian?" It was prying, and a bit impertinent—and she regretted the question the second it came out.

But Nehemia just clicked her tongue. "That pretty boy? He grinned at me far too much—and you should only see how he winked at the other women in the court. I want a husband to warm *my* bed, and my bed alone." She glanced sidelong at the assassin, giving her another head-to-toe examination. Celaena caught the princess's eyes lingering on the few scars on her hands. "Where are you from, Lillian?"

Celaena casually hid her hands in the folds of her gown. "Bellhaven—a city in Fenharrow. It's a fishing port. Smells terrible." That wasn't a lie. Every time she'd visited Bellhaven for a mission, the reek of fish made her gag if she got too near the docks.

The princess chuckled. "Rifthold smells terrible. Too many people. At least in Banjali, the sun burns up everything. And my father's river palace smells like lotus blossoms."

Chaol cleared his throat beside them, obviously tired of being excluded from the conversation, and Celaena grinned at him. "Don't be so glum," she said in the common tongue. "We must cater to the princess."

"Stop your gloating," he said, his brows low. He put a hand on the hilt of his sword, and Nehemia's guards stepped closer to him. Though Chaol might be Captain of the Guard, Celaena didn't doubt for a moment that Nehemia's guards would put him down if he became a threat. "We're only bringing her back to the king's council. I'm going to have a word with them about allowing Kaltain to show her around."

"Do you hunt?" Nehemia interrupted in Eyllwe.

"Me?" The princess nodded. "Oh—er, no," Celaena said, then switched back to Eyllwe. "I'm more of a reader."

Nehemia looked toward a rain-splattered window. "Most of our books were burned five years ago, when Adarlan marched in. It didn't make a difference if the books were about magic"—her voice quieted at the word, even though Chaol and the councilman couldn't understand them—"or history. They just burned the libraries whole, along with the museums and universities . . ."

A familiar ache filled her chest. Celaena nodded. "Eyllwe wasn't the only country where that happened."

Something cold and bitter glittered in Nehemia's eyes. "Now, most of the books we receive are from Adarlan—books in a language I can barely understand. That's also what I must learn while I'm here. There are so many things!" She stomped her foot, her jewelry clinking. "And I hate these shoes! And this miserable dress! I don't care if it's Eyllwe silk and I'm supposed to be representing my kingdom—the material's been itching me ever since I put it on!" She stared at Celaena's elaborate gown. "How can you stand wearing that enormous thing?"

Celaena picked at the skirts of her dress. "It breaks my ribs, to be honest."

"Well, at least I'm not the only one suffering," Nehemia said. Chaol stopped before a door and informed the six sentries posted outside to watch the women and the princess's guards. "What's he doing?"

"Returning you to the council and ensuring that Kaltain doesn't lead you around again."

Nehemia's shoulders slumped slightly. "I've only been here for a day, and I wish to leave." She let out a long sigh through her nose, and again turned to the window, as if she could see all the way back to Eyllwe. Suddenly, she grabbed Celaena's hand and squeezed it. Her fingers were surprisingly calloused—in all the spots where the hilt of a sword or dagger might rest. Celaena's eyes met with those of the princess and she dropped her hand.

Perhaps the rumors were correct about her association with the rebels in Eyllwe . . .

"Will you keep me company while I'm here, Lady Lillian?"

Celaena blinked at the request—feeling, despite herself, honored. "Of course. When I'm available, I'll gladly attend you."

"I have attendants. I wish for someone to talk to."

Celaena couldn't help it—she beamed. Chaol entered into the hallway once more, and bowed to the princess. "The council would like to see you." Celaena translated.

Nehemia let out a low groan, but thanked Chaol before turning to Celaena. "I'm glad we met, Lady Lillian," Nehemia said, her eyes bright. "Peace be with you."

"And with you," the assassin murmured, watching her leave.

She never had many friends, and the ones she had often disappointed her. Sometimes with devastating consequences, as she'd learned that summer with the Silent Assassins of the Red Desert. After that, she'd sworn never to trust girls again, especially girls with agendas and power of their own. Girls who would do *anything* to get what they wanted.

But as the door closed behind the ivory train of the Eyllwe princess, Celaena wondered if she'd been wrong.

~

Chaol Westfall watched the assassin eat lunch, her eyes darting from one plate to the next. She had immediately stripped from her gown upon entering her rooms, and now sat in a rose-and-jade dressing robe that suited her well.

"You're awfully quiet today," she said, her mouth full of food. Would she never stop eating? She ate more than anyone he knew—including his guards. She had multiple helpings of every course at each meal. "Enthralled by the Princess Nehemia?" The words were barely distinguishable from her chewing.

"That headstrong girl?" He immediately regretted the remark as her eyes narrowed. A lecture was coming on, and he was in no mood to be patronized. He had more important things on his mind. Before departing this morning, the king hadn't taken *any* of the guards he'd suggested he bring on his journey, and refused to say where he was going, or to accept his offer of accompaniment.

Not to mention the fact that a few of the royal hounds had gone missing, only to have their half-eaten remains found in the northern wing of the palace. *That* was worrisome; who would do such a gruesome thing?

"And what's wrong with headstrong girls?" she pressed. "Other than the fact that they're not wooden-headed ninnies who can only open their mouths to give orders and gossip?"

"I just prefer a certain type of woman."

Thankfully, it was the right thing to say, because she batted her eyelashes. "And what type of woman is that?"

"Not an arrogant assassin."

She pouted. "Suppose I wasn't an assassin. Would you fancy me then?"

"No."

"Would you prefer *Lady Kaltain*?"

"Don't be a fool." It was easy to be mean, but it was also getting far too easy to be nice. He took a bite of bread. She watched him, her head angled. He sometimes felt that she looked at him the way a cat regards a mouse. He just wondered how long it would take for her to pounce.

She shrugged, and took a bite from an apple. There was something girlish about her, too. Oh, he couldn't stand her contradictions!

"You're staring, Captain."

He almost apologized, but stopped. She was a haughty, vulgar, utterly impertinent assassin. He wished for the months to fly by, for her to be appointed Champion, and then, once her years of servitude were over, to be gone. He hadn't slept well since they'd taken her out of Endovier.

"You have food in your teeth," he said. She picked it out with a sharp nail and turned her head to the window. The rain slid down the glass. Was she looking at the rain, or something beyond?

He sipped from his goblet. Despite her arrogance, she was clever, and relatively kind, and somewhat charming. But where was that writhing darkness? Why didn't it show itself so he could just throw her into the dungeon and call off this ridiculous competition? There was something great and deadly concealed within her, and he didn't like it.

He'd be ready—when the time came, he'd be waiting. He just wondered which one of them would survive.

14

For the next four days, Celaena awoke before dawn to train in her room, using whatever she could to exercise—chairs, the doorway, even her billiards table and cue sticks. The balls made for remarkable balance tools. Around dawn, Chaol usually showed up for breakfast. Afterward, they ran through the game park, where he kept pace at her side. Autumn had fully come, and the wind smelled of crisp leaves and snow. Chaol never said anything when she doubled over, hands on her knees, and vomited up her breakfast, nor did he comment on the fact that she could go farther and farther each day without stopping for breath.

Once they'd finished their run, they trained in a private room far from her competitors' eyes. Until, that is, she collapsed to the ground and cried that she was about to die of hunger and fatigue. At lessons, the knives remained Celaena's favorite, but the wooden staff became dear; naturally, it had to do with the fact that she could freely whack him and not chop off an arm. Since her initial meeting with Princess

Nehemia, she hadn't seen or heard from the princess—not even chatter from the servants.

Chaol always came for lunch, and afterward, she joined the other Champions for a few more hours of training under Brullo's watchful eye. Most of their training was just to make sure they could actually *use* weapons. And, of course, she kept her head down throughout it all, doing enough to keep Brullo from critiquing her, but not enough to make him praise her the way he did Cain.

Cain. How she loathed him! Brullo practically worshipped the man—and even the other Champions nodded their respect when he passed by. No one bothered to comment on how perfect *her* form was. Was this how the other assassins at the Assassins' Keep had felt all those years she had spent hogging Arobynn Hamel's attention? But here, it was hard to focus when Cain was nearby, taunting and sneering, waiting for her to make one mistake. Hopefully he wouldn't distract her at the first elimination test. Brullo hadn't given them any indication *what* they might be tested for, and Chaol was just as clueless.

The day before the first Test, she knew something was wrong long before she got to the training hall. Chaol hadn't shown up for breakfast, but rather sent her guards to bring her to the training hall to practice on her own. He didn't show up for lunch, either, and by the time she was escorted to the hall, she was brimming with questions.

Without Chaol to stand near, she lingered beside a pillar, watching the competitors file in, flanked by guards and their trainers. Brullo wasn't there yet—another oddity. And there were far too many guards in the training hall today.

"What do you suppose this is about?" Nox Owen, the young thief from Perranth, asked from beside her. After proving himself somewhat skilled during practice, many of the other competitors had sought him out, but he still opted to keep to himself.

"Captain Westfall didn't train me this morning," she offered. What was the harm in admitting that?

Nox held out his hand. "Nox Owen."

"I know who you are," she said, but shook his hand anyway. His grip was solid, his hand calloused and scarred. He'd seen his fair share of action.

"Good. I've felt a bit invisible with that hulking lout showing off these past few days." He jerked his chin toward Cain, who was in the middle of examining his bulging biceps. A large ring of black, iridescent stone glimmered on Cain's finger—strange that he'd wear it to practice. Nox went on. "Did you see Verin? He looks like he's going to be sick." He pointed to the loudmouthed thief that Celaena wanted to knock out cold. Normally, Verin could be found near Cain, taunting the other Champions. But today he stood alone by the window, face pale and eyes wide.

"I heard him talking to Cain," said a timid voice behind them, and they found Pelor, the youngest assassin, standing nearby. She'd spent half a day watching Pelor—and while she only pretended to be mediocre, he truly could use the training.

Assassin indeed. His voice hasn't even deepened yet. How did he wind up here?

"What'd he say?" Nox put his hands in his pockets. His clothes weren't as ratty as the other competitors'; the mere fact that she'd actually heard his name implied he must have been a good thief in Perranth.

Pelor's freckled face paled a bit. "Bill Chastain—the Eye Eater—was found stone cold dead this morning."

A Champion was dead? And a notorious killer at that. "How?" she demanded.

Pelor swallowed hard. "Verin said it wasn't pretty. Like someone ripped him wide open. He passed the body on his way here." Nox cursed under his breath, and Celaena studied the other Champions. A hush had fallen on the group, and clusters of them stood together, whispering. Verin's story was spreading fast. Pelor went on. "He said Chastain's body was in *ribbons*."

A chill snaked down her spine, but she shook her head, just as a guard entered and told them that Brullo had ordered them to have free rein of the training hall today and to practice what they wanted. Needing to distract herself from the image forming in her mind, she didn't bother to say good-bye to Nox and Pelor as she strode to the weapons rack and gathered a belt strapped with throwing knives.

She took up a place near the archery targets; Nox joined her a moment later, and started firing his knives at the target. He hit the second ring, but never got any closer to the center. His skill with knives wasn't nearly as good as his archery.

She drew a dagger from the belt. Who would have killed one of the Champions so brutally? And how had they gotten away with it, if the body was in the hall? This castle was swarming with guards. A Champion was dead, and just a day before their first Test; would this start a pattern?

Her focus narrowed to the small, black dot in the center of the target. She steadied her breathing as she cocked her arm, letting her wrist go loose. The sounds of the other Champions faded. The blackness of the bull's-eye beckoned, and as she exhaled, she sent the dagger flying.

It sparkled, a shooting star of steel. She smiled grimly as it struck home.

Beside her, Nox swore colorfully when his dagger hit the third ring on his target, and her smile broadened, despite the shredded corpse that lay somewhere in the castle.

Celaena drew another dagger, but paused as Verin called to her from the ring where he sparred with Cain. "Circus tricks ain't much use when you're the King's Champion." She shifted her gaze to him, but kept positioned toward the target. "You'd be better off on your back, learning tricks useful to a woman. In fact, I can teach you some tonight, if you'd like." He laughed, and Cain joined with him. Celaena gripped the hilt of a dagger so hard that it hurt.

"Don't listen to them," Nox murmured. He tossed another dagger, missing the bull's-eye again. "They wouldn't know the first thing to do with a woman, even if one walked stark naked into their bedroom."

Celaena threw her dagger, and the blade clanged as it landed a hair's breadth from the one she'd already embedded in the bull's-eye.

Nox's dark brows rose, accentuating his gray eyes. He couldn't have been older than twenty-five. "You've got impressive aim."

"For a girl?" she challenged.

"No," he said, and threw another dagger. "For anyone." The dagger yet again missed the mark. He stalked to the target, yanking out all six daggers and shoving them in their sheaths before returning to the throwing line. Celaena cleared her throat.

"You're standing wrong," she said, quietly enough so the other Champions couldn't hear. "And you're holding your wrist incorrectly."

Nox lowered his arm. She took up her stance. "Legs like this," she said. He studied her for a moment, then positioned his legs similarly. "Bend slightly at the knees. Shoulders back; loosen your wrist. Throw when you exhale." She demonstrated for him, and her dagger found its mark.

"Show me again," Nox said appreciatively.

She did so, and struck the target. Then she threw with her left hand, and fought her whoop of triumph as the blade sank into the handle of another dagger.

Nox focused on the target as he brought up his arm. "Well, you've just put me to shame," he said, laughing under his breath as he lifted his dagger higher.

"Keep your wrist even looser," was her reply. "It's all about how you snap it."

Nox obeyed, and as he exhaled a long breath, his dagger flew. It didn't hit the bull's-eye, but it came within the inner circle. His brows rose. "That's a bit of an improvement."

"Just a bit," she said, and held her ground as he gathered their knives from the two targets and handed hers back. She sheathed them in her belt. "You're from Perranth, right?" she asked. Though she'd never been to Perranth, Terrasen's second largest city, the mention of her homeland still spiked a bolt of fear and guilt. It had been ten years since the royal family had been butchered, ten years since the King of Adarlan had marched his army in, ten years since Terrasen met its doom with bowed heads and silence. She shouldn't have mentioned it—she didn't know *why* she mentioned it, actually.

She schooled her features into polite interest as Nox nodded. "This is my first time out of Perranth, actually. You said you were from Bellhaven, didn't you?"

"My father is a merchant," she lied.

"And what does he think about a daughter who steals jewels for a living?"

She conceded a smile and hurled a knife into the target. "He won't be inviting me home for a while, that's for certain."

"Ah, you're in good hands, though. You've got the best trainer out of anyone. I've seen you two running at dawn. I have to beg mine to put down the bottle and let me train outside of lessons." He inclined his head toward his trainer, who sat against the wall, the hood of his cape over his eyes. "Sleeping, yet again."

"The Captain of the Guard is a pain in my ass at times," she said, chucking another knife, "but you're right—he's the best."

Nox was quiet for a moment before he said: "The next time we pair off for lessons, find me, will you?"

"Why?" She reached for another dagger, but found she'd depleted her stock again.

Nox threw another dagger, and it hit the bull's-eye this time. "Because my gold's on you winning this whole damn thing."

She smiled a little. "Let's hope you won't be eliminated at the Test tomorrow." She scanned the training hall for any sign of the challenge to come the following morning, but found nothing out of the ordinary. The other competitors remained mostly quiet—save for Cain and Verin—and many of them were pale as snow. "And let's hope neither of us winds up like the Eye Eater," she added, and meant it.

"Don't you ever do anything other than read?" said Chaol. She started from her chair on the balcony as he took a seat beside her. The late-afternoon sunlight warmed her face, and the last balmy breeze of autumn rushed through her unbound hair.

She stuck out her tongue. "Shouldn't you be looking into the Eye Eater's murder?" He never came to her rooms after lunch.

Something dark flitted across his eyes. "That's none of your business. And don't try to pry details from me about it," he added as she opened her mouth. He pointed to the book in her lap. "I saw at lunch that you're reading *The Wind and the Rain*, and I forgot to ask what you thought."

He'd really come to talk about a book when a Champion's corpse had been found that morning? "It's a bit dense," she admitted, holding up the brown volume in her lap. When he didn't reply, she asked, "Why are you really here?"

"I had a long day."

She massaged an ache in her knee. "Because of Bill's murder?"

"Because the prince dragged me into a council meeting that lasted for three hours," he said, a muscle in his jaw feathering.

"I thought His Royal Highness was your friend."

"He is."

"How long have you been friends?"

He paused, and she knew he was contemplating how she might use the information against him, weighing the risk of telling her the truth. She was about to snap at him when he said: "Since we were young. We were the only boys of our age in the castle—at least of high rank. We had lessons together, played together, trained together. But when I was thirteen, my father moved my family back to our home in Anielle."

"The city on the Silver Lake?" It somehow made sense that Chaol's family ruled Anielle. The citizens of Anielle were warriors from birth, and had been guardians against the hordes of the wild men from the White Fang Mountains for generations. Thankfully, things had gotten a little easier for the warriors of Anielle in the past ten years; the White Fang mountain men had been one of the first peoples to be put down by Adarlan's conquering armies, and very rarely did their rebels make it to slavery. She'd heard tales of mountain men killing their wives and children, then themselves, rather than be taken by Adarlan. The thought of Chaol going up against hundreds of them—against men built like Cain—made her a little sick.

"Yes," Chaol said, fiddling with the long hunting knife at his side. "I was slotted to join the Royal Council, like my father; he wanted me to spend some time among my own people, and learn . . . whatever it is councilmen learn. He said that with the King's army now in the mountains, we could move our interests from fighting the mountain folk to politics." His golden eyes were distant. "But I missed Rifthold."

"So you ran away?" She marveled that he was volunteering this much—hadn't he refused to tell her almost anything about himself while traveling from Endovier?

"Ran away?" Chaol chuckled. "No. Dorian convinced the Captain of the Guard to take me as his apprentice, with the help of Brullo. My father refused. So I abdicated my title as Lord of Anielle to my brother and left the next day."

The captain's silence suggested what he could not say. That his father hadn't objected. What of his mother? He loosed a long breath. "What about you, then?"

She crossed her arms. "I thought you didn't want to know anything about me."

There was a ghost of a smile on his face as he watched the sky melt into a smear of tangerine. "What do your parents make of their daughter being Adarlan's Assassin?"

"My parents are dead," she said. "They died when I was eight."

"So you—"

Her heart thundered in her chest. "I was born in Terrasen, then I became an assassin, then I went to Endovier, and now I'm here. And that's it."

Silence fell; then he asked, "Where'd you get that scar on your right hand?" She didn't need to glance at the jagged line that ran along the top of her hand, just above her wrist. She flexed her fingers.

"When I was twelve, Arobynn Hamel decided I wasn't nearly as skilled at swordplay with my left hand. So he gave me a choice: either he could break my right hand, or I could do it myself." The phantom memory of the blinding pain lanced through her hand. "That night, I put my hand against a doorframe, and slammed the door shut on it. I split my hand wide open and broke two bones. It took months to heal—months during which I could only use my left hand." She gave him a vicious smile. "I bet Brullo never did that to you."

"No," he said quietly. "No, he didn't." He cleared his throat and stood. "The first Test is tomorrow. Are you ready?"

"Of course," she lied.

He remained standing there for a moment longer, studying her. "I'll see you tomorrow morning," he said, and left. In the silence that followed in his wake, she contemplated his story, the paths that had made them so different, but so similar. She wrapped her arms around herself, a cold wind picking up the skirts of her dress and blowing them behind her.

15

Though she'd never admit it, Celaena didn't really know what to expect at their first Test. With all the training over the past five days and fiddling with various weapons and techniques, her body ached. Which was another thing she'd never admit, even though hiding the throbbing pain in her limbs was nearly impossible. As Celaena and Chaol entered the giant sparring room in the morning, she glanced at her competitors and remembered she wasn't the only one who hadn't a clue what to expect. A towering black curtain had been swept across half of the room, blocking the other half from sight. Whatever lay beyond that curtain, she realized, was to decide the fate of one of them.

The normal ruckus had been replaced by a rustling quiet—and rather than mill about, the competitors lingered by their trainers' sides. She kept close to Chaol, which wasn't a change from the ordinary. But the sponsors atop the mezzanine looking over the black-and-white checkered floor were. Her throat tightened as her gaze met with that of the Crown Prince. Aside from sending her his books, she hadn't seen or heard from him since the meeting with the king. He flashed her a grin, those sapphire eyes gleaming in the morning light. She offered him a tight smile in return and quickly looked away.

Brullo stood by the curtain, a scarred hand upon his sword, and Celaena studied the scene. Someone stepped to her side. She knew who it was before he spoke. "It's a bit dramatic, don't you think?"

She glanced sidelong at Nox. Chaol tensed next to her, and she could feel him watching the thief closely, no doubt wondering if she and Nox were formulating some escape plan that would include the deaths of every member of the royal family.

"After five days of mindless training," she replied quietly, all too aware that very few people were speaking in the hall, "I'm glad for a bit of excitement."

Nox laughed under his breath. "What do you think it is?"

She shrugged, keeping her attention on the curtain. More and more competitors were arriving, and soon the clock would strike nine—the time when the Test would begin. Even if she knew what was behind the curtain, she certainly wouldn't help him. "Hopefully it's a pack of man-eating wolves that we have to take on with our bare hands." She looked at him fully now, a half smile on her lips. "Wouldn't that be fun?"

Chaol subtly cleared his throat. Now was not the time for talking. She stuffed her hands into the pockets of her black pants. "Best of luck," she said to Nox before she strode toward the curtain, Chaol following her. When they were far enough away, she asked under her breath, "No idea what's behind that curtain?" Chaol shook his head.

She adjusted the thick leather belt slung low across her hips. It was the kind of belt intended to bear the weight of multiple weapons. Its lightness now only reminded her of what she'd lost—and what she had to gain. The death of the Eye Eater yesterday had been fortunate in one aspect: one less man to compete with.

She glanced up at Dorian. *He* could probably see what was behind the curtain from his place on the mezzanine. Why not help her cheat a little? She flicked her attention to the other sponsors—noblemen in fine clothing—and ground her teeth at the sight of Perrington. He smirked as he watched Cain, who was stretching out his muscular arms. Had he already told Cain what was beyond the curtain?

Brullo cleared his throat. "Attention *now*!" he called to them. All of the competitors tried to look calm as he strode to the center of the curtain. "Your first Test has arrived." He grinned broadly, as if whatever the curtain concealed was going to torment the hell out of them. "As His Majesty has ordered, one of you will be eliminated today—one of you will be deemed *unworthy*."

Just get on with it! she thought, her jaw clenched tight.

As if he'd read her thoughts, Brullo snapped his fingers, and a guard standing by the wall pulled the curtain back. Inch by inch, it swayed away, until—

Celaena bit down her laugh. Archery? It was an *archery* contest?

"Rules are simple," Brullo said. Behind him, five targets were staggered at various distances through the hall. "You get five shots—one per target. The one with the worst aim goes home."

Some competitors began murmuring, but it was all she could do to keep from beaming. Unfortunately, Cain didn't bother to hide his triumphant grin. Why couldn't *he* have been the Champion who was found dead?

"You'll go one at a time," Brullo said, and behind them a pair of soldiers rolled out a cart of bows and quivers loaded with arrows. "Form a line at the table to determine your order. The Test begins now."

She expected them to rush to the long table stacked with identical bows and arrows, but apparently none of the twenty-one other competitors were in much of a hurry to go home. Celaena made to join the forming line, but Chaol grasped her shoulder. "Don't show off," he warned.

She smiled sweetly and pried his fingers off her. "I'll try not to," she purred, and joined the line.

~

It was an enormous leap of faith to give them arrows, even if the tips were blunted. A dull head wouldn't stop it from going through Perrington's throat—or Dorian's, if she wanted.

Though the thought was entertaining, she kept her attention on the competitors. With twenty-two Champions and five shots each, the Test took a dreadfully long time. Thanks to Chaol pulling her aside, she'd been in the back of the line—not dead last, but three from the end. Far enough back that she had to watch everyone else go before her, including Cain.

The other competitors did well enough. The giant circular targets were composed of five colored rings—yellow marking the center, with only a tiny black dot to mark the bull's-eye. Each target got smaller the farther back it was placed, and because the room was so long, the final target was nearly seventy yards away.

Celaena ran her fingers along the smooth curve of her yew bow. Archery was one of the first skills Arobynn had taught her—a staple of any assassin's training. Two of the assassins further proved it with easy, skilled shots. Though they didn't hit the bull's-eyes, and their shots got sloppier the farther the target, whoever their masters had been, they'd known what they were teaching.

Pelor, the gangly assassin, wasn't yet strong enough to manage a longbow, and barely made any shots. When he finished, his eyes gleaming with resentment, the Champions sniggered, and Cain laughed the loudest.

Brullo's face was grim. "Didn't *anyone* ever teach you how to use a bow, boy?"

Pelor lifted his head, glaring at the Weapons Master with surprising brazenness. "I'm more skilled in poisons."

"Poisons!" Brullo threw his hands up. "The king wants a *Champion*—and you couldn't shoot a cow in a pasture!" The Weapons Master waved Pelor off. The other Champions laughed again, and Celaena wanted nothing more than to smile with them. But Pelor took a shuddering breath, his shoulders relaxing, and joined the other finished competitors. If he wound up being eliminated, where would they bring him? To prison—or some other hellhole? Despite herself, Celaena felt badly for the boy. His shots hadn't been *that* bad.

It was Nox, actually, who surprised her most, with three bull's-eyes into the nearer targets and the two final shots along the border of the inner ring. Perhaps she *should* consider him for an ally. From the way the other competitors watched him as he strode to the back of the room, she knew they were thinking the same thing.

Grave, the repulsive assassin, did fine, she supposed. Four bull's-eyes, and the final shot right on the border of the innermost ring. But then Cain stepped up to the white line painted at the back of the room, drew back his yew bow, his black ring glinting, and fired.

Again, and again, and again, within the span of a few seconds.

And when the sound of his final shot stopped echoing in the suddenly silent chamber, Celaena's stomach turned over. Five bull's-eyes.

Her one consolation was that none of them had been on that black dot—the absolute center. One had come close, though.

For some reason, the line started moving quickly. All she could think about was Cain—Cain getting applauded by Perrington, Cain getting clapped on the back by Brullo, Cain getting all of that praise and attention, not because he was a mountain of muscle, but because he actually deserved it.

Suddenly, Celaena found herself standing at the white line, looking at the vast length of the room before her. Some of the men chuckled—albeit quietly—and she kept her head held high as she reached over her shoulder for an arrow and nocked it into her bow.

They'd done some archery practice a few days earlier, and she'd been excellent. Or, as excellent as she could be without attracting attention. And she'd killed men from longer shots than the farthest target. Clean shots, too. Right through the throat.

She tried to swallow, but her mouth was dry.

I am Celaena Sardothien, Adarlan's Assassin. If these men knew who I was, they'd stop laughing. I am Celaena Sardothien. I am going to win. I will not be afraid.

She pulled back her bow, the sore muscles in her arm aching with the effort. She shut out noise, shut out movement, shut out anything other than the sound of her breathing as her focus narrowed on the first target. She took a steady breath. As she exhaled, she let the arrow fly.

Bull's-eye.

The tightness in her stomach abated, and she sighed through her nose. It wasn't an absolute bull's-eye, but she hadn't been aiming for it, anyway.

Some men stopped laughing, but she paid them no heed as she nocked another arrow and fired at the second target. She aimed for the edge of the innermost ring, which she hit with deadly precision. She could have made an entire circle of arrows, if she'd wanted. And if she'd had enough ammunition.

She got another bull's-eye on the third target—aiming for the edge, but landing within the border. She did the same for the fourth target, but aimed for the opposite side of the bull's-eye. Where she aimed, the arrow met its mark.

As she reached for her last arrow, she heard one of the competitors, a red-haired mercenary named Renault, snigger. She clenched her bow tightly enough for the wood to groan, and pulled back her final shot.

The target was little more than a blur of color, so far back that its bull's-eye was a grain of sand in the vastness of the room. She couldn't see the little dot in its center—the dot that no one had yet to touch, even Cain. Celaena's arm trembled with effort as she pulled the string back a bit farther and fired.

The arrow hit the absolute center, obliterating the black dot. They stopped laughing.

No one said anything to her when she stalked away from the line and tossed her bow back onto the cart. Chaol only scowled at her—obviously, she hadn't been *that* inconspicuous—but Dorian smiled. She sighed and joined the competitors waiting for the competition to finish, keeping well away from all of them.

When their marks were compared by Brullo himself, one of the army soldiers, not young Pelor, wound up being eliminated. But though she hadn't lost by any means, Celaena couldn't stand—absolutely could not *stand*—the feeling that she hadn't really won anything at all.

16

Despite her attempt to keep her breathing steady, Celaena gasped for air as she ran beside Chaol in the game park. If he was winded, he didn't show it, other than the gleam of sweat on his face and the dampness of his white shirt.

They ran toward a hill, its top still shrouded in morning mist. Her legs buckled at the sight of the incline, and her stomach rose in her throat. Celaena let out a loud gasp to get Chaol's attention before she slowed to a stop, and braced her hands against a tree trunk.

She took a shuddering breath, holding on tightly to the tree as she vomited. She hated the warmth of the tears that leaked from her eyes, but couldn't wipe them away as she heaved again, gagging. Chaol stood nearby, just watching. She leaned her brow into her upper arm, calming her breathing, willing her body to ease. It had been three days since the first Test, ten since her arrival in Rifthold, and she was still horribly out of shape. The next elimination was in four days, and though training had resumed as usual, she had started waking up a little earlier than normal. She would *not* lose to Cain, or Renault, or any of them.

"Done?" Chaol asked. She lifted her head to give him a withering glare, but everything spun, dragging her down with it, and she retched again. "I told you not to eat before we left."

"Are you done being smug?"

"Are you done vomiting your guts up?"

"For the time being," she snapped. "Perhaps I won't be so courteous next time, and I'll just vomit all over you instead."

"If you can catch me," he said with a half smile.

She wanted to punch the smirk off his face, but as she took a step, her knees shook, and she put her hands against the tree again, waiting for the retching to renew. Out of the corner of her eye she saw him looking at her back, most of which was exposed by her damp, white undershirt. She stood. "Are you enjoying looking at my scars?"

He sucked on his lower lip for a moment. "When did you get those?" She knew he meant the three enormous lines that ran down her back.

"When do you think?" she said. He didn't reply, and she looked up at the canopy of leaves above them. A morning breeze sent them all shuddering, ripping a few from where they clung to the skeletal branches. "Those three, I received my first day in Endovier."

"What did you do to deserve it?"

"Deserve it?" She laughed sharply. "No one deserves to be whipped like an animal." He opened his mouth, but she cut him off. "I arrived in Endovier, and they dragged me into the center of the camp, and tied me between the whipping posts. Twenty-one lashes." She stared at him without entirely seeing him as the ash-gray sky turned into the bleakness of Endovier, and the hiss of the wind became the sighing of slaves. "That was before I had befriended any of the other slaves—and I spent that first night wondering if I would make it until morning, if my back would become infected, or if I would bleed out and die before I knew what was happening."

"No one helped you?"

"Only in the morning. A young woman slipped me a tin of salve while we were waiting in line for breakfast. I never got to thank her. Later that day, four overseers raped and killed her." She clenched her hands into fists as her eyes stung. "The day I snapped, I stopped by their section of the mines to repay them for what they did to her." Something frozen rushed through her veins. "They died too quickly."

"But you were a woman in Endovier," Chaol said, his voice rough and quiet. "No one ever . . ." He trailed off, unable to form the word.

She gave him a slow, bitter smile. "They were afraid of me to begin with. And after the day I almost touched the wall, none of them dared to come too close to me. But if one guard tried to get too friendly . . . Well, he'd become the example that reminded the others I could easily snap again, if I felt like it." The wind stirred around them, ripping strands of hair from her braid. She didn't need to voice her other suspicion—that perhaps somehow Arobynn had bribed the guards in Endovier for her safety. "We each survive in our own way."

Celaena didn't quite understand the softness in the look he gave her as he nodded. She only stared at him for a moment longer before she burst into a run, up toward the hill—where the first rays of sunshine began to peek through.

The following afternoon, the Champions stood gathered around Brullo, who lectured them on different weapons and other nonsense she'd learned years ago and didn't need to hear again. She was just contemplating whether she could sleep while standing up when, from the corner of her eye, a sudden movement by the balcony doors caught her attention. Celaena turned just in time to see one of the larger

Champions—one of the discharged soldiers—shove a nearby guard, knocking him to the ground. The guard's head hit the marble with a crack, and he was instantly unconscious. She didn't dare to move—none of the Champions did—as the man hurtled toward the door, toward the gardens and escape.

But Chaol and his men moved so fast that the fleeing Champion didn't have time to touch the glass door before an arrow went clean through his throat.

Silence fell, and half of the guards encircled the Champions, hands on their swords, while the others, Chaol included, rushed to the dead Champion and fallen guard. Bows groaned as the archers on the mezzanine pulled their strings taut. Celaena kept still, as did Nox, who was standing close beside her. One wrong movement and a spooked guard could kill her. Even Cain didn't breathe too deeply.

Through the wall of Champions, guards, and their weapons, Celaena beheld Chaol kneeling by the unconscious guard. No one touched the fallen Champion, who lay facedown, his hand still outstretched toward the glass door. Sven had been his name—though she didn't know why he'd been expelled from the army.

"Gods above," Nox breathed, so softly that his lips barely moved. "They just . . . killed him." She thought about telling him to shut up, but even snapping at him seemed risky. Some of the other Champions were murmuring to each other, but no one dared to take a step. "I knew they were serious about not letting us leave, but . . ." Nox swore, and she felt him glance sidelong at her. "I was granted immunity by my sponsor. He tracked me down and said I wouldn't go to prison if I lost the competition." At that point, she knew he was speaking more to himself, and when she didn't respond, Nox stopped talking. She stared and stared at the dead Champion.

What had made Sven risk it? And why here, right now? There were still three days until their second Test; what had made this moment so special? The day she snapped at Endovier, she hadn't been thinking about freedom. No, she'd picked the time and place, and started swinging. She'd never meant to escape.

The sunlight shone through the doors, illuminating the Champion's splattered blood like stained glass.

Maybe he'd realized he had no chance of winning, and that this kind of death was far better than returning to whatever place he'd come from. If he'd wanted to escape, he would have waited until dark, when he was away from everyone at the competition. Sven had wanted to prove a point, she understood, and understood only because of that day she had come within a fingertip of touching the wall at Endovier.

Adarlan could take their freedom, it could destroy their lives and beat and break and whip them, it could force them into ridiculous contests, but, criminal or not, they were still human. Dying—rather than playing in the king's game—was the only choice left to him.

Still staring at his outstretched hand, forever pointing toward an unreachable horizon, Celaena said a silent prayer for the dead Champion, and wished him well.

17

With heavy eyelids, Dorian Havilliard tried not to slouch as he sat upon his throne. Music and chatter flitted through the air, wooing him to sleep. Why must his mother insist on his attending court? Even the weekly afternoon visit was too much. But it was better than studying the corpse of the Eye Eater, which Chaol had spent the past few days investigating. He'd worry about that later—if it became an issue. Which it wouldn't, if Chaol was looking into it. It had probably just been a drunken brawl.

And then there was the Champion who'd tried to escape this afternoon. Dorian shuddered at the thought of what it must have been like to witness it—and at the mess Chaol had to deal with, from the injured soldier to the sponsor who'd lost his Champion to the dead man himself. What had his father been thinking when he decided to host this contest?

Dorian glanced at his mother, seated on a throne beside his own.

She certainly didn't know anything about it, and probably would have been horrified if she knew what kind of criminals were living under her roof. His mother was still beautiful, though her face was a bit wrinkled and cracked with powder, and her auburn hair had a few silver streaks. Today she was swathed in yards of forest-green velvet and floating scarves and shawls of gold, and her crown upheld a sparkling veil that gave Dorian the distinct impression she was wearing a tent upon her head.

Before them, the nobility strutted across the floor of the court, gossiping, scheming, seducing. An orchestra played minuets in a corner, and servants slipped through the gathered nobles in a dance of their own as they refilled and cleared plates and cups and silverware.

Dorian felt like an ornament. Of course, he was wearing an outfit of his mother's choosing, sent to him this morning: a vest of dark bluish-green velvet, with almost ridiculously billowy white sleeves bursting from the blue-and-white-striped shoulders. The pants, mercifully, were light gray, though his chestnut suede boots looked *too* new for masculine pride.

"Dorian, my dear. You're sulking." He gave Queen Georgina an apologetic grin. "I received a letter from Hollin. He sends his love."

"Did he say anything of interest?"

"Only that he loathes school and wishes to come home."

"He says that every letter."

The Queen of Adarlan sighed. "If your father didn't prevent me, I'd have him home."

"He's better off at school." When it came to Hollin, the farther away he was, the better.

Georgina surveyed her son. "You were better behaved. You never disobeyed your tutors. Oh, my poor Hollin. When I am dead, you'll care for him, won't you?"

"Dead? Mother, you're only—"

"I know how old I am." She waved a ring-encrusted hand. "Which is why you must marry. And soon."

"Marry?" Dorian ground his teeth. "Marry whom?"

"Dorian, you are the Crown Prince. And already nineteen, at that. Do you wish to become king and die without an heir so Hollin can take the throne?" He didn't answer. "I thought so." After a moment, she said, "There are plenty of young women who might make a good wife. Though a princess would be preferred."

"There are no princesses left," he said a bit sharply.

"Except for the Princess Nehemia." She laughed and put a hand on his. "Oh, don't worry. I wouldn't force you to marry *her*. I'm surprised your father allows for her to still bear the title. The impetuous, haughty girl—do you know she refused to wear the dress I sent her?"

"I'm sure the princess has her reasons," Dorian said warily, disgusted by his mother's unspoken prejudice. "I've only spoken to her once, but she seemed . . . lively."

"Then perhaps you *shall* marry her." His mother laughed again before he could respond.

Dorian smiled weakly. He still couldn't figure out why his father had granted the King of Eyllwe's request that his daughter visit their court to become better acquainted with the ways of Adarlan. As far as ambassadors went, Nehemia wasn't exactly the best choice. Not when he'd heard rumors of her support of the Eyllwe rebels—and her efforts to shut down the labor camp at Calaculla. Dorian couldn't blame her for that, though, not after he'd seen the horror that was Endovier, and the destruction it had wrought upon Celaena Sardothien's body. But his father never did anything without a reason—and from the few words he'd exchanged with Nehemia, he couldn't help but wonder if she had her own motivations in coming here, too.

"It's a pity that Lady Kaltain has an agreement with Duke

Perrington," his mother went on. "She's *such* a beautiful girl—and so polite. Perhaps she has a sister."

Dorian crossed his arms, swallowing his repulsion. Kaltain stood at the far end of the court, and he was all too aware of her eyes creeping over every inch of him. He shifted in his seat, his tailbone aching from sitting for so long.

"What about Elise?" the queen said, indicating a blond young woman clad in lavender. "She's very beautiful. And can be quite playful."

As I've already learned.

"Elise bores me," he said.

"Oh, *Dorian*." She put a hand over her heart. "You're not about to inform me that you wish to marry for *love*, are you? Love does not guarantee a successful marriage."

He *was* bored. Bored of these women, bored of these cavaliers who masqueraded as companions, bored of everything.

He'd hoped his journey to Endovier would quell that boredom, and that he'd be glad to return home, but he found home to be the same. The same ladies still looked at him with pleading eyes, the same serving girls still winked at him, the same councilmen still slipped pieces of potential legislation under his door with hopeful notes. And his father . . . his father would always be preoccupied with conquest—and wouldn't stop until every continent bore Adarlan's flag. Even gambling over the so-called Champions had become achingly dull. It was clear Cain and Celaena would ultimately face each other, and until then . . . well, the other Champions weren't worth his time.

"You're sulking again. Are you upset over something, my pet? Have you heard from Rosamund? My poor child—how she broke your heart!" The queen shook her head. "Though it *was* over a year ago . . ." He didn't reply. He didn't want to think about Rosamund—or about the boorish husband she'd left him for.

Some nobles started dancing, weaving in and out among each

other. Many were his age, but he somehow felt as if there existed a vast distance between them. He didn't feel older, nor did he feel any wiser, but rather he felt . . . He felt . . .

He felt as if there were something inside him that didn't fit in with their merriment, with their willing ignorance of the world outside the castle. It went beyond his title. He had enjoyed their company early in his adolescence, but it had become apparent that he'd always be a step away. The worst of it was that they didn't seem to notice he was different—or that he felt different. Were it not for Chaol, he would have felt immensely lonely.

"Well," his mother said, snapping her ivory fingers at one of her ladies-in-waiting, "I'm sure your father has you busy, but when you find a moment to bother thinking of me, and the fate of your kingdom, look through this." His mother's lady curtsied as she extended to him a folded piece of paper, stamped with his mother's bloodred seal. Dorian ripped it open, and his stomach twisted at the long line of names. All ladies of noble blood, all of marriageable age.

"What is this?" he demanded, fighting the urge to rip up the paper.

She gave him a winning smile. "A list of potential brides. Any one of them would be suitable to take the crown. And all, I've been told, are quite capable of producing heirs."

Dorian stuffed the list of names into the pocket of his vest. The restlessness within him would not cease. "I'll think about it," he said, and before she could reply, he stepped from the awning-covered podium. Immediately, five young women flocked to him and began asking him to dance, how he fared, if he would attend the Samhuinn ball. Around and around their words circled, and Dorian stared at them blankly. What were their names?

He peered over their jewel-encrusted heads to find the path to the door. He'd suffocate if he remained here for too long. With only polite good-byes, the Crown Prince strode from the jangle and jingle of the court, the list of would-be brides burning a hole through his clothes and straight into his skin.

Dorian put his hands in his pockets as he strode down the halls of the castle. The kennels were empty—the dogs were at the track. He'd wished to inspect one of the pregnant hounds, though he knew it was impossible to predict the outcome of the litter until she gave birth. He hoped the pups would be pure, but their mother had a tendency to escape from her pen. She was his fastest, but he'd never been able to quell the wildness within her.

He didn't really know where he was going now; he just needed to walk—anywhere.

Dorian loosened the top button on his vest. The clash of swords echoed from an open doorway, and he paused. He faced the Champions' training room, and even though training was supposed to be over by now, there—

There she was.

Her golden hair shone as she wove in and out of a knot of three guards, her sword little more than a steel extension of her hand. She didn't balk at the guards as she dodged and twirled around them.

Someone began clapping to the left, and the four dueling figures stopped, panting. Dorian watched a grin spread across the assassin's face as she beheld the source. The sheen of sweat illuminated her high cheekbones, and her blue eyes sparkled. Yes, she was truly lovely. But—

Princess Nehemia approached, clapping. She was clad not in her usual white gown, but rather in a dark tunic and loose trousers, and she clutched an ornately carved wooden staff in one hand.

The princess clasped the assassin on the shoulder, and said something to the girl that made her laugh. Dorian looked around. Where was Chaol or Brullo? Why was Adarlan's Assassin here with the Princess of Eyllwe? And with a sword! This could not go on, especially after that Champion's attempted escape the other day.

Dorian approached, and smiled at the princess as he bowed. Nehemia only deigned to give him a terse nod. Not surprising. Dorian took Celaena's hand. It smelled of metal and sweat, but he kissed it anyway, raising his eyes to her face as he did so. "Lady Lillian," he muttered onto her skin.

"Your Highness," she said, trying to pull her hand from his. But Dorian held fast to her calloused palm.

"Might I have a word?" he said, leading her away before she could agree. When they were out of hearing distance, he demanded, "Where's Chaol?"

She crossed her arms. "Is this any way to speak to your beloved Champion?"

He frowned. "Where is he?"

"I don't know. If I were to bet, though, I'd wager that he's inspecting the Eye Eater's mangled corpse, or disposing of Sven's body. Besides, Brullo said I could stay here as long as I liked after we were done. I *do* have another Test tomorrow, you know."

Of course he knew. "Why is Princess Nehemia here?"

"She called on me, and when Philippa told her I was here, she insisted on joining. Apparently, a woman can only go so long without a sword between her hands." She bit her lip.

"I don't recall you being so talkative."

"Well, perhaps if you'd taken the time to speak with me, you'd have found me to be so."

He snorted, but took the bait, gods damn him. "And when would I have spoken to you?"

"You *do* recall the little fact that we traveled together from Endovier, don't you? And that I've been here for weeks now."

"I sent you those books," he offered.

"And did you ever ask me if I had read them?"

Had she forgotten to whom she was speaking? "I've spoken to you once since we've been here."

She shrugged and made to turn away. Irritated, but slightly curious, he grabbed her arm. Her turquoise eyes glittered as she stared at his hand, and his heart quickened when her gaze rose to his face. Yes, sweaty as she was, she was beautiful.

"Aren't you afraid of me?" She glanced at his sword belt. "Or are you as deft at handling your sword as Captain Westfall?"

He stepped closer, tightening his grip. "Better," he whispered in her ear. There: she was blushing and blinking.

"Well," she began, but the timing was off. He'd won. She crossed her arms. "Very amusing, Your Highness."

He bowed dramatically. "I do what I can. But you can't have Princess Nehemia here with you."

"And why is that? Do you believe I'm going to *kill* her? Why would I kill the one person in this castle who isn't a babbling idiot?" She gave him a look that suggested he was part of the majority. "Not to mention, her guards would kill *me* before I even lifted a hand."

"It simply can't happen. She's here to learn our customs, not to spar."

"She's a princess. She can do what she likes."

"And I suppose *you're* going to teach her about weaponry?"

She cocked her head. "Perhaps you're just a *little* bit afraid of me."

"I'll escort her back to her chambers."

She gestured widely for him to pass. "Wyrd help you."

He ran a hand through his black hair and approached the princess, who waited for them with a hand on her hip. "Your Highness," Dorian said, motioning to her personal guard to join them. "I'm afraid we must return you to your chambers."

The princess looked behind his shoulder with a raised eyebrow. To his dismay, Celaena began speaking in Eyllwe to the princess, who stomped her staff. She hissed something at him. Dorian's skill with the Eyllwe language was spotty at best, and the princess spoke too fast for him to understand. Thankfully, the assassin translated.

"She says you can return to your cushions and dancing and leave us be," Celaena said.

He tried his best to look serious. "Tell her it's unacceptable for her to spar."

Celaena said something, to which the princess only waved a hand and strode past them and onto the sparring floor.

"What did you say?" Dorian said.

"I said you volunteered to be her first partner," she said. "Well? You don't want to upset the princess."

"I will not *spar* with the princess."

"Would you rather spar with me?"

"Perhaps if we had a private lesson in your chambers," he said smoothly. "Tonight."

"I'll be waiting." She curled her hair around a finger.

The princess twirled her staff with strength and precision that made him gulp. Deciding that he didn't feel like having the daylights walloped out of him, he walked to the rack of weapons and selected two wooden swords. "How about some basic swordplay instead?" he asked Nehemia. To his relief, the princess nodded and handed her staff to one of her guards, then took the practice sword Dorian extended to her. Celaena would not make a fool out of *him*!

"You stand like this," he said to the princess, taking a defensive stance.

18

Celaena smiled as she watched the Crown Prince of Adarlan lead the Princess of Eyllwe through the basic steps of fencing. He was charming, she supposed. In an arrogant sort of way. But someone with his title could have been far, far worse. It made her uneasy how he'd made her blush. In fact, he was so attractive that she had difficulty *not* thinking about how attractive he was, and again wondered why he wasn't married.

She sort of wanted to kiss him.

She swallowed. She'd been kissed before, of course. By Sam, and often enough that she was no stranger to it. But it'd been over a year since she'd lost the assassin she'd grown up with. And even though the thought of kissing anyone else had once made her sick, when she saw Dorian . . .

Princess Nehemia lunged, slapping Dorian on the wrist with her sword. Celaena bit down her laughter. He grimaced and rubbed the sore joint, but then smiled as the princess began gloating.

Damn him for being so handsome!

She leaned against the wall and would have enjoyed the lesson had someone not grabbed her arm hard enough to hurt.

"*What* is this?" Dragged from the wall, she found herself facing Chaol.

"What is what?"

"*What* is Dorian doing with *her*?"

She shrugged. "Sparring?"

"And *why* are they sparring?"

"Because he volunteered to teach her how to fight?"

Chaol practically shoved her from him as he approached the pair. They stopped, and Dorian followed Chaol to a corner. They spoke quickly—angrily—before Chaol came back to Celaena. "The guards will take you to your chambers."

"What?" She remembered their conversation on the balcony and frowned. So much for swapping stories. "The Test is tomorrow, and I need to train!"

"I think you've had enough training for today—it's almost dinner. Your lesson with Brullo ended two hours ago. Get some rest, or you'll be useless tomorrow. And *no*, I *don't* know what the Test will be, so don't bother asking."

"That's absurd!" she cried, and a pinch from Chaol kept her voice down. Princess Nehemia cast a worried glance in Celaena's direction, but the assassin waved at her to resume her lesson with the Crown Prince. "I'm not going to *do* anything, you insufferable moron."

"Are you honestly so blind that you can't see why we can't allow this?"

"'Can't allow'—you're just afraid of me!"

"Don't flatter yourself."

"You think I *want* to go back to Endovier?" she hissed. "You think I'm not aware of the fact that if I flee, I'll be hunted down for the rest of my life? You think I don't know *why* I vomit when you and I run in the morning? My body is a *wreck*. I *need* to spend these extra hours here, and you shouldn't punish me for it!"

"I'm not going to pretend to know how a criminal mind works."

She threw her hands in the air. "You know, I actually felt guilty. Just a *little* guilty. And now I remember why I shouldn't have. I hate sitting around, locked in my room, bored out of my senses. I hate all these guards and nonsense; I hate you telling me to hold back when Brullo sings Cain's praises and I'm just there, boring and unnoticed in the middle. I hate being told what I *can't* do. And I hate *you* most of all!"

He tapped his foot on the ground. "Are you finished?"

There was no kindness in Chaol's face, and she clicked her tongue as she left, her fists aching to bash his teeth down his throat.

19

Sitting in a chair near the hearth of the great hall, Kaltain watched Duke Perrington converse with Queen Georgina atop her dais. It'd been a shame that Dorian had left so quickly an hour ago; she hadn't even had the chance to speak to him. Which was especially irksome, given that she'd spent the better part of the morning dressing for court: her raven-black hair was neatly coiled around her head, and her skin glowed golden from the subtle shimmering powders she'd dusted on her face. Though the bindings on her pink-and-yellow gown crushed her ribs, and the pearls and diamonds around her neck strangled her, she kept her chin high, poised. Dorian had left, but having Perrington show up was an unexpected surprise. The duke rarely visited court; this had to be important.

Kaltain rose from her chair by the fire as the duke bowed to the queen and strode toward the doors. As she stepped into his path, he paused at the sight of her, his eyes gleaming with a hunger that made her want to cringe. He bowed low. "Milady."

"Your Grace," she smiled, forcing all that repulsion down deep, deep, deep.

"I hope you're well," he said, offering his arm to lead her out of the hall. She smiled again, taking it. Though he was somewhat rotund, hard muscle lay in the arm beneath her hand.

"Very well, thank you. And yourself? I feel I haven't seen you in days and days! What a wonderful surprise to have you visit the court."

Perrington gave her a yellow smile. "I've missed you as well, milady."

She tried not to wince as his hairy, meaty fingers rubbed her pristine skin, and instead delicately inclined her head toward him. "I hope Her Majesty was in good health; was your conversation a pleasant one?"

Oh, it was so dangerous to pry, especially when she was here on his good graces. Meeting him last spring had been a stroke of luck. And convincing him to invite her to court—mostly by implying what might await him once she was out of her father's household and without a chaperone—hadn't been that difficult. But she wasn't here to simply enjoy the pleasures of the court. No, she was tired of being a minor lady, waiting to be married off to the highest bidder, tired of petty politics and easily manipulated fools.

"Her Majesty is quite well, actually," Perrington said, leading Kaltain toward her rooms. Her stomach clenched a bit. Though he didn't hide that he wanted her, he hadn't pushed her into bed—yet. But with a man like Perrington, who always got what he wanted . . . she didn't have much time to find a way to avoid owning up to the subtle promise she'd made him earlier that year. "But," the duke went on, "with a son of marriageable age, she's busy."

Kaltain kept her face plain. Calm. Serene. "Can we expect any news of an engagement in the near future?" Another dangerous question.

"I certainly hope so," the duke grumbled, his face darkening beneath his ruddy hair. The jagged scar along his cheek stood out starkly. "Her

Majesty already has a list of girls deemed appropriate—" The duke halted, remembering whom he spoke to, and Kaltain batted her eyelashes at him.

"Oh, I'm quite sorry," she purred. "I didn't mean to pry into the Royal Household's affairs." She patted his arm, her heart kicking into a full gallop. Dorian had been given a list of appropriate brides? Who was on it? And how could she . . . No, she'd think of that later. For now, she had to find out who stood between her and the crown.

"It's nothing to apologize for," he said, his dark eyes shining. "Come—tell me what you've been doing these past few days."

"Not much of note. Though I met a very interesting young woman," she said casually, leading him down a window-lined stairway into the glass section of the castle. "A friend of Dorian's—the Lady Lillian, he called her."

The duke went positively rigid. "You met her?"

"Oh, yes—she's quite kind." The lie rolled off of her tongue. "When I spoke to her today, she mentioned how much the Crown Prince likes her. I hope for her sake she was on the queen's list." While she'd wanted *some* information about Lillian, she hadn't expected *this*.

"The Lady Lillian? Of course she isn't."

"The poor thing. I suspect her heart will be broken. I know it's not my place to pry," she went on, the duke growing redder and more furious by the moment, "but I heard it not an hour ago from Dorian himself that . . ."

"That what?" A thrill went through her at his anger—not anger at her, but at Lillian. At the weapon she'd just had the good fortune to stumble across.

"That he's very attached to her. Possibly in love with her."

"That's absurd."

"It's true!" She gave a morose shake of the head. "How tragic."

"Foolish is what it is." The duke stopped at the end of the hallway that led to Kaltain's room. His anger loosened his tongue. "Foolish and daft and impossible."

"Impossible?"

"Someday I will explain why." A clock chimed, off-kilter, and Perrington turned in its direction. "I have a council meeting." He leaned close enough to whisper in her ear, his breath hot and damp against her skin. "Perhaps I'll see you tonight?" He dragged a hand down her side before he walked away. She watched him go, and when he disappeared, she let out a shuddering sigh. But if he could get her close to Dorian . . .

She had to find out who her competition was, but first she had to find a way to get Lillian's claws out of the prince. List or no list, she was a threat.

And if the duke hated her as much as it seemed, she might have powerful allies when the time came to make sure Lillian released her hold on Dorian.

Dorian and Chaol didn't say much as they walked to dinner in the Great Hall. Princess Nehemia was safely in her chambers, surrounded by her guards. It'd been quickly agreed that while it was foolish of Celaena to spar with the princess, Chaol's absence was inexcusable, even with the dead Champion to investigate.

"You seemed rather friendly with Sardothien," Chaol said, his voice cold.

"Jealous, are we?" Dorian teased.

"I'm more concerned for your safety. She might be pretty and might impress you with her cleverness, but she's still an *assassin*, Dorian."

"You sound like my father."

"It's common sense. Stay away from her, Champion or no."

"Don't give me orders."

"I'm only doing it for your safety."

"Why would she kill me? I think she likes being pampered. If she hasn't attempted to escape or kill anyone, then why would she do it now?" He patted his friend on the shoulder. "You worry too much."

"It's my occupation to worry."

"Then you'll have gray hair before you're twenty-five, and Sardothien certainly will *not* fall in love with you."

"What nonsense are you talking?"

"Well, if she *does* try to escape, which she *won't*, then she'll break your heart. You'd be forced to throw her in the dungeons, hunt her down, or kill her."

"Dorian, I don't like her."

Sensing his friend's growing irritation, Dorian changed the subject. "What about that dead Champion—the Eye Eater? Any idea yet who did it, or why?"

Chaol's eyes darkened. "I've studied it again and again over the past few days. The body was totally destroyed." The color leeched from Chaol's cheeks. "Innards scooped out and gone; even the brain was . . . missing. I've sent a message to your father about it, but I'll continue investigating in the meantime."

"I bet it was just a drunken brawl," Dorian said, though he had been in plenty of brawls himself and had never known anyone to go about removing someone's innards. A trickle of fear formed in the back of Dorian's mind. "My father will probably be glad to have the Eye Eater dead and gone."

"I hope so."

Dorian grinned and put an arm around the captain's shoulders. "With you looking into it, I'm sure it'll be solved tomorrow," he said, leading his friend into the dining hall.

20

Celaena closed her book and sighed. What a terrible ending. She stood from the chair, unsure where she was going, and walked out of her bedroom. She'd been willing to apologize to Chaol when he found her sparring with Nehemia that afternoon, but his behavior . . . She paced through her rooms. He had more important things to do than guard the world's most famous criminal, did he? She didn't enjoy being cruel, but . . . hadn't he deserved it?

She'd really made a fool out of herself by mentioning the vomiting. And she'd called him all sorts of nasty things. Did he trust her or hate her? Celaena looked at her hands and realized she had wrung them so badly that her fingers were red. How had she gone from the most feared prisoner in Endovier to *this* sappy mess?

She had greater matters to worry about—like the Test tomorrow. And this dead Champion. She'd already altered the hinges on all her doors so that they squealed loudly any time they opened. If someone entered her room, she'd know well in advance. And she'd managed to embed some stolen sewing needles into a bar of soap for a makeshift, miniature pike. It was better than nothing, especially if this murderer had a taste for Champion blood. She forced her hands to her sides, shaking her unease, and strode into the music and gaming room. She could not play billiards or cards by herself, but . . .

Celaena eyed the pianoforte. She used to play—oh, she'd loved to play, loved music, the way music could break and heal and make everything seem possible and heroic.

Carefully, as if approaching a sleeping person, Celaena walked to the large instrument. She pulled out the wooden bench, wincing at the loud scraping sound it made. Folding back the heavy lid, she pushed her feet on the pedals, testing them. She eyed the smooth ivory keys, and then the black keys, which were like the gaps between teeth.

She had been good once—perhaps better than good. Arobynn Hamel made her play for him whenever they saw each other.

She wondered if Arobynn knew she was out of the mines. Would he try to free her if he did? She still didn't dare to face the possibility of *who* might have betrayed her. Things had been such a haze when she'd been captured—in two weeks, she'd lost Sam and her own freedom, and lost something of herself in those blurry days, too.

Sam. What would he make of all this? If he'd been alive when she was captured, he would have had her out of the royal dungeons before the king even got word of her imprisonment. But Sam, like her, had been betrayed—and sometimes the absence of him hit her so hard that she forgot how to breathe. She touched a lower note. It was deep and throbbing, full of sorrow and anger.

Gingerly, with one hand, she tapped out a simple, slow melody on the higher keys. Echoes—shreds of memories arising out of the void of her mind. Her rooms were so silent that the music seemed obtrusive.

She moved her right hand, playing upon the flats and sharps. It was a piece that she used to play again and again until Arobynn would yell at her to play something else. She played a chord, then another, added in a few silver notes from her right hand, pushed once on a pedal, and was gone.

The notes burst from her fingers, staggering at first, but then more confidently as the emotion in the music took over. It was a mournful piece, but it made her into something clean and new. She was surprised that her hands had not forgotten, that somewhere in her mind, after a year of darkness and slavery, music was still alive and breathing. That somewhere, between the notes, was Sam. She forgot about time as she drifted between pieces, voicing the unspeakable, opening old wounds, playing and playing as the sound forgave and saved her.

Leaning against the doorway, Dorian stood, utterly transfixed. She'd been playing for some time with her back to him. He wondered when she'd notice him, or if she'd ever stop at all. He wouldn't mind listening forever. He had come here with the intention of embarrassing a snide assassin, and had instead found a young woman pouring her secrets into a pianoforte.

Dorian peeled himself from the wall. For all her assassinating experience, she didn't notice him until he sat down on the bench beside her. "You play beau—"

Her fingers slipped on the keys, which let out a loud, awful *CLANK*, and she was halfway to the rack of cue sticks when she beheld him. He could have sworn her eyes were damp. "What are you doing here?" She glanced to the door. Was she planning on using one of those cue sticks against him?

"Chaol isn't with me," he said with a quick smile. "If that's what you're wondering. I apologize if I interrupted." He wondered at her discomfort as she turned red. It seemed far too human an emotion for

Adarlan's Assassin. Perhaps his earlier plan to embarrass her wasn't foiled yet. "But you were playing so beautifully that I—"

"It's fine." She walked toward one of the chairs. He stood, blocking her path. She was of surprisingly average height. He glanced down at her form. Average height aside, her curves were enticing. "What are you doing here?" she repeated.

He smiled roguishly. "We decided to meet tonight. Don't you remember?"

"I thought it was a joke."

"I'm Crown Prince of Adarlan." He sank into a chair before the fire. "I never joke."

"Are you allowed to be here?"

"Allowed? Again: I'm a prince. I can do what I like."

"Yes, but I'm Adarlan's Assassin."

He wouldn't be intimidated, even if she could grab that billiards cue and skewer him with it in a matter of seconds. "From your playing, it seems that you're a great deal more than that."

"What do you mean?"

"Well," he said, trying not to get lost in her strange, lovely eyes, "I don't think anyone who plays like that can be *just* a criminal. It seems like you have a soul," he teased.

"Of course I have a soul. Everyone has a soul."

She was still red. He made her that uncomfortable? He fought his grin. This was too much fun. "How'd you like the books?"

"They were very nice," she said quietly. "They were wonderful, actually."

"I'm glad." Their eyes met, and she retreated behind the back of the chair. If he didn't know better, he would have thought *himself* to be the assassin! "How's training going? Any competitors giving you trouble?"

"Excellently," she said, but the corners of her mouth drifted downward. "And no. After today, I don't think any of us will be giving anyone any trouble." It took him a moment to realize she was thinking of the competitor who had been killed while trying to escape. She chewed on her bottom lip, quiet for a heartbeat, before she asked: "Did Chaol give the order to kill Sven?"

"No," he said. "My father commanded all the guards to shoot to kill if any of you tried to escape. I don't think Chaol would ever have given that order," he added, though he wasn't sure why. But the unnerving stillness in her eyes abated, at least. When she didn't say more, Dorian asked as casually as he could: "On that note, how are you and Chaol getting along?" Of course, it was a totally innocent question.

She shrugged, and he tried to not read too far into the gesture. "Fine. I think he hates me a bit, but given his position, I'm not surprised."

"Why do you think he hates you?" For some reason, he couldn't bring himself to deny it.

"Because I'm an assassin, and he's Captain of the Guard, forced to belittle himself by minding the would-be King's Champion."

"Do you wish it were otherwise?" He gave her a lazy grin. That question wasn't so innocent.

She inched around the chair, coming closer to him, and his heart jumped a beat. "Well, who wants to be hated? Though I'd rather be hated than invisible. But it makes no difference." She wasn't convincing.

"You're lonely?" He said it before he could stop himself.

"Lonely?" She shook her head and finally, after all that coaxing, sat down. He fought against the urge to reach across the space between them to see if her hair was as silky as it looked. "No. I can survive well enough on my own—if given proper reading material."

He looked at the fire, trying not to think about where she'd been only weeks before—and what that kind of loneliness might have felt like. There were no books in Endovier. "Still, it can't be pleasant to be one's own companion at all times."

"And what would you do?" She laughed. "I'd rather not be seen as one of your *lovers*."

"And what's wrong with that?"

"I'm already notorious as an assassin—I don't particularly feel like being notorious for sharing your bed." He choked, but she went on. "Would you like me to explain *why*, or is it enough for me to say that I don't take jewels and trinkets as payment for my affection?"

He snarled. "I'm not going to debate morality with an assassin. You kill people for *money*, you know."

Her eyes became hard and she pointed to the door. "You may leave now."

"You're dismissing *me*?" He didn't know whether to laugh or yell.

"Shall I summon Chaol to see what he thinks?" She crossed her arms, knowing she had won. Perhaps she'd also realized that there was fun to be had in riling him, too.

"Why should I be thrown from your rooms for stating the truth? You just called me little more than a whoremonger." He hadn't had this much fun in ages. "Tell me about your life—how you learned to play the pianoforte so masterfully. And what was that piece? It was so sad; were you thinking about a secret lover?" He winked.

"I practiced." She stood, walking toward the door. "And yes," she snapped, "I was."

"You're quite prickly tonight," he said, trailing her. He stopped a foot away, but the space between them felt strangely intimate, especially as he purred, "You're not nearly as chatty as you were this afternoon."

"I'm not some odd commodity that you can gawk at!" She stepped closer. "I'm not some carnival exhibit, and you won't use *me* as part of some unfulfilled desire for adventure and excitement! Which is undoubtedly why you chose me to be your Champion."

His mouth fell open and he conceded a step. "What?" was all he managed.

She stalked past him and dropped into the armchair. At least she wasn't leaving. "Did you honestly think I wouldn't realize why you came here tonight? As someone who gave me *The Crown of a Hero* to read, which suggests a rather fanciful mind that yearns for adventure?"

"I don't think you're an adventure," he muttered.

"Oh? The castle offers so much excitement that the presence of Adarlan's Assassin is nothing unusual? Nothing that would entice a young prince who's been confined to a court all his life? And what does this competition suggest, for that matter? I'm already at your father's disposal. I won't become his son's jester, too."

It was his turn to blush. Had he ever been scolded by anyone like this? His parents and tutors perhaps, but certainly not a young woman. "Don't you know who you're talking to?"

"My dear prince," she drawled, examining her nails, "you're alone in my rooms. The hallway door is very far away. I can say whatever I wish."

He burst out laughing. She sat up and watched him, her head tilted to the side. Her cheeks were flushed, making her blue eyes even brighter. Did she know what he might have wanted to do with her if she wasn't an assassin? "I'll go," he said at last, stopping himself from wondering if he could actually risk it—risk his father's and Chaol's wrath, and what might happen if he decided to damn the consequences. "But I'll return. Soon."

"I'm sure," she said dryly.

"Good night, Sardothien." He looked around her rooms and grinned. "Tell me something before I leave: this mystery lover of yours . . . he doesn't live in the castle, does he?"

He instantly knew he'd said the wrong thing when some of the light vanished from her eyes. "Good night," she said a bit coldly.

Dorian shook his head. "I didn't mean to—"

She just waved him off, looking toward the fire. Understanding his dismissal, he strode to the door, each of his footsteps sounding in the now too-silent room. He was almost to the threshold when she spoke, her voice distant. "His name was Sam."

She was still staring at the fire. *Was* Sam . . . "What happened?"

She looked at him, smiling sadly. "He died."

"When?" he got out. He would have never teased her like that, never said a damn word if he'd known . . .

Her words were strangled as she said, "Thirteen months ago."

A glimmer of pain flashed across her face, so real and endless that he felt it in his gut. "I'm sorry," he breathed.

She shrugged, as if it could somehow diminish the grief he still saw in her eyes, shining so bright in the firelight. "So am I," she whispered, and faced the fire again.

Sensing she was truly done talking this time, Dorian cleared his throat. "Good luck at the Test tomorrow." She didn't say anything as he left the room.

He couldn't banish her heart-wrenching music from his mind, even when he burned his mother's list of eligible maidens, even when he read a book long into the night, even when he finally fell asleep.

21

Celaena dangled from the stone wall of the castle, her legs trembling as she dug her tar-covered fingers and toes into the cracks between the giant blocks. Brullo shouted something at the other nineteen remaining Champions scaling the castle walls, but from seventy feet up, the wind carried his words away. One of the Champions hadn't shown up for the Test—and even his guards hadn't known where he went. Maybe he'd actually managed to escape. Risking it seemed better than this miserably stupid Test, anyway. She gritted her teeth, inching her hand upward, and pulled herself up another foot.

Twenty feet up and about thirty feet away flapped the object of this insane race: a golden flag. The Test was simple: climb the castle to where the flag waved ninety feet in the air and retrieve it. First one who grabbed the flag and brought it back down received a pat on the back. Last one to reach the designated spot would be sent back to whatever gutter they came from.

Surprisingly, no one had fallen yet—perhaps because the path to the flag was fairly easy: balconies, windowsills, and trellises covered most of the space. Celaena scooted up another few feet, her fingers aching. Looking down was always a bad idea, even if Arobynn had forced her to stand on the ledge of his Assassin's Keep for hours on end to become accustomed to heights. She panted as she grasped another window ledge and hoisted herself up. It was deep enough that she could crouch within, and she took a moment to study the other competitors.

Sure enough, Cain was in the lead, and had taken the easiest path toward the flag, Grave and Verin on his trail, Nox close behind, and Pelor, the young assassin, not far below him. There were so many competitors following him that their gear often got tangled together. They'd each been given the opportunity to select one object to aid them in their ascent—rope, spikes, special boots—and sure enough, Cain had gone right for the rope.

She'd taken a small tin of tar, and as Celaena rose from her crouch in the windowsill, her sticky, black hands and bare feet easily gripped the stone wall. She'd used some rope to strap the tin to her belt, and before she stepped out of the shade of the sill, she rubbed a little more on her palms. Someone gasped below, and she swallowed the urge to glance down. She knew she'd taken a more difficult path—but it was better than fighting off all the competitors taking the easy route. She wouldn't put it past Grave or Verin to shove her off the wall.

Her hands suctioned onto the stone, and Celaena heaved herself upward just in time to hear a shriek, a thump, and then silence, followed by the shouting of onlookers. A competitor had fallen—and died. She looked down and beheld the body of Ned Clement, the murderer who'd called himself the Scythe and spent years in the labor camps of Calaculla for his crimes. A shudder went through her. Though the murder of the Eye Eater had made many of the Champions quiet down, the sponsors certainly didn't seem to care that this Test might very well kill a few more of them.

She shimmied up a drainpipe, her thighs clinging to the iron. Cain hooked his long rope around a leering gargoyle's neck and swung across an expanse of flat wall, landing on a balcony ledge fifteen feet below the flag. She fought her frustration as she worked her way up higher and higher, following the course of the drainpipe.

The other competitors shuffled along, following Cain's path. There were a few more shouts, and she looked down long enough to see that Grave was causing a backup because he couldn't manage to toss his rope around the gargoyle's neck as Cain had. Verin nudged the assassin aside and moved past him, easily securing his own rope. Nox, now behind Grave, made to do the same, but Grave started cursing at him, and Nox stopped, lifting his hands in a gesture of placation. Smirking, Celaena braced her blackened feet on a stabilizing bracket holding the pipe in place. She'd soon be directly parallel to the flag. And then only thirty feet of bare stone would separate her from it.

Celaena eased farther up the pipe, her toes sticking to the metal. Fifteen feet below her pipe, a mercenary was clutching the horns of a gargoyle as he set about fastening his rope around its head. He seemed to be taking the faster route across a cluster of gargoyles. Then he'd have to swing onto a landing eighteen feet away, before making his way to the other gargoyles on which Grave and Nox now quarreled. She was in no danger of him trying to scale the drainpipe to bother her. So inch by inch, she moved up, the wind battering her hair this way and that.

It was then that she heard Nox shout, and Celaena looked in time to see Grave shove him from their perch atop the gargoyle's back. Nox swung wide, the rope wrapped around his middle going taut as he collided with the castle wall below. Celaena froze, her breath catching as Nox scraped his hands and feet against the stone to catch hold.

But Grave wasn't done yet. He bent under the guise of adjusting his boot, and Celaena saw a small dagger glint in the sunlight. How he'd gotten the weapon past his guards was a feat in itself. Celaena's warning cry was carried away by the wind as Grave set about sawing Nox's rope from its tether on the gargoyle. None of the other Champions nearby bothered to do anything, though Pelor paused for a moment before easing around Grave. If Nox died, it was one less competitor—and if they interfered, it might cost them this Test. Celaena knew she should keep moving, but something kept her rooted to the spot.

Nox couldn't find a hold on the stone wall, and without a nearby ledge or gargoyle to grasp, he had nowhere to go but down. Once the rope broke, he'd fall.

One by one, the threads of his rope snapped beneath Grave's dagger, and Nox, sensing the vibrations, looked up at the assassin in horror. If he fell, there was no chance of surviving. A few more slices of Grave's blade and the rope would be severed entirely.

The rope groaned. Celaena moved.

She slid down the drainpipe, the flesh of her feet and hands tearing open as the metal cut into her skin, but she didn't let herself think of the pain. The mercenary on the gargoyle below only had time to lean into the wall as she slammed onto the creature's head, gripping its horns to steady herself. The mercenary had already tied one end of his climbing rope around the gargoyle's neck; now she seized it and tied the other around her own waist. The rope was long enough—and strong enough, and the four gargoyles perched beside hers would provide enough space to run. "Touch this rope and I'll gut you," she warned the mercenary, and readied herself.

Nox shouted at Grave, and she dared a look to where the thief dangled. There was a sharp snap of rope breaking, and Nox's cry of fear and rage, and Celaena took off, sprinting across the backs of the four gargoyles before she launched herself into the void.

22

Wind tore at her, but Celaena kept her focus on Nox, falling so fast, so far from her outstretched hands.

People shouted below, and the light bouncing off the glass castle blinded her. But there he was, just a hand's breadth from her fingers, his gray eyes wide, his arms swinging as if he could turn them into wings.

In a heartbeat, her arms were around his middle, and she slammed into him so hard that the breath was knocked from her chest. Together they plummeted like a stone, down, down, down toward the rising ground.

Nox grabbed the rope, but even that wasn't enough to lighten the blinding impact on her torso as the rope went taut. She held on to him with every ounce of strength she had, willing her arms not to let him go. The rope sent them careening toward the wall. Celaena hardly had the sense to lean her head away from the approaching stones, and the impact burst through her side and shoulder. She held tight to him still, focusing on her arms, on her too-shallow breathing. They hung there, flat against the wall, panting as they looked at the ground thirty feet below. The rope held.

"Lillian," Nox said, gasping for breath. He pressed his face onto her hair. "Gods above." But cheers erupted from below and drowned out his words. Celaena's limbs trembled so violently that she had to focus on gripping Nox, and her stomach turned over and over and over.

But they were still in the middle of the Test—still expected to complete it, and Celaena looked up. All the Champions had stopped to see her save the falling thief. All except one, who perched high, high above them.

Celaena could only gape as the flag was ripped down, and Cain howled his triumph. More cheers rose up to meet them as Cain waved the flag for everyone to see. She seethed.

She would have won if she'd taken the easy route—she would have gotten there in half the time it took Cain. But Chaol told her to stay in the middle, anyway. And her path had been far more impressive and demonstrative of her skills. Cain just had to jump and swing—amateur scaling. Besides, if she had won, if she'd gone the easy way, she wouldn't have saved Nox.

She clenched her jaw. Could she get back up there in time? Perhaps Nox could take the rope, and she'd just scale the wall with her bare hands. There was nothing worse than second place. But even as she thought it, Verin, Grave, Pelor, and Renault climbed the last few feet to the spot, tapping it with a hand before descending.

"Lillian. Nox. Hurry up," Brullo called, and she peered down at the Weapons Master.

Celaena scowled, and started sliding her feet along the cracks in the stone, looking for a foothold. Her skin, raw and bleeding in spots, stung as she found a crevice for her toes to squeeze into. Carefully, carefully, she pulled herself up.

"I'm sorry," Nox breathed, his legs knocking into hers as he also sought out a foothold.

"It's fine," she told him. Shaking, numb, Celaena climbed back up the wall, leaving Nox to figure out the way on his own. Foolish. It'd been so foolish to save him. What had she been thinking?

"Cheer up," Chaol said, drinking from his glass of water. "Eighteenth place is fine. At least Nox placed behind you."

Celaena said nothing and pushed her carrots around on her plate. It had taken two baths and an entire bar of soap to get the tar off her aching hands and feet, and Philippa had spent thirty minutes cleaning out and binding the wounds on each. And though Celaena had stopped shaking, she could still hear the shriek and thump of Ned Clement hitting the ground. They'd carried his body away before she finished the test. Only his death had saved Nox from elimination. Grave hadn't even been scolded. There had been no rules against playing dirty.

"You're doing exactly like we planned," Chaol went on. "Though I'd hardly consider your valiant rescue to be entirely discreet."

She glared at him. "Well, I still lost." While Dorian had congratulated her for saving Nox, and while the thief had hugged and thanked her again and again, only Chaol had frowned when the Test was over. Apparently, daring rescues weren't part of a jewel thief's repertoire.

Chaol's brown eyes shone golden in the midday sun. "Wasn't learning to lose gracefully part of your training?"

"No," she said sourly. "Arobynn told me that second place was just a nice title for the first loser."

"Arobynn Hamel?" Chaol asked, setting down his glass. "The King of the Assassins?"

She looked toward the window, and the glittering expanse of Rifthold barely visible beyond it. It was strange to think that Arobynn was in the same city—that he was so close to her now. "You know he was my master, don't you?"

"I'd forgotten," Chaol said. Arobynn would have flogged her for saving Nox, jeopardizing her own safety and place in this competition. "He oversaw your training personally?"

"He trained me himself, and then brought in tutors from all over Erilea. The fighting masters from the rice fields of the southern continent, poison experts from the Bogdano Jungle . . . Once he sent me to the Silent Assassins in the Red Desert. No price was too high for him. Or me," she added, fingering the fine thread on her bathrobe. "He didn't bother to tell me until I was fourteen that I was expected to pay him back for all of it."

"He trained you and then made you pay for it?"

She shrugged, but was unable to hide the flash of anger. "Courtesans go through the same experience: they're taken in at a young age, and are bound to their brothels until they can earn back every coin that went into their training, upkeep, and wardrobe."

"That's despicable," he spat, and she blinked at the anger in his voice—anger that, for once, was not directed at her. "Did you pay it back?"

A cold smile that didn't reach her eyes spread across her face. "Oh, down to the last copper. And he then went out and spent all of it. Over five hundred thousand gold coins. Gone in three hours." Chaol started from his seat. She shoved the memory down so deep that it stopped hurting. "You still haven't apologized," she said, changing the subject before Chaol could inquire further.

"Apologized? For what?"

"For all the horrid things you said yesterday afternoon when I was sparring with Nehemia."

He narrowed his eyes, taking the bait. "I won't apologize for speaking the truth."

"The truth? You treated me like I'm a crazed criminal!"

"And *you* said that you hated me more than anyone alive."

"I meant every word of it." However, a smile began to tug at her lips—and she soon found it reflected on his face. He tossed a piece of bread at her, which she caught in one hand and threw back at him. He caught it with ease. "Idiot," she said, grinning now.

"Crazed criminal," he returned, grinning, too.

"I really do hate you."

"At least I didn't come in eighteenth place," he said. Celaena felt her nostrils flare, and it was all Chaol could do to duck the apple she chucked at his head.

It wasn't until later that Philippa brought the news. The Champion who hadn't shown up for the Test had been found dead in a servants' stairwell, brutally mauled and dismembered.

The new murder cast a pall over the next two weeks, and the two Tests they brought with them. Celaena passed the Tests—stealth and tracking—without drawing much attention to herself or risking her neck to save anyone. No other Champions were murdered, thankfully, but Celaena still found herself looking over her shoulder constantly, even though Chaol seemed to consider the two murders to be just unfortunate incidents.

Every day, she got better at running, going farther and faster, and managed to keep from killing Cain when he taunted her at training. The Crown Prince didn't bother to show his face in her rooms again, and she only saw him during the Tests, when he usually just grinned and winked at her and made her feel ridiculously tingly and warm.

But she had more important things to worry about. There were only nine weeks left until the final duel, and some of the others, including Nox, were doing well enough that those four spots were starting to seem rather precious. Cain would definitely be there, but who would the other final three be? She'd always been so sure she'd make it.

But, if she were honest with herself, Celaena wasn't so sure anymore.

23

Celaena gaped at the ground. She knew these sharp, gray rocks—knew how they crunched beneath her feet, how they smelled after the rain, how they could so easily cut into her skin when she was thrown down. The rocks stretched for miles, rising into jagged, fang-like mountains that pierced the cloudy sky. In the frigid wind, she had little clothing to protect her from its stinging gusts. As she touched the dirty rags, her stomach rose in her throat. What had happened?

She pivoted, shackles clanking, and took in the desolate waste that was Endovier.

She had failed, failed and been sent back here. There was no chance of escape. She had tasted freedom, come so close to it, and now—

Celaena screamed as excruciating pain shot down her back, barely heralded by the crack of the whip. She fell onto the ground, stone slicing into her raw knees.

"Get on your feet," someone barked.

Tears stung her eyes, and the whip creaked as it rose again. She would be killed this time. She would die from the pain of it.

The whip fell, slicing into bone, reverberating through her body, making everything collapse and explode in agony, shifting her body into a graveyard, a dead—

Celaena's eyes flew open. She panted.

"Are you . . . ," someone said beside her, and she jerked.

Where was she?

"It was a dream," said Chaol.

She stared at him, then looked around the room, running a hand through her hair. Rifthold. Rifthold—that's where she was. In the glass castle—no, in the stone castle beneath.

She was sweating, and the sweat on her back felt uncomfortably like blood. She felt dizzy, nauseated, too small and too large all at once. Though her windows were shut, an odd draft from somewhere in her room kissed her face, smelling strangely of roses.

"Celaena. It was a dream," the Captain of the Guard said again. "You were screaming." He gave her a shaky smile. "I thought you were being murdered."

Celaena reached around to touch her back, beneath her nightshirt. She could feel the three ridges—and some smaller ones, but nothing, nothing—

"I was being whipped." She shook her head to remove the memory from her mind. "What are you doing here? It's not even dawn." She crossed her arms, flushing slightly.

"It's Samhuinn. I'm canceling our training today, but I wanted to see if you planned to attend the service."

"Today's—what? It's Samhuinn today? Why has no one mentioned it? Is there a feast tonight?" Could she have become so enmeshed in the competition that she'd lost track of time?

He frowned. "Of course, but you're not invited."

"Of course. And will you be summoning the dead to you this haunted night or lighting a bonfire with your companions?"

"I don't partake in such superstitious nonsense."

"Be careful, my cynical friend!" she warned, putting a hand in the air. "The gods and the dead are closest to the earth this day—they can hear every nasty comment you make!"

He rolled his eyes. "It's a silly holiday to celebrate the coming of winter. The bonfires just produce ash to cover the fields."

"As an offering to the gods to keep them safe!"

"As a way to fertilize them."

Celaena pushed back the covers. "So says you," she said as she stood. She adjusted her drenched nightgown. She reeked of sweat.

He snorted, following after her as she walked. "I never took you for a superstitious person. How does *that* fit into your career?"

She glared at him over her shoulder before she strode into the bathing chamber, Chaol close behind. She paused on the threshold. "Are you going to join me?" she said, and Chaol stiffened, realizing his error. He slammed the door in response.

Celaena found him waiting in her dining room when she emerged, her hair dripping water onto the floor. "Don't you have your own breakfast?"

"You still haven't given me an answer."

"An answer to what?" She sat down across the table and spooned porridge into a bowl. All that was needed was a heap—no, three heaps—of sugar, and some hot cream and—

"Are you going to temple?"

"I'm allowed to go to temple, but not to the feast?" She took a spoonful of the porridge.

"Religious observances shouldn't be denied to anyone."

"And the feast is . . . ?"

"A show of debauchery."

"Ah, I see." She swallowed another bite. Oh, she *loved* porridge! But perhaps it needed another spoonful of sugar.

"Well? Are you going? We need to leave soon if you are."

"No," she said through her food.

"For someone so superstitious, you risk angering the gods by not attending. I imagine that an assassin would take more interest in the day of the dead."

She made a demented face as she continued eating. "I worship in my own way. Perhaps I'll make a sacrifice or two of my own."

He rose, patting his sword. "Mind yourself while I'm gone. Don't bother dressing too elaborately—Brullo told me that you're still training this afternoon. You've got a Test tomorrow."

"Again? Didn't we just have one three days ago?" she moaned. The last Test had been javelin throwing on horseback, and a spot on her wrist was still tender.

But he said nothing more, and her chambers turned silent. Though she tried to forget it, the sound of the whip still snapped in her ears.

Grateful the service was finally over, Dorian Havilliard strode by himself through the castle grounds. Religion neither convinced nor moved him, and after hours of sitting in a pew, muttering prayer after prayer, he was in desperate need of some fresh air. And solitude.

He sighed through his clenched teeth, rubbing a spot on his temple, and headed through the garden. He passed a cluster of ladies, each of whom curtsied and giggled behind their fans. Dorian gave them a terse nod as he strode by. His mother had used the ceremony as a chance to point out all the eligible ladies to him. He'd spent the entire service trying not to scream at the top of his lungs.

Dorian turned around a hedge, almost crashing into a figure of blue-green velvet. It was the color of a mountain lake—that gem-like shade that didn't quite have a name. Not to mention the dress was about a hundred years out of fashion. His gaze rose to her face, and he smiled.

"Hello, Lady Lillian," he said, bowing, and then turned to her two companions. "Princess Nehemia. Captain Westfall." Dorian eyed the assassin's dress again. The folds of fabric—like the flowing waters of a river—were rather attractive. "You're looking festive." Celaena's brows lowered.

"The Lady Lillian's servants were attending the service when she dressed," said Chaol. "There was nothing else to wear." Of course; corsets required assistance to get in and out of—and the dresses were a labyrinth of secret clasps and ties.

"My apologies, my lord prince," Celaena said. Her eyes were bright and angry, and a blush rose to her cheek. "I'm *truly* sorry my clothes don't suit your taste."

"No, no," he said quickly, glancing at her feet. They were clad in red shoes—red like the winter berries beginning to pop out on the bushes. "You look very nice. Just a bit—out of place." Centuries, actually. She gave him an exasperated look. He turned to Nehemia. "Forgive me," he said in his best Eyllwe, which wasn't very impressive at all. "How are you?"

Her eyes shone with amusement at his shoddy Eyllwe, but she nodded in acknowledgment. "I am well, Your Highness," she answered in his language. Dorian's attention flicked to her two guards, who lurked in the shadows nearby—waiting, watching. Dorian's blood thrummed in his veins.

For weeks now, Duke Perrington had been pushing for a plan to bring more forces into Eyllwe—to crush the rebels so efficiently that they wouldn't dare challenge Adarlan's rule again. Just yesterday, the duke presented a plan: they would deploy more legions, and keep

Nehemia here to discourage any retaliation from the rebels. Not particularly inclined to add hostage-taking to his repertoire of abilities, Dorian had spent hours arguing against it. But while some of the council members had also voiced their disapproval, the majority seemed to think the duke's strategy to be a sound one. Still, Dorian had convinced them to back off about it until his father returned. That would give him time to win over some of the duke's supporters.

Now, standing before her, Dorian quickly looked away from the princess. If he were anyone but the Crown Prince, he would warn her. But if Nehemia left before she was supposed to, the duke would know who had told her, and inform his father. Things were bad enough between Dorian and the king; he didn't need to be branded as a rebel sympathizer.

"Are you going to the feast tonight?" Dorian asked the princess, forcing himself to look at her and keep his features neutral.

Nehemia looked to Celaena. "Are *you* attending?"

Celaena gave her a smile that only meant trouble. "Unfortunately, I have other plans. Isn't that right, Your Highness?" She didn't bother to hide the undercurrent of annoyance.

Chaol coughed, suddenly very interested in the berries in the hedges. Dorian was on his own. "Don't blame me," Dorian said smoothly. "*You* accepted an invitation to that party in Rifthold weeks ago." Her eyes flickered, but Dorian wouldn't yield. He couldn't bring her to the feast, not with so many watching. There would be too many questions. Not to mention too many people. Keeping track of her would be difficult.

Nehemia frowned at Celaena. "So you're not going?"

"No, but I'm sure you'll have a lovely time," Celaena said, then switched into Eyllwe and said something else. Dorian's Eyllwe was just competent enough that he understood the gist of it to be: "His Highness certainly knows how to keep women entertained."

Nehemia laughed, and Dorian's face warmed. They made a formidable pair, gods help them all.

"Well, we're very important and very busy," Celaena said to him, linking elbows with the princess. Perhaps allowing them to be friends was a horrible, dangerous idea. "So, we must be off. Good day to you, Your Highness." She curtsied, the red and blue gems in her belt sparkling in the sun. She looked over her shoulder, giving Dorian a sneer as she led the princess deeper into the garden.

Dorian glared at Chaol. "Thanks for your help."

The captain clapped him on the shoulder. "You think that was bad? You should see them when they really get going." With that, he strode after the women.

Dorian wanted to yell, to pull out his hair. He'd enjoyed seeing Celaena the other night—enjoyed it immensely. But for the past few weeks, he'd gotten caught up in council meetings and holding court, and hadn't been able to visit her. Were it not for the feast, he'd go to her again. He hadn't meant to annoy her with talk about the dress—though it *was* outdated—nor had he known she'd be *that* irritated about not being invited to the feast, but . . .

Dorian scowled and walked off to the kennels.

Celaena smiled to herself, running a finger across a neatly trimmed hedge. She thought the dress was lovely. *Festive indeed!*

"No, no, Your Highness," Chaol was saying to Nehemia, slow enough that she could understand. "I'm not a soldier. I'm a guard."

"There is no difference," the princess retorted, her accent thick and a bit unwieldy. Still, Chaol understood enough to bristle, and Celaena could hardly contain her glee.

She'd managed to see Nehemia a fair amount over the past two weeks—mostly just for brief walks and dinners, where they discussed what it was like for Nehemia to grow up in Eyllwe, what she thought of Rifthold, and who at court had managed to annoy the princess that day. Which, to Celaena's delight, was usually everyone.

"I'm not trained to fight in battles," Chaol replied through his teeth.

"You kill on the orders of your king." *Your* king. Nehemia might not be fully versed in their language, but she was smart enough to know the power of saying those two words. "Your king," not hers. While Celaena could listen to Nehemia rant about the King of Adarlan for hours, they were in a garden—other people might be listening. A shudder went through Celaena, and she interrupted before Nehemia could say more.

"I think it's useless arguing with her, Chaol," Celaena said, nudging the Captain of the Guard with her elbow. "Perhaps you shouldn't have given Terrin your title. Can you reclaim it? It'd prevent a lot of confusion."

"How'd you remember my brother's name?"

She shrugged, not quite understanding the gleam in his eye. "You told me. Why wouldn't I remember it?" He looked handsome today. It was in the way his hair met his golden skin—in the tiny gaps between the strands, in the way it fell across his brow.

"I suppose you'll enjoy the feast—without me there, that is," she said morosely.

He snorted. "Are you that upset about missing it?"

"No," she said, sweeping her unbound hair over a shoulder. "But—well, it's a party, and everyone loves parties."

"Shall I bring you a trinket from the revelry?"

"Only if it consists of a sizable portion of roast lamb."

The air was bright and clear around them. "The feast isn't that exciting," he offered. "It's the same as any supper. I can assure you the lamb will be dry and tough."

"As my friend, you should either bring me along, or keep me company."

"Friend?" he asked.

She blushed. "Well, 'scowling escort' is a better description. Or 'reluctant acquaintance,' if you prefer." To her surprise, he smiled.

The princess grabbed Celaena's hand. "You'll teach me!" she said in Eyllwe. "Teach me how to better speak your language—and teach me how to write and read it better than I do now. So I don't have to suffer through those horribly boring old men they call tutors."

"I—" Celaena began in the common tongue, and winced. She felt guilty for leaving Nehemia out of the conversation for so long, and having the princess be fluent in both languages *would* be great fun. But convincing Chaol to let her see Nehemia was always a hassle—because he insisted on being there to keep watch. He'd never agree to sitting through lessons. "I don't know how to properly teach you my language," Celaena lied.

"Nonsense," Nehemia said. "You'll teach me. After . . . whatever it is you do with *this* one. For an hour every day before supper."

Nehemia raised her chin in a way that suggested saying no wasn't an option. Celaena swallowed, and did her best to look pleasant as she turned to Chaol, who observed them with raised brows. "She wishes me to tutor her every day before supper."

"I'm afraid that's not possible," he said. She translated.

Nehemia gave him the withering glare that usually made people start sweating. "Why not?" She fell into Eyllwe. "She's smarter than most of the people in this castle."

Chaol, thankfully, caught the general gist of it. "I don't think that—"

"Am I not Princess of Eyllwe?" Nehemia interrupted in the common tongue.

"Your Highness," Chaol began, but Celaena silenced him with a wave of her hand. They were approaching the clock tower—black and menacing, as always. But kneeling before it was Cain. His head bent, he focused on something on the ground.

At the sound of their footsteps, Cain's head shot up. He grinned broadly and stood. His hands were covered in dirt, but before Celaena could better observe him, or his strange behavior, he nodded to Chaol and stalked away behind the tower.

"Nasty brute," Celaena breathed, still staring in the direction in which he'd disappeared.

"Who is he?" Nehemia asked in Eyllwe.

"A soldier in the king's army," Celaena said, "though he now serves Duke Perrington."

Nehemia looked after Cain, and her dark eyes narrowed. "Something about him makes me want to beat in his face."

Celaena laughed. "I'm glad I'm not the only one."

Chaol said nothing as he began walking again. She and Nehemia took up behind him, and as they crossed the small patio in which the clock tower stood, Celaena looked at the spot where Cain had just been kneeling. He'd dug out the dirt packed into the hollows of the strange mark in the flagstone, making the mark clearer. "What do you think this is?" she asked the princess, pointing at the mark etched into the tile. And why had Cain been cleaning it?

"A Wyrdmark," the princess replied, giving it a name in Celaena's own language.

Celaena's brows rose. It was just a triangle inside of a circle. "Can you read these marks?" she asked. A Wyrdmark . . . how strange!

"No," Nehemia said quickly. "They're a part of an ancient religion that died long ago."

"What religion?" Celaena asked. "Look, there's another." She pointed at another mark a few feet away. It was a vertical line with an inverted peak stretching upward from its middle.

"You should leave it alone," Nehemia said sharply, and Celaena blinked. "Such things were forgotten for a reason."

"What are you talking about?" asked Chaol, and she explained the gist of their conversation. When she finished, he curled his lip, but said nothing.

They continued on, and Celaena saw another mark. It was a strange shape: a small diamond with two inverted points protruding from either side. The top and bottom peaks of the diamond were elongated into a straight line, and it seemed to be symmetrically perfect. Had the king had them carved when he built the clock tower, or did they predate it?

Nehemia was staring at her forehead, and Celaena asked, "Is there dirt on my face?"

"No," Nehemia said a bit distantly, her brows knotting as she studied Celaena's brow. The princess suddenly stared into Celaena's eyes with a ferocity that made the assassin recoil slightly. "You know nothing about the Wyrdmarks?"

The clock tower chimed. "No," Celaena said. "I don't know anything about them."

"You're hiding something," the princess said softly in Eyllwe, though it was not accusatory. "You are much more than you seem, Lillian."

"I—well, I should hope I'm more than just some simpering courtier," she said with as much bravado as she could muster. She grinned broadly, hoping Nehemia would stop looking so strange, and stop staring at her brow. "Can you teach me how to speak Eyllwe properly?"

"If you can teach me more of your ridiculous language," said the princess, though some caution still lingered in her eyes. What had Nehemia seen that caused her to act that way?

"It's a deal," Celaena said with a weak smile. "Just don't tell *him.* Captain Westfall leaves me alone in the midafternoon. The hour before supper is perfect."

"Then I shall come tomorrow at five," Nehemia said. The princess smiled and began to walk once more, a spark appearing in her black eyes. Celaena could only follow after her.

24

Celaena lay on the bed, staring at a pool of moonlight on the floor. It filled in the dusty gaps between the stone tiles, and turned everything a bluish silver that made her feel as if she were frozen in an everlasting moment.

She didn't fear the night, though she found little comfort in its dark hours. It was just the time when she slept, the time when she stalked and killed, the time when the stars emerged with glittering beauty and made her feel wonderfully small and insignificant.

Celaena frowned. It was only midnight, and even though they had another Test tomorrow, she couldn't sleep. Her eyes were too heavy to read, she wouldn't play the pianoforte for fear of another embarrassing encounter, and she most certainly wouldn't amuse herself with fantasies of what the feast was like. She was still wearing her emerald-blue gown, too lazy to change.

She traced the moonlight to where it lapped upon the

tapestry-covered wall. The tapestry was odd, old, and not very carefully preserved. Images of forest animals amongst drooping trees dotted the large expanse. A woman—the only human in the tapestry—stood near the floor.

She was life-size and remarkably beautiful. Though she had silver hair, her face was young, and her flowing white gown seemed to move in the moonlight; it—

Celaena sat up in bed. Did the tapestry sway slightly? She glanced at the window. It was firmly shut. The tapestry was barely blowing outward, not to the side.

Could it be?

Her skin tingled, and she lit a candle before approaching the wall. The tapestry stopped moving. She reached to the end of the fabric and pulled it up. There was only stone. But . . .

Celaena pushed back the heavy folds of the work and tucked it behind a chest to keep it aloft. A vertical groove ran down the face of the wall, different from the rest. And then another one, not three feet from it. They emerged from the floor, and just above Celaena's head they met in a—

It is *a door!*

Celaena leaned her shoulder into the slab of stone. It gave a little, and her heart jumped. She pushed again, the candle flickering in her hand. The door groaned as it moved slightly. Grunting, she shoved, and finally it swung open.

A dark passage loomed before her.

A breeze blew into the black depths, pulling the strands of her hair past her face. A shiver ran down her spine. Why was the wind going inward? Especially when it had blown the tapestry out?

She looked back at the bed, which was littered with books she wasn't going to read tonight. She took a step into the passage.

The light of the candle revealed that it was made of stone and thickly coated in dust. She stepped back into her room. If she were to go exploring, she'd need proper provisions. It was a pity she didn't have a sword or a dagger. Celaena put her candle down. She also needed a torch—or at least some extra candlesticks. While she might be used to darkness, she wasn't foolish enough to trust it.

Moving through her room, trembling with excitement, Celaena gathered two balls of yarn from Philippa's sewing basket, along with three sticks of chalk and one of her makeshift knives. She tucked three extra candlesticks into the pockets of her cape, which she wrapped tightly around herself.

Again, she stood before the dark passage. It *was* terribly dark, and seemed to be beckoning to her. The breeze blew into the passage again.

Celaena pushed a chair into the doorway—it wouldn't do to have it slam shut on her and leave her trapped forever. She tied a string to the back of the chair, knotting it five times, and held the ball in her spare hand. If she got lost, this would lead her back. She carefully folded the tapestry over the door, just in case someone came in.

Striding into the passage, she found it to be cold, but dry. Cobwebs hung everywhere, and there were no windows, only a very long stair that descended far beyond the light of her little candle. She tensed as she stepped down, waiting for a single sound that would send her springing back to her rooms. It was silent—silent and dead and completely forgotten.

Celaena held the candle aloft, her cape trailing behind her, leaving a clean wake on the dust-covered stairs. Minutes passed, and she scanned the walls for any engravings or markings, but saw none. Was this just a forgotten servants' passage? She found herself a bit disappointed.

The bottom of the stairs soon appeared, and she came to a halt before three equally dark and imposing portals. Where was she? She had difficulty imagining that such a space could be forgotten in a castle filled with so many people, but—

The ground was covered with dust. Not even a hint of a footprint.

Knowing how the story always went, Celaena lifted the candle to the arches above the portals, looking for any inscriptions regarding the sure death that would meet her if she walked beneath a specific arch.

She took stock of the ball of yarn in her hand. Now it was little more than a lump of string. She set down her candle and tied another ball to the end of the string. Perhaps she should have taken another. Well, at least she still had the chalk.

She chose the door in the middle, if only because it was closer. On the other side, the staircase continued downward—in fact, it went so far down that she wondered if she were beneath the castle. The passage became very damp and very cold, and Celaena's candle sputtered in the moisture.

There were many archways now, but Celaena chose to go straight, following the moisture that grew by the inch. Water trickled down the walls, and the stone became slick with whatever fungus had grown over the centuries. Her red velvet shoes felt flimsy and thin against the wetness of the chamber. She would have considered turning back were it not for the sound that arose.

It was running water—slow-moving. In fact, as she walked, the passage became lighter. It was not the light of a candle, but rather the smooth, white light of the outdoors—of the moon.

Her yarn ran out, and she left it on the ground. There were no more turns to mark. She knew what this was—rather, she didn't dare to hope that it was actually what she believed it to be. She hurried along, slipping twice, her heart pounding so loudly that she thought her ears would break. An archway appeared, and beyond it, beyond it . . .

Celaena stared at the sewer that ran past, flowing straight out of the castle. It smelled unpleasant, to say the least.

She stood along the side, examining the open gate that led to a wide stream that undoubtedly emptied into the sea or the Avery. There were no guards, and no locks, save for the iron fence that hovered over the surface, raised just enough to allow trash to pass through.

Four little boats were tied to either bank, and there were several other doors—some wooden, some iron—that led to this exit. It was probably an escape route for the king, though from the half-rotted condition of some of the boats, she wondered if he knew that it was here.

She strode to the iron fence, putting her hand through one of the gaps. The night air was chilled but not freezing. Trees loomed just beyond the stream: she must be in the back of the castle—the side that faced the sea . . .

Were there any guards posted outside? She found a stone on the ground—a bit of fallen ceiling—and hurled it into the water beyond the gate. There was no sound of shifting armor, no muttering or cursing. She studied the other side. There was a lever to raise the gate for the boats. Celaena set down her candle, removed her cloak, and emptied her pockets. Holding tightly with her hands, she placed one foot on the gate, then the other.

It would be so easy to raise the gate. She felt reckless—reckless and wild. What was she doing in a palace? Why was she—Adarlan's Assassin!—participating in some absurd competition to prove that she was the best? She *was* the best!

They were undoubtedly drunk now, all of them. She could take one of the less-ancient boats and disappear into the night. Celaena began to climb back over. She needed her cloak. Oh, they were fools for thinking that they could tame *her*!

Her foot slipped on a slick rung, and Celaena barely stifled her cry as she gripped the bars, cursing as her knee banged into the gate. Clinging to the gate, she closed her eyes. It was only water.

She calmed her heart, letting her feet find their support again. The moon was almost blinding, so bright the stars were barely visible.

She knew that she could easily escape, and that it would be foolish to do so. The king would find her, somehow. And Chaol would be disgraced and relieved of his position. And Princess Nehemia would be left alone with moronic company, and, well . . .

Celaena straightened, her chin rising. She would not run from them as a common criminal. She would face them—face the king—and earn her freedom the honorable way. And why not take advantage of the free food and training for a while longer? Not to mention she'd need to stock up on provisions for her escape, and that could take weeks. Why rush any of it?

Celaena returned to her starting side and picked up the cloak. She'd win. And after she won, if she ever wanted to escape her servitude to the king . . . well, now she had a way out.

Still, Celaena had difficulty leaving the chamber. She was grateful for the silence of the passage as she walked upward, her legs burning from so many stairs. It was the right thing to do.

Celaena soon found herself before the other two portals. What other disappointments would she find in them? She had lost interest. But the breeze stirred again, and it blew so hard toward the far right arch that Celaena took a step. The hair on her arms rose as she watched the flame of her candle bend forward, pointing to a darkness that seemed blacker than all the rest. Whispers lay beneath the breeze, speaking to her in forgotten languages. She shuddered, and decided to go in the opposite direction—to take the far left portal. Following whispers on Samhuinn could only lead to trouble.

Despite the breeze, the passage was warm. With each step up the winding stairs, the whispers faded away. Up, and up, and up, her heavy breathing and shuffling steps the only sounds. There were no twisting passages once she reached the top, but rather one straight hall that seemed to lead on forever. She followed it, her feet already tired. After some time, she was surprised to hear music.

Actually, it was the sound of great revelry, and there was golden light ahead. It streamed in through a door or a window.

She rounded the corner and ascended a small set of steps that led into a significantly smaller hallway. In fact, the ceiling was so low that she had to duck as she waddled toward the light. It wasn't a door, nor a window, but rather a bronze grate.

Celaena blinked at the light as she looked, from high above, at the feast in the Great Hall.

Were these tunnels for spying? She frowned at what she saw. Over a hundred people eating, singing, dancing . . . There was Chaol, sitting beside some old man, talking and—

Laughing?

His happiness made her own face flush in response, and Celaena set down her candle. She peered at the other end of the massive hall; there were a few other grates just below the ceiling, though she could see no other squinting eyes beyond their ornate metalwork. Celaena shifted her gaze to the dancers. Among them were a few of the Champions, dressed finely, but not finely enough to conceal their poor dancing. Nox, who had now become her sparring and training partner, danced as well, perhaps a bit more elegantly than the others—though she still pitied the ladies who danced with him. But—

The other Champions were allowed to attend, and she wasn't? She gripped the grate, pressing her face against it to get a better look. Sure enough, there were more Champions seated at the tables—even the pimply-faced Pelor sat near Chaol! A half-rate boy assassin! She bared her teeth. How *dare* she be denied an invitation to the feast? The tightness in her chest abated only slightly when she couldn't find Cain's face among the revelers. At least they kept him locked up in a cage, too.

She spotted the Crown Prince, dancing and laughing with some blond idiot. She wanted to hate him for refusing to invite her; she was *his* Champion, after all! But . . . she had difficulty not staring at him. She had no desire to talk to him, but rather just to look at him, to see that unusual grace, and the kindness in his eyes that had made her tell him about Sam. While he might be a Havilliard, he was . . . Well, she still very much wanted to kiss him.

Celaena scowled as the dance finished and the Crown Prince kissed the hand of the blond woman. She turned away from the grate. Here the hallway ended. She glanced back at the feast, only to see Chaol stand from the table and begin weaving his way out of the Great Hall. What if he came to her rooms and found her missing? Hadn't he promised to bring her something from the feast?

Groaning at the thought of all the stairs she now had to climb, she picked up her candle and yarn and hurried toward the comfort of higher ceilings, rolling up the string as she went. Down and down she ran, taking the steps two by two.

She burst past the portals and darted up the stairs to her room, the small light growing with each bound. Chaol would throw her in the dungeons if he found her in some secret passageway—especially if the passageway led out of the castle!

She was sweating when she reached her chambers. She kicked the chair away, swung the stone door shut, pulled the tapestry over it, and flung herself on the bed.

After hours of enjoying himself at the feast, Dorian entered Celaena's rooms, not sure what, exactly, he was doing in the chambers of an assassin at two in the morning. His head spun from the wine, and he was so tired from all the dancing that he was fairly certain that if he sat down, he'd fall asleep. Her chambers were silent and dark, and he cracked open her bedroom door to peer inside.

Though she was asleep on the bed, she still wore that strange dress. Somehow, it seemed far more fitting now that she lay sprawled upon the red blanket. Her golden hair was spread around her, and a flush of pink bloomed on her cheeks.

A book lay by her side, open and still waiting for her to turn the page. He remained in the doorway, fearful that she'd wake up if he took another step. Some assassin. She hadn't even bothered to stir. But there was nothing of the assassin in her face. Not a trace of aggression or bloodlust lay across her features.

He knew her somehow. And he knew she wouldn't harm him. It made little sense. When they talked, as sharp as her words usually were, he felt at ease, as if he could say anything. And she must have felt the same, after she'd told him about Sam, whoever he'd been. So here he was, in the middle of the night. She flirted with him, but was it real? A footstep sounded, and he found Chaol standing across the foyer.

The captain stalked over to Dorian and grabbed him by the arm. Dorian knew better than to struggle as his friend dragged him through the foyer, and stopped in front of the door to the hall. "What are you doing here?" Chaol hissed softly.

"What are *you* doing here?" Dorian countered, trying to keep his voice quiet. It was the better question, too. If Chaol spent so much time warning him about the dangers of associating with Celaena, what was he doing here in the middle of the night?

"By the Wyrd, Dorian! She's an *assassin*. Please, *please* tell me you haven't been here before." Dorian couldn't help his smirk. "I don't even want an explanation. Just get out, you reckless idiot. Get out." Chaol grabbed him by the collar of his jacket, and Dorian might have punched his friend had Chaol not been so lightning fast. Before he knew it, he was roughly tossed into the hallway, and the door closed and locked behind him.

Dorian, for some reason, didn't sleep well that night.

~

Chaol Westfall took a deep breath. What was he doing here? Had he any right to treat the Crown Prince of Adarlan in such a manner when he himself was going against reason? He didn't understand the rage that arose upon seeing Dorian standing in the doorway, didn't *want* to understand that sort of anger. It wasn't jealousy, but something beyond it. Something that transformed his friend into someone else, someone he didn't know. He was fairly certain she was a virgin, but did Dorian know it? It probably made him more interested. He sighed and eased the door open, wincing as it creaked loudly.

She was still in her clothes, and while she looked beautiful, that did nothing to mask the killing potential that lay beneath. It was present in her strong jaw, in the slope of her eyebrows, in the perfect stillness of her form. She was a honed blade made by the King of Assassins for his own profit. She was a sleeping animal—a mountain cat or a dragon—and her markings of power were everywhere. He shook his head and walked into the bedroom.

At the sound of his step, she opened an eye. "It's not morning," she grumbled, and rolled over.

"I brought you a present." He felt immensely foolish, and for a moment considered running from her rooms.

"A present?" she said more clearly, turning toward him and blinking.

"It's nothing; they were giving them out at the party. Just give me your hand." It was a lie—sort of. They had given them to the women of the nobility as favors, and he'd snagged one from the basket as it was passed around. Most of the women would never wear them—they would be tossed aside or given to a favorite servant.

"Let me see it." She lazily extended an arm.

He fished in his pockets and pulled out the gift. "Here." He placed it in her palm.

She examined it, smiling drowsily. "A ring." She put it on. "How pretty." It was simple: crafted of silver, its only ornamentation lay in the fingernail-sized amethyst embedded in its center. The surface of the gem was smooth and round, and it gleamed up at the assassin like a purple eye. "Thank you," she said, her eyelids drooping.

"You're wearing your gown, Celaena." His blush refused to fade.

"I'll change in a moment." He knew she wouldn't. "I just need . . . to rest." Then she was asleep, a hand upon her breast, the ring hovering over her heart. With a disgruntled sigh, the captain grabbed a blanket from the nearby sofa and tossed it over her. He was half tempted to remove the ring from her finger, but . . . Well, there was something peaceful looking about her. Rubbing his neck, his face still burning, he walked from her rooms, wondering how, exactly, he'd explain this to Dorian tomorrow.

25

Celaena dreamt. She was walking down the long, secret passage again. She didn't have a candle, nor did she have a string to lead her. She chose the portal on the right, for the other two were dank and unwelcoming, and this one seemed to be warm and pleasant. And the smell—it wasn't the smell of mildew, but of roses. The passage twisted and wound, and Celaena found herself descending a narrow set of stairs. For some reason she couldn't name, she avoided brushing against the stone. The staircase swooped down, winding on and on, and she followed the rose scent whenever another door or arch appeared. Just when she grew tired of so much walking, she reached the bottom of a set of stairs and stopped. She stood before an old wooden door.

A bronze knocker in the form of a skull hung in its center. It seemed to be smiling. She waited for that terrible breeze, or to hear someone cry, or for it to become cold and damp. But it was still warm, and it still smelled lovely, and so Celaena, with a bit of mustered courage, turned the handle. Without a sound, the door swung open.

She expected to find a dark, forgotten room, but this was something far different. A shaft of moonlight shot through a small hole in the ceiling, falling upon the face of a beautiful marble statue lying upon a stone slab. No—not a statue. A sarcophagus. It was a tomb.

Trees were carved into the stone ceiling, and they stretched above the sleeping female figure. A second sarcophagus had been placed beside the woman, depicting a man. Why was the woman's face bathed in moonlight and the man's in darkness?

He was handsome, his beard clipped and short, his brow broad and clear, and his nose straight and sturdy. He held a stone sword between his hands, its handle resting upon his chest. Her breath was sucked from her. A crown sat upon his head.

The woman, too, wore a crown. It wasn't a tacky, enormous thing, but rather a slender peak with a blue gem embedded in the center—the only jewel in the statue. Her hair, long and wavy, spilled around her head and tumbled over the side of the lid, so lifelike that Celaena could have sworn it was real. The moonlight fell upon her face, and Celaena's hand trembled as she reached out and touched the smooth, youthful cheek.

It was cold and hard, as a statue should be. "Which queen were you?" she said aloud, her voice reverberating through the still chamber. She ran a hand across the lips, then across the brow. Her eyes narrowed. A mark was faintly carved into the surface, practically invisible to the eye. She traced it with her finger, then traced it again. Deciding that the moonlight must be bleaching it, Celaena shielded the spot with her hand. A diamond, two arrows piercing its side, then a vertical line through its middle . . .

It was the Wyrdmark she'd seen earlier. She stepped back from the sarcophagi, suddenly cold. This was a forbidden place.

She tripped on something, and as she staggered, she noticed the floor. Her mouth fell open. It was covered in stars—raised carvings that mirrored the night sky. And the ceiling depicted the earth. Why were they reversed? She looked at the walls and put a hand to her heart.

Countless Wyrdmarks were etched into their surface. They were in swirls and whorls, in lines and squares. The small Wyrdmarks made up larger ones, and the larger ones made up even larger ones, until it seemed the entire room meant something she couldn't possibly understand.

Celaena looked at the stone coffins. There was something written at the feet of the queen. Celaena inched toward the female figure. There, in stone letters, it read:

Ah! Time's Rift!

It made little sense. They must be important rulers, and immensely old, but . . .

She approached the head again. There was something calming and familiar about the queen's face, something that reminded Celaena of the rose smell. But there was still something off about her—something odd.

Celaena almost cried aloud as she saw them: the pointed, arched ears. The ears of the Fae, the immortal. But no Fae had married into the Havilliard line for a thousand years, and there had been only one, and she was a half-breed at that. If this were true, if she was Fae or half-Fae, then she was . . . she was . . .

Celaena stumbled back from the woman and slammed into the wall. A coating of dust flew into the air around her.

Then this man was Gavin, the first King of Adarlan. And this was Elena, the first princess of Terrasen, Brannon's daughter, and Gavin's wife and queen.

Celaena's heart pounded so violently that she felt sick. But she couldn't make her feet move. She shouldn't have entered the tomb, she shouldn't have strayed into the sacred places of the dead when she was so stained and tainted by her crimes. Something would come after her, and haunt and torture her for disturbing their peace.

But why was their tomb so neglected? Why had no one been to honor the dead this day? Why were there not flowers at her head? Why was Elena Galathynius Havilliard forgotten?

Against the far wall of the chamber sat piles of jewels and weapons. A sword was prominently displayed before a suit of golden armor. She knew that sword. She stepped toward the treasure. It was the legendary sword of Gavin, the sword he had wielded in the fierce wars that had almost ripped apart the continent, the sword that had slain the Dark Lord Erawan. Even after a thousand years, it hadn't rusted. Though magic might have vanished, it seemed that the power that had forged the blade lived on. "Damaris," she whispered, naming the blade.

"You know your history," said a light, female voice, and Celaena jumped, yelping as she tripped over a spear and fell into a gold-filled chest. The voice laughed. Celaena grappled for a dagger, a candlestick, anything. But then she saw the owner of the voice, and froze.

She was beautiful beyond reckoning. Her silver hair flowed around her youthful face like a river of moonlight. Her eyes were a crystal, sparkling blue, and her skin was white as alabaster. And her ears were ever so slightly pointed.

"Who are you?" the assassin breathed, knowing the answer, but wanting to hear it.

"You know who I am," Elena Havilliard said.

Her likeness had been perfectly rendered on the sarcophagus. Celaena didn't move from where she had fallen into the chest, despite her throbbing spine and legs. "Are you a ghost?"

"Not quite," said Queen Elena, helping Celaena rise from the chest. Her hand was cold, but solid. "I'm not alive, but my spirit doesn't haunt this place." She flicked her eyes toward the ceiling, and her face became grave. "I've risked much coming here tonight."

Celaena, despite herself, took a step away. "Risked?"

"I cannot stay here long—and neither can you," said the queen. What sort of absurd dream was this? "They are distracted for now, but . . ." Elena Havilliard looked at her husband's sarcophagus.

Celaena's head ached. Was Gavin Havilliard distracting something above? "Who needs distracting?"

"The eight guardians; you know of whom I speak."

Celaena stared at her blankly, but then understood. "The gargoyles on the clock tower?"

The queen nodded. "They guard the portal between our worlds. We have managed to buy some time, and I was able to slip past . . ." She grasped Celaena's arms. To her surprise, it hurt. "You must listen to what I tell you. Nothing is a coincidence. Everything has a purpose. You were meant to come to this castle, just as you were meant to be an assassin, to learn the skills necessary for survival."

The nausea returned. She hoped Elena wouldn't speak of what her heart refused to remember, hoped that the queen wouldn't mention what she had spent so long forgetting.

"Something evil dwells in this castle, something wicked enough to make the stars quake. Its malice echoes into all worlds," the queen went on. "You must stop it. Forget your friendships, forget your debts and oaths. *Destroy* it, before it is too late, before a portal is ripped open so wide that there can be no undoing it." Her head whipped around, as if she heard something. "Oh, there is no time," she said, the whites of her eyes showing. "You *must* win this competition and become the King's Champion. You understand the people's plight. Erilea needs you as the King's Champion."

"But what is—"

The queen reached into her pockets. "They must not catch you here. If they do—all will be lost. Wear this." She pushed something cold and metallic into Celaena's hand. "It will protect you from harm." She yanked Celaena to the door. "You were led here tonight. But not by me. I was led here, too. Someone wants you to learn; someone wants you to see . . ." Her head snapped to the side as a growl rippled through the air. "They are coming," she whispered.

"But I don't understand! I'm not—I'm not who you think I am!"

Queen Elena put her hands on Celaena's shoulders and kissed her forehead. "Courage of the heart is very rare," she said with sudden calm. "Let it guide you."

A distinct howl shook the walls and made Celaena's blood icy. "*Go*," said the queen, shoving Celaena into the hallway. "*Run!*"

Needing no more encouragement, Celaena staggered up the stairs. She fled so fast that she had little idea of where she was going. There was a scream below, and snarling, and Celaena's stomach rose in her throat as she hurled herself upward. The light of her chambers appeared, and as it neared, she heard a faint voice cry from behind her, almost in sudden realization and anger.

Celaena hurtled into the room, and saw only her bed before everything went dark.

Celaena's eyes opened. She was breathing—hard. And still wearing her gown. But she was safe—safe in her room. Why was she so prone to strange, unpleasant dreams? And why was she out of breath? *Find and destroy the evil lurking in the castle indeed!*

Celaena turned on her side, and would have gladly fallen asleep again were it not for the metal that cut into her palm. *Please tell me this is Chaol's ring.*

But she knew it wasn't. In her hand lay a coin-size gold amulet on a delicate chain. She fought against the urge to scream. Made of intricate bands of metal, within the round border of the amulet lay two overlapping circles, one on top of the other. In the space that they shared was a small blue gem that gave the center of the amulet the appearance of an eye. A line ran straight through the entire thing. It was beautiful, and strange, and—

Celaena faced the tapestry. The door was slightly ajar.

She jumped from the bed, slamming into the wall so hard that her shoulder made an ugly cracking noise. Despite the pain, she rushed to the door and pulled it tightly shut. The last thing she needed was for whatever was down there to wind up in her rooms. Or to have Elena show up again.

Panting, Celaena stepped back, surveying the tapestry. The woman's figure rose up from behind the wooden chest. With a jolt, she realized it was Elena; she stood just where the door was. A clever marker.

Celaena threw more logs onto the fire, quickly changed into her nightgown, and slid into bed, clutching her makeshift knife. The amulet lay where she had left it. *It will protect you . . .*

Celaena glanced at the door again. No screams, no howls—nothing to indicate what had just happened. Still . . .

Celaena cursed herself for it, but hastily attached the chain around her neck. It was light and warm. Pulling the covers up to her chin, she squeezed her eyes shut, waiting for sleep to come, or for a clawed hand to snatch at her, to decapitate her. If it hadn't been a dream—if it hadn't just been some hallucination . . .

Celaena clutched the necklace. Become the King's Champion—she could do that. She was *going* to do that, anyway. But what were Elena's motives? Erilea needed the King's Champion to be someone who understood the suffering of the masses. That seemed simple enough. But why did *Elena* have to be the one to tell her that? And how did it tie to her first command: to find and destroy the evil lurking in the castle?

Celaena took a steadying breath, nestling farther into her pillows. What a fool she was for opening the secret door on Samhuinn! Had she somehow brought all of this upon herself, then? She opened her eyes, watching the tapestry.

Something evil dwells in this castle . . . Destroy it . . .

Didn't she have enough to worry about right now? She was going to fulfill Elena's second command—but the first . . . that might lead her into trouble. It wasn't like she could go poking about the castle whenever and wherever she pleased, either!

But—if there was a threat like that, then not only her life was at risk. And while she'd be more than happy if some dark force somehow destroyed Cain, Perrington, the king, and Kaltain Rompier, if Nehemia, or even Chaol and Dorian, were somehow harmed . . .

Celaena took a shuddering breath. The least she could do was look in the tomb for some clues. Maybe she'd find out something regarding Elena's purpose. And if that didn't yield anything . . . well, at least she'd tried.

The phantom breeze flowed through her room, smelling of roses. It was a long while before Celaena slipped into an uneasy sleep.

26

The doors to her bedroom banged open, and Celaena was on her feet in an instant, a candlestick in hand.

But Chaol took no notice of her as he stormed in, his jaw clenched. She groaned and slumped back onto her bed. "Don't you *ever* sleep?" she grumbled, pulling the covers over herself. "Weren't you celebrating into the wee hours of the morning?"

He put a hand on his sword as he ripped back the blankets and dragged her out of bed by the elbow. "Where were you last night?"

She pushed away the fear that tightened her throat. There was no way he could know about the passages. She smiled at him. "Here, of course. Didn't you visit to give me this?" She yanked her elbow out of his grasp and waved her fingers in front of him, displaying the amethyst ring.

"That was for a few minutes. What about the rest of the night?"

She refused to step back as he studied her face, then her hands, then the rest of her. As he did so, she returned the favor. His black tunic was unbuttoned at the top, and slightly wrinkled—and his short hair needed a combing. Whatever this was, he was in a rush.

"What's all the fuss about? Don't we have a Test this morning?" She picked at her nails as she waited for an answer.

"It's been canceled. A Champion was found dead this morning. Xavier—the thief from Melisande."

She flicked her eyes to him, then back to her nails. "And I suppose you think *I* did it?"

"I'm hoping you didn't, as the body was half-eaten."

"Eaten!" She crinkled her nose. She sat cross-legged on the bed, propping herself on her hands. "How gruesome. Perhaps Cain did it; he's beastly enough to do such a thing." Her stomach felt tight—another Champion murdered. Did it have to do with whatever evil Elena had mentioned? The Eye Eater and the other two Champions' killings hadn't been just a fluke, or a drunken brawl, as the investigation had determined. No, this was a pattern.

Chaol sighed through his nose. "I'm glad you find humor in a man's murder."

She made herself grin at him. "Cain *is* the most likely candidate. You're from Anielle—you should know more than anyone how they are in the White Fang Mountains."

He ran a hand through his short hair. "You should mind who you accuse. While Cain is a brute, he's Duke Perrington's Champion."

"And I'm the Crown Prince's Champion!" She flipped her hair over a shoulder. "I should think that means I can accuse whomever I please."

"Just tell me plainly: where were you last night?"

She straightened, staring into his golden-brown eyes. "As my guards can attest, I was *here* the entire night. Though if the king wants me questioned, I can always tell him that you can vouch for me, too."

Chaol glanced at her ring, and she hid her smile as a faint line of color crept into his cheeks. He said, "I'm sure you'll be even more pleased to hear that you and I won't be having a lesson today."

She grinned at that, and sighed dramatically as she slid back under the blankets and nestled into her pillows. "Immensely pleased." She pulled the blankets up to her chin and batted her eyelashes at him. "Now get out. I'm going to celebrate by sleeping for another five hours." A lie, but he bought it.

She closed her eyes before she could see the glare he gave her, and smiled to herself when she heard him stalk out of the room. It was only when she heard him slam the doors to her room that she sat up.

The Champion had been *eaten*?

Last night in her dream—no, it hadn't been a dream. It had been real. And there had been those screeching creatures . . . Had Xavier been killed by one of them? But they'd been in the tomb; there was no way they could have been in the castle halls without someone noticing. Some vermin probably got to the body before it was found. Very, very hungry vermin.

She shuddered again, and leapt out from under the blankets. She needed a few more makeshift weapons, and a way to fortify the locks on her windows and doors.

Even as she readied her defenses, she kept assuring herself that it was nothing to worry about at all. But with a few hours of freedom ahead of her, she brought as many of them with her as possible as she locked the door to her bedroom and slipped into the tomb.

Celaena paced the length of the tomb, snarling to herself. There was *nothing* here that explained Elena's motives. Or what the source of this mysterious evil might be. Absolutely nothing.

In the daytime, a ray of sunlight shone into the tomb, making all the dust motes she stirred up swirl like falling snow. How was it possible that there was light so far beneath the castle? Celaena paused beneath the grate in the ceiling, peering up at the light flowing through it.

Sure enough, the sides of the shaft shimmered—they were lined with polished gold. A *lot* of gold, if it meant reflecting the sun's rays all the way down here.

Celaena stalked between the two sarcophagi. Though she'd brought three of her makeshift weapons, she'd found no trace of whatever had been growling and screeching last night. And no trace of Elena, either.

Celaena paused beside Elena's sarcophagus. The blue gem embedded in her stone crown pulsed in the faint sunlight.

"What was your purpose in telling *me* to do those things?" she mused aloud, her voice echoing off of the intricately carved walls. "You've been dead for a thousand years. Why still bother with Erilea?"

And why not get Dorian or Chaol or Nehemia or someone *else* to do it?

Celaena rapped a finger on the queen's pert nose. "One would think you'd have better things to do with your afterlife." Though she tried to grin, her voice came out quieter than she would have liked.

She should go; even with her bedroom door locked, someone was bound to come looking for her sooner or later. And she highly doubted that anyone would believe her if she told them that she'd been charged with a *very* important mission by the first Queen of Adarlan. In fact, she realized with a grimace, she'd be lucky if she weren't accused of treason and magic-using. It would certainly guarantee her return to Endovier.

After a final sweep of the tomb, Celaena left. There was nothing useful here. And besides, if Elena wanted her to be the King's Champion so badly, then she couldn't spend all her time hunting down whatever this evil was. It would probably *hurt* her chances of winning, actually. Celaena hurried up the steps, her torch casting odd shadows on the walls. If this evil was as threatening as Elena made it seem, then how could *she* possibly defeat it?

Not that the thought of something wicked dwelling in the castle *scared* her or anything.

No. It wasn't that at all. Celaena huffed. She'd focus on becoming King's Champion. And then, if she won, she'd go about finding this evil.

Maybe.

An hour later, flanked by guards, Celaena held her chin high as they strode through the halls toward the library. She smiled at the young chevaliers they passed—and smirked at the court women who eyed her pink-and-white gown. She couldn't blame them; the dress was spectacular. And she was spectacular in it. Even Ress, one of the handsomer guards posted outside her rooms, had said so. Naturally, it hadn't been too difficult to convince him to escort her to the library.

Celaena smiled smugly to herself as she nodded to a passing nobleman, who raised his eyebrows at the sight of her. He was immensely pale, she noticed as he opened his mouth to say something, but Celaena continued down the hall. Her steps quickened at the rumblings of arguing male voices that echoed off the stones as they neared a bend.

Hurrying farther, Celaena ignored the click of Ress's tongue as she rounded the corner. She knew that smell all too well. The tang of blood and the stinging reek of decomposing flesh.

But she hadn't expected the sight of it. "Half-eaten" was a pleasant way to describe what was left of Xavier's rail-thin body.

One of her escorts cursed under his breath, and Ress stepped closer to her, a light hand on her back, encouraging her to keep walking. None of the gathered men looked at her as she passed, skirting the edge of the scene, and getting a better look at the body in the process.

Xavier's chest cavity had been split open and his vital organs removed. Unless someone had moved them upon finding the body, there was no trace of them. And his long face, stripped of its flesh, was still contorted in a silent scream.

This was no accidental killing. There was a hole in the crown of Xavier's head, and she could see that his brain was gone, too. The smears of blood on the wall looked like someone had been writing, and then rubbed it away. But even now, some of the writing remained, and she tried not to gape at it. Wyrdmarks. Three Wyrdmarks, forming an arcing line that had to have once been a circle near the body.

"Holy Gods," one of her guards muttered as they left behind the throng at the crime scene.

No wonder Chaol had looked so disheveled this morning! She straightened. He'd thought *she* did this? Fool. If she wanted to knock off her competitors one by one, she'd do it quick and clean—a slit throat, a knife in the heart, a poisoned glass of wine. This was just plain tasteless. And strange; the Wyrdmarks made this something more than a brutal killing. Ritualistic, perhaps.

Someone approached from the opposite direction. It was Grave, the vicious assassin, staring at the body from a distance. His eyes, dark and still like a forest pool, met hers. She ignored his rotting teeth as she jerked her chin toward the remnants of Xavier. "Too bad," she said, deliberately not sounding very sorry at all.

Grave chuckled, sticking his gnarled fingers into the pockets of his worn and dirty pants. Didn't his sponsor bother to properly clothe him? *Obviously not, if his sponsor was nasty and foolish enough to pick him as a Champion.*

"Such a pity," Grave said, shrugging as she passed by him.

She nodded tersely, and despite herself, she kept her mouth shut as she continued down the hall. There were only sixteen of them left now—sixteen Champions, and four of them were to duel. The competition was getting steeper. She should thank whatever grim god had decided to end Xavier's life. But for some reason, she couldn't.

Dorian swung his sword, grunting as Chaol easily deflected the blow and parried. His muscles were sore from weeks of not practicing, and his breath was ragged in his throat as he thrust and thrust again.

"This is what comes from such idle behavior," Chaol chuckled, stepping to the side so that Dorian stumbled forward. He remembered a time when they'd been of equal skill—though that had been long ago. Dorian, while he still enjoyed swordplay, had grown to prefer books.

"I've had meetings and important things to read," Dorian said, panting. He lunged.

Chaol deflected, feigned, then thrust so hard that Dorian stepped back. His temper rose. "Meetings which you used as an excuse to start arguing with Duke Perrington." Dorian made a wide sweep of his sword, and Chaol took up the defensive. "Or maybe you're just too busy visiting Sardothien's rooms in the middle of the night." Sweat dripped from Chaol's brow. "How long has *that* been going on?"

Dorian growled as Chaol switched to the offensive, and conceded step after step, his thighs aching. "It's not what you think," he said through his teeth. "I don't spend my nights with her. Aside from last night, I've only visited her once, and she was less than warm, don't worry."

"At least one of you has some common sense." Chaol delivered each blow with such precision that Dorian had to admire him. "Because you've clearly lost your mind."

"And what about you?" Dorian demanded. "Do you want me to comment on how *you* showed up in her rooms last night—the same night another Champion died?" Dorian feinted, but Chaol didn't fall for it. Instead, he struck strongly enough that Dorian staggered back a step, fighting to keep his footing. Dorian grimaced at the rage flickering in Chaol's eyes. "Fine, that was a cheap shot," he admitted, bringing his sword up to deflect another blow. "But I still want an answer."

"Maybe I don't have one. Like you said, it's not what you think." Chaol's brown eyes gleamed, but before Dorian could debate it, his friend switched the subject with brutal aim. "How's court?" Chaol asked, breathing hard. Dorian winced. That was why he was here. If he had to spend another moment sitting in his mother's court, he'd go mad. "That terrible?"

"Shut up," Dorian snarled, and slammed his sword into Chaol's.

"It must be exceptionally awful to be you today. I bet all the ladies were begging you to protect them from the murderer inside our walls." Chaol grinned, but it didn't reach his eyes. Taking the time to spar with him when there was a fresh corpse in the castle was a sacrifice Dorian was surprised Chaol had been willing to make; Dorian knew how much his position meant to him.

Dorian stopped suddenly and straightened. Chaol should be doing more important things right now. "Enough," he said, sheathing his rapier. Not missing a step, Chaol did the same.

They walked from the sparring room in silence. "Any word from your father?" Chaol asked in a voice that indicated he knew something was amiss. "I wonder where he went off to."

Dorian let out a long breath, calming his panting. "No. I haven't the slightest idea. I remember him leaving like this when we were children, but it hasn't happened for some years now. I bet he's doing something particularly nasty."

"Be careful what you say, Dorian."

"Or what? You'll throw me in the dungeons?" He didn't mean to snap, but he'd barely gotten any sleep the night before, and this Champion winding up dead did nothing to improve his mood. When Chaol didn't bother retorting, Dorian asked: "Do you think someone wants to kill all the Champions?"

"Perhaps. I can understand wanting to kill the competition, but to do it so viciously . . . I hope it's not a pattern."

Dorian's blood went a bit cold. "You think they'll try to kill Celaena?"

"I added some extra guards around her rooms."

"To protect her, or to keep her in?"

They stopped at the hallway crossroads where they would part ways to their separate rooms. "What difference does it make?" Chaol said quietly. "You don't seem to care either way. You'll visit her no matter what I say, and the guards won't stop you because you're the prince."

There was something so defeated, so bitter, underlying the captain's words that Dorian, for a heartbeat, felt badly. He *should* stay away from Celaena—Chaol had enough to worry about. But then he thought of the list his mother made and realized he had enough, too.

"I need to inspect Xavier's body again. I'll see you in the hall for dinner tonight," was all Chaol said before he headed to his rooms. Dorian watched him go. The walk back to his tower felt surprisingly long. He opened the wooden door to his rooms, peeling off his clothing as he headed to the bathing room. He had the entire tower to himself, though his chambers occupied only the upper level. They provided a haven from everyone, but today they just felt empty.

27

Late that afternoon, Celaena stared at the ebony clock tower. It grew darker and darker, as if it somehow absorbed the sun's dying rays. On top of it, the gargoyles remained stationary. They hadn't moved. Not even a finger. The Guardians, Elena had called them. But Guardians to what? They'd scared Elena enough to keep her away. Surely, if they'd been the evil Elena mentioned, she would have just said it outright. Not that Celaena was considering looking for it right now—not when it could get her into trouble. And somehow wind up killing her before she could even become the King's Champion.

Still, *why* did Elena have to be so oblique about everything?

"What's your obsession with these ugly things?" Nehemia asked from beside her.

Celaena turned to the princess. "Do you think they move?"

"They're made of stone, Lillian," the princess said in the common tongue, her Eyllwe accent slightly less thick.

"Oh!" Celaena exclaimed, smiling. "That was very good! One lesson, and you're already putting me to shame!" Unfortunately, the same couldn't be said of Celaena's Eyllwe.

Nehemia beamed. "They do look wicked," she said in Eyllwe.

"And I'm afraid the Wyrdmarks don't help," Celaena said. A Wyrdmark was at her feet, and she glanced to the others. There were twelve of them all together, forming a large circle around the solitary tower. She hadn't the faintest idea what any of it meant. None of the marks here matched the three she'd spotted at Xavier's murder site, but there had to be some connection. "So, you truly can't read these?" she asked her friend.

"No," Nehemia said curtly, and headed toward the hedges that bordered the courtyard. "And you shouldn't try to discover what they say," she added over her shoulder. "Nothing good will come of it."

Celaena pulled her cloak tighter around her as she followed after the princess. Snow would start falling in a matter of days, bringing them closer to Yulemas—and the final duel, still two months away. She savored the heat from her cloak, remembering all too well the winter she'd spent in Endovier. Winter was unforgiving when you lived in the shadow of the Ruhnn Mountains. It was a miracle she hadn't gotten frostbite. If she went back, another winter might kill her.

"You look troubled," Nehemia said when Celaena reached her side, and put a hand on her arm.

"I'm fine," Celaena said in Eyllwe, smiling for Nehemia's sake. "I don't like winter."

"I've never seen snow," Nehemia said, looking at the sky. "I wonder how long the novelty will last."

"Hopefully long enough for you to not mind the drafty corridors, freezing mornings, and days without sunshine."

Nehemia laughed. "You should come to Eyllwe with me when I return—and make sure you stay long enough to experience one of our blistering summers. *Then* you'll appreciate your freezing mornings and days without sun."

Celaena had already spent one blistering summer in the heat of the Red Desert, but to tell Nehemia that would only invite difficult questions. Instead, she said: "I'd like to see Eyllwe very much."

Nehemia's gaze lingered on Celaena's brow for a moment before she grinned. "Then it shall be so."

Celaena's eyes brightened, and she tilted her head back so she could see the castle looming above them. "I wonder if Chaol sorted through the mess of that murder."

"My bodyguards tell me that the man was . . . very violently killed."

"To say the least," Celaena murmured, watching the shifting colors of the fading sun turn the castle gold and red and blue. Despite the ostentatious nature of the glass castle, she had to admit that it *did* look rather beautiful at times.

"You saw the body? My guards weren't allowed close enough."

She nodded slowly. "I'm sure you don't want to know the details."

"Indulge me," Nehemia pressed, smiling tightly.

Celaena raised an eyebrow. "Well—there was blood smeared everywhere. On the walls, on the floor."

"Smeared?" Nehemia said, her voice dropping into a hush. "Not splattered?"

"I think so. Like someone had rubbed it on there. There were a few of those Wyrdmarks painted, but most had been rubbed away." She shook her head at the image that arose. "And the man's body was missing its vital organs—like someone had split him open from neck to navel, and—I'm sorry, you look like you're going to be ill. I shouldn't have said anything."

"No. Keep going. What else was missing?"

Celaena paused for a moment before saying: "His brain. Someone had made a hole in the top of his head, and his brain was gone. And the skin from his face had been ripped off."

Nehemia nodded, staring at a barren bush in front of them. The princess chewed on her bottom lip, and Celaena noted that her fingers curled and uncurled at the sides of her long, white gown. A cold breeze blew past them, making Nehemia's multitude of fine, thin braids sway. The gold woven into her braids clinked softly.

"I'm sorry," Celaena said. "I shouldn't have—"

A step fell behind them, and before Celaena could whirl, a male voice said: "Look at this."

She tensed as Cain came to stand nearby, half-hidden in the shadow of the clock tower behind them. Verin, the curly-haired loudmouth thief, was at his side. "What do you want?" she said.

Cain's tan face twisted in a sneer. Somehow, he'd gotten bigger—or maybe her eyes were playing tricks on her. "Pretending to be a lady doesn't mean you are one," he said. Celaena shot Nehemia a look, but the princess's eyes remained upon Cain—narrowed, but her lips strangely slack.

But Cain wasn't done, and his attention shifted to Nehemia. His lips pulled back, revealing his gleaming white teeth. "Neither does wearing a crown make you a real princess—not anymore."

Celaena took a step closer to him. "Shut your stupid mouth, or I'll punch your teeth down your throat and shut it for you."

Cain let out a sharp laugh, which Verin echoed. The thief circled behind them, and Celaena straightened, wondering if they'd actually pick a fight here. "Lots of barking from the prince's lapdog," Cain said. "But does she have any fangs?"

She felt Nehemia's hand on her shoulder, but she shrugged it off as she took another step toward him, close enough for the curls of his breath to touch her face. Inside the castle, the guards remained loitering about, talking amongst themselves. "You'll find out when my fangs are buried in your neck," she said.

"Why not right now?" Cain breathed. "Come on—hit me. Hit me with all that rage you feel every time you force yourself to miss the bull's-eye, or when you slow yourself down so you don't scale walls as fast as me. Hit me, *Lillian*," he whispered so only she could hear, "and let's see what that year in Endovier really taught you."

Celaena's heart leapt into a gallop. He knew. He knew who she was, and what she was doing. She didn't dare to look at Nehemia, and only hoped her understanding of the common language was still weak enough for her not to have understood. Verin still watched from behind them.

"You think you're the only one whose sponsor is willing to do anything to win? You think your prince and captain are the only ones who know what you are?"

Celaena clenched her hand. Two blows, and he'd be on the ground, struggling to breathe. Another blow after that, and Verin would be beside him.

"Lillian," Nehemia said in the common tongue, taking her by the hand. "We have business. Let us go."

"That's right," Cain said. "Follow her around like the lapdog you are."

Celaena's hand trembled. If she hit him . . . If she hit him, if she got into a brawl right here and the guards had to pull them apart, Chaol might not let her see Nehemia again, let alone leave her rooms after lessons, or stay late to practice with Nox. So Celaena smiled and rolled her shoulders as she said brightly: "Shove it up your ass, Cain."

Cain and Verin laughed, but she and Nehemia walked away, the princess holding her hand tightly. Not from fear or anger, but just to tell her that she understood . . . that she was there. Celaena squeezed her hand back. It had been a while since someone had looked out for her, and Celaena had the feeling she could get used to it.

Chaol stood with Dorian in the shadows atop the mezzanine, staring down at the assassin as she punched at the dummy situated in the center of the floor. She'd sent him a message saying she was going to train for a few hours after dinner, and he'd invited Dorian to come along to watch. Perhaps Dorian would now see *why* she was such a threat to him. To everyone.

Celaena grunted, throwing punch after punch, left-right-left-left-right. On and on, as if she had something burning inside of her that she couldn't quite get out.

"She looks stronger than before," the prince said quietly. "You've done a good job getting her back in shape." Celaena punched and kicked at the dummy, dodging invisible blows. The guards at the door just watched, their faces impassive. "Do you think she stands a chance against Cain?"

Celaena swung her leg through the air, connecting with the dummy's head. It rocked back. The blow would have knocked out a man. "I think if she doesn't get too riled and keeps a cool head when they duel, she might. But she's . . . wild. And unpredictable. She needs to learn to control her feelings—especially that impossible anger."

Which was true. Chaol didn't know if it was because of Endovier, or just being an assassin; whatever the cause of that unyielding rage, she could never entirely leash herself.

"Who's that?" Dorian asked sharply as Nox entered the room and walked over to Celaena. She paused, rubbing her wrapped knuckles, and wiped the sweat from her eyes as she waved to him.

"Nox," Chaol said. "A thief from Perranth. Minister Joval's Champion."

Nox said something to Celaena that set her chuckling. Nox laughed, too. "She made another friend?" Dorian said, raising his brows as Celaena demonstrated a move for Nox. "She's *helping* him?"

"Every day. They usually stay after lessons with the others are over."

"And you allow this?"

Chaol hid his glower at Dorian's tone. "If you want me to put an end to it, I will."

Dorian watched them for another moment. "No. Let her train with him. The other Champions are brutes—she could use an ally."

"That she could."

Dorian turned from the balcony and strode off into the darkness of the hall beyond. Chaol watched the prince disappear, his red cape billowing behind him, and sighed. He knew jealousy when he saw it, and while Dorian was clever, he was just as bad as Celaena at hiding his emotions. Perhaps bringing the prince along had done the opposite of what he'd intended.

His feet heavy, Chaol followed after the prince, hoping Dorian wasn't about to drag them all into serious trouble.

~

A few days later, Celaena turned the crisp yellow pages of a heavy tome, squirming in her seat. Like the countless others she'd tried, it was just page after page of scribbled nonsense. But it was worth researching, if there were Wyrdmarks at Xavier's crime scene and Wyrdmarks at the clock tower. The more she knew about what this killer wanted—*why* and *how* he was killing—the better. *That* was the real threat to be dealing with, not some mysterious, inexplicable evil Elena had mentioned. Of course, there was little to nothing to be found. Her eyes sore, the assassin looked up from the book and sighed. The library was gloomy, and were it not for the sound of Chaol flipping pages, it would have been wholly silent.

"Done?" he asked, closing the novel he was reading. She hadn't told him about Cain revealing that he knew who she really was, or the possible murder connection to the Wyrdmarks—not yet. Inside the library, she didn't have to think about competitions and brutes. Here, she could savor the quiet and the calm.

"No," she grumbled, drumming her fingers on the table.

"This is *actually* how you spend your spare time?" A hint of a smile appeared on his lips. "You should hope no one else hears about this—it would ruin your reputation. Nox would leave you for Cain." He chuckled to himself and opened his book again, leaning back in his chair. She stared at him for a moment, wondering if he'd stop laughing at her if he knew what she was researching. How it might help him, too.

Celaena straightened in her chair, rubbing a nasty bruise on her leg. Naturally, it was from an intentional blow of Chaol's wooden staff. She glared at him, but he continued reading.

He was merciless during their lessons. He had her doing all sorts of activities: walking on her hands, juggling blades . . . It wasn't anything new, but it was unpleasant. But his temper had improved somewhat. He did *seem* a bit sorry for hitting her leg so hard. Celaena supposed she liked him.

The assassin slammed shut the tome, dust flying into the air. It was pointless.

"What?" he asked, straightening.

"Nothing," she grumbled.

What *were* Wyrdmarks, and where did they come from? And more importantly, why had she never heard of them before? They'd been all over Elena's tomb, too. An ancient religion from a forgotten time—what were they doing *here*? And at the crime scene! There had to be a connection.

So far, she hadn't learned much: according to one book, Wyrdmarks were an alphabet. Though, according to *this* book, no grammar existed with the Wyrdmarks: everything was just symbols that one had to string together. And they changed meaning depending on the marks around them. They were painfully difficult to draw; they required precise lengths and angles, or they became something else entirely.

"Stop glowering and sulking," Chaol chided. He looked at the title of the book. Neither of them had mentioned Xavier's murder, and she'd gleaned no more information about it. "Remind me what you're reading."

"Nothing," she said again, covering the book with her arms. But his brown eyes narrowed farther, and she sighed. "It's just—just about Wyrdmarks—those sundial-things by the clock tower. I was interested, so I started learning about them." A half truth, at least.

She waited for the sneer and sarcasm, but it didn't come. He only said: "And? Why the frustration?"

She looked at the ceiling, pouting. "All I can find is just . . . just radical and outlandish theories. I never knew *any* of this! *Why?* Some books claim the Wyrd is the force that holds together and governs Erilea—and not just Erilea! Countless other worlds, too."

"I've heard of it before," he said, picking up his book. But his eyes remained fixed on her face. "I always thought the Wyrd was an old term for Fate—or Destiny."

"So did I. But the Wyrd isn't a religion, at least not in the northern parts of the continent, and it's not included in the worship of the Goddess or the gods."

He set the book in his lap. "Is there a point to this, beyond your obsession with those marks in the garden? Are you *that* bored?"

Worried for my safety is more like it!

"No. Yes. It's interesting: some theories suggest the Mother Goddess is just a spirit from one of these other worlds, and that she strayed through something called a Wyrdgate and found Erilea in need of form and life."

"That sounds a little sacrilegious," he warned. He was old enough to more vividly recall the burnings and executions ten years ago. What had it been like to grow up in the shadow of the king who had ordered so much destruction? To have lived here when royal families were slaughtered, when seers and magic-wielders were burned alive, and the world fell into darkness and sorrow?

But she went on, needing to dump the contents of her mind in case all the pieces somehow assembled by speaking them aloud. "There's an idea that before the Goddess arrived, there *was* life—an ancient civilization, but somehow, they disappeared. Perhaps through that Wyrdgate thing. Ruins exist—ruins too old to be of Fae making." How this connected to the Champion murders was beyond her. She was definitely grasping at straws.

He set his feet down and put the book on the table. "Can I be honest with you?" Chaol leaned closer, and Celaena leaned to meet him as he whispered: "You sound like a raving lunatic."

Celaena made a disgusted noise and sat back, seething. "Sorry for having *some* interest in the history of our world!"

"As you said, these sound like radical and outlandish theories." He started reading once more, and said without looking at her, "Again: why the frustration?"

She rubbed her eyes. "Because," she said, almost whining. "Because I just want a straightforward answer to *what* the Wyrdmarks are, and why they're in the garden *here*, of all places." Magic had been wiped away on the king's orders; so why had something like the Wyrdmarks been allowed to remain? To have them show up at the murder scene meant something.

"You should find another way to occupy your time," he said, returning to his book. Usually, guards watched her in the library for hours on end, day after day. What was he doing here? She smiled—her heart skipping a beat—and then looked at the books on the table.

She ran again through the information she'd gathered. There was also the idea of the Wyrdgates, which appeared numerous times alongside the mention of Wyrdmarks, but she'd never heard of them. When she'd first stumbled across the notion of Wyrdgates, days ago, it had seemed interesting, and so she'd researched, digging through piles of old parchment, only to find more puzzling theories.

The gates were both real and invisible things. Humans could not see them, but they could be summoned and accessed using the Wyrdmarks. They opened into other realms, some of them good, some of them bad. Things could come through from the other side and slither into Erilea. It was due to this that many of the strange and fell creatures of Erilea existed.

Celaena pulled another book toward her and grinned. It was as if someone had read her mind. It was a large black volume entitled *The Walking Dead* in tarnished silver letters. Thankfully, the captain didn't see the title before she opened it. But . . .

She didn't remember selecting this from the shelves. It reeked, almost like soil, and Celaena's nose crinkled as she turned the pages. She scanned for any sign of the Wyrdmarks, or any mention of a Wyrdgate, but she soon found something far more interesting.

An illustration of a twisted, half-decayed face grinned at her, flesh falling from its bones. The air chilled, and Celaena rubbed her arms. Where had she found this? How had this escaped the burnings? How had *any* of these books escaped the purging fires ten years ago?

She shivered again, almost twitching. The hollow, mad eyes of the monster were full of malice. It seemed to look at her. She closed the book and pushed it to the end of the table. If the king knew this kind of book still existed in his library, he'd have it all destroyed. Unlike the Great Library of Orynth, here there were no Master Scholars to protect the invaluable books. Chaol kept reading. Something groaned, and Celaena's head swung toward the back of the library. It was a guttural noise, an animalistic noise—

"Did you hear anything?" she asked.

"When do you plan on leaving?" was his only reply.

"When I grow tired of reading." She pulled the black book back to her, leafed past the terrifying portrait of the dead thing, and drew the candle closer to read the descriptions of various monsters.

There was a scraping noise somewhere beneath her feet—close, as if someone were running a fingernail along the ceiling below. Celaena slammed the book shut and stepped away from the table. The hair on her arms rose, and she almost stumbled into the nearest table as she waited for something—a hand; a wing; a gaping, fanged mouth—to appear and grab her.

"Do you feel that?" she asked Chaol, who slowly, maliciously grinned. He held out his dagger and dragged it on the marble floor, creating the exact sound and feeling.

"Damned idiot," she snarled. She grabbed two heavy books from the table and stalked from the library, making sure to leave *The Walking Dead* far behind.

28

Brows narrowed, Celaena aimed the cue at the white ball. The pole slid easily between her fingers as she steadied her hand on the felt surface of the table. With an awkward lurch of her arm, she jabbed the rod forward. She missed completely.

Cursing, Celaena tried again. She hit the cue ball in such a way that it gave a pathetic half roll to the side, gently knocking into a colored ball with a faint click. Well, at least she'd hit something. It was more successful than her research on the Wyrdmarks had been.

It was past ten, and, in need of a break from hours of training and researching and fretting about Cain and Elena, she'd come into the gaming room. She was too tired for music, she couldn't play cards alone, and—well, billiards seemed to be the only plausible activity. She'd picked up the cue with high hopes that the game wouldn't be too difficult to learn.

The assassin pivoted around the table and took aim again. She missed. Gritting her teeth, she considered snapping the cue in half across her knee. But she'd been attempting to play for only an hour. She'd be incredible by midnight! She'd master this ridiculous game or she'd turn the table into firewood. And use it to burn Cain alive.

Celaena jabbed the cue, and hit the ball with such force that it zoomed toward the back wall of the table, knocking three colored balls out of its way before it collided with the number three ball, sending it shooting straight for a hole.

It stopped rolling at the edge of the pocket.

A shriek of rage ripped from her throat, and Celaena ran over to the pocket. She first screamed at the ball, then took the cue in her hands and bit down upon the shaft, still screaming through her clamped teeth. Finally the assassin stopped and slapped the three ball into the pocket.

"For the world's greatest assassin, this is pathetic," said Dorian, stepping from the doorway.

She yelped and swung toward him. She wore a tunic and pants, and her hair was unbound. He leaned against the table, smiling as she turned a deep shade of red. "If you're going to insult me, you can shove this—" She lifted the cue in the air and made an obscene gesture that finished her sentence.

He rolled his sleeves before picking up a cue from the rack on the wall. "Are you planning on biting the cue again? Because if you are, I'd like to invite the court painter so I can forever remember the sight."

"Don't you dare mock me!"

"Don't be so serious." He aimed at the ball and sent it gracefully into a green one, which dropped into a pocket. "You're immensely entertaining when you're hopping mad."

To his surprise and delight, she laughed. "Funny to you," she said, "infuriating for me." She moved and took another shot. And missed.

"Let me show you how to do it." He strode over to where she stood and set his stick down, taking hers in his hand. Nudging her out of the way, his heart beating a bit faster, he positioned himself where she stood. "You see how my thumb and index finger are always holding the upper end of the cue? All you have to do is—"

She knocked him out of the way with a swish of her hips and took the rod from him. "I know how to hold it, you buffoon." She tried to hit the ball and missed yet again.

"You're not moving your body the correct way. Here, just let me show you."

Though it was the oldest and most shameless trick in the book, he reached over her and put his hand on top of the one that gripped the cue. He then positioned the fingers of her other hand on the wood before lightly gripping her wrist. To Dorian's dismay, his face became warm.

His eyes shifted to her, and, to his relief, he found that she was as red as he, if not more so.

"If you don't stop feeling and start instructing, I'm going to rip out your eyes and replace them with these billiard balls."

"Look, all you have to do is . . ." He walked her through the steps, and she hit the ball smoothly. It went into a corner and rebounded into a pocket. He removed himself from her and smirked. "See? If you do it properly, it'll work. Try again." He picked up his cue. She snorted, but still positioned herself, aimed, and hit it. The cue ball shot all around the table, creating general chaos. But at least she made contact.

He grabbed the triangle and held it in the air. "Care for a game?"

The clock struck two before they stopped. He had ordered an array of desserts to be brought in the midst of their playing, and though she protested, she gobbled down a large piece of chocolate cake and then ate half of his piece, too.

He won every game, yet she hardly noticed. As long as she hit the ball, it resulted in shameless bragging. When she missed—well, even the fires of Hell couldn't compare to the rage that burst from her mouth. He couldn't remember a time when he'd laughed so hard.

When she wasn't cursing and sputtering, they spoke of the books they'd both read, and as she jabbered on and on, he felt as if she hadn't spoken a word in years and was afraid she'd suddenly go mute again. She was frighteningly smart. She understood him when he spoke of history, or of politics—though she claimed to loathe the subject—and even had a great deal to say about the theater. He somehow wound up promising to take her to a play after the competition. An awkward silence arose at that, but it quickly passed.

Dorian was slumped in an armchair, resting his head on a hand. She lay sprawled across the chair facing his, her legs dangling off an arm. She stared at the fire, her eyelids half-closed. "What are you thinking?" he asked.

"I don't know," she said. She let her head drop onto the arm of the chair. "Do you think Xavier and the other Champion murders were intentional?"

"Perhaps. Does it make a difference?"

"No." She lazily waved her hand in the air. "Never mind."

Before he could ask more, she fell asleep.

He wished he knew more about her past. Chaol had only told him that she came from Terrasen, and that her family was dead. He hadn't the faintest clue what her life was like, how she became an assassin, how she learned to play the pianoforte . . . It was all a mystery.

He wanted to know everything about her. He wished she'd just tell him. Dorian stood and stretched. He placed their cues on the rack, arranged the balls, and returned to the slumbering assassin. He shook her gently, and she groaned in protest. "You may want to sleep there, but you'll sorely regret it in the morning."

Barely opening her eyes, she stood and shuffled to the door. When she nearly walked into the doorpost, he decided that a guiding arm was needed before she broke something. Trying not to think of the warmth of her skin beneath his hand, he directed her to her bedroom and watched her stagger into bed, where she collapsed on top of the blankets.

"Your books are there," she mumbled, pointing at a stack by her bed. He slowly entered the chamber. She lay still, her eyes closed. Three candles burned on various surfaces. With a sigh, he moved to blow them out before approaching her bed. Was she sleeping?

"Good night, Celaena," he said. It was the first time he'd addressed her by her name. It came off his tongue nicely. She mumbled something that sounded like "nahnuh," and did not move. A curious necklace glittered in the hollow of her throat. He felt as if it were familiar somehow, like he'd seen it before. With a final glance, he picked up the stack of books and left the room.

If she became his father's Champion, and later gained her freedom, would she remain the same? Or was this all a facade to get what she wanted? But he couldn't imagine that she was pretending. Didn't *want* to imagine that she was pretending.

The castle was silent and dark as he walked back to his room.

29

At their Test the next afternoon, Celaena stood in the training hall with her arms crossed, watching Cain spar with Grave. Cain knew who she was; all of her simpering and pretending and holding back had been for nothing. It had *amused* him.

She clenched her jaw as Cain and Grave flew across the sparring ring, swords clanging. The Test was fairly simple: they were each given a sparring partner, and if they won their duel, they needn't worry about being eliminated. The losers, however, would face judgment by Brullo. Whoever had performed the worst would be sent packing.

To his credit, Grave held up well against Cain, even though she saw how his knees trembled from the effort. Nox, standing beside her, hissed as Cain shoved into Grave and sent him staggering back.

Cain smiled throughout the entire thing, barely panting. Celaena clenched her hands into fists, pushing them hard against her ribs. In a flash of steel, Cain had his blade at Grave's throat, and the pockmarked assassin bared his rotting teeth at him. "Excellent, Cain," Brullo said, clapping. Celaena struggled to control her breathing.

"Look out, Cain," Verin said from beside her. The curly-headed thief grinned at her. She hadn't been thrilled when it had been announced she was to spar against Verin. But at least it wasn't Nox. "Little lady wants a piece of you."

"Watch yourself, Verin," Nox warned, his gray eyes burning.

"What?" Verin said. Now the other Champions—and everyone else—were turning to them. Pelor, who had been lingering nearby, retreated a few steps. Smart move. "Defending her, are you?" Verin taunted. "Is that the bargain? She opens her legs, and you keep an eye on her during practice?"

"Shut your mouth, you damned pig," Celaena snapped. Chaol and Dorian pushed off from where they both leaned against the wall, coming closer to the ring.

"Or what?" Verin said, nearing her. Nox stiffened, his hand drifting to his sword.

But Celaena refused to back down. "Or I'll rip out your tongue."

"That's enough!" Brullo barked. "Take it out in the ring. Verin. Lillian. Now."

Verin gave her a snakelike smile, and Cain clapped him on the back as he entered the chalk-etched circle, drawing his sword.

Nox put a hand on her shoulder, and out of the corner of her eye, she spied Chaol and Dorian watching them closely. She ignored them.

It was enough. Enough of the pretending and the meekness. Enough of Cain.

Verin raised his sword, shaking his blond curls out of his eyes. "Let's see what you've got."

She stalked toward him, keeping her sword sheathed at her side. Verin's grin widened as he lifted his blade.

He swung, but Celaena struck, ramming her fist into his arm, sending the blade soaring through the air. In the same breath, her palm hit his left arm, knocking it aside, too. As he staggered back, her leg came up, and Verin's eyes bulged as her foot slammed into his chest. The kick sent him flying, and his body crunched as it hit the floor and slid out of the ring, instantly eliminating him. The hall was utterly silent.

"Mock me again," she spat at Verin, "and I'll do that with my sword the next time." She turned from him, and found Brullo's face slack. "Here's a lesson for you, Weapons Master," she said, stalking past him. "Give me *real* men to fight. Then maybe I'll bother trying."

She strode away, past the grinning Nox, and stopped before Cain. She stared up at his face—a face that might have been handsome had he not been a bastard—and smiled with sweet venom. "Here I am," she said, squaring her shoulders. "Just a little lapdog."

Cain's black eyes gleamed. "All I hear is yapping."

Her hand itched toward her sword, but she kept it at her side. "Let's see if you still hear yapping when I win this competition." Before he could say more, she stalked to the water table.

Only Nox dared speak to her after that. Surprisingly, Chaol didn't reprimand her, either.

When she was safely back in her rooms after the Test, Celaena watched the snowflakes drift from the hills beyond Rifthold. They swept toward her, harbingers of the storm that was to come. The late afternoon sun, trapped beneath a wall of pewter, stained the clouds a yellowish gray, making the sky unusually bright. It felt surreal, as if the horizon had disappeared beyond the hills. She was stranded in a world of glass.

Celaena left the window, but stopped before the tapestry and its depiction of Queen Elena. She had often wished for adventure, for old spells and wicked kings. But she hadn't realized it would be like this—a fight for her freedom. And she'd always imagined that there'd be someone to help her—a loyal friend or a one-armed soldier or something. She hadn't imagined she would be so . . . alone.

She wished Sam were with her. He'd always known what to do, always had her back, whether she wanted him to or not. She would give anything—anything in the world—to have him still with her.

Her eyes burned, and Celaena put a hand to the amulet. The metal was warm beneath her fingers—comforting, somehow. She took a step back from the tapestry to better study the entire scope of it.

In the center stood a stag, magnificent and virile, gazing sideways at Elena. The symbol of the royal house of Terrasen, of the kingdom that Brannon, Elena's father, had founded. A reminder that though Elena had become Queen of Adarlan, she still belonged to Terrasen. Like Celaena, no matter where Elena went, no matter how far, Terrasen would *always* own a part of her.

Celaena listened to the wind howl. With a sigh, she shook her head and turned away.

Find the evil in the castle . . . But the only truly evil thing in this world is the man ruling it.

Across the castle, Kaltain Rompier clapped lightly as a troupe of acrobats finished their tumbling. The performance had stopped at last. She didn't feel inclined to watch peasants bouncing about in bright colors for hours, but Queen Georgina enjoyed it, and had invited her to sit beside the throne today. It was an honor, and had been arranged through Perrington.

Perrington wanted her; she knew it. And if she pushed, she could easily get him to offer to make her his duchess. But duchess wasn't enough—not when Dorian was still unmarried. Her head had been pounding for the past week, and today it seemed to throb with the words: *Not enough. Not enough. Not enough.* Even in her sleep, the pain seeped in, warping her dreams into nightmares so vivid she couldn't remember where she was when she awoke.

"How delightful, Your Majesty," Kaltain said as the acrobats gathered their things.

"Yes, they were rather exciting, weren't they?" The queen's green eyes were bright, and she smiled at Kaltain. Just then Kaltain's head gave a bolt of pain so strong she clenched her fists, hiding them in the folds of her tangerine-colored gown.

"I do wish Prince Dorian could have seen them," Kaltain got out. "His Highness told me only yesterday how much he enjoyed coming here." The lie was easy enough, and it somehow made the pain of the headache ease.

"Dorian said that?" Queen Georgina raised an auburn eyebrow.

"Does that surprise Your Majesty?"

The queen put a hand to her chest. "I thought my son had a distaste for such things."

"Your Majesty," she whispered, "will you swear not to say a word?"

"A word about what?" the queen whispered back.

"Well, Prince Dorian told me something."

"What did he say?" The queen touched Kaltain's arm.

"He said that the reason he doesn't come to court so often is because he's rather shy."

The queen withdrew, the light in her eyes fading. "Oh, he's told me that a hundred times. I was so hoping you'd tell me something interesting, Lady Kaltain. Like if he's found a young woman he favors."

Kaltain's face warmed, and her head pounded mercilessly. She wished for her pipe, but hours remained of this court session, and it wouldn't be proper to leave until Georgina departed.

"I heard," said the queen under her breath, "that there's a young lady, but no one knows who! Or at least when they hear her name, it's nothing *familiar*. Do you know her?"

"No, Your Majesty." Kaltain fought to keep the frustration from her face.

"What a pity. I had hoped that you of all people would know. You're such a clever girl, Kaltain."

"Thank you, Your Majesty. You are too kind."

"Nonsense. I'm an excellent judge of character; I knew how extraordinary you were the moment you entered the court. Only you are suitable for a man of Perrington's prowess. What a pity you didn't meet my Dorian first!"

Not enough, not enough, the pain sang. This was her time. "Even if I had," Kaltain chuckled, "Your Majesty surely would not have approved—I'm far too lowly for the attentions of your son."

"Your beauty and wealth compensate for it."

"Thank you, Your Majesty." Kaltain's heart pounded quickly.

If the queen approved of her . . . Kaltain could scarcely think as the queen nestled into her throne, then clapped her hands twice. The music began. Kaltain didn't hear it.

Perrington had given her the shoes. Now was her time to dance.

30

"You're not *focusing*."

"Yes, I am!" Celaena said through her teeth, pulling the bowstring back even farther.

"Then go ahead," Chaol said, pointing to a distant target along the far wall of the abandoned hallway. An outrageous distance for anyone—except her. "Let's see you make that."

She rolled her eyes and straightened her spine a bit. The bowstring quivered in her hand, and she lifted the tip of her arrow slightly.

"You're going to hit the left wall," he said, crossing his arms.

"I'm going to hit you in the head if you don't shut up." She turned her head to meet his gaze. His brows rose, and, still staring at him, she smiled wickedly as she blindly fired the arrow.

The whiz of the arrow's flight filled the stone hallway before the faint, dull thud of impact. But they remained gazing at each other. His eyes were slightly purple beneath—hadn't he gotten any sleep in the three weeks since Xavier had died?

She certainly hadn't been sleeping well, either. Every noise woke her, and Chaol hadn't yet discovered who might be targeting the Champions one by one. The *who* didn't matter as much to her as the *how*—how was the killer selecting them? There was no pattern; five were dead, and they had no connection to each other, aside from the competition. She hadn't been able to see another crime scene to determine if Wyrdmarks had been painted in blood there as well. Celaena sighed, rolling her shoulders. "Cain knows who I am," she said quietly, lowering her bow.

His face remained blank. "How?"

"Perrington told him. And Cain told me."

"When?" She'd never seen him look so serious. It made something within her strain.

"A few days ago," she lied. It had been weeks since their confrontation. "I was in the garden with Nehemia—with my guards, don't worry—and he approached us. He knows all about me—and knows that I hold back when we're with the other Champions."

"Did he lead you to believe that the other Champions know about you?"

"No," she said. "I don't think they do. Nox doesn't have a clue."

Chaol put a hand on the hilt of his sword. "It's going to be fine. The element of surprise is gone, that's all. You'll still beat Cain in the duels."

She half smiled. "You know, it's starting to sound like you actually believe in me. You'd better be careful."

He began to say something, but running footsteps sounded from around the corner, and he paused. Two guards skidded to a stop and saluted them. Chaol gave them a moment to collect their breath before he said, "Yes?"

One of the guards, an aging man with thinning hair, saluted a second time and said, "Captain—you're needed."

Though his features remained neutral, Chaol's shoulders shifted, and his chin rose a bit higher. "What is it?" he said, a bit too quickly to pass for unconcerned.

"Another body," replied the guard. "In the servant's passages."

The second guard, a slender, frail-looking young man, was deathly pale. "You saw the body?" Celaena asked him. The guard nodded. "How fresh?"

Chaol gave her a sharp look. The guard said, "They think it's from last night—from the way the blood's half-dried."

Chaol's eyes were unfocused. Thinking—he was figuring out what to do. He straightened. "You want to prove how good you are?" he asked her.

She put her hands on her hips. "Do I even need to?"

He motioned the guards to lead the way. "Come with me," he said to her over his shoulder, and—despite the body—she smiled a bit and followed him.

As they departed, Celaena looked back at the target.

Chaol had been right. She'd missed the center by six inches—to the left.

Thankfully, someone had created some semblance of order before they arrived. Even still, Chaol had to push his way through a crowd of gathered guards and servants, Celaena keeping close behind him. When they reached the edge of the crowd and beheld the body, her hands slackened at her sides. Chaol cursed with impressive violence.

She didn't know where to look first. At the body, with the gaping chest cavity and missing brain and face, at the claw marks gouged into the ground, or at the two Wyrdmarks, drawn on either side of the body in chalk. Her blood went cold. There was no denying their connection now.

The crowd continued talking as the captain approached the body, then turned to one of the guards watching him. "Who is it?"

"Verin Ysslych," Celaena said before the guard could reply. She'd recognize Verin's curly hair anywhere. Verin had been at the head of the pack since this competition started. Whatever had killed him . . .

"What kind of animal makes scratches like those?" she asked Chaol, but didn't need to hear his reply to know that his guess was as good as hers. The claw marks were deep—a quarter of an inch at least. She crouched beside one and ran her finger along the interior edge. It was jagged, but cut clean into the stone floor. Her brows knotting, she scanned the other claw marks.

"There's no blood in these claw marks," she said, twisting her head to look over her shoulder at Chaol. He knelt beside her as she pointed to them. "They're clean."

"Which means?"

She frowned, fighting the chill that ran down her arms. "Whatever did this sharpened its nails before it gutted him."

"And why is *that* important?"

She stood, looking up and down the hallway, then squatted again. "It means this thing had time to do that before it attacked him."

"It could have done it while lying in wait."

She shook her head. "Those torches along the wall are almost burnt to stubs. There aren't any signs of them being extinguished before the attack—there are no traces of sooty water. If Verin died last night, then those torches were still burning when he died."

"And?"

"And look at this hallway. The nearest doorway is fifty feet down, and the nearest corner is a bit farther than that. If those torches were burning—"

"Then Verin would have seen whatever it was long before he got to this spot."

"So why get near it?" she asked, more to herself than anything. "What if it wasn't an animal, but a person? And what if that person disabled Verin long enough for them to summon this creature?" She pointed to Verin's legs. "Those are clean cuts around his ankles. His tendons were snapped by a knife, to keep him from running." She moved next to the body, taking care not to disturb the Wyrdmarks etched into the ground as she lifted Verin's rigid, cold hand. "Look at his fingernails." She swallowed hard. "The tips are cracked and shattered." She used her own nail to scrape out the dirt beneath his nails, and smeared it across her palm. "See?" She held out her hand for Chaol to observe. "Dust and bits of stone." She pulled aside Verin's arm, revealing faint lines in the stone beneath. "Fingernail marks. He was desperate to get away—to drag himself by his fingertips, if necessary. He was alive the entire time that thing sharpened its claws on the stone while its master watched."

"So what does that mean?"

She smiled grimly at him. "It means that you're in a lot of trouble."

And, as Chaol's face paled, Celaena realized with a jolt that perhaps the Champions' killer and Elena's mysterious evil force might be one and the same.

Seated at the dining table, Celaena flipped through the book.

Nothing, nothing, nothing. She scanned page after page for any sign of the two Wyrdmarks that had been drawn beside Verin's body. There had to be a connection.

She stopped as a map of Erilea appeared. Maps had always interested her; there was something bewitching in knowing one's precise location in relation to others on the earth. She gently traced a finger along the eastern coast. She began in the south—at Banjali, the Eyllwe capital, then went up, curving and snaking, all the way to Rifthold.

Her finger then traveled through Meah, then north and inland to Orynth, then back, back to the sea, to the Surian Coast, and finally to the very tip of the continent and the North Sea beyond.

She stared at Orynth, that city of light and learning, the pearl of Erilea and capital of Terrasen. Her birthplace. Celaena slammed shut the book.

Glancing around her room, the assassin let out a long sigh. When she managed to sleep, her dreams were haunted by ancient battles, by swords with eyes, by Wyrdmarks that swirled around her head and blinded her with their bright colors. She could see the gleaming armor of Fae and mortal warriors, hear the clash of shields and the snarl of vicious beasts, and smell blood and rotting corpses all around her. Carnage trailed in her wake. Adarlan's Assassin shuddered.

"Oh, good. I hoped you'd still be awake," the Crown Prince said, and Celaena jumped from her seat to find Dorian approaching. He looked tired and a bit ruffled.

She opened her mouth, then shook her head. "What are you doing here? It's almost midnight, and I've got a Test tomorrow." She couldn't deny having him here was a bit of a relief—the murderer only seemed to attack Champions when they were alone.

"Have you moved from literature to history?" He surveyed the books on the table. "*A Brief History of Modern Erilea*," he read. "*Symbols and Power. Eyllwe Culture and Customs.*" He raised an eyebrow.

"I read what I like."

He slid into the seat beside her, his leg brushing hers. "Is there a connection between all of these?"

"No." It wasn't quite a lie—though she had hoped for all of them to contain *something* about Wyrdmarks, or what they meant beside a corpse. "I assume you heard about Verin's death."

"Of course," he said, a dark expression crossing his handsome face.

She was all too aware of how close his leg was, but she couldn't bring herself to shift away.

"And you're not at all concerned that so many Champions have been brutally murdered at the hands of someone's feral beast?"

Dorian leaned in, his eyes fixed on hers. "All of those murders occurred in dark, isolated hallways. You're never without guards—and your chambers are well-watched."

"I'm not concerned for myself," she said sharply, pulling back a bit. Which wasn't entirely true. "I just think it reflects poorly on your esteemed father to have all of this going on."

"When was the last time you bothered to care for the reputation of my 'esteemed' father?"

"Since I became his son's Champion. So perhaps you ought to devote some additional resources to solving these murders, before I win this absurd competition just because I'm the last one left alive."

"Any more demands?" he asked, still close enough for her lips to graze his if she dared.

"I'll let you know if I think of any." Their eyes locked. A slow smile spread across her face. What sort of a man was the Crown Prince? Though she didn't want to admit it, it was nice to have someone around, even if he was a Havilliard.

She pushed claw marks and brainless corpses from her thoughts. "Why are you so disheveled? Has Kaltain been clawing at you?"

"Kaltain? Thankfully, not recently. But what a miserable day it was! The pups are mutts, and—" He put his head in his hands.

"Pups?"

"One of my bitches gave birth to a litter of mongrels. Before, they were too young to tell. But now . . . Well, I'd hoped for purebreds."

"Are we speaking of dogs or of women?"

"Which would you prefer?" He gave her an impish grin.

"Oh, hush up," she hissed, and he chuckled.

"Why, might I ask, are *you* so disheveled?" His smile faltered. "Chaol told me he took you to see the body; I hope it wasn't too harrowing."

"Not at all. It's just that I haven't slept well."

"Me, neither," he admitted. He straightened. "Will you play the pianoforte for me?" Celaena tapped her foot on the floor, wondering how he had moved on to such a different subject.

"Of course not."

"You played beautifully."

"If I had known someone was spying on me, I wouldn't have played at all."

"Why is playing so personal for you?" He leaned back in his chair.

"I can't hear or play music without— Never mind."

"No, tell me what you were going to say."

"Nothing interesting," she said, stacking the books.

"Does it stir up memories?"

She eyed him, searching for any sign of mockery. "Sometimes."

"Memories of your parents?" He reached to help her stack the remaining books.

Celaena stood suddenly. "Don't ask such stupid questions."

"I'm sorry if I pried."

She didn't respond. The door in her mind that she kept locked at all times had been cracked open by the question, and now she tried frantically to close it. Seeing his face, seeing him so near to her . . . The door shut and she turned the key.

"It's just," he said, oblivious to the battle that had just occurred, "it's just that I don't know anything about you."

"I'm an assassin." Her heartbeat calmed. "That's all there is to know."

"Yes," he said with a sigh. "But why is it so wrong for me to want to know more? Like how you became an assassin—and what things were like for you before that."

"It's not interesting."

"I wouldn't find it boring." She didn't say anything. "Please? One question—and I promise, nothing too sensitive."

Her mouth twisted to the side and she looked at the table. What harm was there in a question? She could choose not to reply. "Very well."

He grinned. "I need a moment to think of a good one." She rolled her eyes, but sat down. After a few seconds, he asked, "Why do you like music so much?"

She made a face. "You said nothing sensitive!"

"Is it *that* prying? How different is that from asking why you like to read?"

"No, no. That question is fine." She let out a long breath through her nose and stared at the table. "I like music," she said slowly, "because when I hear it, I . . . I lose myself within myself, if that makes sense. I become empty and full all at once, and I can feel the whole earth roiling around me. When I play, I'm not . . . for once, I'm not destroying. I'm creating." She chewed on her lip. "I used to want to be a healer. Back when I was . . . Back before this became my profession, when I was almost too young to remember, I wanted to be a healer." She shrugged. "Music reminds me of that feeling." She laughed under her breath. "I've never told anyone that," she admitted, then saw his smile. "Don't mock me."

He shook his head, wiping the smile from his lips. "I'm not mocking you—I'm just . . ."

"Unused to hearing people speak from the heart?"

"Well, yes."

She smiled slightly. "Now it's my turn. Are there any limitations?"

"No." He tucked his hands behind his head. "I'm not nearly as private as you are."

She made a face as she thought of the question. "Why aren't you married yet?"

"Married? I'm nineteen!"

"Yes, but you're the Crown Prince."

He crossed his arms. She tried not to notice the cut of muscle that shifted just beneath the fabric of his shirt. "Ask another question."

"I want to hear your answer—it must be interesting if you're so ardently resisting."

He looked at the window and the snow that swirled beyond. "I'm not married," he said softly, "because I can't stomach the idea of marrying a woman inferior to me in mind and spirit. It would mean the death of my soul."

"Marriage is a legal contract—it's not a sacred thing. As Crown Prince, you should have given up such fanciful notions. What if you're ordered to marry for the sake of alliance? Would you start a war because of your romantic ideals?"

"It's not like that."

"Oh? Your father wouldn't command you to marry some princess in order to strengthen his empire?"

"My father has an army to do that for him."

"You could easily love some woman on the side. Marriage doesn't mean you can't love other people."

His sapphire eyes flashed. "You marry the person you love—and none other," he said, and she laughed. "You're mocking *me*! You're laughing in my face!"

"You deserve to be laughed at for such foolish thoughts! I spoke from my soul; you speak only from selfishness."

"You're remarkably judgmental."

"What's the point in having a mind if you don't use it to make judgments?"

"What's the point in having a heart if you don't use it to spare others from the harsh judgments of your mind?"

"Oh, well said, Your Highness!" He stared at her sullenly. "Come now. I didn't wound you that severely."

"You've attempted to ruin my dreams and ideals. I get enough from my mother as it is. You're just being cruel."

"I'm being practical. There's a difference. And you're the Crown Prince of Adarlan. You're in a position where it's possible for you to change Erilea for the better. You could help create a world where *true love* isn't needed to secure a happy ending."

"And what sort of world would I need to create for that to happen?"

"A world where men govern themselves."

"You speak of anarchy and treason."

"I do *not* speak of anarchy. Call me a traitor all you like—I've been convicted as an assassin already."

He sidled closer to her, and his fingers brushed hers—calloused, warm, and hard. "You can't resist the opportunity to respond to everything I say, can you?" She felt restless—but at the same time remarkably still. Something was brought to life and laid to sleep in his gaze. "Your eyes are very strange," he said. "I've never seen any with such a bright ring of gold."

"If you're attempting to woo me with flattery, I'm afraid it won't work."

"I was merely observing; I have no agenda." He looked at his hand, still touching hers. "Where did you get that ring?"

She contracted her hand into a fist as she pulled it away from him. The amethyst in her ring glowed in the firelight. "It was a gift."

"From whom?"

"That's none of your concern."

He shrugged, though she knew better than to tell him who'd really given it to her—rather, she knew *Chaol* wouldn't want Dorian to know. "I'd like to know who's been giving *rings* to my Champion."

The way the collar of his black jacket lay across his neck made her unable to sit still. She wanted to touch him, to trace the line between his tan skin and the golden lining of the fabric.

"Billiards?" she asked, rising to her feet. "I could use another lesson." Celaena didn't wait for his answer as she strode toward the gaming room. She very much wanted to stand close to him and have her skin warm under his breath. She liked that. Worse than that, she realized, she liked *him*.

Chaol watched Perrington at his table in the dining hall. When he had approached the duke about Verin's death, he hadn't seemed bothered. Chaol looked around the cavernous hall; in fact, most of the Champions' sponsors went about as usual. Idiots. If Celaena was actually right about it, then whoever was responsible for killing the Champions could be among them. But which of the members of the king's council would be so desperate to win that he'd do such a thing? Chaol stretched his legs beneath the table and shifted his attention back to Perrington.

He'd seen how the duke used his size and title to win allies on the king's council and keep opponents from challenging him. But it wasn't his maneuverings that had captured the interest of the Captain of the Guard tonight. Rather, it was the moments between the grins and laughter, when a shadow passed across the duke's face. It wasn't an expression of anger or of disgust, but a shade that clouded his eyes. It was so strange that when Chaol had first seen it, he'd extended his dinner just to see if it happened again.

A few moments later, it did. Perrington's eyes became dark and his face cleared, as if he saw everything in the world for what it was and found no joy or amusement in it. Chaol leaned back in his chair, sipping his water.

He knew little of the duke, and had never entirely trusted him. Neither had Dorian, especially not after all his talk of using Nehemia as a hostage to get the Eyllwe rebels to cooperate. But the duke was the king's most trusted advisor—and had offered no cause for mistrust other than a fierce belief in Adarlan's right to conquest.

Kaltain Rompier sat a few chairs away. Chaol's brows rose slightly. Her eyes were upon Perrington as well—filled not with the longing of a beloved, but with cold contemplation. Chaol stretched again, lifting his arms over his head. Where was Dorian? The prince hadn't come to dinner, nor was he in the kennels with the bitch and her pups. His gaze returned to the duke. There it was—for a moment!

Perrington's eyes fell upon the black ring on his left hand and darkened, as if his pupils had expanded to encompass all of each eye. Then it was gone—his eyes returned to normal. Chaol looked to Kaltain. Had she noticed the odd change?

No—her face remained the same. There was no bewilderment, no surprise. Her look became shallow, as if she were more interested in how his jacket might complement her dress. Chaol stretched and rose, finishing his apple as he strode from the dining hall. Strange as it was, he had enough to worry about. The duke was ambitious, but certainly not a threat to the castle or its inhabitants. But even as the Captain of the Guard walked to his rooms, he couldn't shake the feeling that Duke Perrington had been watching him, too.

31

Someone was standing at the foot of her bed.

Celaena knew this long before she opened her eyes, and she eased her hand beneath her pillow, pulling out the makeshift knife she'd crafted of pins, string, and soap.

"That's unnecessary," a woman said, and Celaena sat upright at the sound of Elena's voice. "And would be wholly ineffective."

Her blood went cold at the sight of the shimmering specter of the first Queen of Adarlan. Though Elena looked fully formed, the edges of her body gleamed as though made from starlight. Her long, silver hair flowed around her beautiful face, and she smiled as Celaena set down her miserably pathetic knife. "Hello, child," the queen said.

"What do you want?" Celaena demanded, but kept her voice down. Was she dreaming, or could the guards hear her? She tensed, her legs preparing to leap from the bed—perhaps toward the balcony, since Elena stood between her and the door.

"Simply to remind you that you *must* win this competition."

"I already plan to." She'd been woken up for *this*? "And it's not for you," she added coldly. "I'm doing it for my freedom. Do you have anything useful to say, or are you just here to bother me? Or maybe you could just *tell* me more about this evil thing that's hunting the Champions down one by one."

Elena sighed, lifting her eyes to the ceiling. "I know as little as you." When Celaena's frown didn't disappear, Elena said, "You don't trust me yet. I understand. But you and I are on the same side, whether you allow yourself to believe it or not." She lowered her gaze to the assassin, pinning her with the intensity of it. "I came here to warn you to keep an eye on your right."

"Excuse me?" Celaena cocked her head. "What does that mean?"

"Look to your right. You'll find the answers there."

Celaena looked to her right, but all she saw was the tapestry that concealed the tomb. She opened her mouth to snap a response, but when she looked back at Elena, the queen was gone.

At her Test the next day, Celaena studied the small table before her and all the goblets it contained. It had been over two weeks since Samhuinn, and while she'd passed yet another Test—knife-throwing, to her relief—another Champion had been found dead just two days ago. To say she was getting little sleep these days was an understatement. When she wasn't searching for an indication of what the Wyrdmarks around the corpses had meant, she spent most of the night wide awake, watching her windows and doors, listening for the scrape of claw on stone. The royal guards outside her rooms didn't help; if this beast was capable of gouging marble, it could take down a few men.

Brullo stood at the front of the sparring hall, his hands clasped behind his back, watching the thirteen remaining competitors standing at thirteen individual tables. He glanced at the clock. Celaena looked at it, too. She had five minutes left—five minutes during which she not only had to identify the poisons in seven goblets, but arrange them in the order of the most benign to the deadliest.

The true test, however, would come at the end of the five minutes, when they were to drink from the goblet they deemed the most harmless. If they got the answer wrong . . . Even with antidotes on hand, it would be unpleasant. Celaena rolled her neck and lifted one of the goblets to her nose, sniffing. Sweet—too sweet. She swirled the dessert wine they'd used to conceal the sweetness, but in the bronze goblet, it was difficult to see the color. She dipped her finger into the cup, studying the purple liquid as it dripped off her nail. Definitely belladonna.

She looked at the other goblets she'd identified. Hemlock. Bloodroot. Monkshood. Oleander. She shifted the goblets into order, squeezing in belladonna just before the goblet containing a lethal dose of oleander. Three minutes left.

Celaena picked up the penultimate goblet and sniffed. And sniffed again. It didn't smell like anything.

She shifted her face away from the table and sniffed the air, hoping to clear her nostrils. When trying perfumes, people sometimes lose their sense of smell after sniffing too many. Which was why perfumers usually kept something on site to help clear the scent from the nose. She sniffed the goblet again, and dunked her finger. It smelled like water, looked like water . . .

Perhaps it *was* just water. She set down the glass and picked up the final goblet. But when she sniffed it, the wine inside didn't have any unusual smell. It seemed fine. She bit her lip and glanced at the clock. Two minutes left.

Some of the other Champions were cursing under their breath. Whoever got the order most wrong went home.

Celaena sniffed the water goblet again, racing through a list of odorless poisons. None of them could be combined with water, not without coloring it. She picked up the wine goblet, swirling the liquid. Wine could conceal any number of advanced poisons—but which one was it?

At the table to the left of her, Nox ran his hands through his dark hair. He had three goblets in front of him, the other four in line behind them. Ninety seconds left.

Poisons, poisons, poisons. Her mouth went dry. If she lost, would Elena haunt her from spite?

Celaena glanced to the right to find Pelor, the gangly young assassin, watching her. He was down to the same two goblets that she struggled with, and she watched as he put the water glass at the very end of the spectrum—the most poisonous—and the wine glass at the other.

His eyes flicked to hers, and his chin drooped in a barely detectible nod. He put his hands in his pockets. He was done. Celaena turned to her own goblets before Brullo could catch her.

Poisons. That's what Pelor had said during their first Test. He was trained in poisons.

She glanced at him sidelong. He stood to her right.

Look to your right. You'll find the answers there.

A chill went down her spine. Elena had been telling the truth.

Pelor stared at the clock, watching it count down the seconds until the Test was over. But why help her?

She moved the water glass to the end of the line, and put the wine glass first.

Because aside from her, Cain's favorite Champion to torment was Pelor. And because when she'd been in Endovier, the allies she'd made hadn't been the darlings of the overseers, but the ones the overseers had hated most. The outsiders looked out for each other. None of the other Champions had bothered to pay attention to Pelor—even Brullo, it seemed, had forgotten Pelor's claim that first day. If he'd known, he never would have allowed them to do the Test so publicly.

"Time's up. Make your final order," Brullo said, and Celaena stared at her line of goblets for a moment longer. On the side of the room, Dorian and Chaol watched with crossed arms. Had they noticed Pelor's help?

Nox cursed colorfully and shoved his remaining glasses into the line, many of the competitors doing the same. Antidotes were on hand in case mistakes were made—and as Brullo began going through the tables, telling the Champions to drink, he handed them out frequently. Most of them had assumed the wine with nothing in it was a trap and placed it toward the end of the spectrum. Even Nox wound up chugging a vial of antidote; he'd put monkshood first.

And Cain, to her delight, wound up going purple in the face after consuming belladonna. As he guzzled down the antidote, she wished Brullo had somehow run out. So far, no one had won the Test. One Champion drank the water and was on the ground before Brullo could hand him the antidote. Bloodbane—a horrible, painful poison. Even consuming just a little could cause vivid hallucinations and disorientation. Thankfully, the Weapons Master forced him to swallow the antidote, though the Champion still had to be rushed to the castle infirmary.

At last, Brullo stopped at her table to survey her line of goblets. His face revealed nothing as he said, "On with it, then."

Celaena glanced at Pelor, whose hazel eyes shone as she lifted the glass of wine to her lips and drank a sip.

Nothing. No strange taste, no immediate sensation. Some poisons could take longer to affect you, but . . .

Brullo extended a fist to her, and her stomach clenched. Was the antidote inside?

But his fingers splayed, and he only clapped her on the back. "The right one—just wine," he said, and the Champions murmured behind him.

He moved on to Pelor—the last Champion—and the youth drank

the glass of wine. Brullo grinned at him, grasping his shoulder. "Another winner."

Applause rippled through the sponsors and trainers, and Celaena flashed an appreciative grin in the assassin's direction. He grinned back, going red from his neck to his copper hair.

So she'd cheated a little, but she'd won. She could handle sharing the victory with an ally. And, yes, Elena was looking out for her—but that didn't change anything. Even if her path and Elena's demands were now tied closely together, she wouldn't become the King's Champion just to serve some ghost's agenda—an agenda that Elena had twice now failed to reveal.

Even if Elena had told her how to win the Test.

32

After cutting short their lesson in favor of a stroll, Celaena and Nehemia walked through the spacious halls of the castle, guards trailing behind them. Whatever Nehemia thought of the flock of guards that followed Celaena everywhere, she didn't say anything. Despite the fact that Yulemas was a month away—and the final duel five days after that—every evening, for an hour before dinner, Celaena and the princess divided their time equally between Eyllwe and the common tongue. Celaena had Nehemia read from her library books, and then forced her to copy letter after letter until they looked flawless.

Since they'd begun their lessons, the princess had greatly improved her fluency in the common tongue, though the girls still spoke Eyllwe. Perhaps it was for ease and comfort, perhaps it was to see the raised eyebrows and gaping mouths when others overheard them, perhaps it was to keep their conversations private—whichever reason, the assassin found the language preferable. At least Endovier had taught her *something*.

"You're quiet today," Nehemia said. "Is something the matter?"

Celaena smiled weakly. Something *was* the matter. She'd slept so poorly the previous night that she'd wished for dawn to arrive early. Another Champion was dead. Not to mention, there was still the matter of Elena's commands. "I was up late reading, is all."

They entered a part of the castle that Celaena had never seen before. "I sense much worry in you," Nehemia said suddenly, "and I hear much that you do not say. You never voice any of your troubles, though your eyes betray them." Was she so transparent? "We're friends," Nehemia said softly. "When you need me, I'll be there."

Celaena's throat tightened, and she put a hand on Nehemia's shoulder. "No one has called me friend in a long time," the assassin said. "I—" An inky black crept into the corner of her memory, and she struggled against it. "There are parts of me that I . . ." She heard it then, the sound that haunted her dreams. Hooves pounding, thunderous hooves. Celaena shook her head and the sound stopped. "Thank you, Nehemia," she said with sincerity. "You're a true friend."

Her heart was raw and trembling, and the darkness faded.

Nehemia suddenly groaned. "The queen asked me to watch some acting troupe perform one of her favorite plays tonight. Will you go with me? I could use a translator."

Celaena frowned. "I'm afraid that—"

"You cannot go." Nehemia's voice was tinted with annoyance, and Celaena gave her friend an apologetic look.

"There are certain things that—" Celaena began, but the princess shook her head.

"We all have our secrets—though I'm curious why you're so closely watched by that captain and locked in your rooms at night. If I were a fool, I'd say they're afraid of you."

The assassin smiled. "Men will always be silly about such things." She thought about what the princess had said, and worry slipped into her stomach. "So are you actually on good terms with the Queen of Adarlan? You didn't really . . . make an effort to start off that way."

The princess nodded, lifting her chin. "You know that the situation between our countries isn't pleasant right now. While I might have been a little distant with Georgina at first, I realized that it might be in Eyllwe's best interest if I make more of an effort. So, I've been speaking with her for some weeks now, hoping to make her aware of how we might improve our relations. I think inviting me tonight is a sign that I might be making some progress." And, Celaena realized, through Georgina, Nehemia would also get the King of Adarlan's ear.

Celaena bit her lip, but then quickly smiled. "I'm sure your parents are pleased." They turned down a hall and the sound of barking dogs filled the air. "Where *are* we?"

"The kennels." Nehemia beamed. "The prince showed me the pups yesterday—though I think he was just looking for an excuse to get out of his mother's court for a while."

It was bad enough they were walking together without Chaol, but to enter the kennels . . . "Are we allowed to be here?"

Nehemia straightened. "I am Princess of Eyllwe," she said. "I can go wherever I please."

Celaena followed the princess through a large wooden door. Wrinkling her nose at the sudden smell, the assassin walked past cages and stalls filled with dogs of many different breeds.

Some were so large that they came up to her hip, while others had legs the length of her hand with bodies as long as her arm. The breeds were all fascinating and beautiful, but the sleek hounds aroused awe within her breast. Their arched undersides and slender, long legs were full of grace and speed; they did not yap as the other dogs did, but sat perfectly still and watched her with dark, wise eyes.

"Are these all hunting dogs?" Celaena asked, but Nehemia had disappeared. She could hear her voice, and the voice of another, and then saw a hand extended from within a stall to beckon Celaena inside. The assassin hurried to the pen and looked down over the gate.

Dorian Havilliard smiled at her as Nehemia took a seat. "Why, hello, Lady Lillian," he purred, and set aside a brown-and-gold puppy. "I didn't expect to see *you* here. Though with Nehemia's passion for hunting, I can't say I'm surprised she finally dragged you along."

Celaena stared at the four dogs. "These are the mutts?"

Dorian picked one up and stroked its head. "Pity, isn't it? I still can't resist their charm."

Carefully, watching Nehemia laugh as two dogs leapt upon her and buried her beneath tongues and wagging tails, the assassin opened the pen door and slipped inside.

Nehemia pointed to the corner. "Is that dog sick?" she asked. There was a fifth pup, a bit larger than the others, and its coat was a silky, silvery gold that shimmered in the shadows. It opened its dark eyes, as if it knew it was being spoken about, and watched them. It was a beautiful animal, and had Celaena not known better, she would have thought it purebred.

"It's not sick," Dorian said. "It just has a foul disposition. It won't come near anyone—human or canine."

"With good reason," Celaena said, stepping over the legs of the Crown Prince and nearing the fifth pup. "Why should it touch someone like you?"

"If it won't respond to humans, then it will have to be killed," Dorian said offhandedly, and a spark went through Celaena.

"Kill it? *Kill* it? For what reason? What did it do to you?"

"It won't make a suitable pet, which is what all of these dogs will become."

"So you'd kill it because of its temperament? It can't help being that way!" She looked around. "Where's its mother? Perhaps it needs her."

"Its mother only sees them to nurse and for a few hours of

socialization. I usually raise these dogs for racing and hunting—not for cuddling."

"It's cruel to keep it from its mother!" The assassin reached into the shadow and scooped the puppy into her arms. She held it against her chest. "I won't let you harm it."

"If its spirit is strange," Nehemia offered, "it would be a burden."

"A burden to whom?"

"It's nothing to be upset about," Dorian said. "Plenty of dogs are painlessly laid to rest each day. I don't see why *you* would object to that."

"Well, don't kill this one!" she said. "Let me keep it—if only so you don't kill it."

Dorian observed her. "If it upsets you so much, I won't have it killed. I'll arrange for a home, and I'll even ask for your approval before I make a final decision."

"You'd do that?"

"What's the dog's life to me? If it pleases you, then it shall happen."

Her face burned as he rose to his feet, standing close. "You—you promise?"

He put a hand on his heart. "I swear on my crown that the pup shall live."

She was suddenly aware of how near to touching they were. "Thank you."

Nehemia watched them from the floor, her brows raised, until one of her personal guards appeared at the gate. "It's time to go, Princess," he said in Eyllwe. "You must dress for your evening with the queen." The princess stood, pushing past the bouncing puppies.

"Do you want to walk with me?" Nehemia said in the common tongue to Celaena.

Celaena nodded and opened the gate for them. Shutting the gate, she looked back at the Crown Prince. "Well? Aren't you coming with us?"

He slumped down into the pen, and the puppies immediately leapt on him. "Perhaps I'll see you later tonight."

"If you're lucky," Celaena purred, and walked away. She smiled to herself as they strode through the castle.

Eventually Nehemia turned to her. "Do you like him?"

Celaena made a face. "Of course not. Why would I?"

"You converse easily. It seems as if you have . . . a connection."

"A connection?" Celaena choked on the word. "I just enjoy teasing him."

"It's not a crime if you consider him handsome. I'll admit I judged him wrong; I thought him to be a pompous, selfish idiot, but he's not so bad."

"He's a Havilliard."

"My mother was the daughter of a chief who sought to overthrow my grandfather."

"We're both silly. It's nothing."

"He seems to take great interest in you."

Celaena's head whipped around, her eyes full of long-forgotten fury that made her belly ache and twist. "I would sooner cut out my own heart than love a Havilliard," she snarled.

They completed their walk in silence, and when they parted ways, Celaena quickly wished Nehemia a pleasant evening before striding to her part of the castle.

The few guards that followed her remained a respectful distance away—a distance that grew greater each day. Based on Chaol's orders? Night had recently fallen, and the sky remained a deep blue, staining the snow piled upon the panes of the windows. She could easily walk right out of the castle, stock up on supplies in Rifthold, and be on a ship to the south by morning.

Celaena stopped at a window, leaning in close to the panes. The guards stopped, too, and said nothing as they waited. The coldness from outside seeped in, kissing her face. Would they expect her to go south? Perhaps going north would be the unexpected choice; no one went north in winter unless they had a death wish.

Something shifted in the reflection of the window, and she whirled as she beheld the man standing behind her.

But Cain didn't smile at her, not in that mocking way. Instead, he panted, his mouth opening and closing like a fish wrenched from water. His dark eyes were wide, and he had a hand around his enormous throat. Hopefully, he was choking to death.

"Is something wrong?" she asked sweetly, leaning against the wall. He glanced from side to side, at the guards, at the window, before his eyes snapped to hers. His grip on his throat tightened, as if to silence the words that fought to come out, and the ebony ring on his finger gleamed dully. Even though it should have been impossible, he seemed to have packed on an additional ten pounds of muscle in the past few days. In fact, every time she saw him, Cain seemed bigger and bigger.

Her brows knotted, and she uncrossed her arms. "Cain," she said, but he took off down the hall like a jackrabbit, faster than he should have any ability to run. He peered a few times over his shoulder—not at her, or the confused and murmuring guards, but at something beyond.

Celaena waited until the sounds of his fleeing footsteps faded, then hurried back to her own rooms. She sent messages to Nox and Pelor, not explaining why, but just telling them to stay in their chambers that night and not open the door for anyone.

33

Kaltain pinched her cheeks as she emerged from the dressing room. Her servants sprayed perfume, and the young woman gulped down sugar water before putting her hand on the door. She'd been in the midst of smoking a pipe when Duke Perrington had been announced. She'd fled into the dressing room and changed her clothes, hoping the scent wouldn't linger. If he found out about the opium, she could just blame it on the horrible headaches she'd been having lately. Kaltain passed through her bedroom into the foyer, and then into the sitting room.

He looked ready for battle, as always. "Your Grace," she said, curtsying. The world was foggy around the edges, and her body felt heavy. He kissed her hand when she offered it, his lips soggy against her skin. Their eyes met as he looked up from her hand, and a piece of the world slipped away. How far would she go to secure her position at Dorian's side?

"I hope I didn't disturb you," he said, releasing her hand. The walls of the room appeared, and then the floor and the ceiling, and she had the distinct feeling that she was trapped in a box, a lovely cage filled with tapestries and cushions.

"I was only napping, milord," she said, sitting down. He sniffed, and Kaltain would have felt immensely nervous were it not for the drug curling around her mind. "To what do I owe the pleasure of this unexpected visit?"

"I wished to inquire after you—I didn't see you at dinner." Perrington crossed his arms—arms that looked capable of crushing her skull.

"I was indisposed." She resisted the urge to rest her too-heavy head on the couch.

He said something to her, but she found that her ears had stopped hearing. His skin seemed to harden and glaze over, and his eyes became unforgiving marble orbs. Even the thinning hair was frozen in stone. She gaped as the white mouth continued to move, revealing a throat of carved marble. "I'm sorry," she said. "I'm not feeling well."

"Shall I fetch you water?" The duke stood. "Or shall I go?"

"No!" she said, almost crying out. Her heart twitched. "What I mean is—I'm well enough to enjoy your company, but you must forgive my absentmindedness."

"I wouldn't call you absentminded, Lady Kaltain," he said, sitting down. "You're one of the cleverest women I've met. His Highness told me the same thing yesterday."

Kaltain's spine snapped and straightened. She saw Dorian's face and the crown that sat upon his head. "The prince said that—about me?"

The duke put a hand on her knee, stroking it with his thumb. "Of course, then Lady Lillian interrupted before he could say more."

Her head spun. "Why was she with him?"

"I don't know. I wish it were otherwise."

She must do something, something to stop this. The girl moved fast—too fast for her maneuvering. Lillian had snared the Crown Prince in her net, and now Kaltain must cut him free. Perrington could do it. He could make Lillian disappear and never be found. No—Lillian was a lady, and a man with as much honor as Perrington would never harm one of noble birth. Or would he? Skeletons danced in circles around her head. But what if he thought Lillian weren't a lady . . . ? Her headache flared to life with a sudden burst that sucked the air from her lungs.

"I had the same reaction," she said, rubbing her temple. "It's hard to believe someone as disreputable as the Lady Lillian won the heart of the prince." Maybe the headaches would stop once she was at Dorian's side. "Perhaps it would do some good if someone spoke to His Highness."

"Disreputable?"

"I heard from someone that her background is not as . . . pure as it should be."

"What have you heard?" Perrington demanded.

Kaltain played with a jewel hanging from her bracelet. "I didn't get specifics, but some of the nobility don't believe her to be a worthy companion of anyone in this court. I'd like to learn more about the Lady Lillian, wouldn't you? It's our duty as loyal subjects of the crown to protect our prince from such forces."

"Indeed it is," the duke said quietly.

Something wild and foreign issued a cry within her, shattering through the pain in her head, and thoughts of poppies and cages faded away.

She must do what was necessary to save the crown—and her future.

Celaena looked up from an ancient book of Wyrdmark theories as the door creaked open, the hinges squealing loud enough to wake the dead. Her heart skipped a beat, and she tried to appear as casual as possible. But it was not Dorian Havilliard who entered, nor was it a ferocious creature.

The door finished opening and Nehemia, clad in a gold-worked wonder, stood before her. She didn't look at Celaena, nor did she move as she stood in the doorway. Her eyes were upon the floor, and rivers of kohl ran down her cheeks.

"Nehemia?" Celaena asked, getting to her feet. "What happened to the play?"

Nehemia's shoulders rose and fell. Slowly, she lifted her head, revealing red-rimmed eyes. "I—I didn't know where else to go," she said in Eyllwe.

Celaena found breathing a bit difficult as she asked, "What happened?"

It was then that Celaena noticed the piece of paper in Nehemia's hands. It trembled in her grasp.

"They massacred them," Nehemia whispered, her eyes wide. She shook her head, as if she were denying her own words.

Celaena went still. "Who?"

Nehemia let out a strangled sob, and a part of Celaena broke at the agony in the sound.

"A legion of Adarlan's army captured five hundred Eyllwe rebels hiding on the border of Oakwald Forest and the Stone Marshes." Tears dripped from Nehemia's cheeks and onto her white dress. She crumpled the piece of paper in her hand. "My father says they were to go to Calaculla as prisoners of war. But some of the rebels tried to escape on the journey, and . . ." Nehemia breathed hard, fighting to get the words out. "And the soldiers killed them all as punishment, even the children."

Celaena's dinner rose in her throat. Five hundred—butchered.

Celaena became aware of Nehemia's personal guards standing in the doorway, their eyes gleaming. How many of the rebels had been people that they knew—that Nehemia had somehow helped and protected?

"What is the point in being a princess of Eyllwe if I cannot help my people?" Nehemia said. "How can I call myself their princess, when such things happen?"

"I'm so sorry," Celaena whispered. As if those words broke the spell that had been holding the princess in place, Nehemia rushed into her arms. Her gold jewelry pressed hard into Celaena's skin. Nehemia wept. Unable to say anything, the assassin simply held her—for as long as it took for the pain to ease.

34

Celaena sat by a window in her bedroom, watching the snow dance in the night air. Nehemia had long since returned to her own rooms, tears dried and shoulders squared once more. The clock chimed eleven and Celaena stretched, but then stopped as pain seized her stomach. She bent over, focusing on her breathing, and waited for the cramp to pass. She'd been like this for over an hour now, and she pulled her blanket tighter around herself, the heat of the roaring fire not adequately reaching her seat by the window. Thankfully, Philippa entered, extending a cup of tea.

"Here, child," she said. "This will help." She placed it on the table beside the assassin and rested a hand on the armchair. "Pity what happened to those Eyllwe rebels," she said quietly enough that no listening ears might hear. "I can't imagine what the princess must be feeling." Celaena felt anger bubble alongside the pain in her stomach. "She's fortunate to have a good friend like you, though."

Celaena touched Philippa's hand. "Thank you." She grabbed her teacup and hissed, almost dropping it into her lap as the scalding-hot cup bit into her hand.

"Careful now." Philippa chuckled. "I didn't know assassins could be so clumsy. If you need anything, send word. I've had my fair share of monthly pains." Philippa ruffled Celaena's hair and left. Celaena would have thanked her again, but another wave of cramping took over and she leaned forward as the door closed.

Her weight gain over the past three and a half months had allowed for her monthly cycles to return after near-starvation in Endovier had made them vanish. Celaena groaned. How was she going to train like this? The duel was four weeks away.

The snowflakes sparkled and shimmered beyond the glass panes of the window, twirling and weaving as they flew to the ground in a waltz that was beyond human comprehension.

How could Elena expect her to defeat some evil in this castle, when there was so much more of it out there? What was any of this compared to what was occurring in other kingdoms? As close as Endovier and Calaculla, even? The door to her bedroom opened, and someone approached.

"I heard about Nehemia." It was Chaol.

"What are you—isn't it late for you to be here?" she asked, pulling the blankets tight.

"I—are you sick?"

"I'm indisposed."

"Because of what happened to those rebels?"

Didn't he get it? Celaena grimaced. "No. I'm *truly* feeling unwell."

"It makes me sick, too," Chaol murmured, glaring at the floor. "All of it. And after seeing Endovier . . ." He rubbed his face, as if he could clear away the memories of it. "Five hundred people," he whispered. Stunned at what he was admitting, she could only watch.

"Listen," he began, and started to pace. "I know that I'm sometimes aloof with you, and I know you complain about it to Dorian, but—" He turned to her. "It's a good thing that you befriended the princess, and I appreciate your honesty and unwavering friendship with her. I know there are rumors about Nehemia's connection to the rebels in Eyllwe, but . . . but I'd like to think that if my country was conquered, I would stop at nothing to win back my people's freedom, too."

She would have replied were it not for the deep pain that wrapped around her lower spine, and the sudden churning in her stomach.

"I might—" he started, looking at the window. "I might have been wrong." The world began to spin and tilt, and Celaena closed her eyes. She'd always had horrible cramping, usually accompanied by nausea. But she wouldn't vomit. Not right now.

"Chaol," she began, putting a hand over her mouth as nausea swelled and took control.

"It's just that I take great pride in my job," he continued.

"Chaol," she said again. Oh, she was going to vomit.

"And you're Adarlan's Assassin. But I was wondering if—if you wanted to—"

"*Chaol,*" she warned. As he pivoted, Celaena vomited all over the floor.

He made a disgusted noise, jumping back a foot. Tears sprang up as the bitter, sharp taste filled her mouth. She hung over her knees, letting drool and bile spill on the floor.

"Are you—by the Wyrd, you're really sick, aren't you?" He called for a servant, helping her from the chair. The world was clearer now. What had he been asking? "Come on. Let's get you into bed."

"I'm not ill like *that*," she groaned. He sat her on the bed, peeling back the blanket. A servant entered, frowning at the mess on the floor, and shouted for help.

"Then in what way?"

"I, uh . . ." Her face was so hot she thought it would melt onto the floor. *Oh, you idiot!* "My monthly cycles finally came back."

His face suddenly matched hers and he stepped away, dragging a hand through his short brown hair. "I—if . . . Then I'll take my leave," he stammered, and bowed. Celaena raised an eyebrow, and then, despite herself, smiled as he left the room as quickly as his feet could go without running, tripping slightly in the doorway as he staggered into the rooms beyond.

Celaena looked at the servants cleaning. "I'm so sorry," she started, but they waved her off. Embarrassed and aching, the assassin climbed farther onto her bed and nestled beneath the covers, hoping sleep would soon come.

But sleep wouldn't soon come, and a while later, the door opened again, and someone laughed. "I intercepted Chaol, and he informed me of your 'condition.' You'd think a man in his position wouldn't be so squeamish, especially after examining all of those corpses."

Celaena opened an eye and frowned as Dorian sat on her bed. "I'm in a state of absolute agony and I can't be bothered."

"It can't be that bad," he said, fishing a deck of cards from his jacket. "Want to play?"

"I already told you that I don't feel well."

"You look fine to me." He skillfully shuffled the deck. "Just one game."

"Don't you pay people to entertain you?"

He glowered, breaking the deck. "You should be honored by my company."

"I'd be honored if you would *leave*."

"For someone who relies on my good graces, you're very bold."

"Bold? I've barely begun." Lying on her side, she curled her knees to her chest.

He laughed, pocketing the deck of cards. "Your new canine companion is doing well, if you wish to know."

She moaned into her pillow. "Go away. I feel like dying."

"No fair maiden should die alone," he said, putting a hand on hers. "Shall I read to you in your final moments? What story would you like?"

She snatched her hand back. "How about the story of the idiotic prince who won't leave the assassin alone?"

"Oh! I *love* that story! It has such a happy ending, too—why, the assassin was really feigning her illness in order to get the prince's attention! Who would have guessed it? Such a clever girl. And the bedroom scene is *so* lovely—it's worth reading through all of their ceaseless banter!"

"Out! Out! Out! Leave me be and go womanize someone else!" She grabbed a book and chucked it at him. He caught it before it broke his nose, and her eyes widened. "I didn't mean—that wasn't an attack! It was a joke—I didn't mean to actually hurt you, Your Highness," she said in a jumble.

"I'd hope that Adarlan's Assassin would choose to attack me in a more *dignified* manner. At least with a sword or a knife, though preferably not in the back."

She clutched her belly and bent over. Sometimes she hated being a woman.

"It's Dorian, by the way. Not 'Your Highness.'"

"Very well."

"Say it."

"Say what?"

"Say my name. Say, 'Very well, Dorian.'"

She rolled her eyes. "If it pleases Your Magnanimous Holiness, I shall call you by your first name."

"'Magnanimous Holiness'? Oh, I like that one." A ghost of a smile appeared on her face, and Dorian looked down at the book. "This isn't one of the books that *I* sent you! I don't even *own* books like these!"

She laughed weakly and took the tea from the servant as she

approached. "Of course you don't, *Dorian*. I had the maids send for a copy today."

"*Sunset's Passions*," he read, and opened the book to a random page to read aloud. "'His hands gently caressed her ivory, silky br—'" His eyes widened. "By the Wyrd! Do you actually *read* this rubbish? What happened to *Symbols and Power* and *Eyllwe Customs and Culture*?"

She finished her drink, the ginger tea easing her stomach. "You may borrow it when I'm done. If you read it, your literary experience will be complete. And," she added with a coy smile, "it will give you some creative ideas of things to do with your lady friends."

He hissed through his teeth. "I will *not* read this."

She took the book from his hands, leaning back. "Then I suppose you're just like Chaol."

"Chaol?" he asked, falling into the trap. "You asked *Chaol* to read this?"

"He refused, of course," she lied. "He said it wasn't right for him to read this sort of material if I gave it to him."

Dorian snatched the book from her hands. "Give me that, you demon-woman. I'll not have *you* matching us against each other." He glanced once more at the novel, then turned it over, concealing the title. She smiled, and resumed watching the falling snow. It was blisteringly cold now, and even the fire could not warm the blasts of wind that crept through the cracks of her balcony doors. She felt Dorian watching her—and not in the cautious way that Chaol sometimes watched her. Rather, Dorian just seemed to be watching her because he *enjoyed* watching her.

And she enjoyed watching him, too.

Dorian didn't realize he'd been transfixed by her until she straightened and demanded, "What are you staring at?"

"You're beautiful," Dorian said before he could think.

"Don't be stupid."

"Did I offend you?" His blood pumped through him in a strange rhythm.

"No," she said, and quickly faced the window. Dorian watched her face turn redder and redder. He'd never known an attractive woman for so long without courting her—save for Kaltain. And he couldn't deny that he was aching to learn what Celaena's lips felt like, what her bare skin smelled like, how she'd react to the touch of his fingers along her body.

The week surrounding Yulemas was a time of relaxation, a time to celebrate the carnal pleasures that kept one warm on a winter's night. Women wore their hair down; some even refused to don a corset. It was a holiday to feast on the fruits of the harvest and those of the flesh. Naturally, he looked forward to it every year. But now . . .

Now he had a sinking feeling in his stomach. How could he celebrate when word had just arrived of what his father's soldiers had done to those Eyllwe rebels? They hadn't spared a single life. Five hundred people—all dead. How could he ever look Nehemia in the face again? And how could he someday rule a country whose soldiers had been trained to have so little compassion for human life?

Dorian's mouth went dry. Celaena was from Terrasen—another conquered country, and his father's first conquest. It was a miracle Celaena bothered to acknowledge his existence—or perhaps she'd spent so long in Adarlan that she'd stopped caring. Somehow, Dorian didn't think that was the case—not when she had the three giant scars on her back to forever remind her of his father's brutality.

"Is there something the matter?" she asked. Cautiously; curiously. As if she cared. He took a deep breath and walked to the window, unable to look at her. The glass was cold beneath his hand, and he watched the snowflakes come crashing down to earth.

"You must hate me," he murmured. "Hate me and my court for our frivolity and mindlessness when so many horrible things are going on outside of this city. I heard about those butchered rebels, and I—I'm ashamed," he said, leaning his head against the window. He heard her rise and then slump into a chair. The words came out in a river, one flowing after the other, and he couldn't stop himself from speaking. "I understand why you have such ease when killing my kind. And I don't blame you for it."

"Dorian," she said gently.

The world outside the castle was dark. "I know you'll never tell me," he continued, voicing what he had wanted to say for some time. "But I know something terrible happened to you when you were young, something perhaps of my father's own doing. You have a right to hate Adarlan for seizing control of Terrasen as it did—for taking all of the countries, and the country of your friend."

He swallowed, his eyes stinging. "You won't believe me. But . . . I don't want to be a part of that. I can't call myself a man when I allow my father to encourage such unforgivable atrocities. Yet even if I pleaded for clemency on behalf of the conquered kingdoms, he wouldn't listen. Not in this world. This is the world where I only picked you to be my Champion because I knew it would annoy my father." She shook her head, but he kept going. "But if I had refused to sponsor a Champion, my father would have seen it as a sign of dissent, and I'm not yet enough of a man to stand against him like that. So I chose Adarlan's Assassin to be my Champion, because the choice of my Champion was the only choice I had."

Yes, it was all clear now. "Life shouldn't be like this," he said, their eyes meeting as he gestured at the room. "And . . . and the *world* shouldn't be like this."

The assassin was silent, listening to the throbbing of her heart before she spoke. "I don't hate you," she said in little more than a whisper. He dropped into the chair across from her and put his head in a hand. He seemed remarkably lonely. "And I don't think you're like them. I'm—I'm sorry if I've hurt you. I'm joking most of the time."

"Hurt me?" he said. "*You* haven't hurt me! You've just . . . you've made things a little more entertaining."

She cocked her head. "Just a little?"

"Maybe a tad more than that." He stretched out his legs. "Ah, if only you could come to the Yulemas ball with me. Be grateful you can't attend."

"Why can't I attend? And what's the Yulemas ball?"

He groaned. "Nothing all that special. Just a masked ball that happens to be on Yulemas. And I think you know exactly why you can't come."

"You and Chaol really delight in ruining any fun I might have, don't you? I *like* attending parties."

"When you're my father's Champion, you can attend all the balls you want."

She made a face. He wanted to tell her then that if he could, he would have asked her to go with him; that he wanted to spend time with her, that he thought of her even when they were apart; but he knew she would have laughed.

The clock chimed midnight. "I should probably go," he said, stretching his arms. "I have a day of council meetings to look forward to tomorrow, and I don't think Duke Perrington will be pleased if I'm half-asleep for all of them."

Celaena smirked. "Be sure to give the duke my warmest regards." There was no way she'd forgotten how the duke had treated her that first day in Endovier. Dorian hadn't forgotten it, either. And the thought of the duke treating her like that again made him burn with cold rage.

Without thinking, he leaned down and kissed her cheek. She stiffened as his mouth touched her skin, and though the kiss was brief, he breathed in the scent of her. Pulling away was surprisingly hard. "Rest well, Celaena," he said.

"Good night, Dorian." As he left, he wondered why she suddenly looked so sad, and why she'd pronounced his name not with tenderness, but with resignation.

Celaena stared at the moonlight as it streamed across the ceiling. A masked ball on Yulemas! Even if it was the most corrupt and ostentatious court in Erilea, it sounded dreadfully romantic. And of course, she wasn't allowed to go. She let out a long sigh through her nose and tucked her hands beneath her head. Was that what Chaol had wanted to ask her before she vomited—a true invitation to the ball?

She shook her head. No. The last thing he'd ever do would be to invite her to a royal ball. Besides, both of them had more important things to worry about. Like whoever was killing the Champions. Perhaps she should have sent word to him about Cain's strange behavior earlier that afternoon.

Celaena closed her eyes and smiled. She could think of no nicer Yulemas gift than for Cain to be found dead the next morning. Still, as the clock marked the passing hours, Celaena kept her vigil—waiting, wondering what truly lurked in the castle, and unable to stop thinking of those five hundred dead Eyllwe rebels, buried in some unmarked grave.

35

The next evening, Chaol Westfall stood on the second floor of the castle, looking over the courtyard. Below him, two figures slowly wove through the hedges. Celaena's white cloak made her easy to spot, and Dorian could always be noticed by the empty circle of space around him.

He should be down there, a foot behind, watching them, making sure she didn't seize Dorian and use him to escape. Logic and years of experience screamed at him to be with them, even though six guards trailed them. She was deceitful, cunning, vicious.

But he couldn't make his feet move.

With each day, he felt the barriers melting. He *let* them melt. Because of her genuine laugh, because he caught her one afternoon sleeping with her face in the middle of a book, because he knew that she would win.

She was a criminal—a prodigy at killing, a Queen of the

Underworld—and yet . . . yet she was just a girl, sent at seventeen to Endovier.

It made him sick every time he thought about it. He'd been training with the guards at seventeen, but he'd still lived here, still had a roof over his head and good food and friends.

Dorian had been in the middle of courting Rosamund when he was that age, not caring about anything.

But she—at *seventeen*—had gone to a death camp. And survived.

He wasn't sure if *he* could survive Endovier, let alone during the winter months. He'd never been whipped, never seen anyone die. He'd never been cold and starving.

Celaena laughed at something Dorian said. She'd survived Endovier, and yet could still laugh.

While it terrified him to see her down there, a hand's breadth from Dorian's unprotected throat, what terrified him even more was that he trusted her. And he didn't know what that meant about himself.

Celaena walked between the hedges, and couldn't help the smile that spread across her face. They walked closely, but not close enough to touch. Dorian had found her just moments after dinner and invited her for a walk. In fact, he'd showed up so quickly after the servants cleared away her food that she might have thought he'd been waiting outside.

Of course, it was due entirely to the cold that she longed to link arms with him and absorb his warmth. The white, fur-lined cloak did little to keep the frigid air from freezing all of her. She could only imagine how Nehemia would react to such temperatures. But after learning about the fate of those rebels, the princess was spending most of her time in her rooms, and had declined Celaena's repeated offers to go for walks.

It had been over three weeks since her last encounter with Elena, and she hadn't seen or heard her at all, despite the three Tests she'd had, the most exciting of which being an obstacle course, which she passed with only a few minor scratches and bruises. Unfortunately, Pelor hadn't done so well, and had been sent home at long last. But he'd been lucky: three other competitors had died. All found in forgotten hallways; all mutilated beyond recognition. Even Celaena had taken to jumping at every strange sound.

There were only six of them left now: Cain, Grave, Nox, a soldier, and Renault, a vicious mercenary who'd stepped up to replace Verin as Cain's right-hand man. Not surprisingly, Renault's favorite new activity was taunting Celaena.

She shoved thoughts of the murders aside as they strode past a fountain and she caught Dorian giving her an admiring glance from the corner of his eye. Of course, she hadn't been thinking of Dorian when she chose such a fine lavender gown to wear tonight, or when she made sure her hair was so carefully arranged, or that her white gloves were spotless.

"What to do now?" Dorian said. "We've walked twice around the garden."

"Don't you have princely duties to attend to?" Celaena winced as a gust of icy wind blew back her hood and froze her ears. When she recovered the hood, she found Dorian staring at her throat. "What?" she asked, pulling her cloak tightly around her.

"You always wear that necklace," he said. "Is it another gift?" Though she wore gloves, he glanced at her hand—where the amethyst ring always sat—and the spark died from his eyes.

"No." She covered the amulet with her hand. "I found it in my jewelry box and liked the look of it, you insufferably territorial man."

"It's very old looking. Been robbing the royal coffer, have you?" He winked, but she didn't feel any warmth behind it.

"No," she repeated sharply. Even though a necklace wouldn't protect her from the murderer, and even though Elena had some agenda she was being cagey about, Celaena wouldn't take it off. Its presence somehow comforted her in the long hours she sat up, watching her door.

He continued staring at her hand until she lowered it from her throat. He studied the necklace. "When I was a boy, I used to read tales about the dawn of Adarlan; Gavin was my hero. I must have read every legend regarding the war with Erawan."

How can he be that smart? He can't *have figured it out so quickly.* She tried her best to look innocently interested. "And?"

"Elena, First Queen of Adarlan, had a magical amulet. In the battle with the Dark Lord, Gavin and Elena found themselves defenseless against him. He was about to kill the princess when a spirit appeared and gave her the necklace. And when she put it on, Erawan couldn't harm her. She saw the Dark Lord for what he was and called him by his true name. It surprised him so much that he became distracted, and Gavin slew him." Dorian looked to the ground. "They called her necklace the Eye of Elena; it's been lost for centuries."

How strange it was to hear Dorian, son of the man who had banished and outlawed all traces of magic, talking about powerful amulets. Still, she laughed as best she could. "And you think this trinket is the Eye? I think it'd be dust by now."

"I suppose not," he said, and vigorously rubbed his arms for warmth. "But I've seen a few illustrations of the Eye, and your necklace looks like it. Perhaps it's a replica."

"Perhaps." She quickly found another subject. "When's your brother arriving?"

He looked skyward. "I'm lucky. We received a letter this morning that snows in the mountains prevented Hollin from coming home. He's stuck at school until after his spring term, and he's beside himself."

"Your poor mother," Celaena said, half-smiling.

"She'll probably send servants to deliver his Yulemas presents, regardless of the storm."

Celaena didn't hear him, and though they talked for a good hour afterward meandering through the grounds, she couldn't get her heart to calm. Elena had to have known someone would recognize her amulet—and if this was the real thing . . . The king could kill her on the spot for wearing not only an heirloom of his house, but something of power.

Yet again, she could only wonder what Elena's motives actually were.

Celaena glanced from her book to the tapestry on the wall. The chest of drawers remained where she'd shoved it in front of the passageway. She shook her head and returned to her book. Though she scanned the lines, none of the words registered.

What did Elena want with her? Dead queens usually didn't come back to give orders to the living. Celaena clenched her book. It wasn't like she wasn't fulfilling Elena's command to win, either—she would have fought this hard to become the King's Champion anyway. And as for finding and defeating the evil in the castle . . . well, now that it seemed tied to who was murdering the Champions, how could she *not* try to figure out where it was coming from?

A door shut somewhere inside her rooms, and Celaena jumped, the book flying from her hands. She grabbed the brass candlestick beside her bed, ready to leap off the mattress, but lowered it as Philippa's humming filtered through the doors to her bedroom. She groaned as she climbed out of the warmth of her bed to retrieve her book.

It had fallen under the bed, and Celaena knelt upon the icy floor, straining to reach the book. She couldn't feel it anywhere, so she grabbed the candle. She saw the book immediately, tucked against the back wall, but as her fingers grappled onto the cover, a glimmer of candlelight traced a white line across the floor beneath her bed.

Celaena yanked the book back to her and stood with a jolt. Her hands trembled as she pushed the bed out of position, her feet slipping on the half-frozen floor. It moved slowly, but eventually, she had shifted it enough to see what had been sketched on the floor beneath.

Everything inside of her turned to ice.

Wyrdmarks.

Dozens of Wyrdmarks had been drawn onto the floor with chalk. They formed a giant spiral, with a large mark in its center. Celaena stumbled back, slamming into her dresser.

What was this? She ran a shaking hand through her hair, staring at the center mark.

She'd seen that mark. It had been etched on one side of Verin's body.

Her stomach rising in her throat, she rushed to her nightstand and grabbed the pitcher of water atop it. Without a thought, she tossed the water onto the marks, then raced to her bathing chamber to draw more water. When the water had finished loosening the chalk, she took a towel and scrubbed the floor until her back ached and her legs and hands were frozen.

Then, only then, did she throw on a pair of pants and a tunic and head out the door.

Thankfully, the guards didn't say anything when she asked them to escort her to the library at midnight. They remained in the main room of the library as she set off through the stacks, heading toward the musty, forgotten alcove where she'd found the majority of the books on the Wyrdmarks. She couldn't walk fast enough, and kept looking over her shoulder.

Was she next? What did any of it mean? She wrung her fingers. She rounded a corner, not ten stacks from the alcove, and came to a halt.

Nehemia, seated at a small desk, stared at her with wide eyes.

Celaena put a hand on her racing heart. "Damn," she said. "You gave me a fright!"

Nehemia smiled, but not very well. Celaena cocked her head as she approached the table. "What are you doing here?" Nehemia demanded in Eyllwe.

"I couldn't sleep." She shifted her eyes to the princess's book. That wasn't the book they used during their lessons. No, it was a thick, aging book, crammed with dense lines of text. "What are you reading?"

Nehemia slammed the book shut and stood. "Nothing."

Celaena observed her face; her lips were pursed, and the princess lifted her chin. "I thought you couldn't read at that level yet."

Nehemia tucked the book into the crook of her arm. "Then you're like every ignorant fool in this castle, Lillian," she said with perfect pronunciation in the common tongue. Not giving her a chance to reply, the princess strode away.

Celaena watched her go. It didn't make sense. Nehemia *couldn't* read books that advanced, not when she still stumbled through lines of text. And Nehemia never spoke with that kind of flawless accent, and—

In the shadows behind the desk, a piece of paper had fallen between the wood and the stone wall. Easing it out, Celaena unfolded the crumpled paper.

She whirled around, to the direction where Nehemia had disappeared. Her throat constricting, Celaena tucked the piece of paper into her pocket and hurried back toward the great room, the Wyrdmark drawn on the paper burning a hole in her clothing.

Celaena rushed down a staircase, then strode along a hallway lined with books.

No, Nehemia couldn't have played her like that—Nehemia wouldn't have lied day after day about how little she knew. Nehemia had been the one to tell her that the etchings in the garden were Wyrdmarks. She knew what they were—she'd *warned* her to stay away from the Wyrdmarks, again and again. Because Nehemia was her friend—because

Nehemia had wept when her people had been murdered, because she'd come to *her* for comfort.

But Nehemia came from a conquered kingdom. And the King of Adarlan had ripped the crown off her father's head and stripped his title from him. And the people of Eyllwe were being kidnapped in the night and sold into slavery, right along with the rebels that rumor claimed Nehemia supported so fiercely. And five hundred Eyllwe citizens had just been butchered.

Celaena's eyes stung as she spotted the guards loitering in armchairs in the great room.

Nehemia had every reason to deceive them, to plot against them. To tear apart this stupid competition and send everyone into a tizzy. Who better to target than the criminals living here? No one would miss them, but the fear would seep into the castle.

But why would Nehemia plot against *her*?

36

Days passed without seeing Nehemia, and Celaena kept her mouth shut about the incident to Chaol or Dorian or anyone who visited her chambers. She couldn't confront Nehemia—not without more concrete proof, not without ruining everything. So she spent her spare time researching the Wyrdmarks, desperate for a way to decipher them, to find those symbols, to learn what it all meant, and how it connected to the killer and the killer's beast. Amidst her worrying, another Test passed without incident or embarrassment—though she couldn't say the same for the soldier who'd been sent home—and she kept up her intense training with Chaol and the other Champions. There were five of them left now. The final Test was three days away, and the duel two days after that.

Celaena awoke on Yulemas morning and relished the silence.

There was something inherently peaceful about the day, despite the darkness of her encounter with Nehemia. For the moment, the whole castle had quieted to hear the falling snow. Frost laced each windowpane, a fire already crackled in the fireplace, and shadows of snowflakes drifted across the floor. It was as peaceful and lovely a winter morning as she could imagine. She wouldn't ruin it with thoughts of Nehemia, or of the duel, or of the ball she wasn't allowed to attend tonight. No, it was Yulemas morning, and she would be happy.

It didn't feel like a holiday to celebrate the darkness that gave birth to the spring light, nor did it feel like a holiday to celebrate the birth of the Goddess's firstborn son. It was simply a day when people were more courteous, looked twice at a beggar in the street, remembered that love was a living thing. Celaena smiled and rolled over. But something got in her way. It was crinkly and harsh against her face, and had the distinct odor of—

"Candy!" A large paper bag sat on a pillow, and she found that it was filled with all sorts of confectionary goodies. There was no note, not even a name scribbled on the bag. With a shrug and glowing eyes, Celaena pulled out a handful of sweets. Oh, how she *adored* candy!

Celaena issued a jolly laugh and crammed some of the candy into her mouth. One by one, she chewed through the assortment, and she closed her eyes and breathed in deeply as she tasted all of the flavors and textures.

When she finally stopped chewing, her jaw ached. She emptied the contents of the bag onto the bed, ignoring the dunes of sugar that poured out with it, and surveyed the land of goodness before her.

All of her favorites were there: chocolate-covered gummies, chocolate almond bark, berry-shaped chews, gem–shaped hard sugar, peanut brittle, plain brittle, sugarlace, frosted red licorice, and, most importantly, chocolate. She popped a hazelnut truffle into her mouth.

"Someone," she said in between chews, "is *very* good to me."

She paused to examine the bag again. Who had sent it? Maybe Dorian. Certainly not Nehemia or Chaol. Nor the Frost Faeries that delivered presents to good children. They'd stopped coming to her when she'd first drawn blood from another human being. Maybe Nox. He liked her well enough.

"*Miss Celaena!*" Philippa exclaimed from the doorway, gaping.

"Happy Yulemas, Philippa!" she said. "Care for a candy?"

Philippa stormed toward Celaena. "Happy Yulemas indeed! Look at this bed! Look at this mess!" Celaena winced.

"Your teeth are *red*!" Philippa cried. She reached for the hand mirror that Celaena kept by her bed and held it for the assassin to see.

Sure enough, her teeth were tinged with crimson. She ran her tongue over her teeth, then tried to brush away the stains with a finger. They remained. "Damn those sugar suckers!"

"Yes," Philippa snapped. "And that's *chocolate* all over your mouth. Even my grandson doesn't eat his candy like this!"

Celaena laughed. "You have a grandson?"

"Yes, and he can eat his food without getting it on the bed, on his teeth, and on his *face*!"

Celaena pushed back the covers, sugar spraying into the air. "Have a candy, Philippa."

"It's seven in the morning." Philippa swept the sugar into her cupped palm. "You'll make yourself sick."

"Sick? Who can get sick from candy?" Celaena made a face and exposed her crimson teeth.

"You look like a demon," said Philippa. "Just don't open your mouth and no one will notice."

"You and I both know that's not possible."

To her surprise, Philippa laughed. "Happy Yulemas, Celaena," she said. Hearing Philippa call her by her name sent an unexpected burst of pleasure through her. "Come," the servant clucked. "Let's get you dressed—the ceremony begins at nine." Philippa bustled toward the dressing room, and Celaena watched her go. Her heart was big and as red as her teeth. There was good in people—deep down, there was always a shred of good. There *had* to be.

Celaena emerged a while later, clad in a solemn-looking green dress that Philippa had deemed the only appropriate gown for temple attendance. Celaena's teeth were, of course, still red, and now she felt queasy as she stared at the bag of candy. However, she quickly forgot about her sickness when she saw Dorian Havilliard sitting at the table in her bedroom with crossed legs. He wore a beautiful white-and-gold jacket.

"Are you my present, or is there something in that basket at your feet?" she asked.

"If you'd like to unwrap me," he said, lifting the large wicker basket onto the table, "we still have an hour until the temple service."

She laughed. "Happy Yulemas, Dorian."

"And to you as well. I can see that I— Are your teeth red?"

She clamped her mouth shut, shaking her head in violent protestation.

He grabbed her nose and pinched it closed, and try as she might, she could not dislodge his fingers. She opened her mouth, and he burst into laughter. "Been eating candies, have you?"

"You sent those?" She kept her mouth closed as much as possible.

"Of course." He picked up the brown bag of candy on the table. "What's your . . ." He trailed off as he weighed the bag in his hands. "Didn't I give you three pounds of candy?"

She smiled impishly.

"You ate half the bag!"

"Was I supposed to save it?"

"I would have liked some!"

"You never told me that."

"Because I didn't expect you to consume all of it before breakfast!"

She snatched the bag from him and put it on the table. "Well, that just shows poor judgment on your part, doesn't it?"

Dorian opened his mouth to reply, but the bag of candy tipped over and spilled across the table. Celaena turned just in time to see the slender golden snout protruding from the basket, inching toward the candy. "What is that?" she asked flatly.

Dorian grinned. "A Yulemas present for you."

The assassin flipped back the lid of the basket. The nose instantly shot inward, and Celaena found the strange golden-haired pup quivering in a corner with a red bow around her neck.

"Oh, *puppy*," she crooned, and petted her. The dog trembled, and she glared at Dorian over her shoulder. "What did you do, you buffoon?" she hissed.

Dorian threw his hands in the air. "It's a *gift*! I almost lost my arm—and more important parts—trying to put that bow on, and then she howled all the way up here!"

Celaena looked piteously at the dog, which was now licking the sugar off her fingers. "What am I going to do with her? You couldn't find an owner, so you decided to give her to me?"

"No!" he said. "Well, yes. But—she didn't seem so frightened when you were around, and I remembered how my hounds followed you when we traveled from Endovier. Perhaps she'll trust you enough to become adapted to humans. Some people have those kinds of gifts." She raised an eyebrow as he paced. "It's a lousy present, I know. I should have gotten you something better."

The dog peered up at Celaena. Her eyes were a golden-brown color, like molten caramel. She seemed to be waiting for a blow to fall. She was a beautiful thing, and her huge paws hinted that she might someday grow large—and swift. A slight smile spread on Celaena's lips. The dog swished her tail—once, then another time.

"She's yours," Dorian said, "if you want her."

"What shall I do with her if I'm sent back to Endovier?"

"I'll worry about that." Celaena stroked her folded velvet-soft ears, then ventured low enough to scratch her chin. The pup's tail wagged in earnest. Yes, there was life in her.

"So you don't want her?" he muttered.

"Of course I want her," Celaena said, then realized what the implications would be. "But I want her trained. I don't want her urinating on everything and chewing on furniture and shoes and books. And I want her to sit when I tell her to and lay down and roll over and whatever it is that dogs do. And I want her to run—run with the other dogs when they're practicing. I want her to put those long legs to use."

Dorian crossed his arms as Celaena scooped up the dog. "That's a long list of demands. Perhaps I should have bought you jewelry after all."

"When I'm training"—she kissed the pup's soft head, and the dog nestled her cold nose against Celaena's neck—"I want her in the kennels, training as well. When I return in the afternoon, she may be brought to me. I'll keep her in the night." Celaena held the dog at eye level. The dog kicked her legs in the air. "If you ruin any of my shoes," she said to the pup, "I'll turn you into a pair of slippers. Understood?"

The dog stared at her, her wrinkled brow lifting, and Celaena smiled and set her down on the floor. She began sniffing about, though she stayed far from Dorian, and she soon disappeared beneath the bed. The assassin lifted the dust ruffle to peer underneath. Thankfully, the Wyrdmarks had been washed away entirely. The dog continued her exploration, sniffing everywhere. "I'll have to think of a name for you," she said to her, and then stood. "Thank you," she said to Dorian. "It's a lovely gift."

He was kind—unnaturally kind, for someone of his upbringing. He had a heart, she realized, and a conscience. He was different from the others. Timidly, almost clumsily, the assassin strode over to the

Crown Prince and kissed him on the cheek. His skin was surprisingly hot, and she wondered if she'd kissed him properly as she pulled away and found his eyes bright and wide. Had she been sloppy? Too wet? Were her lips sticky from the candy? She hoped he wouldn't wipe his cheek.

"I'm sorry I don't have a present for you," she said.

"I—er, I didn't expect you to." He blushed madly and glanced at the clock. "I have to go. I'll see you at the ceremony—or perhaps tonight after the ball? I'll try to get away as early as I can. Though I bet that without you there, Nehemia will probably do the same—so it won't look so bad if I leave early, too."

She'd never seen him *babble* like this. "Enjoy yourself," she said as he took a step back and almost crashed into the table.

"I'll see you tonight, then," he said. "After the ball."

She hid her smile behind a hand. Had her kiss thrown him into such a tizzy?

"Good-bye, Celaena." He looked back when he reached the door. She smiled at him, flashing her red teeth, and he laughed before he bowed and disappeared. Alone in her rooms, Celaena was about to see what her new companion was up to when the thought struck her:

Nehemia would be at the ball.

It was a simple enough thought at first, but then worse thoughts followed it. Celaena began pacing. If Nehemia were truly somehow behind the Champions' murders—and worse, had some feral beast at her command to destroy them—and also just learned about the massacre of her people . . . then what better place to punish Adarlan than at the ball, where so many of its royals would be celebrating and unguarded?

It was irrational, Celaena knew. But what if . . . what if Nehemia unleashed whatever creature she controlled at the ball? Fine, she wouldn't mind if Kaltain and Perrington met horrible deaths, but Dorian would be there. And Chaol.

Celaena strode into her bedroom, wringing her fingers. She couldn't warn Chaol—because if she were wrong, then it would ruin not just her friendship with Nehemia, but also the princess's efforts at diplomacy. But she couldn't just do *nothing.*

Oh, she shouldn't even be thinking this. But she'd seen friends do terrible things before, and it had become safer for her to believe the worst. She'd witnessed firsthand how far a need for revenge could drive someone. Perhaps Nehemia wouldn't do anything—perhaps she was just being paranoid and ridiculous. But if something happened tonight . . .

Celaena opened the doors to her dressing room, surveying the glittering gowns hanging along the walls. Chaol would be beyond furious if she infiltrated the ball, but she could handle it. She could handle it if he decided to throw her in the dungeons for a little while, too.

Because somehow, the thought of him getting hurt—or worse—made her willing to risk just about anything.

~

"Will you not even smile on Yulemas?" she asked Chaol as they walked out of the castle and toward the glass temple at the center of the eastern garden.

"If my teeth were crimson, I wouldn't be smiling at all," he said. "Be content with an occasional grimace." She flashed her teeth at him, then closed her mouth as several courtiers strode past, servants in tow. "I'm surprised you're not complaining more."

"Complaining about what?" Why did Chaol never joke with her as Dorian did? Perhaps he truly didn't find her attractive. The possibility of it stung more than she would have liked.

"About not going to the ball tonight." He glanced sidelong at her. He couldn't know what she was planning. Philippa had promised to keep it a secret—promised not to ask questions when Celaena requested she find a gown and matching mask.

"Well, apparently you still don't trust me enough." She meant to sound sassy, but couldn't keep the snap from her tone. She couldn't waste her time worrying about someone who clearly had no interest in her beyond the ridiculous competition.

Chaol snorted, though a hint of a smile appeared on his lips. At least the Crown Prince never made her feel stupid or rotten. Chaol just provoked her . . . though he had his good side, too. And she had no idea when she'd stopped loathing him so much.

Still, she knew he wouldn't be pleased when she appeared at the ball tonight. Mask or no mask, Chaol would know it was her. She just hoped he wouldn't punish her too severely.

37

Seated in a pew in the rear of the spacious temple, Celaena kept her mouth closed so tightly that it hurt. Her teeth were still red; she didn't need anyone else noticing.

The temple was a beautiful space, built entirely from glass. The limestone covering the floor was all that remained of the original stone temple, which the King of Adarlan had destroyed when he decided to replace it with the glass structure. Two columns of about a hundred rosewood pews stretched beneath a vaulted glass ceiling that let in so much light that no candles were needed during the day. Snow lay piled upon the translucent roof, casting patterns of sunshine throughout. As the walls were also glass, the stained windows above the altar appeared to hover in midair.

She stood to peer over the heads of those sitting in front of her. Dorian and the queen sat in the first pew, a row of guards immediately behind. The duke and Kaltain sat on the other side of the aisle, and behind them were Nehemia and several others she didn't recognize. She didn't spy Nox, or the other remaining Champions—or Cain. They'd let her come to *this*, but not to the ball?

"Sit *down*," Chaol growled, pulling at her green gown. She made a face and dropped onto the cushioned bench. Several people stared at her. They wore gowns and jackets so elaborate that she wondered if the ball had been moved to lunchtime.

The High Priestess walked onto the stone platform and raised her hands above her head. The folds of her midnight-blue gossamer robe fell around her, and her white hair was long and unbound. An eight-pointed star was tattooed upon her brow in a shade of blue that matched her gown, its sharp lines extending to her hairline. "Welcome all, and may the blessings of the Goddess and all her gods be upon you." Her voice echoed across the chamber to reach even those in the back.

Celaena stifled a yawn. She respected the gods—if they existed, and when it suited her to ask for their assistance—but religious ceremonies were . . . *brutal.*

It had been years and years since she'd attended anything of this sort, and as the High Priestess lowered her arms and stared at the crowd, the assassin shifted in her seat. It would be the usual prayers, then the Yulemas prayers, then the sermon, then the songs, and then the procession of the gods.

"You're squirming already," Chaol said under his breath.

"What time is it?" she whispered, and he pinched her arm.

"Today," the priestess said, "is the day on which we celebrate the end and the beginning of the great cycle. Today is the day on which the Great Goddess gave birth to her firstborn, Lumas, Lord of the Gods. With his birth, love was brought into Erilea, and it banished the chaos that arose from the Gates of the Wyrd."

A weight pressed on her eyelids. She had woken up so early—and slept so little after that encounter with Nehemia . . . Unable to stop, Celaena wandered into the Land of Sleep.

"Get up," Chaol snarled in her ear. "Now."

She sat up with a jolt, the world bright and foggy. Several lesser nobles in her pew laughed silently. She gave Chaol an apologetic look and turned her gaze to the altar. The High Priestess had finished her sermon, and the songs of Yulemas were over. She only had to sit through the procession of the gods, and then she would be free.

"How long was I asleep?" she whispered. He didn't respond. "How long was I asleep?" she asked again, and noticed a hint of red in his cheeks. "You were asleep, too?"

"Until you began drooling on my shoulder."

"Such a self-righteous young man," she cooed, and he poked her leg.

"Pay attention."

A choir of priestesses stepped off the platform. Celaena yawned, but nodded with the rest of the congregation as the choir gave their blessings. An organ sounded, and everyone leaned to stare down the aisle for the procession of the gods.

The sound of pattering footsteps filled the temple, and the congregation stood. Each blindfolded child was no more than ten years old, and though they looked rather foolish dressed in the costumes of the gods, there was something charming about it. Every year, nine children were chosen. If a child stopped before you, you received the blessings of the god and the small gift the child carried as a symbol of the god's favor.

Farnor, God of War, stopped at the front row near Dorian, but then moved to the right, across the aisle, to give the miniature silver sword to Duke Perrington. *Not surprising.*

Clad in glistening wings, Lumas, God of Love, strode past her. She crossed her arms.

What a foolish tradition.

Deanna, Goddess of the Hunt and Maidens, approached. Celaena shifted from one foot to the other, wishing she hadn't demanded that Chaol give her the aisle seat. To her dread and dismay, the girl stopped before her and removed the blindfold.

She was a pretty little thing: her blond hair hung in loose curls, and her brown eyes were flecked with green. The girl smiled at Celaena and reached to touch the assassin's forehead. Celaena's back began sweating as she felt hundreds of eyes upon her. "May Deanna, the Huntress and Protector of the Young, bless and keep you this year. I bestow upon you this golden arrow as a symbol of her power and good graces." The girl bowed as she extended the slender arrow. Chaol prodded her back and Celaena grabbed the arrow. "Yulemas blessings to you," the girl said, and Celaena nodded her thanks. She gripped the arrow as the girl bounded away. It couldn't be used, of course. But it was made of solid gold.

It'll fetch a nice price.

With a shrug, Celaena handed the arrow to Chaol. "I suppose I'm not allowed to have this," she said, sitting down with the rest of the crowd.

He put it back in her lap. "I wouldn't want to test the gods." She stared at him for a moment. Did he look different? Something had changed in his face. Nudging him with an elbow, Celaena grinned.

38

Yards of silk, clouds of powder, brushes, combs, pearls, and diamonds glistened before Celaena's eyes. As Philippa arranged the last strand of Celaena's hair neatly around her face, secured a mask over her eyes and nose, and placed a small crystal tiara on her head, Celaena couldn't help but feel, despite herself, like a princess.

Philippa knelt to polish the lump of crystal on Celaena's silver slippers. "If I didn't know better, I'd call myself a Faerie Queen. It's like m—" Philippa caught herself before she spoke the word the King of Adarlan had so effectively outlawed, then quickly said, "I barely recognize you!"

"Good," Celaena said. This would be her first ball where she wasn't there to kill someone. True, she was mostly going to make sure Nehemia didn't hurt herself or the court. But . . . a ball was a ball. Maybe if she was lucky, she could dance a little.

"Are you certain this is a good idea?" Philippa asked quietly, standing. "Captain Westfall won't be pleased."

Celaena gave the servant a sharp look. "I told you not to ask questions."

Philippa huffed. "Just don't tell them *I* helped you when you get dragged back here."

Checking her irritation, Celaena strode to the mirror, Philippa bustling after her. Standing before her reflection, Celaena wondered if she was seeing correctly. "This is the most beautiful dress I've ever worn," she admitted, her eyes filling with light.

It was not pure white, but rather a grayish offset, and its wide skirts and bodice were encrusted with thousands of minuscule crystals that reminded Celaena of the surface of the sea. Swirls of silk thread on the bodice made rose-like designs that could have passed for a work by any master painter. A border of ermine lined the neck and provided slender sleeves that only covered her shoulders. Tiny diamond droplets fell from her ears, and her hair was curled and swept up onto her head, strands of pearls woven in. Her gray silk mask had been secured tightly against her face. It wasn't fashioned after anything, but the delicate crystal and pearl whorls had been crafted by a skilled hand.

"You could win the hand of a king, looking like that," said Philippa. "Or perhaps a Crown Prince will do."

"Where in Erilea did you find this dress?" Celaena murmured.

"Don't ask questions," clucked the old woman.

Celaena smirked. "Fair enough." She wondered why her heart now felt too large for her body, and why she was so unstable in her shoes. She had to remember why she was going—she had to keep her wits about her.

The clock struck nine, and Philippa glanced toward the doorway, giving Celaena the opportunity to slip her makeshift knife down her bodice without being noticed. "How, exactly, are you going to get to the ball? I don't think your guards will let you just walk out."

Celaena shot Philippa a sly look. "We're both going to pretend that

I was invited by the Crown Prince—and right now *you* are going to make such a fuss about me being late that they won't object."

Philippa fanned herself, her face reddening. Celaena grasped her hand. "I promise," she said, "if I get into any sort of trouble, I will swear to my last breath that you were deceived by me, and had no knowledge of anything."

"But *are* you going to get into trouble?"

Celaena gave her most winning smile. "No. I'm just sick of being left to sit around while they have grand parties." It wasn't quite a lie.

"Gods help me," Philippa muttered, and took a deep breath. "Go!" she suddenly cried, herding Celaena toward the door to the hall. "Go, you'll be late!" She was a bit too loud to be totally convincing, but . . . Philippa flung open the door to the hallway. "The Crown Prince won't be pleased if you're late!" Celaena paused in the doorway, nodding at the five guards who were posted outside, then looked back at Philippa.

"Thank you," Celaena said.

"No more dawdling!" the servant woman cried, and almost knocked Celaena off her feet as she pushed her out the doorway and slammed it shut.

Celaena turned to the guards. "You look nice," one of them—Ress—said shyly. "Off to the ball?" grinned another. "Save a dance for me, will you?" the third added. Not one of them questioned her.

Celaena smiled and took Ress's arm as he extended it to her. She tried not to laugh when he puffed out his chest. But as they neared the Great Hall and the sounds of a waltz could be heard, a swarm of bees took flight in her stomach. She couldn't forget why she was here. She'd played this part in the past, but it had ended in killing a stranger—not confronting a friend.

The red-and-gold glass doors appeared, and she could see the wreaths and candles that bedecked the massive hall. It would have been easier if she could have slipped into the ball through a side door and remained unnoticed, but she hadn't had time to go exploring through the secret tunnels to find another way out of her rooms, and she certainly couldn't find another way into the ball now without raising suspicions. Ress stopped and bowed. "This is where I leave you," he said as seriously as he could, though he kept looking at the ball that lay at the foot of the stairs. "Have a lovely night, Miss Sardothien."

"Thank you, Ress." She felt an urge to vomit and run back to her rooms. Instead, she graciously nodded her farewell. She just had to make it down the stairs, and find a way to convince Chaol to let her stay. Then she could keep an eye on Nehemia all night.

Her shoes seemed frail, and Celaena took a few steps back, ignoring the guards at the door as she lifted her feet high and set them down to test the strength of the shoes. When she was assured that not even a jump through the air could snap the heel, she approached the top of the stairs.

Tucked into her bodice, the makeshift knife poked her skin. She prayed to the Goddess, to every god she knew, to the Wyrd, to whatever was responsible for her fate, that she wouldn't have to use it.

Celaena squared her shoulders and stepped forward.

What was *she* doing here?

Dorian almost dropped his drink as he saw Celaena Sardothien atop the stairs. Even with the mask, he recognized her. She might have her faults, but Celaena never did anything half-heartedly. She'd outdone herself with that dress. But what was she doing *here*?

He couldn't tell if it were a dream or reality until several heads, then many, turned to look. Though the waltz was playing, those not dancing quieted themselves as the mysterious masked girl lifted her skirts and took a step, then another. Her dress was made of stars plucked from the sky, and the whorls of crystals in her gray mask glittered.

"Who is *that*?" breathed a young courtier beside him.

She looked at no one as she descended the staircase, and even the Queen of Adarlan stood to see the late arrival, Nehemia also rising from her seat beside her. Had Celaena lost her mind?

Walk to her. Take her hand. But his feet were leaden, and Dorian could do nothing except watch her. His skin flushed beneath his small black mask. He didn't know why, but seeing her made him feel like a man. She was something out of a dream—a dream in which he was not a spoiled young prince, but a king. She reached the bottom of the stairs, and Dorian took a step forward.

But someone had already arrived, and Dorian clenched his jaw tight enough for it to hurt as she smiled and bowed to Chaol. The Captain of the Guard, who hadn't bothered to wear a mask, extended his hand. Celaena stared only at Chaol with those starlit eyes, and her long, white fingers floated through the air to meet his. The crowd began chattering as Chaol led her from the stairs, and they disappeared into the throng. Whatever conversation they were about to have, it wasn't going to be pleasant. He'd be better off staying out of it.

"Please," said another courtier, "tell me that Chaol doesn't suddenly have a wife."

"Captain Westfall?" said the courtier who had spoken earlier. "Why would a pretty thing like that marry a guard?" Remembering who stood beside him, he glanced at Dorian, who was still staring, wide-eyed, at the stairs. "Who is she, Your Highness? Do you know her?"

"No, I don't," whispered Dorian, and walked away.

The waltz was driving and so loud she had difficulty hearing herself think as Chaol pulled her into a shadowy alcove. Not surprisingly, he hadn't worn a mask—it would be too silly for him. Which made the fury on his face all too visible.

"So," he seethed, holding tightly to her wrist, "do you want to tell me how you got it into your mind that this was a good idea?"

She tried shaking off his hand, but he wouldn't let go. Across the great hall, Nehemia sat with the Queen of Adarlan, occasionally glancing in Celaena's direction. Because she was nervous—or just surprised to see her?

"Relax," she hissed at the Captain of the Guard. "I only wanted to have some fun."

"Fun? Crashing a royal ball is your idea of *fun*?"

Arguing wouldn't help; she could tell that his anger was mostly about being embarrassed that she'd managed to slip out of her rooms in the first place. So she gave him a pitiful pout. "I was lonely."

He choked. "You couldn't spend one evening on your own?"

She twisted her wrist out of his grasp. "Nox is here—and he's a thief! How could you let him come—with all this jewelry flashing about—and not me? How can I be the King's Champion if you don't *trust* me?" Actually, that was a question she really wanted to know the answer to.

Chaol covered his face with a hand and let out a long, long sigh. She tried not to smile. She'd won. "If you take one step out of line—"

She grinned in earnest. "Consider it your Yulemas present to me."

Chaol gave her a weighing look, but slumped his shoulders. "Please don't make me regret this."

She patted his cheek, sweeping past him. "I knew I liked you for some reason."

He said nothing, but followed her back into the crowd. She'd been to masked balls before, but there was still something unnerving about not being able to see the faces of those around her. Most of the court, Dorian included, wore masks of varying sizes, shapes, and colors—some of simple design, others elaborate and animal-shaped. Nehemia still sat with the queen, wearing a gold-and-turquoise mask with a lotus motif. They appeared to be engaged in polite conversation, and Nehemia's guards stood to the side of the dais, already looking bored.

Chaol kept close to her as she found an empty spot in the crowd and stopped. It was a good vantage point. She could see everything from here—the dais, the main stairs, the dance floor . . .

Dorian was dancing with a small brunette with outrageously large breasts that he took no pains to avoid glancing at every so often. Hadn't he noticed her arrival? Even Perrington had seen her when Chaol dragged her into that corner. Thankfully, the captain had subtly moved her away before she had to interact with him.

Across the room, she met Nox's eye. He was flirting with a young woman wearing a dove mask, and he raised his glass in salute before turning back to the girl. He'd opted for a blue mask that concealed only his eyes.

"Well, try not to have too much fun," Chaol said beside her, crossing his arms.

Hiding her scowl, Celaena crossed her arms as well and began her vigil.

An hour later, Celaena was beginning to curse herself for being a fool. Nehemia was still sitting with the queen, and hadn't looked again in Celaena's direction. How had she even considered that Nehemia—Nehemia, of all people!—would attack everyone?

Celaena's face burned with shame beneath the mask. She didn't deserve to call herself a friend. All the dead Champions and mysterious evil powers and this ridiculous competition had made her go mad.

Celaena smoothed the fur on her dress, frowning slightly. Chaol remained beside her, saying nothing. Though he'd allowed her to stay, she doubted he'd soon forget this. Or that the guards wouldn't get the tongue-lashing of their lives later tonight.

Celaena straightened as Nehemia suddenly rose from her seat beside the queen's throne, her guards snapping to attention. She bowed her head to the queen, the light of the chandeliers making her mask glisten, and then strode off the dais.

Celaena felt each of her heartbeats hammering in her veins as Nehemia wove through the crowd, her guards close behind—and halted in front of Celaena and Chaol.

"You look beautiful, Lillian," Nehemia said in the common tongue, her accent as thick as it had ever been. It felt like a slap in the face; she'd spoken with perfect fluency that night in the library. Was she warning Celaena to keep quiet about it?

"As do you," Celaena said tightly. "Are you enjoying the ball?"

Nehemia played with a fold in her dress. And, from the look of the rich blue fabric, it was probably a gift from the Queen of Adarlan. "Yes, but I'm not feeling well," the princess said. "I'm going back to my rooms."

Celaena gave her a stiff nod. "I hope you feel better," was all she could think of to say. Nehemia looked at her for a long moment, her eyes shining with what seemed like pain, and then left. Celaena watched her walk up the stairs, and didn't tear her gaze away until the princess was gone.

Chaol cleared his throat. "Do you want to tell me what that was all about?"

"None of your business," she replied. Something could still happen—even if Nehemia wasn't here, something could happen. But no. Nehemia wouldn't repay pain with more pain. She was too good for that. Celaena swallowed hard. The makeshift knife in her bodice felt like a dead weight.

Even if Nehemia wasn't going to hurt anyone tonight, that didn't prove her innocence.

"What's wrong?" Chaol pressed.

Forcing herself to push aside her shame and worry, Celaena lifted her chin. With Nehemia gone, she still had to keep watch, but maybe she could attempt to have a little fun, too. "With you scowling at everyone, no one will ask me to dance."

Chaol's dark brows rose. "I'm not scowling at everyone." Even as he said it, she spotted him frowning at a passing courtier who looked too long in Celaena's direction.

"Stop it!" she hissed. "No one will ever ask me to dance if you keep doing that!"

He gave her an exasperated look and strode off. She followed him to the border of the dance floor. "Here," he said, standing at the edge of the sea of swirling gowns. "If anyone wants to ask you to dance, you're in plain sight."

From this spot she could also still make sure no feral beasts were about to rip into the crowd. But he didn't need to know that. She glanced at him. "Would you like to dance with me?"

He laughed. "With you? No."

She looked at the marble floor, her chest tight. "You needn't be so cruel."

"Cruel? Celaena, Perrington is just over there. I'm sure he's not happy about you being here, so I wouldn't risk drawing his attention any more than necessary."

"Coward."

Chaol's eyes softened. "If he weren't here, I would have said yes."

"I can easily arrange that, you know."

He shook his head as he adjusted the lapel on his black tunic. Just then Dorian waltzed by, sweeping the brunette with him. He didn't even glance at her.

"Anyway," Chaol added, jerking his chin at Dorian, "I think you have far more attractive suitors vying for your attention. I'm boring company to keep."

"I don't mind being here with you."

"I'm sure you don't," Chaol said dryly, though he met her stare.

"I mean it. Why aren't *you* dancing with anyone? Aren't there ladies whom you like?"

"I'm the Captain of the Guard—I'm not exactly a catch for any of them." There was some sorrow in his eyes, though it was well concealed.

"Are you mad? You're better than everyone in here. And you're—you're very handsome," she said, taking his hand in her free one. There was beauty in Chaol's face—and strength, and honor, and loyalty. She stopped hearing the crowd, and her mouth became dry as he stared at her. How had she missed it for so long?

"You think so?" he said after a moment, looking at their clasped hands.

She tightened her grasp. "Why, if I wasn't—"

"Why aren't you two dancing?"

Chaol dropped her hand. She had difficulty turning away from him. "And with whom would I dance, Your Highness?"

Dorian was alarmingly handsome in his pewter tunic. One might say it matched her dress. "You look radiant," he said. "And you look radiant as well, Chaol." He winked at his friend. Then Dorian's gaze met hers, and Celaena's blood turned into shooting stars. "Well? Do I need to lecture you about how stupid it was to sneak into the ball, or can I just ask you to dance with me instead?"

"I don't think that's a good idea," Chaol said.

"Why?" they asked in unison. Dorian stepped a little closer to her. Even though she was ashamed of herself for believing such awful things about Nehemia, knowing that Dorian and Chaol were safe made the misery worth it.

"Because it attracts too much attention, that's why." Celaena rolled her eyes, and Chaol glared at her. "Do I have to remind you who you are?"

"No. You remind me every day," she retorted. His brown eyes darkened. What was the point in being nice to her if he was only going to insult her the next moment?

Dorian put a hand on her shoulder and gave Chaol a charming smile. "Relax, Chaol," he said, and his hand slipped to rest on her back, his fingers grazing her bare skin. "Just take the night off." Dorian turned her from the captain. "It'll do you some good," he said over his shoulder, though the merriness faded from his tone.

"I'm getting a drink," muttered Chaol, and walked away. She watched the captain for a moment. It would be a miracle if he considered her a friend. Dorian caressed her back, and she looked at him. Her heart jumped into a gallop, and Chaol dissolved from her thoughts, like dew beneath the morning sun. She felt bad for forgetting him—but . . . but . . . Oh, she wanted Dorian, she couldn't deny it. She *wanted* him.

"You look beautiful," Dorian said quietly, running an eye over her in a way that made her ears burn. "I haven't been able to stop staring at you."

"Oh? And I thought you hadn't even noticed me."

"Chaol got there first when you arrived. And besides, I had to work up the nerve to approach you." He grinned. "You're very intimidating. Especially with the mask."

"And I suppose it didn't help that you had a line of ladies waiting to dance with you."

"I'm here now, aren't I?" Her heart tightened, and she realized it wasn't the answer she'd been hoping for. What *did* she want from him?

He held out his hand, inclining his head. "Dance with me?"

Was there music playing? She'd forgotten. The world had shrunk into nothing, dissolved by the golden glow of candles. But there were her feet, and here was her arm, and her neck, and her mouth. She smiled and took his hand, still keeping one eye on the ball around them.

39

He was lost—lost in a world of which he'd always dreamed. Her body was warm beneath his hand, and her fingers were soft around his. He spun her and led her about the floor, waltzing as smoothly as he could. She didn't falter a single step, nor did she seem to care about the many angry female faces that watched as dance after dance passed and they didn't switch partners.

Of course, it wasn't polite for a prince to dance with only one lady, but he couldn't focus on anything beyond his partner and the music that carried them onward.

"You certainly have a lot of stamina," she said. When had they last spoken? It could have been ten minutes or an hour ago. The masked faces around them blurred together.

"While some parents hit their children, mine also punished me with dancing lessons."

"Then you must have been a very naughty boy." She glanced around the ball, as if she were looking for something—or someone.

"You're gracious with your compliments tonight." He twirled her. The skirts of her gown sparkled underneath the chandelier.

"It's Yulemas," she said. "Everyone's kind on Yulemas." A flash of what he could have sworn was pain shone in her eyes, but it was gone before he could be certain of it.

He caught her around the waist, his feet moving to the beat of the waltz. "And how's your present?"

"Oh, she hid under my bed, then in the dining room, which is where I left her."

"You locked the dog in your dining room?"

"Should I have kept her in my bedroom, where she could ruin the carpets? Or in the gaming room, where she might eat the chess pieces and choke?"

"Perhaps you should have sent her to the kennels, where dogs belong."

"On Yulemas? I couldn't think of sending her back to that wretched place!"

He suddenly felt the urge to kiss her—hard—upon the mouth. But this—what he felt, it could never be real. Because once the ball was over, she would go back to being an assassin, and he would still be a prince. Dorian swallowed hard. For tonight, though . . .

He held her closer. Everyone transformed into mere shadows on the wall.

Frowning, Chaol watched his friend dance with the assassin. He wouldn't have danced with her, anyway. And he was glad he hadn't worked up the nerve to ask her, not after seeing the color that Duke Perrington's face turned upon discovering the pair.

A courtier named Otho stepped beside Chaol. "I thought she was with you."

"Who? Lady Lillian?"

"So that's her name! I've never seen her before. Is she newly arrived to court?"

"Yes," said Chaol. Tomorrow, he'd have a word with her guards about letting Celaena out tonight. Hopefully by then, he'd be less inclined to knock their heads together.

"How are you doing, Captain Westfall?" Otho said, clapping him on the back a bit too hard. His breath reeked of wine. "You don't dine with us anymore."

"I stopped dining at your table three years ago, Otho."

"You should come back—we miss your conversation." It was a lie. Otho only wanted information about the foreign young lady. His reputation with women was well known in the castle—so well known that he had to seize courtiers as they arrived or go into Rifthold for a different sort of woman.

Chaol watched Dorian dip Celaena, watched the way her lips widened in a smile and her eyes burst with light as the Crown Prince said something. Even with the mask on, Chaol could see the happiness written across her face. "Is *he* with her?" Otho asked.

"The Lady Lillian belongs to herself, and no one else."

"So she's not with him?"

"No."

Otho shrugged. "That's strange."

"Why?" Chaol had the sudden urge to strangle him.

"Because it looks like he's in love with her," he said, and walked away.

Chaol's eyes lost focus for a moment. Then Celaena laughed, and Dorian kept staring at her. The prince hadn't once taken his eyes off her. Dorian's expression was full of—something. Joy? Wonder? His shoulders were straight, his back erect. He looked like a man. Like a king.

It was impossible for such a thing to have occurred; and when would it have happened? Otho was a drunk and a womanizer. What did he know of love?

Dorian spun Celaena with speed and dexterity, and she snapped into his arms, her shoulders rising with exhilaration. But *she* wasn't in love with *him*—Otho hadn't said that. He had seen no attachment on her part. And Celaena would never be that stupid. It was Dorian who was the fool—Dorian who would have his heart broken, if he did actually love her.

Unable to look at his friend any longer, the Captain of the Guard left the ball.

Kaltain watched in rage and agony as Lillian Gordaina and the Crown Prince of Adarlan danced and danced and danced. Even with a much more concealing mask, she would have recognized the upstart. And what sort of a person wore gray to a ball? Kaltain looked down at her dress and smiled. Bright shades of blue, emerald, and soft brown, her gown and matching peacock mask had cost as much as a small house. It was all a gift from Perrington, of course, along with the jewelry that decorated much of her neck and arms. It was certainly not the dull, drab mess of crystal that the conniving harlot wore.

Perrington stroked her arm, and Kaltain turned to him with fluttering eyelashes. "You look handsome tonight, my love," she said, adjusting a gold chain across his red tunic. His face quickly matched the color of his clothes. She wondered if she could bear the repulsion of kissing him. She could always keep refusing, just as she had for the past month; but when he was this drunk . . .

She would have to think of a way out as soon as possible. But she was no closer to Dorian than she'd been in early autumn, and would certainly make no progress with Lillian in the way.

A precipice opened before her. Her head gave a brief, faint throb of pain. There were no other options now. Lillian had to be eliminated.

When the clock chimed three and most of the guests—including the queen and Chaol—had left, Celaena finally decided that it was safe for her to leave. So she slipped from the ball when Dorian went to get a drink and found Ress waiting outside to escort her back. The halls of the castle were silent as they strode to her room, taking the empty servants' passages to avoid any too-curious courtiers learning more about her. Even if she'd gone to the ball for the wrong reasons, she *had* had some fun dancing with Dorian. More than some, actually. She smiled to herself, picking at her nails as they entered the hallway that led to her rooms. The rush of having Dorian look only at her, talk only to her, treat her as if she were his equal and more hadn't yet worn off. Maybe her plan hadn't been such a failure after all.

Ress cleared his throat, and Celaena looked up to see Dorian standing outside her rooms, chatting with the guards. He couldn't have stayed long at the ball if he'd beaten her back here. Her heart pounded, but she managed a coy smile as Dorian bowed to her, opened the door, and they went inside. Let Ress and the guards think what they wanted.

She unfastened the mask from her face, tossing it onto the table in the center of the foyer, and sighed as the cool air met her flushed skin. "Well?" she asked, leaning against the wall beside the door to her bedroom.

Dorian approached her slowly, halting only a hand's breath away. "You left the ball without saying good-bye," he said, and braced an arm against the wall beside her head. She raised her eyes, examining the black detail on the sleeve that fell just above her hair.

"I'm impressed you got up here so quickly—and without a pack of court ladies hounding after you. Perhaps you should try your hand at being an assassin."

He shook the hair out of his face. "I'm not interested in court ladies," he said thickly, and kissed her.

His mouth was warm, and his lips were smooth, and Celaena lost all sense of time and place as she slowly kissed him back. He pulled away for a moment, looked into her eyes as they opened, and kissed her again. It was different this time—deeper, full of need.

Her arms were heavy and light all at once, and the room twirled round and round. She couldn't stop. She liked this—liked being kissed by him, liked the smell and the taste and the feel of him.

His arm slipped around her waist and he held her tightly to him as his lips moved against hers. She put a hand on his shoulder, her fingers digging into the muscle that lay beneath. How different things were between them than when she'd first seen him in Endovier!

Her eyes opened. Endovier. Why was she kissing the Crown Prince of Adarlan? Her fingers loosened and her arm dropped to her side.

He removed his mouth from hers and smiled. It was infectious. Dorian leaned forward again, but she smoothly put two fingers against his lips.

"I should go to bed," she said. He raised his eyebrows. "Alone," she added. He removed her fingers from his mouth. He tried to kiss her, but she easily swung under his arm and reached for the door handle. She had opened the bedroom door and slid inside before he could stop her. She peered into the foyer, watching as he continued to smile. "Good night."

Dorian leaned against the door, bringing his face close to hers. "Good night," he whispered, and she didn't stop him as he kissed her again. He broke it off before she was ready, and she almost fell onto the ground as he removed his weight from the door. He laughed softly.

"Good night," she said again, heat rushing to her face. Then he was gone.

Celaena strode to the balcony and flung open the doors, embracing the chill air. Her hand rose to her lips and she stared up at the stars, feeling her heart grow, and grow, and grow.

Dorian walked slowly back to his rooms, his heart racing. He could still feel her lips on his, smell the scent of her hair, and see the gold in her eyes flickering in the candlelight.

Consequences be damned. He'd find a way to make it work; he'd find a way to be with her. He had to.

He had leapt from the cliff. He could only wait for the net.

In the garden, the Captain of the Guard stared up at the young woman's balcony, watching as she waltzed alone, lost in her dreams. But he knew that her thoughts weren't of him.

She stopped and stared upward. Even from a distance, he could see the blush upon her cheeks. She seemed young—no, new. It made his chest ache.

Still, he watched, watched until she sighed and went inside. She never bothered to look below.

40

Celaena groaned as something cold and wet brushed her cheek and moved to lick her face. She opened an eye and found the puppy looking down at her, its tail wagging. Adjusting herself in the bed, she winced at the sunlight. She hadn't meant to sleep in. They had a Test in two days, and she needed to train. It was their last Test before the final duel—the Test that decided who the four finalists would be.

Celaena rubbed an eye and then scratched the dog behind the ears. "Have you peed somewhere and wish to tell me about it?"

"Oh no," said someone as the bedroom door swung open—Dorian. "I took her out at dawn with the other dogs."

She smiled weakly as he approached. "Isn't it rather early for a visit?"

"Early?" He laughed, sitting on the bed. She inched away. "It's almost one in the afternoon! Philippa told me you've been sleeping like the dead all morning."

One! She'd slept that long? What about lessons with Chaol? She scratched her nose and pulled the puppy onto her lap. At least nothing had happened last night; if there had been another attack, she would have heard about it already. She almost sighed with relief, though the guilt of what she'd done—how little faith she'd had in Nehemia—still made her a tad miserable.

"Have you named her yet?" he asked—casual, calm, collected. Was he acting that way for show, or was their kiss just not that important to him?

"No," she said, keeping her face neutral, even though she wanted to scream from the awkwardness. "I can't think of anything appropriate."

"What about," he said, tapping his chin, "Gold . . . ie?"

"That's the stupidest name I've ever heard."

"Can you think of something better?"

She picked up one of the dog's legs and examined the soft paws. She squished the padded foot beneath her thumb. "Fleetfoot." It was a perfect name. In fact, it felt as if the name had existed all along, and she'd finally been clairvoyant enough to stumble across it. "Yes, Fleetfoot it is."

"Does it mean anything?" he asked, and the dog raised her head to look at him.

"It'll mean something when she outruns all of your *purebreds*." Celaena scooped the dog into her arms and kissed her head. She bounced her arms up and down, and Fleetfoot stared up into her eyes with a wrinkled brow. She was absurdly soft and cuddly.

Dorian chuckled. "We'll see." Celaena set the dog down on the bed. Fleetfoot promptly crawled under the blankets and disappeared.

"Did you sleep well?" he asked.

"Yes. Though it seems you didn't, if you were up so early."

"Listen," he began, and Celaena wanted to throw herself from the balcony. "Last night . . . I'm sorry if I was too forward with you." He paused. "Celaena, you're grimacing."

Had she been making a face? "Er—sorry."

"It *did* upset you, then!"

"What did?"

"The kiss!"

Phlegm caught in her throat, and the assassin coughed. "Oh, it was nothing," she said, thumping her chest as she cleared her throat. "I didn't mind it. But I didn't hate it, if that's what you're thinking!" She immediately regretted saying it.

"So, you *liked* it?" He grinned lazily.

"No! Oh, go away!" She flung herself onto her pillows, pulling the blankets above her head. She was going to die from embarrassment.

Fleetfoot licked her face as she hid in the darkness of the sheets. "Come now," he said. "From your reaction, one would think you'd never been kissed."

She threw back the blankets, and Fleetfoot burrowed farther beneath. "Of course I've been kissed," she snapped, trying not to think about Sam and what she'd shared with him. "But it wasn't by some stuffed shirt, pompous, arrogant princeling!"

He looked down at his chest. "Stuffed shirt?"

"Oh, hush up," she said, hitting him with a pillow. She moved to the other side of the bed, got up, and walked to the balcony.

She felt him watching her, staring at her back and the three scars she knew her low-cut nightgown did nothing to hide. "Are you going to remain here while I change?"

She faced him. He wasn't looking at her the way he had the night before. There was something wary in his gaze—and something unspeakably sad. Her blood thrummed in her veins. "Well?"

"Your scars are awful," he said, almost whispering.

She put a hand on a hip and walked to the dressing room door.

"We all bear scars, Dorian. Mine just happen to be more visible than most. Sit there if you like, but I'm going to get dressed." She strode from the room.

Kaltain walked beside Duke Perrington through the endless tables of the palace greenhouse. The giant glass building was full of shadows and light, and she fanned herself as the steamy heat smothered her face. The man picked the most absurd places to walk. She had about as much interest in the plants and flowers as she did in a mud puddle on the side of a street.

He picked a lily—snow white—and handed it to her with a bow of his head. "For you." She tried not to cringe at the sight of his pocked, ruddy skin and orange mustache. The thought of being stuck with *him* made her want to rip all the plants out by their roots and throw them into the snow.

"Thank you," she said huskily.

But Perrington studied her closely. "You seem out of spirits today, Lady Kaltain."

"Do I?" She cocked her head in her coyest expression. "Perhaps today pales in comparison to the fun I had at the ball last night."

The duke's black eyes bored into her, though, and he frowned as he put a hand on her elbow and steered her on. "You needn't pretend with me. I noticed you watching the Crown Prince."

Kaltain gave away nothing as she raised her manicured brows and looked sidelong at him. "Was I?"

Perrington ran a meaty finger down the spine of a fern. The black ring on his finger pulsed, and her head gave a throb of pain in response. "I noticed him, too. The girl, specifically. She's troublesome, isn't she?"

"Lady Lillian?" Kaltain blinked this time, unsure whether she could sag with relief just yet. He hadn't noticed her *wanting* the prince, but rather that she'd noticed how Lillian and Dorian clung to each other all night.

"So she calls herself," Perrington murmured.

"That's not her name?" Kaltain asked before she could think.

The duke turned to her, his eyes as black as his ring. "You don't honestly believe that girl is a purebred lady?"

Kaltain's heart stopped. "She's truly not?" And then Perrington smiled, and finally told her everything.

When Perrington finished, Kaltain could only stare at him. An assassin. Lillian Gordaina was Celaena Sardothien, the world's most notorious assassin. And she had her claws in Dorian's heart. If Kaltain wanted Dorian's hand, then she'd need to be far, far cleverer. Simply revealing who Lillian truly was might be enough. But it might not. Kaltain couldn't afford to take risks. The greenhouse was silent, as if it held its breath.

"How can we let this go on? How can we allow the prince to endanger himself like that?" Perrington's face shifted for a moment, toward something pained and ugly—but it was so fast she barely noticed it above the pounding rising in her head. She needed her pipe—needed to calm down before she had a fit.

"We can't," Perrington said.

"But how can we stop them? Tell the king?"

Perrington shook his head, putting a hand on his broadsword as he thought for a moment. She examined a rosebush and traced a long nail along the curve of a thorn. "She's to face the remaining Champions in a duel," he said slowly. "And in the duel, she'll drink a toast in honor of the Goddess and gods." It wasn't just her too-tight corset that stole the breath from Kaltain as the duke went on. She lowered her hand from the thorn. "I was going to ask you to preside over the toast—as a representation of the Goddess. Perhaps you could slip something into her drink."

"Kill her myself?" Hiring someone was one thing, but to do it herself . . .

The duke raised his hands. "No, no. But the king has agreed that drastic measures should be taken, in a way that will make Dorian believe things were . . . an accident. If we were merely to give her a dose of bloodbane, not lethal, but just enough to cause her to lose control, it would give Cain the advantage he needs."

"Cain can't kill her on his own? Accidents happen all the time in duels." Her head gave a sharp, intense throb that echoed through her body. Maybe drugging her might be easier . . .

"Cain thinks he can, but I don't like taking risks." Perrington grasped her hands. His ring was ice-cold against her skin, and she fought the urge to rip her hands from his grip. "Don't you want to help Dorian? Once he's free of her . . ."

Then he'll be mine. He'll be mine, as he should be.

But to kill for it . . . *He'll be mine.*

"Then we'll be able to get him on the right path, won't we?" Perrington finished with a broad smile that made her instincts tell her to run and run and never look back.

But all her mind could see was a crown and throne, and the prince who would sit by her side. "Tell me what I need to do," she said.

41

The clock chimed ten, and Celaena, seated at the small desk in her bedroom, looked up from her book. She should be sleeping, or at least trying to. Fleetfoot, dozing in her lap, yawned widely. Celaena scratched her behind the ears and ran a hand along the page of the book. Wyrdmarks stared up at her, their intricate curves and angles speaking a language she couldn't yet begin to decipher. How long had it taken Nehemia to learn them? And, she wondered darkly, how could their power possibly still work when magic itself was gone?

She hadn't seen Nehemia since the ball last night, hadn't dared to approach her, or tell Chaol what she'd learned. Nehemia had been deceitful about her language skills, and how much she knew about the Wyrdmarks, but she could have any number of reasons for that. Celaena had been wrong to go to the ball last night, wrong to believe Nehemia was capable of such bad things. Nehemia was one of the good ones. She wouldn't target Celaena, not when they'd been friends. They *had* been friends. Celaena swallowed the tightness in her throat and turned the page. Her heart stopped.

There, looking up at her, were the symbols she'd seen near the bodies. And in the margin, written by someone centuries ago, was the explanation: *For sacrifices to the ridderak: using the victim's blood, mark the area around it accordingly. Once the creature has been summoned, these marks guide the exchange: for the flesh of the sacrifice, the beast will grant you the victim's strength.*

Celaena fought to keep her hands from trembling as she flipped through the pages, searching for anything about the marks under her bed. When the book yielded nothing, she returned to the summoning spell. A ridderak—that was the name of the beast? What was it? Where had it been summoned from, if it wasn't—

The Wyrdgates. She pressed the heels of her palms into her eyes. Someone was actually using the Wyrdmarks to open a portal to summon this creature. It was impossible, because magic was gone, but the texts said Wyrdmarks existed *outside* of magic. What if their power still worked? But . . . but Nehemia? How could her friend do such a thing? Why did she need the Champions' strength? And how could she keep everything hidden so well?

Yet Nehemia could easily be a cunning actress. And maybe Celaena had *wanted* a friend—wanted someone as different and outsiderly as she was. Maybe she'd been too willing, too desperate, to see anything but what she wanted to see. Celaena took a steadying breath. Nehemia loved Eyllwe—that was certainly true—and Celaena knew there was nothing Nehemia wouldn't do to keep her country safe. Unless . . .

Ice moved through Celaena's veins. Unless Nehemia was here to start something bigger—unless she didn't want to make sure the king spared Eyllwe at all. Unless she wanted what few dared whisper: *rebellion.* And not rebellion as it was now, with rebel groups hiding out in the wilderness, but rather rebellion in the sense of entire kingdoms rising up against Adarlan—as it should have been from the start.

But why kill the Champions? Why not target royals? The ball would have been perfect for that. Why use Wyrdmarks? She'd seen Nehemia's rooms; there were no signs of a demon beast lurking about, and nowhere in the castle where she could—

Celaena's eyes rose from the book. Blocked by the giant chest of drawers, the tapestry still rippled in a phantom breeze. There was nowhere in the castle to summon or hide a creature like that, except for the endless, forgotten chambers and tunnels running beneath it.

"No," she said, standing so fast that it was all Fleetfoot could do to leap out of the way as her chair toppled over. No, it *wasn't* true. Because it was Nehemia. Because . . . because . . .

Celaena grunted as she pushed the chest to the side and folded the tapestry back from the wall. Just as it had two months ago, a cold, damp breeze leaked through the cracks, but it smelled nothing of roses. All of the murders had occurred within two days of a Test. That meant tonight, or tomorrow, something would happen. The ridderak, whatever it was, would strike again. And with the marks that she'd found painted under her bed . . . there was no way in hell she'd wait for it to show up.

After shutting the whining Fleetfoot out of the bedroom, Celaena covered the passage entry with the tapestry, wedged a book in the doorway to keep from getting locked in, and only once wished she had a weapon beyond the candlestick she carried and the makeshift knife in her pocket.

Because if Nehemia had truly lied to her like that, and if Nehemia was murdering the Champions, then Celaena had to see it herself. If only so she could kill her with her bare hands.

Down and down she went, her breath thick in the frigid air. Water dripped somewhere, and Celaena looked longingly at the middle archway as she approached the crossroads. There was no thought of escape now. What would be the point, when she was so close to winning? If she lost, she'd sneak back here before they had a chance to ship her off to Endovier again.

Celaena studied the left- and right-side passages. The one to her left only led to a dead end. But the one on the right . . . that was the passage she'd taken to Elena's tomb. There she'd seen countless other passageways leading to unknown places.

She stepped closer to the archway and froze when she saw the steps that descended into the murky darkness. The centuries-old dust had been disturbed. Footprints led up and down.

Nehemia and her creature must have been creeping around down here, just floors below everyone else. Hadn't Verin died just after he taunted her in front of Nehemia? Celaena clutched her candlestick tighter, and pulled her makeshift knife out of her pocket.

Step after step, she began her descent down the stairwell. Soon, she could no longer see the top landing, and the bottom never came any closer. But then whispers filled the corridor, slithering off the walls. She quieted her steps and shielded her candle as she neared. It wasn't the idle chat of servants, but someone speaking rapidly, almost chanting.

Not Nehemia. A man.

A landing approached below, opening into a room to her left. A greenish light seeped out of it onto the stones of the stairwell, which continued on past the landing and into darkness. The hair on her arms rose as the voice became clearer. It didn't speak any tongue that she recognized; it was guttural and harsh, and grated against her ears, as if it sucked the very warmth from her bones. The man panted as he spoke, like the words burned his throat, and finally he gasped for air.

Silence fell. Setting down her candle, Celaena crept toward the landing and peered inside the room. The oaken door had been thrown open, a giant key turned in its rusting lock. And inside the small chamber, kneeling before a darkness so black that it seemed poised to devour the world, was Cain.

42

Cain.

The person who'd gotten stronger and better as the competition went on. She'd thought it was his training, but . . . it was because he'd been using the Wyrdmarks and the beast they summoned to steal the dead Champions' strength.

He dragged a hand across the floor before the darkness, and greenish lights sprung up from where his fingers passed before being sucked into the void like wraiths on the wind. One of his hands was bleeding.

She didn't dare to breathe as something stirred in the darkness. There was a click of claw on stone, and a hiss like an extinguished flame. And then, stepping toward Cain on knees that bent the wrong way—like an animal's hind legs—the ridderak emerged.

It was something out of an ancient god's nightmares. Its hairless gray skin was stretched tightly across its misshapen head, displaying a gaping mouth filled with black fangs.

Fangs that had ripped out and eaten Verin and Xavier's internal organs; fangs that had feasted on their brains. Its vaguely human body sank onto its haunches, and it slid its long front arms across the stone floor. The stones whined under the claws. Cain raised his head and stood slowly as the creature knelt before him and lowered its dark eyes. Submission.

Celaena only realized she was trembling when she made to step away, to flee as far and as fast as she could. Elena had been right: this was evil, plain and simple. The amulet pulsed at her neck, as if urging her to run. Her mouth dry, her blood pounding in her veins, she stepped back.

Cain whirled to look at her, and the ridderak's head shot up, its slitted nostrils sniffing twice. She froze, but as she did so, a massive wind shoved into her from behind, making her stagger into the room.

"It wasn't meant to be you tonight," Cain said, but Celaena's eyes remained on the beast, who began panting. "But this opportunity is too good to go to waste."

"Cain," was all she could say. The ridderak's eyes . . . she'd never seen anything like them. There was nothing in them but hunger—endless, ageless hunger. The creature was not of this world. The Wyrdmarks worked. The gates were real. She pulled the makeshift knife out of her pocket. It was pitifully small; how could hairpins make a dent in that creature's hide?

Cain moved so quickly that she could only blink before he was behind her, her knife somehow now in his hand. No one—no one human—could move that quickly; it was as if he were no more than shadows and wind.

"Pity," Cain whispered from the doorway, pocketing her knife. Celaena glanced to the creature, to him, and then back. "I'll never get to know how you wound up down here in the first place." His fingers wrapped around the door handle. "Not that I care. Good-bye, Celaena." The door slammed shut.

The greenish light still seeped from the marks on the floor—marks Cain had etched with his own blood—illuminating the creature who stared at her with those starving, relentless eyes.

"Cain," she whispered, backing into the door as she fumbled with the handle. She twisted and yanked. It was locked. There was nothing in this room but stone and dust. How had she let him disarm her that easily? "*Cain*." The door wouldn't budge. "*Cain!*" she shouted, and banged on the door with a fist, hard enough to hurt.

The ridderak stalked back and forth on its four long, spidery limbs, sniffing at her, and Celaena paused. Why didn't it attack immediately? It sniffed at her again, and swiped at the ground with a clawed hand—striking deep enough to take out a chunk of stone.

It wanted her alive. Cain had incapacitated Verin while he summoned the creature; it liked its blood hot. So it would find the easiest way to immobilize her, and then . . .

She couldn't breathe. No, not like this. Not in this chamber, where no one would find her, where Chaol would never know why she disappeared, and would forever curse her for it, where she'd never get the chance to tell Nehemia she had been wrong. And Elena—Elena said someone wanted her in the tomb, to see . . . to see what?

And then she knew.

The answer lay on her right—the right passageway, the passage that led to the tomb a few levels below.

The creature sank back onto its haunches, poised to spring, and in that moment, Celaena came up with the most reckless and brave plan she'd ever concocted. She dropped her cape to the floor.

With a roar that shook the castle, the ridderak ran for her.

Celaena remained before the door, watching as it galloped at her, sparks flying from its claws as they struck stone. Ten feet away, it leapt straight toward her legs.

But Celaena was already running, running straight at those

black, rotting fangs. The ridderak jumped for her, and she hurtled over the snarling thing. A thunderous, splintering boom erupted through the chamber as the ridderak shattered the wooden door. She could only imagine what it would have done to her legs. She didn't have time to think. She landed and whirled, charging back to where the creature had crashed through the door and now sought to shake itself free of the pile of wood.

She threw herself through the doorway and turned left, flying down the stairwell. She'd never make it back to her chambers alive, but if she was fast enough, perhaps she could make it to the tomb.

The ridderak roared again, and the stairwell shuddered. She didn't dare to look behind. She focused on her feet, on keeping upright as she bounded down the stairs, making for the landing below, illuminated by moonlight leaking from the tomb.

Celaena hit the landing, ran for the tomb door, and prayed to gods whose names she'd forgotten, but who she hoped had not yet forgotten her.

Someone wanted me to come here on Samhuinn. Someone knew this would happen. Elena wanted me to see it—so I could survive.

The creature hit the bottom landing and charged after her, so close she could smell its reeking breath. The door to the tomb was wide open. As if someone had been waiting.

Please—please . . .

Grabbing onto the side of the doorway, she swung herself inside. She gained precious time as the ridderak skidded to a halt, missing the tomb. It only took a moment for it to recover and charge, taking off a chunk of the door as it entered.

The pounding of her feet echoed through the tomb as she ran between the sarcophagi for Damaris, the sword of the ancient king.

Displayed atop its stand, the blade shone in the moonlight—the metal still gleaming after a thousand years.

The creature snarled, and she heard its deep intake of breath and the scrape of nails departing stone as the ridderak leapt for her. She lunged for the sword, her left hand wrapping around the cool hilt as she twisted in the air and swung.

She only had time to see its eyes and the blur of its skin before she drove Damaris through the ridderak's face.

Pain lanced through her hand as they slammed into the wall and fell to the ground, scattering treasure. Black blood that stank of waste sprayed onto her.

She didn't move, not as she stared at those black eyes barely inches from her own, not as she saw her right hand held between its black teeth, her blood already oozing down its chin. She just panted and shook, not taking her left hand from the hilt of the sword, even after those hungry eyes turned dull and its body sagged atop hers.

It was only when the amulet throbbed again that she blinked. Everything after that became a series of steps, a dance that she had to execute perfectly or else she'd fall apart right there in that tomb and never get up.

She first pried her hand from its teeth. It burned mercilessly. An arc of gushing puncture wounds encircled her thumb, and she swayed on her feet as she shoved the ridderak off her. It was surprisingly light—as if its bones were hollow, or there were nothing inside of it. Though the world became foggy around the edges, she yanked Damaris from its skull.

She used her shirt to wipe Gavin's blade clean, and set it back where it belonged. That was why they'd brought her to the tomb on Samhuinn, wasn't it? So she could see Damaris, and have a way to save herself?

She left the creature where it lay in a crumpled heap atop piles of jewels. Whoever had wanted to save her could clean it up. She'd had enough.

Still, Celaena paused beside Elena's sarcophagus and looked at the beautiful face carved from marble. "Thank you," she said hoarsely. Her vision blurring, she left the tomb and staggered up the stairs, clutching her bleeding hand to her chest.

When she was at last safely inside her chambers, Celaena crossed to her bedroom door and leaned there, panting, as she unlocked it. Her wound hadn't clotted, and blood was still pouring down her wrist. She listened to it drip onto the floor. She should go into the bathing room and wash her hand. Her palm felt like ice. She should—

Her legs gave out and Celaena collapsed. Her eyelids became heavy, so she closed them. Why did her heart beat so slowly?

She opened her eyes to look at her hand. Her eyesight was blurry, and all she could make out was a mess of pink and red. The ice in her hand reached up her arm, down to her legs.

She heard a booming, thunderous noise. A thump-thump-thump, followed by a whine. Through her eyelids she could see the light in the room darken.

She heard a cry—female—and warm hands grabbed her face. She was so cold it almost burned. Had someone left the window open?

"Lillian!" It was Nehemia. She shook Celaena's shoulders. "Lillian! What happened to you?"

Celaena remembered little of the next few moments. Strong arms lifted her up and rushed her into the bathing chamber. Nehemia strained as she carried Celaena into the bathing pool, where she stripped away Celaena's clothes. Celaena's hand burned when it touched the water, and she thrashed, but the princess held her firm, saying words in a tongue the assassin didn't understand. The light in the room pulsed, and her skin tingled. Celaena found her arms covered in glowing turquoise marks—Wyrdmarks. Nehemia held her in the water, rocking back and forth.

Blackness swallowed her up.

43

Celaena opened her eyes.

She was warm, and the candlelight was golden. She could smell lotus blossoms and a bit of nutmeg. She made a small noise and blinked, attempting to raise herself from the bed. What had happened? She could only recall climbing the stairs, then concealing the secret door behind the tapestry—

Celaena gave a start and grabbed at her tunic, gaping as she found that it had somehow turned into a nightgown, and then marveled at her hand as she lifted it into the air. It was healed—completely healed. The only remnants of the wounds were a half-moon-shaped scar between her thumb and index finger and little bite marks from the ridderak's lower teeth. She ran a finger over each of the chalk-white scars, tracing their curve, then wiggled her fingers to ensure no nerves had been severed.

How was this possible? It was magic—someone had healed her. She lifted herself and saw she was not alone.

Nehemia sat in a chair nearby, staring at her. There was no smile on her lips, and Celaena shifted as she beheld the mistrust in the young woman's eyes. Fleetfoot lay at her feet.

"What happened?" Celaena asked.

"That's what I have been waiting to ask you," said the princess in Eyllwe. She gestured at Celaena's body. "If I hadn't found you, you would have died from that bite within a few minutes."

Even the blood she'd dropped on the floor had been cleaned. "Thank you," she said, then started as she looked to the darkened sky beyond the windows. "What day is it?" If somehow two days had passed and she'd missed the last Test—

"It's only been three hours."

Celaena's shoulders sagged. She hadn't missed it. She still had tomorrow to train, and the Test the day after that. "I don't understand. How did—"

"That is not important," Nehemia interrupted. "I want to know where you received that bite. There was blood only in your bedroom—no traces of it in the hallway or anywhere else."

Celaena clenched and unclenched her right hand, watching the scars stretch and contract. She had come so close to dying. She flicked her eyes to the princess, then back to her hand. Whatever Nehemia's involvement was, it wasn't with Cain.

"I'm not who I pretend to be," Celaena said quietly, unable to meet her friend's eyes. "Lillian Gordaina doesn't exist." Nehemia didn't say anything. Celaena made herself look her in the eye. Nehemia had saved her; how had she dared to believe that Nehemia might be the one controlling that creature? The truth was the least she owed her friend. "My name is Celaena Sardothien."

Nehemia's mouth parted. Slowly, she shook her head. "But they sent you to Endovier. You were supposed to be in Endovier with—" Nehemia's eyes widened. "You speak the Eyllwe of the peasants—of those enslaved in Endovier. That was how you learned." Celaena's breathing became a bit difficult. Nehemia's lips trembled. "You went . . . you went to *Endovier*? Endovier is a death camp. But . . . why did you not tell me? Do you not trust me?"

"Of course I do," she said. Especially now that she'd proven beyond a doubt that she wasn't the one responsible for those murders. "I was ordered by the king not to speak a word of it."

"A word of what?" Nehemia said sharply, blinking back her tears. "The *king* knows you're here? He gives you orders?"

"I'm here for his amusement." Celaena sat up straighter in bed. "I'm here because he's hosting a competition to be the King's Champion. And after I win—*if* I win, I'm to work for the king for four years as his lackey and assassin. And then I'll be freed, and my name cleared."

Nehemia just looked at her, damning her with that blank stare.

"You think I want to be here?" Celaena shouted, even though it made her head pound. "It was either this or Endovier! I had no choice." She put her hands on her chest. "Before you start lecturing me on my morality, or before you run away and hide behind your bodyguards, just know that there's not a moment that goes by when I don't wonder what it will be like to kill for him—the man who destroyed *everything* that I loved!"

She couldn't breathe fast enough, not as the door inside her mind opened and closed, and the images that Celaena had made herself forget flashed before her eyes. She closed them, wishing for darkness. Nehemia remained silent. Fleetfoot whined. In the quiet, people, places, words echoed in her mind.

Then, footsteps. They brought her back. The mattress groaned and sighed as Nehemia sat. A second, lighter weight joined her—Fleetfoot.

Nehemia took Celaena's hand in her warm, dry one. Celaena opened her eyes, but stared at the wall across the room.

Nehemia squeezed her hand. "You're my dearest friend, Celaena. It hurt me—hurt me more than I realized it would—to have things become so cold between us. To see you look at me with such distrust in your eyes. And I don't want to ever see you look at me like that again. So I wish to give to you what I have given to few before." Her dark eyes shone. "Names are not important. It's what lies inside of you that matters. I know what you went through in Endovier. I know what my people endure there, day after day. But you did not let the mines harden you; you did not let it shame your soul into cruelty."

The princess traced a mark on her hand, her fingers pressing into Celaena's skin. "You bear many names, and so I shall name you as well." Her hand rose to Celaena's forehead and she drew an invisible mark. "I name you Elentiya." She kissed the assassin's brow. "I give you this name to use with honor, to use when other names grow too heavy. I name you Elentiya, 'Spirit That Could Not Be Broken.'"

Celaena was held in place. She could feel the name fall upon her like a shimmering veil. This was unconditional love. Friends like this did not exist. Why was she so fortunate as to have found one?

"Come," Nehemia said brightly. "Tell me about how you became Adarlan's Assassin, and how you wound up in this castle, exactly—and what the details are of this absurd competition." Celaena smiled slightly as Fleetfoot wagged her tail and licked Nehemia's arm.

She had saved her life—somehow. Answers for that would come later. So Celaena spoke.

The following morning, Celaena walked beside Chaol, her eyes on the marble floor of the hallway. The sun radiated off of the snow in the garden, making the light in the hall nearly blinding. She'd told Nehemia almost everything. There were certain things she'd never tell anyone, and she hadn't mentioned Cain or the creature, either. Nehemia hadn't asked her again what had bitten her hand, but had stayed with her, curled up in bed as they talked long into the night. Celaena, unsure how she'd ever sleep again now that she knew what Cain could do, had been grateful for the company. She pulled her cloak tighter around her. The morning was unnaturally frigid.

"You're quiet today." Chaol kept his gaze ahead of them. "Did you and Dorian have a fight?"

Dorian. He'd stopped by last night, but Nehemia had shooed him off before he could enter the bedroom. "No. I haven't seen him since yesterday morning." After the events of last night, yesterday morning seemed like a week ago.

"Did you enjoy dancing with him at the ball?"

Were his words a bit sharp? She turned to him as they rounded a corner, heading toward a private training room. "You left rather early. I would have thought you'd want to guard me the whole night."

"You don't need me to watch you anymore."

"I didn't need you to watch me from the start."

He shrugged. "Now I know you're not going anywhere."

Outside, a howling wind kicked up a flurry of snow, sending a sparkling wave into the air. "I could go back to Endovier."

"You won't."

"How do you know that?"

"I just know."

"That gives me heaps of confidence."

He chuckled, continuing toward the sparring room. "I'm surprised your dog didn't run after you, for all the crying she did just now."

"If you had a pet, you wouldn't make fun," she said gloomily.

"I've never had a pet; I never wanted one."

"That's probably a blessing for whatever dog might have wound up as your companion."

He jabbed her with an elbow. She grinned and elbowed him back. She wanted to tell him about Cain. She'd wanted to tell him when she saw him at her door this morning. She wanted to tell him everything.

But he couldn't know. Because, she'd realized last night, if she told him about Cain and the creature he'd unleashed, then he'd ask to see the remains of the creature. And that meant taking him into the secret passage. While he might trust her enough to leave her alone with Dorian, knowing that she had access to an unguarded escape route was a test she wasn't ready to give Chaol.

Besides, I killed it. It's over. Elena's mysterious evil is vanquished. Now I'll just defeat Cain in the duel, and then no one needs to know.

Chaol stopped before the unmarked door of their practice room, and whirled to face her. "I'm only going to ask you this once, and then I won't ask it again," he said, staring at her so intensely that she shifted on her feet. "Do you know what you're getting into with Dorian?"

She laughed, a harsh, cawing noise. "Are you giving *me* romantic advice? And is this for my sake or Dorian's?"

"Both."

"I didn't realize that you cared enough about me to bother. Or even notice."

To his credit, he didn't take the bait. Instead, he just unlocked the door. "Just remember to use your brain, will you?" he said over his shoulder, and entered the room.

~

An hour later, sweating and still panting from the swordplay practice, Celaena wiped her brow on her sleeve as they made their way back to her rooms.

"The other day, I saw you were reading *Elric and Emide*," he said. "I thought you hated poetry."

"It's different." She swung her arms. "Epic poetry isn't boring—or pretentious."

"Oh?" A crooked smile twisted across his face. "A poem about massive battles and boundless love isn't pretentious?" She playfully punched his shoulder, and he laughed. Surprisingly delighted at his laughter, she cackled. But then they turned a corner, and guards filled the hall, and she saw him.

The King of Adarlan.

44

The king. Celaena's heart gave a screech and dove behind her spine. Each of the little scars on her hand throbbed. He strode toward them, his monstrous form filling the too-small hallway, and their eyes met. She went cold and hot at once. Chaol halted and bowed low.

Slowly, not wishing to find herself swinging from the gallows just yet, Celaena bowed, too. He stared at her with eyes of iron. The hair on her arms rose. She could feel him searching, looking for something inside of her. He knew that something was wrong, that something had changed in his castle—something to do with her. Celaena and Chaol rose and stepped aside.

His head turned to examine her as he strode past. Could he see what lay beyond her flesh? Did he know that Cain had the ability to open portals, real portals, to other worlds? Did he know that even though he'd banned magic, the Wyrdmarks still commanded a power of their own? Power the king could wield if he learned to summon demons like the ridderak . . .

There was a darkness in his eyes that felt cold and foreign, like the gaps between the stars. Could one man destroy a world? Was his ambition so consuming? She could hear the din of war. The king's head shifted to look at the hallway ahead.

Something dangerous lurked about him. It was an air of death that she'd felt standing before that black void summoned by Cain. It was the stench of another world, a dead world. What was Elena's goal in demanding that she get close to him?

Celaena managed to walk, one step at a time, away from the king. Her eyes were far away and distant, and though she didn't look at Chaol, she felt him studying her face. Thankfully, he didn't say a word. It was nice to have someone who understood.

Chaol also didn't say anything when she moved closer to him for the remainder of their walk.

Chaol paced through his room, his time with Celaena over until she'd train with the other Champions that afternoon. After lunch, he'd returned to his room to read the report detailing the king's journey. And in the past ten minutes, he'd read the thing three times. He crumpled the paper in his fist. Why had the king arrived alone? And, more importantly, how had everyone in his traveling party died? It wasn't clear where he'd gone. He'd mentioned the White Fang Mountains, but . . . Why were they all dead?

The king had vaguely hinted at some sort of issue with rebels poisoning their food stores, but the details were murky enough to suggest that the truth was buried somewhere else. Perhaps he hadn't explained it fully because it would upset his subjects. But Chaol was his Captain of the Guard. If the king didn't trust him . . .

The clock struck and Chaol's shoulders sagged. Poor Celaena. Did she know that she looked like a frightened animal when the king appeared? He'd almost wanted to pat her on the back. And the effect the king had on her lasted long after their encounter; she'd been distant during lunch.

She was incredible now, so fast he had difficulty keeping up with her. She could scale a wall with ease, and had even demonstrated by climbing up to her own balcony with nothing but her bare hands. It unnerved him, especially when he remembered she was only eighteen. He wondered if this was how she'd been before Endovier. She never hesitated when they sparred, but she seemed to sink far within herself, into a place that was calm and cool, but also angry and burning. She could kill anyone, Cain included, in a matter of seconds.

But if she became Champion, could they let her loose into Erilea once more? He was fond of her, but Chaol didn't know if he could sleep at night knowing that he had retrained and released the world's greatest assassin. If she won, though, she'd be here for four years.

What had the king thought when he saw them together, laughing? Surely, that hadn't been his reason for neglecting to tell him what happened to his men. No—the king wouldn't bother to care about that kind of thing, especially if Celaena might soon be his Champion.

Chaol rubbed his shoulder. She'd looked so small when she saw the king.

Since returning from his travels, the king hadn't seemed any different, and was just as gruff with Chaol as he'd always been. But the sudden disappearance, then returning without a single soul . . . There was something brewing, a cauldron that the king had journeyed to stir. Celaena somehow knew it, too.

The Captain of the Guard leaned against a wall, staring at the ceiling. He shouldn't press into the king's business. Right now, his focus was on solving the murders of the Champions, and on making sure

Celaena won. It wasn't even about Dorian's pride anymore; Celaena wouldn't survive another year in Endovier.

Chaol smiled slightly. She'd stirred up enough trouble in the months she'd been in the castle. He could only imagine what would happen over the next four years.

45

Celaena panted as she and Nox lowered their swords, the Weapons Master shouting at the five Champions to get some water. Tomorrow was their last Test before the duel. She kept her distance when Cain lumbered toward the water jug on the table by the far wall, watching his every movement. She eyed his muscles, his height, his girth—all strength stolen from the dead Champions. She studied the black ring on his finger. Did it somehow have a connection to his horrible abilities? He hadn't even looked all that surprised to see her alive when she'd entered the training hall. He'd just given her a small, taunting smile and picked up his practice sword.

"Is something the matter?" Nox said, his breathing ragged as he stopped by her side. Cain, Grave, and Renault were talking amongst themselves. "You were a bit off-balance."

How had Cain learned to summon that creature—and what was that blackness from whence it had appeared? Was it truly just so he could win the competition?

"Or," Nox continued, "do you have other thoughts on your mind?"

She shoved Cain out of her head. "What?"

He grinned at her. "It seemed like you were rather enjoying the Crown Prince's attention at the ball."

"Mind your own business," she snapped.

Nox held up his hands. "I didn't mean to pry." She walked to the water jug, not saying a word to Nox as she poured herself a glass and didn't bother to offer him one. He leaned in as she set down the jug. "Those scars on your hand are new."

She stuffed her hand into a pocket, her eyes flashing. "Mind your own business," she repeated. She stepped away, but Nox grabbed her arm.

"You told me to stay in my rooms the other night. And those scars look like bite marks. They say Verin and Xavier were killed by animals." His gray eyes narrowed. "You know something."

She glanced over her shoulder at Cain, who was joking with Grave as if he weren't a demon-summoning psychopath. "There are only five of us left. Four make it to the duels, and the Test's tomorrow. Whatever happened to Verin and Xavier, it wasn't an accident, not when their deaths occurred within two days of the Tests." She shook her arm out of his grasp. "*Be careful*," she hissed.

"Tell me what you know."

She couldn't, not without sounding insane. "If you were smart, you'd get out of this castle."

"Why?" He shot a look at Cain. "What aren't you saying?"

Brullo finished his water and went to retrieve his sword. She didn't have much time before he called them to resume. "I'm saying that if I didn't have any other choice but to be here—if it wasn't between this and death, I would be halfway across Erilea by now, and not looking back."

Nox rubbed his neck. "I don't understand a word of what you just said. Why don't you have a choice? I know things are bad with your father, but surely he won't—" She silenced him with a pointed stare. "And you're not a jewel thief, are you?" She shook her head. Nox glanced again at Cain. "Cain knows, too. That's why he always tries to rile you—to get you to show who you truly are."

She nodded. What difference did it make if he knew? She had more important things to worry about now. Like how she'd survive until the duels. Or stop Cain.

"But who are you?" Nox said. She bit her lip. "You said your father moved you to Endovier, that much is true. The prince went there to retrieve you—there's evidence of that journey." Even as he said it, his eyes slid toward her back. She could practically see the revelations as they bloomed in his mind. "And—you weren't in the town of Endovier. You were *in* Endovier. The Salt Mines. That explains why you were so painfully thin when I first saw you."

Brullo clapped his hands. "Come on, you lot! Drills!"

Nox and Celaena remained by the table. His eyes were wide. "You were a slave in Endovier?" She couldn't form the words to confirm it. Nox was too smart for his own good. "But you're barely a woman—what did you do to . . ." His gaze fell on Chaol, and the guards who stood near him. "Would I have heard your name before? Would I have heard that you were shipped to Endovier?"

"Yes. Everyone heard when I went," she breathed, and watched as he sorted through every name he'd ever heard associated with the place, then put the pieces together. He took a step back.

"You're a *girl*?"

"Surprising, I know. Everyone thinks I'm older."

Nox ran a hand through his black hair. "And you can either be the King's Champion, or go back to Endovier?"

"That's why I can't leave." Brullo shouted at them to start their drills. "And why I'm telling you to get out of the castle while you can." She took her hand from her pocket and showed it to him. "I received this from a creature I can't even begin to describe to you, nor would you believe me if I tried. But there are five of us now, and because the Test is tomorrow, that means one more night we're at risk."

"I don't understand *any* of this," Nox said, still keeping back a step.

"You don't have to. But you're not going back to prison if you fail, and you're not going to be the Champion, even if you make it to the duels. So you need to *leave*."

"Do I want to know what's killing the Champions?"

She fought her shudder as she recalled the fangs and stench of the creature. "No," she said, unable to keep the fear from her voice. "You don't. You just have to trust me—and trust that I'm not trying to eliminate my competition by tricking you."

Whatever he read in her expression made his shoulders sag. "All of this time, I thought you were just some pretty girl from Bellhaven who stole jewels to get her father's attention. Little did I know that the blond-haired girl was Queen of the Underworld." He smiled ruefully. "Thank you for warning me. You could have opted to say nothing."

"You were the only one who bothered to take me seriously," she said, smiling with warmth that she meant. "I'm surprised you even believe me."

Brullo shouted at them, and they began walking back to the group. Chaol's eyes were hard upon them. She knew he'd question her about their conversation later.

"Do me a favor, Celaena," Nox said. The sound of her name startled her. He brought his mouth close to her ear. "Rip Cain's head off," he whispered with a wicked grin. Celaena only smiled back at him and nodded.

Nox left early that night, slipping out of the castle without a word to anyone.

The clock chimed five, and Kaltain fought the urge to rub her eyes as the opium oozed through every pore of her body. In the light of the setting sun, the castle hallways were awash with red and orange and gold, the colors bleeding together. Perrington had asked her to join his dinner table in the Great Hall, and she normally wouldn't have dared to smoke before a public meal, but the headache that had plagued her all afternoon hadn't gotten any better.

The hall seemed to stretch on forever. She ignored the passing courtiers and servants, focusing instead on the fading day. Someone approached from the other end, a smear of black against the gold and orange light. Shadows seemed to leak from him, flowing onto the stones and the windows and the walls like spilled ink.

She tried to swallow as she neared him, but found her tongue to be leaden and paper-dry.

Each step brought him closer—made him bigger and taller—and her heartbeat thundered in her ears. Perhaps the opium had gone bad—perhaps she'd smoked too much this time. Amid the pounding in her ears and her head, the whisper of wings filled the air.

In the space between blinks, she could have sworn she saw *things* swooping past him in swift, vicious circles, hovering above him, waiting, waiting, waiting . . .

"Milady," Cain said, bowing his head as he strode by.

Kaltain said nothing. She clenched her sweaty palms and continued toward the Great Hall. It took a while for the sound of flapping wings to fade, but by the time she reached the duke's table, she'd forgotten all about it.

After dinner that night, Celaena sat across the chessboard from Dorian. The kiss following the ball two days ago hadn't been so bad. Nice, actually, if she was being honest. Of course, he'd returned tonight, and so far there had been no mention of the fresh scars on her hand, or the kiss. And she'd never, not in a million years, tell him about the ridderak. She might feel something for him, but if he told his father about the power of the Wyrdmarks and Wyrdgates . . . Her blood chilled at the thought.

But looking at him, with his face illuminated by firelight, she couldn't see any resemblance to his father. No, she could only see his kindness, and intelligence, and maybe he was a tad arrogant, but . . . Celaena's toes scratched Fleetfoot's ears. She'd expected him to stay away, to move on to another woman now that he'd tasted her.

Well, did he even want to taste *you in the first place?*

He moved his High Priestess, and Celaena laughed. "Do you *really* wish to do that?" she asked. His face contorted with confusion, and she picked up her pawn, moving it diagonally, and easily knocked over the piece.

"Damn!" he cried, and she cackled.

"Here." She handed him the piece. "Take it and try another move."

"No. I'll play like a man and accept my losses!"

They laughed, but silence soon crept over them. A smile still played about her lips, and he reached for her hand. She wanted to pull it away, but couldn't bring herself to do it. He held her hand over the board and smoothly flattened their palms against each other, interlocking his fingers with hers. His hand was calloused but sturdy. Their entwined hands rested on the side of the table.

"One needs both hands to play chess," she said, wondering if it were possible for her heart to explode. Fleetfoot huffed and trotted away, probably to disappear under the bed.

"I think you only need one." He moved a piece all over the board. "See?"

She chewed her lip. Still, she didn't pull her hand from his. "Are you going to kiss me again?"

"I'd like to." She couldn't move as he leaned toward her, closer and closer, the table groaning beneath him, until he stopped, his lips just a hair's breadth from hers.

"I ran into your father in the hall today," she blurted.

Dorian slowly sat back in his chair. "And?"

"And it was fine," she lied. His eyes narrowed.

He lifted her chin with a finger. "You didn't say that to avoid the inevitable, did you?" No, she'd said that just to keep talking, to keep him here as long as he would be willing to stay, so she didn't have to face a night alone with the threat of Cain hovering over her. Who better to keep at her side in the dark hours of the night than the son of the king? Cain wouldn't dare harm him.

But all of this . . . everything that had happened with the ridderak meant all the books she'd read were true. What if Cain could summon *anything* to him—like the dead? There were many people who lost their fortunes when magic vanished. Even the king himself might be intrigued by this sort of power.

"You're trembling," Dorian said. She was. Like a damned idiot, she was trembling. "Are you all right?" He moved around the table to sit beside her.

She couldn't tell him; no, he could never know. Just as he couldn't know that when she'd checked under her bed before dinner, there were fresh chalk marks for her to wash away. Cain knew that she'd discovered how he was eliminating the competition. Perhaps he'd hunt her down tonight, or perhaps not—she hadn't the faintest idea. But she'd get little sleep tonight—or until Cain was impaled on the end of her sword.

"I'm fine," she said, though her voice was little more than a whisper. But if he kept asking, she was bound to tell him.

"Are you sure that you're feeling—" he began, but she surged forward and kissed him.

She almost knocked him to the floor. But he shot out an arm to the back of the chair and braced himself as his spare arm wrapped around her middle. She let the touch, the taste of him fill the room of her mind with water. She kissed him, hoping to steal some of his air. Her fingers entangled themselves in his hair, and as he kissed her fiercely, she let everything fade away.

The clock chimed three. Celaena sat on her bed, knees curled to her chest. After hours of kissing and talking and more kissing on her bed, Dorian had left only minutes before. She'd been tempted to ask him to stay—the smart thing would have been to ask him to stay—but the thought of Dorian being here when Cain or the ridderak came for her, of Dorian being hurt, made her let him go.

Too tired to read, but too awake to sleep, she just stared at the crackling fire. Every bump and footstep made her jolt, and she'd managed to swipe a few pins from Philippa's sewing basket when she wasn't looking. But a makeshift knife, a heavy book, and a candlestick weren't protection against what Cain could summon.

You shouldn't have left Damaris in the tomb. Going back down there wasn't an option—not while Cain lived. She hugged her knees, shivering as she recalled the utter blackness from which the thing had come.

Cain must have learned about the Wyrdmarks in the White Fang Mountains—that cursed borderland between Adarlan and the Western Wastes. They said that evil still crept out of the ruins of the Witch Kingdom—and that old women with iron teeth still wandered the lonely roads in the mountain passes.

The hair on her arms rose, and she grabbed a fur blanket from her bed to wrap around herself. If she could stay alive until the duels, she'd defeat Cain, and this would all be over. Then she could sleep soundly again—unless Elena had something else, something bigger in mind.

Celaena rested her cheek against her knee, listening to the clock *tick-tick-tick* long into the night.

~

Thundering hooves beat the frozen ground, faster and faster as the rider whipped the horse. Snow and mud lay thick on the earth, and rogue snowflakes drifted through the night sky.

Celaena ran—swifter than her young legs could manage. Everything hurt. Trees ripped at her dress and hair; stones sliced her feet. She scrambled through the woods, breathing so hard she couldn't muster the air to cry for help. She must reach the bridge. It couldn't cross the bridge.

Behind her, a sword shrieked as it was drawn from its sheath.

She fell, slamming into mud and rock. The sound of the approaching demon filled the air as she struggled to rise. But the mud held fast, and she could not run.

Reaching for a bush, her small hands bleeding, the horse now close behind, she—

~

Celaena gasped and awoke. She put a hand to her heart and pushed against her chest as it lifted and fell. It was a dream.

The fire had dwindled to embers; a cold gray light seeped in through her curtains. It was only a nightmare. She must have dozed off at some point during the night. She clutched her amulet, running a thumb across the stone in the center.

Some protection you were when that thing attacked me the other night.

Frowning, she gently arranged her covers around Fleetfoot, and stroked the dog's head for a moment. Dawn was near. She'd made it through another night.

Sighing, Celaena lay back and closed her eyes.

A few hours later, when news of Nox's departure spread, she received notice that the last Test had been canceled. She would duel against Grave, Renault, and Cain tomorrow.

Tomorrow—and then her freedom would be decided.

46

The forest was still and frozen around Dorian, and snow collapsed from the trees in large clumps as he passed by. His eyes darted among the branches and bushes. He'd needed to come out for a hunt today, if only to let the freezing air rush through him.

He saw her face each time he closed his eyes. She haunted his thoughts, made him wish to do grand and wonderful things in her name, made him want to be a man who deserved to wear a crown.

But Celaena—he didn't know how she felt. She kissed him—greedily, at that—but the women he'd loved in the past had always been eager. They'd gazed at him adoringly, while she just looked at him like a cat watching a mouse. Dorian straightened, detecting nearby movement. A stag stood ten yards away, feeding on bark. He stopped his horse and drew an arrow from its quiver. But he slackened the bow.

She was to duel tomorrow.

If harm came to her . . . No, she could hold her own; she was strong and smart and quick. He'd gone too far; he should never have kissed her. Because now, no matter how he might have once envisioned his future, or who he thought he'd spend it with, he couldn't imagine being with anyone else—wanting anyone else.

Snow began falling. Dorian glanced at the gray sky and rode on through the silent game park.

~

Celaena stood before her balcony doors, staring down at Rifthold. The roofs were still snow-covered, and lights twinkled in every home. It might have looked beautiful, had she not known what corruption and filth dwelt within it. And what monstrosity ruled over it all. She hoped Nox was far, far away. She'd told her guards she didn't want any visitors tonight, and to turn away even Chaol and Dorian if they arrived. Someone had knocked, once, but she didn't answer, and they had soon left without trying again. She put her hand on a pane of glass, savoring its frozen bite. The clock struck twelve.

Tomorrow—or was it today already?—she'd face Cain. She'd never sparred with him in practice. The other Champions had been too eager to get a piece of him. While Cain was strong, he wasn't as fast as she was. But he had stamina. She'd have to dodge him for a while. She just prayed all that running with Chaol would keep her from tiring before him. If she lost—

Don't even give yourself that option.

She leaned her forehead against the glass. Would it be more honorable to fall in the duel than to return to Endovier? Or would it be more honorable to die than to become the King's Champion? Who would he have her kill?

She'd had a say as Adarlan's Assassin. Even with Arobynn Hamel running her life, she'd always had a say in what jobs she took. No children. No one from Terrasen. But the king could tell her to kill anyone.

Did Elena expect her to say no to him when she was his Champion? Her stomach rose in her throat. Now wasn't the time for this. She had to focus on Cain, on wearing him down.

But try as she might, all she could think about was that half-starved, hopeless assassin who'd been dragged out of Endovier one autumn day by a snarling Captain of the Guard. What would she have said to the prince's bargain, had she known she would come to stand poised to lose so much? Would she have laughed if she'd known that other things—other people—would come to mean as much as her freedom?

Celaena swallowed the lump in her throat. Perhaps there were other reasons to fight tomorrow. Perhaps a few months in the castle hadn't been enough. Perhaps . . . perhaps she wanted to stay here for reasons other than her eventual freedom. *That* was one thing that hopeless assassin from Endovier would have never believed.

But it was true. She wanted to stay.

And that would make tomorrow so much harder.

47

Kaltain pulled her red cape around her, savoring its warmth. Why were the duels outside? She'd freeze before the assassin arrived! She fingered the vial in her pocket, and glanced at the two goblets on the wooden table. The one on the right was for Sardothien. She must not confuse them.

She looked to Perrington, who stood near the king. He had no idea what she'd do once Sardothien was out of the way—once Dorian was free again. Her blood grew warm and glittering.

The duke moved toward her, and Kaltain kept her eyes on the tiled veranda where the duel was to occur. He stopped in front of her, making a wall between her and the other council members so that none could see.

"A bit chilly for an outside duel," he said. Kaltain smiled and let the folds of her cloak fall over the table as he kissed her hand. With a veil of red to conceal her stealthy, free hand, Kaltain flicked off the lid of the vial and dumped the contents into the wine. The vial was back in her pocket as he raised himself. Just enough to weaken Sardothien—to make her dizzy and disoriented.

A guard appeared in the doorway, and then another. Between them strode a figure. She wore men's clothes, though Kaltain was forced to admit that her black-and-gold jacket was of fine make. It was strange to think of this woman as an assassin, but seeing her now, all of her oddities and faults made sense. Kaltain ran a finger along the base of the goblet and grinned.

Duke Perrington's Champion emerged from behind the clock tower. Kaltain's brows rose. They thought Sardothien could defeat such a man if she wasn't drugged?

Kaltain took a step back from the table, and Perrington moved to sit beside the king as the other two Champions arrived. With eager faces, they waited for blood.

Standing on the wide veranda that encompassed the obsidian clock tower, Celaena tried not to shiver. She couldn't see the point in having the duels outside—well, apart from making the Champions even more uncomfortable. She glanced longingly at the glass windows that lined the wall of the castle, and then at the frost-covered garden. Her hands were already numb. Tucking them into her fur-lined pockets, she approached Chaol, who was standing near the edge of the giant chalk circle that had been drawn on the flagstones.

"It's freezing out here," she said. The collar and sleeves of her black jacket were lined with rabbit fur, but it wasn't enough. "Why didn't you tell me it was outside?"

Chaol shook his head, looking at Grave, and at Renault—the mercenary from Skull's Bay, who, to her satisfaction, also seemed fairly miserable in the cold. "We didn't know; the king decided just now,"

Chaol said. "At least it should be over quickly." He smiled slightly, though she didn't return it.

The sky was bright blue, and she gritted her teeth as a strong gust of wind ripped into her. The thirteen seats of the table were filling up, and at the center of the table sat the king and Perrington. Kaltain stood behind Perrington, wearing a beautiful red cloak lined with white fur. Their eyes met, and Celaena wondered why the woman smiled at her. Kaltain then looked away—toward the tower, and Celaena followed her gaze and understood.

Cain was leaning against the clock tower. His muscles were barely contained within his tunic. All that stolen strength . . . what would have happened if the ridderak had killed her, too? How much stronger would he be today? Worse, he was wearing the red-and-gold garb of a member of the royal guard—the wyvern emblazoned across his broad chest. The sword at his side was beautiful. A gift from Perrington, no doubt. Did the duke know the power his Champion wielded? Even if she tried to reveal him, no one would ever believe her.

Nausea gripped her, but Chaol took her by the elbow and escorted her to the far end of the veranda. At the table, she noticed two aging men casting anxious glances at her. She nodded to them.

Lords Urizen and Garnel. It seems you obtained what you desired enough to kill for. And it seems someone told you who I actually am.

It had been two years ago that they hired her, separately, to kill the same man. She hadn't bothered to tell them, of course, and accepted both their payments. She winked at Lord Garnel, and he paled, knocking over his goblet of hot cocoa and ruining the papers before him. Oh, she'd keep their secrets; it would tarnish her reputation otherwise. But if her freedom came down to a vote . . . She smiled at Lord Urizen, who looked away. Her gaze shifted to another man, who she found staring at her.

The king. Deep inside, she quaked, but she bowed her head.

"Are you ready?" Chaol asked. Celaena blinked, remembering that he was beside her.

"Yes," she said, though she didn't mean it. The wind whipped through her hair, knotting it with frozen fingers. Dorian appeared by the table, heartbreakingly handsome as always, and gave her a grim smile as he stuffed his hands in his pockets and looked toward his father.

The last of the king's councilmen sat down at the table. Celaena cocked her head as Nehemia emerged to stand along the sidelines of the large white circle. The princess met her stare and lifted her chin in encouragement. She wore a spectacular outfit: close-fitting pants, a layered tunic studded with whorls of iron, and knee-high boots; she carried her wooden staff, which stretched as high as her head. To honor her, Celaena realized, her eyes stinging. One fellow warrior acknowledging the other.

Everyone grew silent as the king rose. Her insides turned to stone, and she felt clumsy and thick, but also light and weak as a newborn.

Chaol nudged her with an elbow, motioning for her to stand before the table. She focused on her feet as she moved, and wouldn't look at the king's face. Thankfully, Renault and Grave flanked her. If Cain had been standing beside her, she might have snapped his neck just to end it there. There were so many people watching her . . .

She stood not ten feet from the King of Adarlan. Freedom or death lay at this table. Her past and future were seated on a glass throne.

Her gaze shifted to Nehemia, whose fierce and graceful eyes warmed the marrow of her bones and steadied her arms.

The King of Adarlan spoke. Knowing that seeing his face would only weaken the strength she'd found in Nehemia's eyes, she looked not at him, but at the throne behind him. She wondered if Kaltain's presence meant that Duke Perrington had told her who Celaena truly was.

"You were taken from your miserable lives so you might prove yourself worthy of becoming a sacred warrior to the Crown. After months of training, the moment has come to decide who my Champion shall be. You will face each other in a duel. You can win only by trapping your opponent in a position of sure death. And *no further*," he added with a sharp glance in her direction. "Cain and Councilman Garnel's Champion will go first. Then my son's Champion will face Councilman Mullison's Champion."

Of course, the king would know Cain's name. He might as well have just declared the brute his Champion. "The winners will face each other in a final duel. Whoever wins will be crowned King's Champion. Is that clear?"

They nodded. For a heartbeat, she saw the king with stark clarity. He was just a man—a man with too much power. And in that one heartbeat, she didn't fear him. *I will not be afraid,* she vowed, wrapping the familiar words around her heart. "Then let the duels commence on my command," the king said.

Taking that as a sign that she could clear out of the ring, Celaena stalked to where Chaol stood and took up a place beside him.

Cain and Renault bowed to the king, then to each other, and drew their swords. She ran an eye down Renault's body as he took his stance. She'd seen him square off against Cain before; he'd never won, but he always managed to hold out longer than she would have thought possible. Perhaps he'd win.

But Cain lifted his sword. He had the better weapon. And he had half a foot on Renault.

"Begin," the king said. Metal flashed. They struck each other and danced back. Renault, refusing to take up the defensive, swept forward again, landing a few strong blows on Cain's blade. She forced her shoulders to relax, forced herself to breathe down the cold air.

"Do you think it was just poor luck," she murmured to Chaol, "that I'm the one going second?"

He kept his attention on the duel. "I think you'll be allowed proper time to rest." He jerked his chin at the dueling men. "Cain sometimes forgets to guard his right side. Look there." Celaena watched as Cain struck, twisting his body so his right side was wide open. "Renault doesn't even notice." Cain grunted and pressed Renault's blade, forcing the mercenary to take a step back. "He just missed his chance."

The wind roared around them. "Keep your wits about you," Chaol said, still watching the duel. Renault was retreating, each swing of Cain's blade taking him closer and closer to the line of chalk that had been drawn on the ground. One step outside of that ring and he'd be disqualified. "He'll try to provoke you. Don't get angry. Focus only on his blade, and that unprotected side of his."

"I know," she said, and shifted her gaze back to the duel just in time to see Renault cry out and stumble back. Blood sprayed from his nose, and he hit the ground hard. Cain, his fist smeared with Renault's blood, only smiled as he pointed the blade at Renault's heart. The mercenary's bloody face went white, and he bared his teeth as he stared up at his conqueror.

She looked at the clock tower. He hadn't lasted three minutes.

There was polite clapping, and Celaena noticed that Lord Garnel's face was set with fury. She could only guess how much money he'd just lost.

"A valiant effort," said the king. Cain bowed and didn't offer Renault a hand to help him rise before he stalked toward the opposite end of the veranda. With more dignity than Celaena had expected, Renault got to his feet and bowed to the king, mumbling his thanks. Clutching his nose, the mercenary slunk away. What had he stood to lose—and where would he return to now?

Across the ring, Grave smiled at her as he wrapped a hand around the hilt of his sword. She bit down on her grimace at the sight of his teeth. Of course, she'd have to duel the grotesque one. At least Renault had been clean looking.

"We will begin in a moment," the king said. "Prepare your weapons." With that, he turned to Perrington and began speaking too quietly for anyone else to hear in the blustering wind.

Celaena turned to Chaol. But instead of handing her the plain-as-porridge sword she usually wielded in practice, he drew his own blade. The eagle-shaped pommel glinted in the midday sun. "Here," he said.

She blinked at the blade, and slowly raised her face to look at him. She found the rolling earthen hills of the north in his eyes. It was a sense of loyalty to his country that went beyond the man seated at the table. Far inside of her, she found a golden chain that bound them together.

"Take it," he said.

Her heartbeat thundered in her ears. She lifted a hand to grab the blade, but someone touched her elbow.

"If I may," Nehemia said in Eyllwe, "I'd like to offer this to you instead." The princess held out her beautifully carved iron-tipped staff. Celaena glanced between Chaol's sword and her friend's weapon. The sword, obviously, was the wiser choice—and for Chaol to offer his own weapon made her feel strangely lightheaded—but the staff . . .

Nehemia leaned in to whisper in Celaena's ear. "Let it be with an Eyllwe weapon that you take them down." Her voice hitched. "Let wood from the forests of Eyllwe defeat steel from Adarlan. Let the King's Champion be someone who understands how the innocents suffer."

Hadn't Elena said almost the same thing, all those months ago? Celaena swallowed hard, and Chaol lowered his sword, taking a step back from them. Nehemia didn't break her stare.

She knew what the princess was asking of her. As the King's Champion, she might find ways to save countless lives—ways to undermine the king's authority.

And that, Celaena realized, was what Elena, the king's own ancestor, might want, too.

Though a bolt of fear went through her at the thought, though standing against the king was the one thing Celaena had thought she'd never be brave enough to do, she couldn't forget the three scars on her back, or the slaves she'd left in Endovier, or the five hundred butchered Eyllwe rebels.

Celaena took the staff from Nehemia's hands. The princess gave her a fierce grin.

Chaol, surprisingly enough, didn't object. He only sheathed his sword and bowed his head to Nehemia as she clapped Celaena on the shoulder before she walked off.

Celaena gave the staff a few experimental sweeps in the space around her. Balanced, solid, strong. The rounded iron tip could knock a man out cold.

She could feel the lingering oil from Nehemia's hands and smell her friend's lotus-blossom scent on the engraved wood. Yes, the staff would do just fine. She'd taken down Verin with her bare hands. She could defeat Grave and Cain with this.

She glanced at the king, who was still speaking with Perrington, and found Dorian watching her instead. His sapphire eyes reflected the brilliance of the sky, though they darkened slightly as he flicked them toward Nehemia. Dorian was many things, but he wasn't stupid; had he realized the symbolism in Nehemia's offer? She quickly dropped his stare.

She'd worry about that later. Across the ring, Grave began pacing, waiting for the king to return his attention to the duel and give the order to begin.

She loosed a shuddering breath. Here she was, at long last. She gripped the staff in her left hand, taking in the strength of the wood, the strength of her friend. A lot could happen in a few minutes—a lot could change.

She faced Chaol. The wind ripped a few strands of hair from her braid, and she tucked them behind her ears.

"No matter what happens," she said quietly, "I want to thank you."

Chaol tilted his head to the side. "For what?"

Her eyes stung, but she blamed it on the fierce wind and blinked away the dampness. "For making my freedom mean something."

He didn't say anything; he just took the fingers of her right hand and held them in his, his thumb brushing the ring she wore.

"Let the second duel commence," the king boomed, waving a hand toward the veranda.

Chaol squeezed her hand, his skin warm in the frigid air. "Give him hell," he said. Grave entered the ring and drew his sword.

Pulling her hand from Chaol's, Celaena straightened her spine as she stepped into the ring. She quickly bowed to the king, then to her opponent.

She met Grave's stare and smiled as she bent her knees, holding the staff in two hands.

You have no idea what you're getting yourself into, little man.

48

As she expected, Grave launched himself at her, going straight for the center of the staff in his hope to break it.

But Celaena whirled away. As Grave struck nothing but air, she slammed the butt of the staff into his spine. He staggered, but kept upright, turning on one foot as he charged after her again.

She took the blow this time, angling her staff so he hit the bottom half. His blade wedged in the wood, and she jumped toward him, letting the force of his own blow snap the upper part of the staff straight into his face. He stumbled, but her fist was waiting. As it met with his nose, she savored the rush of pain through her hand and the crunch of his bones beneath her knuckles. She leapt back before he had a chance to strike. Blood gleamed as it trickled from his nose. "Bitch!" he hissed, and swung.

She met his blade, holding the staff with both hands, pushing the wood shaft into his sword, even when it let out a splintering groan.

She shoved him, grunting, and spun. She whacked the back of his head with the top of the staff, and he teetered, but regained his footing. He wiped at his bloody nose, eyes gleaming as he panted. His pock-marked face became feral, and he charged, aiming a direct blow to her heart. Too fast, too wild for him to stop.

She dropped into a crouch. As the blade sailed overhead, she lashed out at his legs. He didn't even have time to cry out as she swept his feet out from under him, nor did he have time to raise his weapon before she crouched over his chest, the iron-coated tip of the staff at his throat.

She brought her mouth close to his ear. "My name is Celaena Sardothien," she whispered. "But it makes no difference if my name's Celaena or Lillian or Bitch, because I'd still beat you, no matter what you call me." She smiled at him as she stood. He just stared up at her, his bloody nose leaking down the side of his cheek. She took the handkerchief from her pocket and dropped it on his chest. "You can keep that," she said before she walked off the veranda.

She intercepted Chaol as soon as she crossed the line of chalk. "How long did that take?" she asked. She found Nehemia beaming at her, and Celaena lifted her staff a little in salute.

"Two minutes."

She grinned at the captain. She was hardly winded. "Better than Cain's time."

"And certainly more dramatic," Chaol said. "Was the handkerchief really necessary?"

She bit down on her lip and was about to reply when the king stood, the crowd quieting. "Wine for the winners," he said, and Cain stalked from his place on the sidelines to stand before the king's table. Celaena remained with Chaol.

The king gestured at Kaltain, who obediently picked up a silver tray containing two goblets. She gave one to Cain, then walked over to Celaena and handed the other to her before pausing in front of the king's table.

"Out of good faith, and honor to the Great Goddess," Kaltain said in a dramatic voice. Celaena wanted to punch her. "May it be your offering to the Mother who bore us all. Drink, and let Her bless you, and replenish your strength." Who had written *that* little script? Kaltain bowed to them, and Celaena raised the goblet to her lips. The king smiled at her, and she tried not to flinch as she drank. Kaltain took the goblet when she finished, and curtsied to Cain as she accepted his and slunk away.

Win. Win. Win. Take him down quickly.

"Ready yourselves," the king ordered. "And begin on my mark."

Celaena looked to Chaol. Wasn't she to be allowed a moment to rest? Even Dorian raised his brows at his father, but the king refused to acknowledge his son's silent questioning.

Cain drew his sword, a crooked grin on his face as he crouched in a defensive stance in the center of the ring.

Insults would have risen to her lips if Chaol hadn't touched her shoulder, his chestnut eyes filled with some emotion she couldn't yet understand. There was strength in his face that she found to be achingly beautiful.

"Don't lose," he whispered so only she could hear. "I don't feel like having to escort you all the way back to Endovier." The world became foggy around the edges as he stepped away, his head held high as he ignored the white-hot glare of the king.

Cain edged closer, his broadsword gleaming. Celaena took a deep breath and entered the ring.

The conqueror of Erilea raised his hands. "Begin!" he roared, and Celaena shook her head, trying to clear her blurry vision. She steadied herself, wielding the staff like a sword as Cain began circling. Nausea flashed through her as his muscles flexed. For some reason, the world was still hazy. She clenched her teeth, blinking. She'd use his strength against him.

Cain charged faster than she anticipated. She caught his sword on the broad side with the staff, avoiding the sharp edges, and leapt back as she heard the wood groan.

He struck so quickly that she had to concede to the edge of his blade. It sank deep into the staff. Her arms ached from the impact. Before she could recover, Cain yanked his sword from her weapon and surged toward her. She could only bound back, deflecting the blow with the iron tip of the staff. Her blood felt slow and thick, and her head spun. Was she ill? The nausea would not ease.

Grunting, Celaena pulled away with an effort of skill and force. If she were truly ill, she must finish this as quickly as possible. It was not a showcase of her abilities, especially if that book had been right and Cain had been granted the strength of all those dead Champions.

Switching onto the offensive, she nimbly swept toward him. He parried Celaena's attack with a brush of his blade. She brought the staff down upon his sword, splinters flying into the air.

Her heart pounded in her ears, and the sound of wood against steel became almost unbearable. Why were things slowing down?

She attacked—faster and faster, stronger and stronger. Cain laughed, and she almost screamed in anger. Each time she moved a foot to trip him, each time they came too close, she either became clumsy or he stepped away, as if he knew what she planned all along. She had the infuriating feeling that he was toying with her, that there was some joke she didn't understand.

Celaena whipped the staff through the air, hoping to catch him upon his unprotected neck. But he deflected, and though she spun and tried to knock him in his stomach, he blocked her again.

"Not feeling well?" he said, showing his white, gleaming teeth. "Perhaps you shouldn't have been holding back all those—"

WHAM!

She grinned as the shaft of her staff slammed into his side. He bent over, and her leg lashed out and swept him off his feet, sending him crashing to the ground. She raised her staff, but a sick feeling rushed through her so powerful that her muscles slackened. She had no strength.

He knocked aside her blow as if it was nothing, and she retreated while he rose. And that's when she heard the laugh—soft, feminine, and vicious. Kaltain. Celaena's feet stumbled, but she stayed upright as she dared a glance at the lady, and the goblets on the table before her. And that's when she knew that it hadn't been wine in that glass, but bloodbane, the very drug she'd missed in the Test. At best, it caused hallucinations and disorientation. At worst . . .

She had difficulty holding the staff. Cain came at her, and she had no choice but to meet his blows, barely having the strength to raise the weapon each time. How much bloodbane had they given her? The staff cracked, splintered, and groaned. If it were a lethal dose, she'd be dead by now. They must have given her enough to disorient her, but not enough that it would be easy to prove. She couldn't focus, and her body became hot and cold. Cain was so large—he was a mountain, and his blows . . . they made Chaol seem like a child . . .

"Tired already?" he asked. "It's a pity all of that yapping didn't amount to much."

He knew. He knew they'd drugged her. She snarled and lunged. He stepped aside, and her eyes went wide as she hit nothing but air, air, air, until—

He slammed his fist into her spine, and she only saw the blur of the slate tiles before they collided with her face.

"Pathetic," he said, his shadow falling over her as she flipped onto her back, scrambling away before he could get closer. She could taste the blood in her mouth. This couldn't be happening—they couldn't have betrayed her like this. "If I were Grave, I'd be insulted that you'd beaten me."

Her breath came fast and hard, and her knees ached as she

stumbled upright, charging at him. Too fast for her to block, he grabbed her by the collar of her shirt and hurled her back. She kept upright as she tripped, and stopped a few feet from him.

Cain circled her, swinging his sword idly. His eyes were dark—dark like that portal to that other world. He was drawing out the inevitable, a predator playing with his meal before eating it. He wanted to enjoy every moment.

She had to end this now, before the hallucinations started. She knew they'd be powerful: seers had once used bloodbane as a drug to view spirits from other worlds. Celaena shot forward with a sweep of the staff. Wood slammed into steel.

The staff snapped in two.

The iron-tipped head soared to the other side of the veranda, leaving Celaena with a piece of useless wood. Cain's black eyes met with hers for a moment before his other arm lashed out and connected with her shoulder.

She heard the crack before she felt the pain, and Celaena screamed, dropping to her knees as her shoulder dislocated. His foot met with the shoulder, and she went flying backward, falling so hard that her shoulder relocated with a sickening crunch. The agony blinded her; the world went in and out of focus. Things were so slow . . .

Cain grabbed the collar of her jacket to pull her to her feet. She staggered back out of his grasp, the ground rushing beneath her, and then fell—hard.

She raised the shaft of broken wood with her left hand. Cain, panting and grinning, approached.

Dorian clenched his teeth. Something was terribly wrong. He'd known it from the moment the duel started, and began sweating when she had the opportunity to bestow a winning blow and failed to deliver it. But now . . .

He couldn't watch as Cain kicked her shoulder, and felt as if he'd vomit when the brute picked her up and she fell to the ground. She kept wiping her eyes, and sweat shone on her forehead. What was wrong?

He should stop it—he should call off the duel now. Let her start tomorrow, with a sword and her senses. Chaol hissed, and Dorian almost cried out as Celaena attempted to stand, but collapsed. Cain teased her—breaking not only her body, but her will . . . He had to stop it.

Cain swung his sword at Celaena, who threw herself backward—but not fast enough. She yelped as the blade sliced across her thigh, clothing and flesh ripping. Blood colored her pants. Despite it, she stood again, her face set in defiant rage.

Dorian had to help her. But if he interfered, they might just proclaim Cain the victor. So he watched, in growing horror and despair, as Cain's fist slammed into her jaw.

Her knees twisted as she fell.

Something in Chaol began fraying as Celaena raised her bloodied face to look at Cain.

"I expected better," Cain said as Celaena crawled into a kneeling position, still clutching at her useless piece of wood. She panted through her teeth, blood leaking from her lip. Cain studied her face as if he could read it, as if he could hear something Chaol couldn't. "And what would your father say?"

An expression flashed across Celaena's eyes that bordered on fear and confusion. "Shut your mouth," she said, her words trembling as she fought the pain of her wounds.

But Cain kept staring at her, his smile growing. "It's all there," he said. "Right under that wall you built on top of it. I can see it clear as day."

What was he talking about? Cain lifted his sword and ran his finger through the blood—her blood. Chaol reined in his disgust and anger.

Cain let out a breathy laugh. "What was it like when you woke up between your parents, covered in their blood?"

"Shut your mouth!" she said again, her free hand clawing at the ground, her face twisted with rage and anguish. Whatever wound Cain was touching, it burned.

"Your mother was a pretty young thing, wasn't she?" Cain said.

"*Be quiet!*" She tried to surge to her feet, but her injured leg kept her down. She gasped for breath. How did Cain know these things about Celaena's past? Chaol's heart pounded wildly, but he could do nothing to help her.

She let out a wordless scream that shattered through the frozen wind as she scrambled to her feet. Her pain lost in her fury, she swung at his blade with the remnant of the staff.

"Good," Cain panted, pressing her staff so hard that his blade sank into the wood. "But not good enough." He shoved her, and as she staggered back a step, he brought up his leg and kicked her in the ribs. She went flying.

Chaol had never seen anyone struck that hard. Celaena hit the ground and flipped, over and over and over, until she slammed into the clock tower. Her head whacked against the black stone, and he bit down on his yell, forcing himself to remain on the sidelines, forcing himself to watch as Cain broke her apart, piece by piece. How had it gone wrong so quickly?

She trembled as she raised herself to her knees, clutching her side. She still held on to the remnant of Nehemia's staff, as if it were a rock in the middle of a violent sea.

Celaena tasted blood as Cain seized her again, dragging her across the floor. She didn't try to fight him. He could have pointed his sword at her heart at any point. This wasn't a duel—it was an execution. And no one was doing anything to stop it. They'd drugged her. It wasn't fair. The sunlight flickered, and she thrashed in Cain's grip, despite the agony shooting through her body.

All around her were whispering, laughing, otherworldly voices. They called to her—but called a different name, a dangerous name . . .

She glanced skyward, seeing the tip of Cain's chin before he hoisted her onto her feet and slammed her—face-first—into a wall of freezing, smooth stone. She was enveloped in familiar darkness. Her skull ached with the impact, but Celaena's cry of pain was cut short as she opened her eyes to the dark and saw what appeared. Something—something dead stood before her.

It was a man, his skin pale and rotting. His eyes burned red, and he pointed at her in a broken, stiff way. His teeth were all sharp and so long they barely fit into his mouth.

Where had the world gone? The hallucinations must be starting. Light flashed as she was yanked back, and her eyes bulged as Cain threw her to the ground near the edge of the ring.

A shadow passed across the sun. It was over. She would die now—die, or lose and be sent back to Endovier. It was over. Over.

Two black boots came into view, then a pair of knees as someone crouched on the edge of the ring.

"Get up," Chaol whispered. She couldn't bring herself to look him in the face. It was over.

Cain began laughing, and she felt the reverberations of his steps as he walked around the ring. "Is *this* all you have to offer?" he shouted triumphantly. Celaena trembled. The world was awash with fog and darkness and voices.

"*Get up*," Chaol said again, louder. She could only stare at the white line of chalk that marked the ring.

Cain had said things he couldn't possibly know—he'd *seen* it in her eyes. And if he knew about her past . . . She whimpered, hating herself for it, and for the tears that began sliding down her face, across the bridge of her nose and onto the floor. It was all over.

"Celaena," Chaol said gently. And then she heard the scraping noise as his hand came into view, sliding across the flagstones. His fingertips stopped just at the edge of the white line. "*Celaena*," he breathed, his voice laced with pain—and hope. This was all she had left—his outstretched hand, and the promise of hope, of something better waiting on the other side of that line.

Moving her arm made sparks dance before her eyes, but she extended it until her fingertips reached the line of chalk, and stayed there, not a quarter of an inch from Chaol, the thick white mark separating them.

She lifted her eyes to his face, and found his gaze lined with silver. "Get up," was all he said.

And in that moment, somehow his face was the only thing that mattered. She stirred, and couldn't stop her sob as her body erupted with pain that made her lie still again. But she kept her focus on his brown eyes, on his tightly pressed lips as they parted and whispered, "Get up."

She pulled her arm away from the line, bracing her palm against the frozen ground. She kept his gaze when she moved her other hand beneath her chest, and bit down on the scream of pain as she pushed upward, her shoulder nearly buckling. She slid her good leg under her. As she made to stand, she felt the thud of Cain's steps, and Chaol's eyes went wide.

The world spun black and mist and blue as Cain grabbed her and shoved her against the clock tower once more, her face smashing into the stone. When she opened her eyes, the world shifted. Blackness was everywhere. Deep down, she knew it wasn't just a hallucination—what she saw, who she saw, truly existed just beyond the veil of her world, and the poisonous drug had somehow opened her mind to see them.

There were two creatures now, and the second one had wings. It was grinning—grinning just as—

Celaena didn't have time to shout as it launched into flight. It threw her to the ground, and its claws ripped at her. She thrashed. Where had the world gone? Where was she?

There were more of them—more appeared. The dead, demons, monsters—they wanted her. They called her name. Most of them had wings, and the ones that didn't were carried in the talons of others.

They struck as they passed, their claws slicing her flesh. They were going to bring her inside their realm, and the tower was the gaping portal. She would be devoured. Terror—terror like she'd never known—took over. Celaena covered her head as they swept upon her, and she kicked blindly. Where had the world gone? How much poison had they given her? She was going to die. *Freedom or death.*

Defiance and rage mixed in her blood. She swung her free arm, and it met with a shadowy face with burning coals for eyes. The darkness rippled, and Cain's gaping features appeared. There was sun here—this was reality. How long did she have before another wave of the poison-induced visions took over?

Cain reached for her throat, and she flung herself backward. All that he managed to grab was her amulet. With a resounding snap, the Eye of Elena ripped from her neck.

The sunlight disappeared, the bloodbane seizing control of her mind again, and Celaena found herself before an army of the dead. The shadowy figure that was Cain raised his arm, dropping the amulet upon the ground.

They came for her.

49

Dorian watched in wide-eyed terror as Celaena thrashed on the ground, waving away things they couldn't see. What was happening? Had there been something in that wine? But there was also something abnormal about the way Cain just stood there, smiling. Was there . . . was there actually something there that they couldn't see?

She screamed. It was the most horrible noise he'd ever heard. "Stop it, now," he said to Chaol as his friend rose from his spot near the ring. But Chaol only gaped at the flailing assassin, his face pale as death.

She kicked and punched at nothing as Cain squatted over her and hit her in the mouth. Blood flowed freely. It wouldn't stop until his father said something or Cain knocked her truly unconscious. Or worse. He had to remind himself that any interference—even trying to say that her wine had been drugged—might result in her disqualification.

She crawled away from Cain, her blood and saliva pooling onto the ground.

Someone stepped beside Dorian, and from her intake of breath, he knew it was Nehemia. She said something in Eyllwe, and walked to the very edge of the ring. Tucked close to the folds of her cloak, nearly concealed there, her fingers were rapidly moving—tracing symbols in the air.

Cain stalked to where Celaena panted, her face white and red. She eased herself into a kneeling position and stared without seeing at the ring, at everyone, at something beyond them, perhaps.

She was waiting for him. Waiting for him to—

Kill her.

Kneeling on the ground, Celaena gasped for breath, unable to find her way out of the hallucination and back into reality. Here, the dead surrounded her, waiting. The shadow-thing that was Cain stood nearby, watching, his burning eyes his only distinguishing feature. Darkness rippled around Cain like shreds of clothing in the wind.

She would die soon.

Light and darkness. Life and death. Where do I fit in?

The thought sent a jolt through her so strong that her hands fumbled for anything to use against him. Not like this. She'd find a way—she could find a way to survive. *I will not be afraid.* She'd whispered that every morning in Endovier; but what good were those words now?

A demon came at her, and a scream—not of terror or of despair, but rather a plea—burst from her throat. A call for help.

The demon flapped back, as if her scream had startled it. Cain motioned it forward again.

But then something extraordinary happened.

Doors, doors, doors all burst open. Doors of wood, doors of iron, doors of air and magic.

And from another world, Elena swept down, cloaked in golden

light. The ancient queen's hair glittered like a shooting star as she plummeted into Erilea.

Cain chuckled as he stepped toward the panting assassin and raised his sword, aiming at the assassin's chest.

Elena exploded through the ranks of the dead, scattering them.

Cain's sword came down.

A gust of wind slammed into Cain so hard he was sent sprawling to the ground, his sword flying across the veranda. But, locked in that dark, horrible world, Celaena only saw the ancient queen barrel into Cain, knocking him down, before the dead charged. Yet they were too late.

Golden light erupted around her, shielding her from them, making the dead step back.

Wind mightier than anything the onlookers had witnessed still roared through the veranda. They shielded their faces as the wind howled.

The demons bellowed and surged again. But a sword rang, and a demon fell. Black blood dripped from the blade, and the lips of Queen Elena were set in a feral snarl as she lifted her sword. It was a challenge; a dare to them to try to pass, to tempt her rage.

Through fading eyes, Celaena saw a crown of stars glittering atop Elena's head, her silver armor shining like a beacon in the blackness. The demons shrieked, and Elena stretched out a hand, golden light bursting from her palm, forming a wall between them and the dead as she rushed to Celaena's side and cupped her face in her hands.

"I cannot protect you," whispered the queen, her skin glowing. Her face was different, too—sharper, more beautiful. Her Fae heritage. "I cannot give you my strength." She traced her fingers across Celaena's brow. "But I can remove this poison from your body."

Beyond them, Cain struggled to his feet. Wind slammed into him from all directions, keeping him trapped in place.

From the far end of the veranda, a gust of wind sent the head of the staff rolling in her direction. It clattered to a stop, still a few tantalizing feet away.

Elena put a hand on Celaena's forehead. "Take it," said the queen. Celaena strained to reach the remnant of the staff, her vision flashing between the sunny veranda and the endless dark. Her shoulder shifted slightly, and she stifled her scream of pain. At last, she felt the smooth carved wood—but also the pain from her aching fingers.

"Once the poison is gone, you will not see me. You will not see the demons," said the queen, sketching marks on Celaena's brow.

Cain looked to the king as he retrieved his sword. The king nodded.

Elena held Celaena's face in her hands. "Do not be afraid." Beyond the golden wall of light, the dead shrieked and moaned Celaena's name. But then Cain—bearing the shadowy, dark thing that dwelled inside of him—stepped through the wall as if it were nothing, shattering it completely.

"Petty tricks, Your Majesty," Cain said to Elena. "Just petty tricks."

Elena was on her feet in an instant, blocking Cain's path to Celaena. Shadows rippled along the edges of his form, and his ember-like eyes flared. Cain's attention was on Celaena as he said, "You were brought here—all of you were. All the players in the unfinished game. My friends," he gestured to the dead, "have told me so."

"Be gone," Elena barked, forming a symbol with her fingers. A bright blue light burst from her hands.

Cain howled as it bit into him, the light slashing his shadow-body into ribbons. Then it was gone, leaving the swirling crowd of the dead and damned, and Elena still before them. They charged, but she blasted them back with that golden shield, panting through her gritted teeth. Elena then dropped to her knees and grabbed Celaena by the shoulders.

"The poison is almost gone," Elena said. The world grew less dark; Celaena could see cracks of sunlight.

Celaena nodded, pain replacing panic. She could feel the coldness of winter, feel her aching leg and the warm stickiness of her own blood all over her body. Why was Elena here, and what was Nehemia doing at the edge of the circle, her hands moving about so strangely?

"Stand," Elena said. She was becoming translucent. Her hands drifted from Celaena's cheeks, and a white light filled the sky. The poison left Celaena's body.

Cain, once again a man of flesh and blood, walked over to the sprawled assassin.

Pain, pain, pain. Pain from her leg, from her head, from her shoulder and arm and ribs . . .

"*Stand*," Elena whispered again, and was gone. The world appeared.

Cain was close, not a trace of shadow around him. Celaena lifted the jagged remnant of the staff in her hand. Her gaze cleared.

And so, struggling and shaking, Celaena stood.

50

Celaena's right leg could barely support her, but she gritted her teeth and rose. She squared her shoulders as Cain halted.

The wind caressed her face and swept her hair behind her in a billowing sheet of gold. *I will not be afraid.* A mark burned on her forehead in blinding blue light.

"What's that on your face?" Cain asked. The king rose, his brows narrowed, and nearby, Nehemia gasped.

With her aching, almost useless arm, she wiped the blood from her mouth. Cain growled as he swung his sword, making to behead her.

Celaena shot forward, as fast as an arrow of Deanna.

Cain's eyes went wide as she buried the jagged end of the staff in his right side, exactly where Chaol had said he would be unguarded.

Blood poured onto her hands as she yanked it out, and Cain staggered back, clutching his ribs.

She forgot pain, forgot fear, forgot the tyrant who stared at the burning mark on her head with dark eyes. She leapt back a step and sliced open Cain's arm with the broken end of the staff, ripping through muscle and sinew. He swatted at her with his other arm, but she moved aside, cutting the limb as well.

He lunged, but she dashed away. Cain sprawled upon the ground. She slammed her foot into his back, and as he lifted his head, he found the knife-sharp remnant of the staff pressed against his neck.

"Move, and I'll spill your throat on the ground," she said, her jaw aching.

Cain went still, and for a moment, she could have sworn his eyes glowed like coals. For a heartbeat, she considered killing him right there, so he couldn't tell anyone what he knew—about her, about her parents, about the Wyrdmarks and their power. If the king knew any of that . . . Her hand trembled with the effort to keep from driving the spearhead into his neck, but Celaena lifted her bruised face to the king.

The councilmen began nervously clapping. None of them had seen the spectacle; none of them had seen the shadows in the gusting wind. The king looked her over, and Celaena willed herself to remain upright, to stand tall as he judged. She felt each second of silence like a blow to her gut. Was he considering whether there was a way out? After what seemed to be a lifetime, the king spoke.

"My son's Champion is the victor," the king growled. The world spun beneath her feet.

She'd won. She'd won. She was free—or as close to it as she could come. She would become the King's Champion, and then she would be free . . .

It came crashing down upon her, and Celaena dropped the bloody remnant of the staff on the ground as she removed her foot from Cain's back. She limped away, her breathing hard and ragged. She'd been saved. Elena had saved her. And she had . . . she had won.

Nehemia was exactly where she'd been standing before, smiling faintly, only—

The princess collapsed, and her bodyguards rushed to her side. Celaena made a move to her friend, but her legs gave out, and she fell to the tiles. Dorian, as if released from a spell, dashed to her, throwing himself to his knees beside her, murmuring her name again and again.

But she barely heard him. Huddled on the ground, hot tears slid down Celaena's face. She'd won. Through the pain, Celaena began laughing.

As the assassin laughed quietly to herself, head bowed to the ground, Dorian surveyed her body. The cut along her thigh wouldn't stop bleeding, her arm hung limp, and her face and arms were a patchwork of cuts and rapidly forming bruises. Cain, his features set with fury, stood not too far behind, blood seeping through his fingers as he clutched his side. Let him suffer.

"She needs a healer," he said to his father. The king said nothing. "You, boy," Dorian snapped to a page. "Fetch a healer—as fast as you can!" Dorian found it difficult to breathe. He should have stopped it when Cain first hit her. He should have done something other than watch when she had so clearly been drugged. She would have helped him; she wouldn't have hesitated. Chaol, even, had helped her—he'd knelt down beside the edge of the ring. And who had drugged her?

Carefully putting his arms around Celaena, Dorian glanced toward Kaltain and Perrington. In doing so, he missed the look exchanged between Cain and his father. The soldier pulled out his dagger.

But Chaol saw. Cain raised his dagger to strike the girl in the back.

Without thinking, without understanding, Chaol leapt between them and plunged his sword through Cain's heart.

Blood erupted everywhere, showering Chaol's arms, his head, his clothes. The blood reeked, somehow, of death and decay. Cain fell, hitting the ground hard.

The world became silent. Chaol watched the last breath issue from Cain's mouth, watched him die. When it was over and Cain's eyes stopped seeing him, Chaol's sword clattered to the ground. He dropped to his knees beside Cain, but didn't touch him. What had he done?

Chaol couldn't stop staring at his blood-soaked hands. He'd killed him.

"Chaol," Dorian breathed. In his arms, Celaena had gone utterly still.

"What have I done?" Chaol asked him. Celaena made a small noise and began shaking.

Two guards helped lift him up, but Chaol could only stare at his bloody hands as they helped him away.

Dorian watched his friend disappear into the castle, and then returned to the assassin. His father was already yelling about something.

She trembled so badly that her wounds leaked further. "He shouldn't have killed him . . . Now he—he . . ." She let out a gasping breath. "She saved me," she said, burying her face in his chest. "Dorian, she took the poison out of me. She—she . . . Oh, gods, I don't even know what happened." Dorian had no idea what she was speaking about, but he held her tighter.

Dorian felt the eyes of the council upon them, weighing and considering every word out of her mouth, every move or reaction of his. Damning the council to hell, Dorian kissed her hair. The mark on her brow had faded. What had that meant? What had any of it meant? Cain had touched a nerve in her today—when he had mentioned her parents, she'd lost control entirely. He'd never seen her that wild, that frantic.

He hated himself for not acting, for standing like a damned coward. He would make it up to her—he would see to it that she was freed, and after that . . . After that . . .

She didn't fight him when he carried her to her rooms, instructing the physician to follow.

He was done with politics and intrigue. He loved her, and no empire, no king, and no earthly fear would keep him from her. No, if they tried to take her from him, he'd rip the world apart with his bare hands. And for some reason, that didn't terrify him.

Kaltain watched in despair and bewilderment as Dorian carried the weeping assassin in his arms. How had she beaten Cain, when she'd been drugged? Why was she not dead?

Seated beside the glowering king, Perrington fumed. The councilmen scribbled on paper. Kaltain drew the empty vial from her pocket. Hadn't the duke given her enough bloodbane to seriously impair the assassin? Why wasn't Dorian crying over her corpse? Why wasn't she holding Dorian, comforting him? The pain in her head erupted, so violent that her vision went obsidian, and she stopped thinking clearly.

Kaltain approached the duke and hissed in his ear. "I thought you said this would work." She fought to keep her voice in a whisper. "I thought you said this damned drug would work!"

The king and the duke stared at her, and the councilmen exchanged glances as Kaltain straightened. Then, slowly, the duke rose from his seat. "What is that in your hand?" the duke asked a bit too loudly.

"You know what it is!" she seethed, still trying to keep her voice down, even as the pain in her head turned into a thunderous roar. She could scarcely think straight; she could only answer to the fury inside of her. "The damned poison I gave her," she murmured so only Perrington could hear.

"Poison?" Perrington asked, so loud Kaltain's eyes grew wide. "You poisoned her? Why would you do that?" He motioned to three guards.

Why did the king not speak? Why did he not come to her aid? Perrington had given her the poison based on the king's command, hadn't he? The council members looked at her accusingly, whispering among themselves.

"You gave it to me!" she said to the duke.

Perrington's orange brows furrowed. "What are you talking about?"

Kaltain started forward. "You scheming son of a harlot!"

"Restrain her, please," the duke said, blandly, calmly—as if she were no more than a hysterical servant. As if she were nobody.

"I told you," the duke said into the king's ear, "that she'd do anything to get the Cro—" The words were lost as she was dragged away. There was nothing—no emotion at all—in the duke's face. He had played her for a fool.

Kaltain struggled against the guards. "Your Majesty, *please*! His Grace told me that *you*—"

The duke merely looked away.

"I'll kill you!" she screamed at Perrington. She turned to the king, beseechingly, but he, too, looked away, his face crumpled with distaste. He wouldn't listen to anything she said, no matter what the truth was. Perrington had been planning this for too long. And she'd played right into his hands. He'd acted the besotted fool only to plunge a dagger into her back.

Kaltain kicked and thrashed against the guards' grip, but the king's table became smaller and smaller. As she reached the doors to the castle, the duke grinned at her, and her dreams shattered.

51

The next morning, Dorian kept his chin high as his father stared at him. He didn't lower his gaze, no matter how many silent seconds ticked by. After his father had allowed Cain to toy with and hurt Celaena for so long, when she'd clearly been drugged . . . It was a miracle Dorian hadn't snapped yet, but he needed this audience with his father.

"Well?" asked the king at last.

"I wish to know what will happen to Chaol. For killing Cain."

His father's black eyes gleamed. "What do *you* think should happen to him?"

"Nothing," said Dorian. "I think he killed him to defend Cel—to defend the assassin."

"You think the life of an assassin is worth more than that of a soldier?"

Dorian's sapphire gaze darkened. "No, but I believe there was no honor in stabbing her in the back after she'd won." And if he ever found out that Perrington or his father had sanctioned it, or somehow played a hand in Kaltain drugging her . . . Dorian's hands clenched into fists at his sides.

"Honor?" The King of Adarlan stroked his beard. "And would you have slain me if I tried to kill her in such a manner?"

"You're my father," he said carefully. "I would trust that the choice you made was correct."

"What a cunning liar you are! Almost as good as Perrington."

"So you won't punish Chaol?"

"I see no reason why I should rid myself of a perfectly capable Captain of the Guard."

Dorian sighed. "Thank you, Father." The gratitude in his eyes was genuine.

"Is there anything else?" asked the king offhandedly.

"I—" Dorian glanced at the window, then back at his father, steeling his nerve once more. The second reason he'd come. "I want to know what you're going to do with the assassin," he said, and his father smiled in a way that made Dorian's blood run cold.

"The assassin . . . ," his father mused. "She was rather disgraceful at the duel; I don't know if I can have a blubbering woman as my Champion, poison or no. If she'd been *really* good, she would have noticed the poison before she drank. Perhaps I should send her back to Endovier."

Dorian's temper flared with dizzying speed. "You're wrong about her," he began, but then shook his head. "You'll not see her otherwise, no matter what I tell you."

"Why should I see an assassin as anything but a monster? I brought her here to do my bidding, not to meddle in the life of my son and empire."

Dorian bared his teeth. He'd never dared look at his father like this. It thrilled him, and as his father slowly sat down, Dorian wondered if the king was considering whether he had become a genuine concern. To Dorian's surprise, he realized that he didn't care. Perhaps the time had come for him to start questioning his father.

"She's not a monster," Dorian said. "Everything she's done, she did to survive."

"Survive? Is that the lie she told you? She could have done anything to survive, but she *chose* killing. She *enjoyed* killing. She has you at her beck and call, doesn't she? Oh, how clever she is! What a politician she'd have made if she had been born a man!"

A deep-throated growl rippled from Dorian. "You don't know what you're talking about. I have no attachment to her."

But in that one sentence, Dorian made his mistake, and he knew that his father had found his new weak spot: the overwhelming terror that Celaena would be ripped from him. His hands slackened at his sides.

The King of Adarlan looked at the Crown Prince. "I shall send her my contract whenever I get around to it. Until then, you'd do well to keep your mouth shut about it, boy."

Dorian drowned in the cold rage that lay inside of him. Yet an image came vividly to his mind: Nehemia handing Celaena her staff at the duel. Nehemia was no fool; like him, she knew that symbols held a special kind of power. Though Celaena might be his father's Champion, she'd gained the title using a weapon from Eyllwe. And while Nehemia might be playing a game that she had no chance of winning, Dorian couldn't deny that he greatly admired the princess for daring to play in the first place.

Perhaps he might someday work up the nerve to demand retribution for what his father had done to those rebels in Eyllwe. Not today. Not yet. But maybe he could make a start.

So he faced his father, and kept his head held high as he said, "Perrington wishes to use Nehemia as some sort of hostage in order to make the Eyllwe rebels obey."

His father cocked his head. "Does he now? It's an interesting idea. Do you agree?"

Though Dorian's palms began sweating, he schooled his features into neutrality as he said, "No, I don't. I think we're better than that."

"Are we? Do you know how many soldiers and supplies I've lost thanks to those rebels?"

"I do, but to use Nehemia like that is too risky. The rebels might use it to gain allies in other kingdoms. And Nehemia is beloved by her people. If you're worried about losing soldiers and supplies, then you'll lose far more if Perrington's plan ignites a full-on rebellion in Eyllwe. We'd be better off trying to win over Nehemia—trying to work with her to get the rebels to back off. That won't happen if we hold her hostage."

Silence fell, and Dorian tried not to fidget as his father studied him. Every heartbeat felt like a hammer striking his body.

At last, his father nodded. "I shall order Perrington to stop his planning, then."

Dorian almost sagged with relief, but he kept his face blank, kept his words steady as he said, "Thank you for hearing me out."

His father didn't reply, and without waiting for his dismissal, the prince turned on his heel and left.

Celaena tried not to wince at the pain that shot through her shoulder and leg as she awoke. Swaddled in blankets and bandages, she glanced at the clock on the mantelpiece. It was almost one in the afternoon.

Her jaw hurt as she opened her mouth. Celaena didn't need a mirror to know that she was covered in nasty bruises. She frowned, and her face throbbed at the movement. Undoubtedly, she looked hideous. She tried unsuccessfully to sit up. Everything hurt.

Her arm was in a sling, and her thigh stung as her legs moved under the covers. She didn't remember much of what had happened after the duel yesterday, but at least she wasn't dead—either by Cain or the king's order.

Her dreams last night had been filled with Nehemia and Elena—though, more often than not, they disappeared into visions of demons and the dead. And those things Cain had said. The nightmares were so terrible that Celaena barely slept, despite her pain and exhaustion. She wondered what had become of Elena's amulet. She had a feeling the nightmares were due to its absence, and wished repeatedly for it to be restored to her, even though Cain was now dead.

The door to her chambers opened, and she found Nehemia standing in the doorway. The princess only smiled slightly at her as she closed the bedroom door and approached. Fleetfoot lifted her head, her tail slapping against the bed as she wagged it in earnest.

"Hello," Celaena said in Eyllwe.

"How are you feeling?" Nehemia replied in the common tongue, without a hint of her accent. Fleetfoot climbed over Celaena's sore legs to greet the princess.

"Exactly how I look," Celaena said, her mouth aching at the movement.

Nehemia took a seat on the edge of the mattress. As it shifted beneath her, Celaena winced. Recovery wasn't going to be easy. Fleetfoot, done licking and sniffing at Nehemia, curled up in a ball between them and went to sleep. Celaena buried her fingers in her velvet-soft ears.

"I won't waste time dancing around the truth," Nehemia said. "I saved your life at the duel."

She had a hazy memory of Nehemia's fingers making strange symbols in the air. "I didn't hallucinate all of that? And—and you saw everything, too?" Celaena tried to sit up a little higher, but found it too painful to even move an inch.

"No, you didn't," the princess said. "And yes, I saw everything that you saw; my gifts enable me to see what others normally cannot. Yesterday, the bloodbane Kaltain put in your wine made you see it, too: what lurks beyond the veil of this world. I don't think Kaltain intended that effect, but it reacted to your blood in that way. Magic calls to magic." Celaena shifted uncomfortably at the words.

"Why did you pretend to not understand our language all these months?" Celaena asked, eager to change the subject, but also wondering why the question stung as much as her wounds.

"It was originally a defense," Nehemia said, gently setting her hand on Celaena's good arm. "You'd be surprised how much people are willing to reveal when they think you can't understand them. But with each day that I pretended to not know anything, being around you became harder and harder."

"But why make me give you lessons?"

Nehemia looked up at the ceiling. "Because I wanted a friend. Because I liked you."

"So you truly were reading that book when I came across you in the library."

Nehemia nodded. "I . . . I was doing research. On the Wyrdmarks, as you call them in your language. I lied to you when I said I didn't know anything about them. I know all about them. I know how to read them—and how to use them. My entire family does, but we keep it a secret, passed down from generation to generation. They are *only* to be used as a last defense against evil, or in the gravest of illnesses. And here, with magic banned . . . well, even though the Wyrdmarks are a different kind of power, I'm sure that if people discovered I was using them, I'd be imprisoned for it."

Celaena tried to sit up straighter, cursing herself for being unable to move without wanting to faint from pain. "You were using them?"

Nehemia nodded gravely. "We keep them a secret because of the terrible power that they wield. Terrible, in that it can be used for good or evil—though most have used their power for wicked deeds. Since the moment I arrived here, I was aware that someone was using the Wyrdmarks to call forth demons from the Otherworlds—realms beyond our realm. That fool Cain knew enough about the Wyrdmarks to summon the creatures, but didn't know how to control them and send them back. I've spent months banishing and destroying the creatures he summoned; that is why I've sometimes been so absent."

Shame burned on Celaena's cheeks. How could she ever have believed Nehemia was the one killing the Champions? Celaena lifted her right hand so she could see the scars on it. "That was why you didn't ask questions the night my hand was bitten. You—you used the Wyrdmarks to heal me."

"I still don't know how or where you came across the ridderak—but I think that's a tale for another time." Nehemia clicked her tongue. "The marks you found under your bed were drawn by me." Celaena jolted a bit at that. She hissed as her body gave a collective, miserable throb of pain.

"Those symbols are for protection. You have no idea what a nuisance it was to have to keep redrawing them every time you washed them away." A smile tugged on the edges of Nehemia's full lips. "Without them, I think the ridderak would have been drawn to you far sooner."

"Why?"

"Because Cain hated you, of course. And wanted to eliminate you from the competition. I wish he weren't dead, so I might ask him where he learned to rip open portals like that. When the poison made you hover between worlds, his very presence somehow brought those creatures to the In-Between to shred you apart. Though after all he's done, I think he deserved Chaol running him through like that."

Celaena looked toward the bedroom door. She still hadn't seen Chaol since yesterday. Had the king punished him for all that he had done to help her?

"That man cares for you more than either of you realize," Nehemia said, a smile in her voice. Celaena's face burned.

Nehemia cleared her throat. "I suppose you wish to know how I saved you."

"If you're so willing," Celaena said, and the princess grinned.

"With the Wyrdmarks, I was able to open a portal into one of the realms of the Otherworld—and let through Elena, first queen of Adarlan."

"You know her?" Celaena raised an eyebrow.

"No—but she answered my call for help. Not all realms are full of darkness and death. Some are filled with creatures of good—beings that, if our need is great enough, will follow us into Erilea to help in our task. She heard your plea for help long before I opened the portal."

"Is it . . . is it possible to *go* to these other worlds?" Celaena vaguely recalled the Wyrdgates that she'd stumbled across in that book months and months ago.

Nehemia studied her carefully. "I don't know. My schooling isn't yet completed. But the queen was both in and not in this world. She was in the In-Between, where she could not fully cross over, nor could the creatures that you saw. It takes an enormous amount of power to open a true portal to let something through—and even then, the portal will close after a moment. Cain could open it long enough for the ridderak to come through, but then it would shut. So I had to open it long enough to send it *back*. We've been playing a cat-and-mouse game for months." She rubbed her temples. "You have no idea how exhausting it's been."

"Cain summoned all of those things at the duel, didn't he?"

Nehemia contemplated the question. "Perhaps. They might have already been waiting."

"But I could only see them because of the bloodbane that Kaltain gave me?"

"I don't know, Elentiya." Nehemia sighed and stood. "All I know is that Cain knew the secrets of my people's power—power that has long been forgotten in the lands of the North. And that troubles me."

"At least he's dead," Celaena offered, then swallowed. "But . . . but in that . . . place—Cain didn't look like Cain. He looked like a demon. Why?"

"Perhaps the evil he kept summoning seeped into his soul and twisted him into something he was not."

"He talked about me. Like he knew everything." Celaena clenched the blankets.

Something flickered in Nehemia's gaze. "Sometimes, the wicked will tell us things just to confuse us—to haunt our thoughts long after we've faced them. He would be delighted to know you're still fretting over whatever nonsense he said." Nehemia patted her hand. "Don't give him the satisfaction of knowing that he's still troubling you; put those thoughts from your mind."

"At least the king doesn't know about any of this; I can't imagine what he'd do if he had access to that kind of power."

"I can imagine a great deal," Nehemia said softly. "Do you know what the Wyrdmark is that burned on your forehead?"

Celaena stiffened. "No. Do you?"

Nehemia gave her a weighing look. "No, I do not. But I have seen it there before. It seems to be a part of you. And I do worry what the king thinks of it. It's a miracle he hasn't questioned it further." Celaena's blood went cold, and Nehemia quickly added, "Don't worry. If he wanted to question you, he would have done it already."

Celaena let out a shuddering breath. "Why are you really here, Nehemia?"

The princess was quiet for a moment. "I will not claim ties of allegiance to the King of Adarlan. You know this already. And I'm not afraid to tell you that I came to Rifthold only for the excellent view it offered of his movements—of his plans."

"You truly came here to spy?" Celaena whispered.

"If you want to put it that way. There is nothing I wouldn't do for my country—no sacrifice too great to keep my people alive and out of slavery, to keep another massacre from happening." Pain flickered across her eyes.

Celaena's heart twisted. "You're the bravest person I've ever met."

Nehemia stroked Fleetfoot's coat. "My love for Eyllwe drowns out my fear of the King of Adarlan. But I will not involve you, Elentiya." Celaena almost sighed with relief, though it shamed her to feel that way. "Our paths might be entwined, but . . . but I think you must continue to travel your own road for now. Adjust to your new position."

Celaena nodded and cleared her throat. "I won't tell anyone about your powers."

Nehemia smiled sadly. "And there shall be no more secrets between us. When you are better, I'd like to hear how you got entangled with Elena." She glanced down at Fleetfoot. "Do you mind if I take her for a walk? I need to feel the wind on my face today."

"Of course," Celaena said. "She's been cooped up here all morning."

As if the dog understood, she jumped off the bed and sat at Nehemia's feet.

"I'm glad to have you as my friend, Elentiya," the princess said.

"I'm even gladder to have you guarding my back," Celaena said, fighting a yawn. "Thank you for saving my life. Twice now, actually. Or perhaps more." Celaena frowned. "Do I even want to know how many times you secretly saved me from one of Cain's creatures?"

"Not if you want to sleep tonight." Nehemia kissed the top of her head before walking to the door, Fleetfoot in tow. The princess paused in the doorway, though, and tossed something to Celaena. "This belongs to you. One of my guards picked it up after the duel." It was the Eye of Elena.

Celaena wrapped a hand around the hard metal of the amulet. "Thank you."

When Nehemia had left, Celaena smiled, despite all that she had just learned, and closed her eyes. The amulet gripped in her hand, she slept more soundly than she had in months.

52

Celaena awoke the next day, unsure what time it was. There had been a knock on her door, and she blinked the sleep from her eyes in time to see Dorian enter. He stared at her for a moment from the doorway, and she managed a smile. "Hello," she said hoarsely. She remembered him carrying her, holding her down as the healers stitched her leg . . .

He came forward, his steps heavy. "You look even worse today," he whispered. Despite the pain, Celaena sat up.

"I'm fine," she lied. She wasn't. Cain had cracked one of her ribs, and it ached every time she breathed. He clenched his jaw, staring out the window. "What's the matter with you?" she asked. She tried to reach out to grab his jacket, but it hurt too much and he was too far.

"I—I don't know," he said. The vacant, lost look in his eyes increased the tempo of her heart. "I haven't been able to sleep since the duel."

"Here," she said as gently as she could, patting a space beside her. "Come sit."

Obediently, he sat, though he kept his back to her as he put his head in his hands and took several deep breaths. Celaena gingerly touched his back. He stiffened, and she almost pulled away. But his spine relaxed, and he continued his controlled breathing. "Are you ill?" she asked.

"No," he mumbled.

"Dorian. What happened?"

"What do you mean, 'what happened'?" he said, keeping his face in his hands. "One minute, you were walloping Grave, and the next, Cain was beating the living daylights out of you—"

"You lost sleep because of *that*?"

"I can't—I can't . . ." He groaned. She gave him a moment, letting him sort through his thoughts. "I'm sorry," he said, removing his hands from his face and straightening. She nodded. She wouldn't push him. "How are you truly feeling?" The fear still lay beneath his words.

"Awful," she said cautiously. "And I suspect I look as bad as I feel."

He smiled slightly. He was trying to fight it—whatever feeling had been hounding him. "I've never seen you look lovelier." He eyed the bed. "Do you mind if I lie down? I'm exhausted."

She didn't object as he removed his boots and unbuttoned his jacket. With a groan, he stretched out beside her, putting his hands on his stomach. She watched him close his eyes and let out a long breath through his nose. Some semblance of normalcy returned to his face.

"How's Chaol?" she asked, tensing. She remembered the spray of blood and his staring, horrified face.

Dorian opened an eye. "He'll be fine. He took yesterday and today off. I think he needs it." Celaena's heart tightened. "You shouldn't feel responsible," he said, turning onto his side to look directly into her face. "He did what he saw fit."

"Yes, but—"

"No," insisted Dorian. "Chaol knew what he was doing." He

brushed a finger down her cheek. His finger was icy, but she held in her shiver. "I'm sorry," he said again, taking his finger from her face. "I'm sorry I didn't save you."

"What are you talking about? *That* is what you've been agonizing over?"

"I'm sorry I didn't stop Cain the moment I knew something was wrong. Kaltain drugged you, and I should have known—I should have found a way to prevent her from doing it. And when I realized you were hallucinating, I . . . I'm sorry I didn't find a way to stop it."

Green skin and yellow fangs flashed before her eyes, and Celaena's aching fingers curled into a fist. "You shouldn't be sorry," she said, not wanting to speak about the horrors that she'd seen, or of Kaltain's treachery, or what Nehemia had confided in her. "You did as anyone would have—should have done. If you'd interfered, I would have been disqualified."

"I should have sliced Cain open the moment he laid a hand on you. Instead, I stood there as Chaol knelt at the sidelines. I should have been the one to kill Cain."

The demons faded, and a smirk spread. "You're starting to sound like an assassin, my friend."

"Perhaps I spend too much time around you." Celaena moved her head from the pillow to rest in the soft space between his shoulder and chest. Heat rushed through her. Though her body almost seized up in agony as she turned over, Celaena put her injured hand on his stomach. Dorian's breath was warm on her head, and she smiled as he brought his arm around her, cupping her shoulder. They were silent for a while.

"Dorian," she began, and he flicked her on the nose. "Ow," she said, wrinkling her nose. Though her face was peppered with bruises, miraculously, Cain hadn't marred her in any permanent way, though the cut on the leg would leave yet another scar.

"Yes?" he said, resting his chin on her head.

She listened to the sound of his heart beating, the steadiness of it. "When you retrieved me from Endovier—did you actually think I'd win?"

"Of course. Why else would I have bothered to journey so far to find you?"

She snorted onto his chest, but he gently lifted her chin. His eyes were familiar—like something she'd forgotten. "I knew you'd win the moment I met you," he whispered, and her heart writhed as she understood what lay before them. "Though I'll admit that I didn't quite see *this* coming. And . . . no matter how frivolous and twisted that competition was, I'm grateful it brought you into my life. As long as I live, I'll always be thankful for that."

"Do you intend to make me cry, or are you just foolish?"

Dorian leaned forward and kissed her. It made her jaw hurt.

Seated on his glass throne, the King of Adarlan stroked Nothung's pommel. Perrington knelt before him, waiting. Let him wait.

Though the assassin was his Champion, he had yet to send her contract. She was close with both his son and Princess Nehemia; would appointing her somehow be a risk?

But the Captain of the Guard trusted the assassin well enough to save her life. The king's face became like stone. He wouldn't punish Chaol Westfall—if only to avoid Dorian raising hell in the captain's defense. If only Dorian had been born a soldier, not a reader.

But there was a man somewhere in Dorian—a man who could be honed into a warrior. Perhaps a few months at the battlefront would do him some good. A helmet and a sword could do wondrous things to a young man's temperament. And after that show of will and power in his throne room . . . Dorian could be a strong general, if he was pushed.

And as for the assassin . . . once her injuries were healed, what better person to have at his bidding? Besides, there were no others in whom he could place his trust. Celaena Sardothien was his best and only choice now that Cain was dead.

The king traced a mark on the glass arm of his seat. He was well versed in Wyrdmarks, but he'd never seen one like hers. He would find out. And if it were an indication of some fell deed or prophecy, he'd have the girl hanging by nightfall. Seeing her thrash about while drugged had almost convinced him to order her death. But then he'd felt them—felt the angry and furious eyes of the dead . . . Someone had interfered and saved her. And if these creatures both protected and attacked her . . .

Perhaps she was not a person to die at his command. Not before he discovered the meaning of her mark. For now, though, he had more important things to worry about.

"Your manipulation of Kaltain was interesting," said the king at last. Perrington remained kneeling. "Were you using the power on her?"

"No; I've relaxed it recently, as you suggested," the duke replied, rotating the obsidian ring around his thick finger. "Besides, she was starting to look noticeably affected—drained and pale, and she even mentioned the headaches."

The treachery of Lady Kaltain was disturbing, but had he known of Perrington's plan to reveal her character—even to prove how easily she'd adapt to their plans, and how strong her determination ran—he would have prevented it. Such a public revelation only brought about irritating questions.

"It was clever of you to experiment on her. She's become a strong ally—and still suspects nothing of our influence. I have high hopes for this power," the king confided, looking at his own black ring. "Cain proved the physical transformative effects, and Kaltain proves the ability to influence thoughts and emotions. I would like to test its full ability to hone the minds of a few others."

"Part of me wishes Kaltain hadn't been so susceptible," grumbled Perrington. "She wanted to use me to get to your son, but I don't want the power to turn her into Cain. Despite myself, I don't like the thought of her rotting in those dungeons for long."

"Do not fear for Kaltain, my friend. She won't remain in the dungeons forever. When the scandal has been forgotten and the assassin is busy with my work, we'll make Kaltain an offer she can't refuse. But there are ways of controlling her, if you think she can't be trusted."

"Let's first see how the dungeons change her mind," Perrington said quickly.

"Of course, of course. It's only a suggestion."

They were silent, and the duke rose.

"Duke," the king said, his voice echoing through the chamber. The fire in the mouth-shaped fireplace flickered, and green light filled the shadows of the room. "We will soon have much to do in Erilea. Prepare yourself. And stop pushing your plan to use the Eyllwe princess—it's attracting too much attention."

The duke only nodded, bowed, and strode out of the chamber.

53

Celaena leaned back in her seat and propped her feet on the table, balancing the chair precariously on its hind legs. She savored the stretch and release of tension in her stiff muscles, and turned the page in the book she was holding aloft. Fleetfoot dozed beneath the table, snoring faintly. Outside, the sunny afternoon had transformed the snow into dripping, shimmering water that cast light about the whole bedroom. Her injuries had stopped being so irksome, but she still couldn't walk without limping. With any luck, she'd start running again soon.

It had been a week since the duel. Philippa was already busy with the task of cleaning out Celaena's closet to accommodate *more* clothing. All the clothing Celaena planned to buy when she was free to venture into Rifthold and do some shopping for herself, once she had her outrageous salary as King's Champion. Which she'd hopefully start receiving as soon as she signed her contract . . . whenever that would be.

With Philippa occupied, Nehemia and Dorian had taken to

attending her—and the prince often read aloud to her long into the night. When she finally did sleep, her dreams were filled with archaic words and long-forgotten faces, with Wyrdmarks that glowed blue, with the king, and with a dead army summoned from the realms of Hell. Upon waking, she did her best to forget them—especially the magic.

Her doorknob clicked and her heart leapt into her throat. Was it time to finally sign her contract with the king? But it wasn't Dorian or Nehemia, not even a page. The world stopped when Chaol entered instead.

Fleetfoot rushed to him, tail wagging. Celaena almost fell out of her chair as she removed her feet from the table, and winced at the pain that shot through the wound on her leg. She was standing in an instant, but when she opened her mouth, she had nothing to say.

After Chaol gave Fleetfoot a friendly rub on the head, the dog trotted back beneath the table, circled twice, and curled up.

Why wouldn't he move from the doorway? Celaena glanced at her nightgown and blushed as she noticed him staring at her bare legs.

"How are your injuries?" he asked. His voice was soft—and she realized he wasn't staring at the amount of skin she was showing, but rather the bandage wrapped around her thigh.

"I'm all right," she said quickly. "The bandage is just to elicit sympathy now." She tried to smile, but failed. "I—I haven't seen you in a week." It had felt like a lifetime. "Have you . . . Are you all right?"

His brown eyes met hers. Suddenly, she was back at the duel, prostrate on the ground, Cain laughing behind her, but all she could see, all she could hear, was Chaol as he knelt and reached for her. Her throat tightened. She had understood something in that moment. But she couldn't remember what. Maybe it had been a hallucination, too.

"I'm fine," he said, and she took a step toward him, all too aware of how short her nightgown was. "I just . . . wanted to apologize for not checking in on you sooner."

She stopped barely a foot away from him and cocked her head. He wasn't wearing his sword. "I'm sure you've been busy," she said.

He only stood there. She swallowed, and tucked a strand of her unbound hair behind an ear. She took another step closer to him, now having to tip her head back to look into his face. His eyes were so sorrowful. She bit her lip. "You—you saved my life, you know. Twice."

Chaol's brows narrowed slightly. "I did what I had to."

"And that's why I owe you my gratitude."

"You don't owe me anything," he said, his voice strained. And when his eyes flickered, her heart tightened.

She took his hand in hers, but he pulled it away. "I just wanted to see how you were. I have to go to a meeting," he said, and she knew he was lying.

"Thank you for killing Cain." He stiffened. "I—I still remember how it felt when I made my first kill. It wasn't easy."

He dropped his gaze to the floor. "That's why I can't stop thinking about it. Because it *was* easy. I just took my sword and killed him. I *wanted* to kill him." He pinned her with his stare. "He knew about your parents. How?"

"I don't know," she lied. She knew very well. Cain's access to the Otherworlds, to the In-Between, to whatever all that nonsense was, had given him the ability to see into her mind, her memories, her soul. Beyond, perhaps. A chill went through her.

Chaol's face softened. "I'm sorry they died like that."

She shut down everything but her voice as she said, "It was very long ago. It had been raining, and I thought the dampness on their bed as I climbed in was from the open window. I awoke the next morning and realized it wasn't rain." She took a jagged breath, one that erased the feeling of their blood on her skin. "Arobynn Hamel found me soon after that."

"I'm still sorry," he said.

"It was very long ago," she repeated. "I don't even remember what they looked like." That was another lie. She remembered every detail of her parents' faces. "Sometimes, I forget that they ever existed."

He nodded, more to confirm that he'd heard her than that he understood.

"What you did for me, Chaol," she tried again. "Not even with Cain, but when you—"

"I have to go," he interrupted, and half turned away.

"Chaol," she said, grabbing his hand and whirling him to face her. She only saw the haunted gleam in his eyes before she threw her arms around his neck and held him tightly. He straightened, but she crushed her body into his, even though it still aggravated her wounds to do so. Then, after a moment, his arms wrapped around her, keeping her close to him, so close that as she shut her eyes and breathed him in, she couldn't tell where he ended and she began.

His breath was warm on her neck as he bent his head, resting his cheek against her hair. Her heart beat so quickly, and yet she felt utterly calm—as if she could have stayed there forever and not minded, stayed there forever and let the world fall apart around them. She pictured his fingers, pushing against that line of chalk, reaching for her despite the barrier between them.

"Is everything all right?" Dorian's voice sounded from the doorway.

Chaol pulled away from her so fast that she nearly stumbled back. "Everything's fine," he said, squaring his shoulders. The air had turned cold, and Celaena's skin prickled as his warmth vacated her body. She had a hard time looking at Dorian as Chaol nodded to the prince and left her chambers.

Dorian faced her as Chaol left. But Celaena remained watching the door, even after Chaol had shut it behind him. "I don't think he's recovered well from killing Cain," Dorian said.

"Obviously," she snapped. Dorian raised his brows, and she sighed. "I'm sorry."

"You two looked like you were in the middle of . . . something," Dorian said cautiously.

"It's nothing. I just felt bad for him, is all."

"I wish he hadn't run off that quickly. I have some good news." Her stomach twisted. "My father stopped dragging his feet about drawing up your contract. You're to sign it in his council chamber tomorrow."

"You mean—you mean I'm *officially* the King's Champion?"

"It turns out he doesn't hate you as much as he let on. It's a miracle he didn't make you wait longer." Dorian winked.

Four years. Four years of servitude, and then she'd be free. Why had Chaol left so soon? She looked to the door, wondering if she could catch him in the hall.

Dorian put his hands on her waist. "I suppose this means we'll be stuck with each other for a while longer." He lowered his face to hers.

He kissed her, but she stepped out of his arms. "I—Dorian, I'm the King's Champion." She choked on a laugh as she said it.

"Yes, you are," Dorian replied, approaching her again. But she kept her distance as she looked out the window, to the dazzling day beyond. The world was wide open—and hers for the taking. She could step over that white line.

She shifted her gaze to him. "I can't be with you if I'm the King's Champion."

"Of course you can. We'll still have to keep it a secret, but—"

"I have enough secrets. I don't need another one."

"So I'll find a way to tell my father. And mother." He winced slightly.

"To what end? Dorian, I'm your father's minion. You're the Crown Prince."

It was true—and if this relationship became something *more*, then it would only complicate matters when she eventually left the castle.

Not to mention the complications of being with Dorian while she served as his father's Champion. And whether he admitted it or not, Dorian had his own obligations to fulfill. Though she wanted him, though she cared for him, she knew a lasting relationship wouldn't end well. Not when he was the heir to the throne.

His eyes darkened. "Are you saying that you don't want to be with me?"

"I'm saying that . . . that I'm going to leave in four years, and I don't know how this could possibly end well for either of us. I'm saying I don't want to think about the options." The sunlight warmed her skin, and the weight around her shoulders drifted away. "I'm saying that in four years, I'm going to be free, and I've never been free in my entire *life*." Her smile grew. "And I want to know what that feels like."

He opened his mouth, but stopped as he beheld her smile. Though she had no regrets about her choice, she felt something strangely like disappointment when he said, "As you wish."

"But I'd like to remain your friend."

He put his hands in his pockets. "Always."

She thought about touching his arm, or about kissing his cheek, but "free" kept echoing through her again and again and again, and she couldn't stop smiling.

He rolled his neck, and his smile was a bit strained. "I think Nehemia is on her way here to tell you about the contract. She'll be mad at me for telling you first; apologize for me, will you?" He paused when he opened the door, his hand still upon the knob. "Congratulations, Celaena," he said quietly. Before she could reply, he shut the door and left.

Alone, Celaena looked to the window and put a hand on her heart, whispering the word to herself again and again.

Free.

54

Several hours later, Chaol stared at the door to her dining room. He didn't entirely know what he was doing back here. But he'd looked for Dorian in his rooms, and he hadn't been there, and he *needed* to tell him that things weren't as they'd seemed when he walked in on them earlier. He glanced at his hands.

The king had barely said anything to him over the past week, and Cain's name hadn't been mentioned in any of their meetings. Not that it would be, as Cain was little more than a pawn in a game to amuse the king, and certainly not a member of the royal guard.

But he was still dead. Cain's eyes would open no more because of him . . . He would not draw breath because of him . . . His heart had stopped beating because of him . . .

Chaol's hand drifted to where his sword should have been. He'd thrown it in the corner of his room as soon as he'd returned from the duel last week. Mercifully, someone had cleaned the blood from it.

Perhaps the guards who had taken Chaol to his chambers and given him a strong drink. They'd sat in silence until some semblance of reality returned, and then left without a word, not waiting for Chaol to thank them.

Chaol ran a hand through his short hair and opened the dining room door.

Celaena was picking at her dinner, slouched in her seat. Her brows rose. "Two visits in one day?" she said, setting down her fork. "To what do I owe this pleasure?"

He frowned. "Where's Dorian?"

"Why would Dorian be here?"

"I thought he usually came here at this hour."

"Well, don't expect to find him here after today."

He approached, stopping at the edge of the table. "Why?"

She popped a piece of bread into her mouth. "Because I ended it."

"You did what?"

"I'm the King's Champion. Surely you realize how inappropriate it would be for me to have a relationship with a prince." Her blue eyes glittered, and he wondered at the slight emphasis she put on *prince*, and why it made his heart skip a beat.

Chaol fought his own smile. "I was wondering when you'd come to your senses." Did she fret as he did? Did she constantly think about her blood-covered hands? But for all of her swaggering, for all of her gloating and parading about with hands on her hips . . .

There was still something soft in her face. It gave him hope—hope that he had not lost his soul in the act of killing, hope that humanity could still be found, and honor could be regained . . . She had come out of Endovier and could still laugh.

She twirled her hair around a finger. She was still wearing that absurdly short nightgown, which slid up her thighs as she propped her feet on the edge of the table. He focused on her face.

"Would you like to join me?" she asked, gesturing with one hand to the table. "It's a shame for me to celebrate alone."

He looked at her, at that half grin on her face. Whatever had happened with Cain, whatever had happened at the duel . . . that would haunt him. But right now . . .

He pulled out the chair in front of him and sat down. She filled a goblet with wine and handed it to him. "To four years until freedom," she said, lifting her glass.

He raised his in salute. "To you, Celaena."

Their eyes met, and Chaol didn't hide his smile as she grinned at him. Perhaps four years with her might not be enough.

Celaena stood in the tomb, and knew she was dreaming. She often visited the tomb in her dreams—to slay the ridderak again, to be trapped inside Elena's sarcophagus, to face a featureless young woman with golden hair and a crown far too heavy for her to bear—but tonight . . . tonight, it was just her and Elena, and the tomb was filled with moonlight, not a sign to be seen of the ridderak's corpse.

"How are you recovering?" the queen asked, leaning against the side of her own sarcophagus.

Celaena stayed in the doorway. The queen's armor was gone, replaced by her usual flowing gown. None of the fierceness twisted her features, either. "Fine," Celaena said, but glanced down at herself. In this dream world, her injuries were gone. "I didn't know you were a warrior," she said, jerking her chin toward the stand where Damaris stood.

"There are many things history has forgotten about me." Elena's blue eyes glowed with sorrow and anger. "I fought on the battlefields during the demon wars against Erawan—at Gavin's side. That's how we fell in love. But your legends portray me as a damsel who waited in a tower with a magic necklace that would help the heroic prince."

Celaena touched the amulet. "I'm sorry."

"You could be different," Elena said quietly. "You could be great. Greater than me—than any of us."

Celaena opened her mouth, but no words came out.

Elena took a step toward her. "You could rattle the stars," she whispered. "You could do anything, if you only dared. And deep down, you know it, too. That's what scares you most."

She walked to Celaena, and it was all the assassin could do to keep from backing out of the tomb and running away. The queen's blazing, glacier-blue eyes were as ethereal as her lovely face. "You found and defeated the evil Cain was bringing into the world. And now you're the King's Champion. You did as I asked."

"I did it for my freedom," Celaena said. Elena gave her a knowing smile that made her want to scream, but Celaena kept her face blank.

"So you say. But when you called for help—when the amulet snapped, and you let your need be felt—you knew someone would answer. You knew *I* would answer."

"Why?" Celaena dared ask. "Why answer? *Why* do I need to be the King's Champion?"

Elena lifted her face toward the moonlight streaming into the tomb. "Because there are people who need you to save them as much as you yourself need to be saved," she said. "Deny it all you want, but there are people—your friends—who need you here. Your friend, Nehemia, needs you here. Because I was sleeping—a long, endless sleep—and I was awoken by a voice. And the voice didn't belong to one person, but to many. Some whispering, some screaming, some not even aware that they were crying out. But they all want the same thing." She touched the center of Celaena's forehead. Heat flared, and a blue light flashed across Elena's face as Celaena's mark burned and then faded. "And when you are ready—when you start to hear them crying out as well—then you will know why I came to you, and why I have stood by you, and will continue to watch over you, no matter how many times you shove me away."

Celaena's eyes stung, and she took a step back toward the hall.

Elena smiled sadly. "Until that day comes, you're exactly where you need to be. From the king's side, you'll be able to see what needs to be done. But for now—enjoy the accomplishment."

Celaena felt ill at the thought of what else might be asked of her, but she nodded. "Fine," she breathed, making to leave, but paused in the hall. She looked over her shoulder, to where the queen still stood, watching her with those sad eyes. "Thank you for saving my life."

Elena bowed her head. "Blood ties can't be broken," she whispered, and then vanished, her words echoing in the silent tomb.

55

The following day, Celaena approached the glass throne, casting a wary glance about the council chamber. It was the same one in which she'd seen the king those many months ago. A greenish fire burned in the mouthlike fireplace, and thirteen men sat at a long table, each staring at her. But there were no other Champions left—only her. The victor. Dorian stood beside his father and smiled at her.

Hopefully that's a good sign.

Despite the hope his grin provided, she couldn't ignore the terror that welled in her heart as the king, with dark eyes, watched her walk forward. The gold skirts of her dress were the only sound in the chamber. Celaena kept her hands pressed against the maroon bodice, trying not to wring them.

She stopped, and bowed. Chaol, standing beside her, did the same. The captain stood closer to her than he needed to.

"You have come to sign your contract," the king said, and his voice made her bones splinter.

How can such a beastly man possess this sort of power over the world?

"Yes, Your Majesty," she said as submissively as possible, staring at the man's boots.

"Be my Champion, and you'll find yourself a free woman. Four years of service was the bargain you set with my son, though I cannot imagine why he felt the need to bargain with *you*," he said with a deadly glare in Dorian's direction. Dorian bit his lip, but said nothing.

Her heart dropped and rose inside of her like a buoy. She would do whatever the king asked—every foul mission he could throw at her, and then when the four years were over, she'd be free to live her own life, without fear of pursuit or enslavement. She could begin again—far away from Adarlan. She could go away and forget this awful kingdom.

She didn't know whether to smile, or to laugh, or to nod, or to cry and dance about. She could live off of her fortune until old age. She wouldn't have to kill. She could say good-bye to Arobynn and leave Adarlan forever.

"Aren't you going to thank me?" the king barked.

She dropped into a low bow, barely able to contain her joy. She had defeated him—she had sinned against his empire and now would emerge victorious. "Thank you for such an honor and gift, Your Majesty. I am your humble servant."

The king snorted. "Lying won't help you. Bring the contract forward." A councilman dutifully placed a piece of parchment on the table before her.

She stared at the quill and the blank line where her name was to go.

The king's eyes flashed, but she didn't bite. Just one sign of rebellion, one movement of aggression, and he'd hang her. "There will be no questioning on your part. When I tell you to do something, you will do it. I don't need to explain myself to you. And if you somehow are caught, you will deny any connection to me to your last breath. Is that clear?"

"Perfectly, Your Majesty."

He strode from the dais. Dorian started to move, but Chaol shook his head.

Celaena looked at the floor as the king stopped before her. "Now understand this, assassin," the king said. She felt small and frail, so close to him. "Should you fail any of my tasks, should you forget to return, you will pay dearly." The king's voice became so soft that even she could barely hear it. "If you don't return from the missions on which I send you, I'll have your friend, the captain"—he paused for emphasis—"killed."

Her eyes were wide as she stared at his empty throne.

"If you fail to return after that, I'll have Nehemia killed. Then, I'll have her brothers executed. Not long after that, I'll bury their mother beside them. Don't believe I'm not as cunning and stealthy as you are." She could feel him smile. "You get the picture, don't you?" He pulled away. "Sign it."

She looked at the blank space, and what it offered. She took a silent, long breath, and with a prayer for her soul, she signed. Each letter was harder to form than the last. Finally, she let the quill drop onto the table.

"Good. Now get out," the king said, pointing at the door. "I'll summon you when you're needed."

The king sat on his throne again. Celaena bowed carefully, not taking her stare from his face. Only for an instant did she glance at Dorian, whose sapphire eyes gleamed with what she could have sworn was sadness before he smiled at her. She felt Chaol's hand graze her arm.

Chaol would die. She couldn't send him to his death. Or the Ytger family. With feet both heavy and light, she left the chamber.

Outside, the wind bellowed and raged against the glass spire, but it could do nothing to shatter the walls.

With each step away from the chamber, the weight on her shoulders lifted. Chaol remained silent until they entered the stone castle, when he turned to her.

"Well, Champion," he said. He still wasn't wearing his sword.

"Yes, Captain?"

The corners of his mouth tugged upward. "Are you happy now?"

She didn't fight her own grin. "I may have just signed away my soul, but . . . yes. Or as happy as I can be."

"Celaena Sardothien, the King's Champion," he mused.

"What about it?"

"I like the sound of it," he said, shrugging. "Do you want to know what your first mission will be?"

She looked at his golden-brown eyes and all of the promises that lay within them, and linked her arm with his as she smiled. "Tell me tomorrow."

ACKNOWLEDGMENTS

It's taken a decade for *Throne of Glass* to go from inception to publication, and I have far more people to thank than I could ever fit within this space.

Endless gratitude to my agent and very own Champion, Tamar Rydzinski, who understood Celaena from page one. Thank you for the phone call that changed my life.

To my brilliant and daring editor, Margaret Miller—how can I ever thank you enough for believing in me and *Throne of Glass*? I'm so proud to be working with you. To Michelle Nagler and the rest of the absolutely fantastic team at Bloomsbury—thank you so, so much for all of your hard work and support!

I owe a huge debt to Mandy Hubbard for giving me that initial shove out the door. Mandy, you are—and will always be—my Yoda.

To my wonderful husband, Josh—you give me a reason to wake up every morning. You are my better half in every possible way.

Thank you to my parents, Brian and Carol, for reading me fairy tales and never telling me that I was too old for them; to my little brother, Aaron—you are the kind of person I wish I could be.

To Stanlee Brimberg and Janelle Schwartz—you have no idea how far your encouragement went (though maybe this book offers some proof). I wish there were more teachers like you.

To Susan Dennard, for the incredible revision suggestions and for being a true friend through thick and thin. You came into my life when I needed you most, and my world is now brighter because you're in it.

Thanks to Alex Bracken, an amazing critique partner, a phenomenal writer, and an even better friend—words can't express how grateful I am to call you that. Or how grateful I am for all of the candy you sent me during revisions!

To Kat Zhang, for always making time to critique my work and for being a stellar friend. To Brigid Kemmerer, for all the e-mails that kept me sane. To Biljana Likic—because talking with you about the characters and plot made it real. To Leigh Bardugo, my bunker buddy extraordinaire—I couldn't have gotten through this process without you.

To Erin Bowman, Amie Kaufman, Vanessa Di Gregorio, Meg Spooner, Courtney Allison Moulton, Aimée Carter, and the ladies at Pub(lishing) Crawl—you're such talented writers and wonderful people, thank you for being a part of my life.

To Meredith Anderson, Rae Buchanan, Renee Carter, Anna Deles, Gordana Likic, Sarah Liu, Juliann Ma, Chantal Mason, Arianna Sterling, Samantha Walker, Diyana Wan, and Jane Zhao: I've never met any of you face-to-face, but the years of your unfailing enthusiasm have meant so much to me. Kelly De Groot, thanks for the incredible map of Erilea!

Lastly, and perhaps most importantly, thank you to all my readers from FictionPress.com. Your letters, fan art, and encouragement gave me the confidence to try to get published. I'm honored to have you as fans—but even more honored to have you as my friends. It's been a long journey, but we made it! Here's looking at you!

READ ON FOR
AN EXCERPT FROM
THE NEXT BOOK
IN THE

THRONE OF GLASS

SERIES

The shutters swinging in the storm winds were the only sign of her entry. No one had noticed her scaling the garden wall of the darkened manor house, and with the thunder and the gusting wind off the nearby sea, no one heard her as she shimmied up the drainpipe, swung onto the windowsill, and slithered into the second-floor hallway.

The King's Champion pressed herself into an alcove at the thud of approaching steps. Concealed beneath a black mask and hood, she willed herself to melt into the shadows, to become nothing more than a slip of darkness. A servant girl trudged past to the open window, grumbling as she latched it shut. Seconds later, she disappeared down the stairwell at the other end of the hall. The girl hadn't noticed the wet footprints on the floorboards.

Lightning flashed, illuminating the hallway. The assassin took a long breath, going over the plans she'd painstakingly memorized in the three days she'd been watching the manor house on the outskirts of

Bellhaven. Five doors on each side. Lord Nirall's bedroom was the third on the left.

She listened for the approach of any other servants, but the house remained hushed as the storm raged around them.

Silent and smooth as a wraith, she moved down the hall. Lord Nirall's bedroom door swung open with a slight groan. She waited until the next rumble of thunder before easing the door shut behind her.

Another flash of lightning illuminated two figures sleeping in the four-poster bed. Lord Nirall was no older than thirty-five, and his wife, dark haired and beautiful, slept soundly in his arms. What had they done to offend the king so gravely that he wanted them dead?

She crept to the edge of the bed. It wasn't her place to ask questions. Her job was to obey. Her freedom depended on it. With each step toward Lord Nirall, she ran through the plan again.

Her sword slid out of its sheath with barely a whine. She took a shuddering breath, bracing herself for what would come next.

Lord Nirall's eyes flew open just as the King's Champion raised her sword over his head.

Celaena Sardothien stalked down the halls of the glass castle of Rifthold. The heavy sack clenched in her hand swung with each step, banging every so often into her knees. Despite the hooded black cloak that concealed much of her face, the guards didn't stop her as she strode toward the King of Adarlan's council chamber. They knew very well who she was—and what she did for the king. As the King's Champion, she outranked them. Actually, there were few in the castle she didn't outrank now. And fewer still who didn't fear her.

She approached the open glass doors, her cloak sweeping behind her. The guards posted on either side straightened as she gave them a nod before entering the council chamber. Her black boots were nearly silent against the red marble floor.

On the glass throne in the center of the room sat the King of Adarlan, his dark gaze locked on the sack dangling from her fingers. Just as she had the last three times, Celaena dropped to one knee before his throne and bowed her head.

Dorian Havilliard stood beside his father's throne—and she could feel his sapphire eyes fixed on her. At the foot of the dais, always between her and the royal family, stood Chaol Westfall, Captain of the Guard. She looked up at him from the shadows of her hood, taking in the lines of his face. For all the expression he showed, she might as well have been a stranger. But that was expected, and it was just part of the game they'd become so skilled at playing these past few months. Chaol might be her friend, might be someone she'd somehow come to trust, but he was still captain—still responsible for the royal lives in this room above all others. The king spoke.

"Rise."

Celaena kept her chin high as she stood and pulled off her hood.

The king waved a hand at her, the obsidian ring on his finger gleaming in the afternoon light. "Is it done?"

Celaena reached a gloved hand into the sack and tossed the severed head toward him. No one spoke as it bounced, a vulgar thudding of stiff and rotting flesh on marble. It rolled to a stop at the foot of the dais, milky eyes turned toward the ornate glass chandelier overhead.

Dorian straightened, glancing away from the head. Chaol just stared at her.

"He put up a fight," Celaena said.

The king leaned forward, examining the mauled face and the jagged cuts in the neck. "I can barely recognize him."

Celaena gave him a crooked smile, though her throat tightened. "I'm afraid severed heads don't travel well." She fished in her sack again, pulling out a hand. "Here's his seal ring." She tried not to focus too much on the decaying flesh she held, the reek that had worsened with each passing day. She extended the hand to Chaol, whose bronze eyes were distant as he took it from her and offered it to the king. The king's lip curled, but he pried the ring off the stiff finger. He tossed the hand at her feet as he examined the ring.

Beside his father, Dorian shifted. When she'd been dueling in the competition, he hadn't seemed to mind her history. What did he *expect* would happen when she became the King's Champion? Though she supposed severed limbs and heads would turn the stomachs of most people—even after living for a decade under Adarlan's rule. And Dorian, who had never seen battle, never witnessed the chained lines shuffling their way to the butchering blocks . . . Perhaps she should be impressed he hadn't vomited yet.

"What of his wife?" the king demanded, turning the ring over in his fingers again and again.

"Chained to what's left of her husband at the bottom of the sea," Celaena replied with a wicked grin, and removed the slender, pale hand from her sack. It bore a golden wedding band, engraved with the date of the marriage. She offered it to the king, but he shook his head. She didn't dare look at Dorian or Chaol as she put the woman's hand back in the thick canvas sack.

"Very well, then," the king murmured. She remained still as his eyes roved over her, the sack, the head. After a too-long moment, he spoke again. "There is a growing rebel movement here in Rifthold, a group of individuals who are willing to do anything to get me off the throne—and who are attempting to interfere with my plans. Your next assignment is to root out and dispatch them all before they become a true threat to my empire."

Celaena clenched the sack so tightly her fingers ached. Chaol and Dorian were staring at the king now, as if this were the first they were hearing of this, too.

She'd heard whispers of rebel forces before she'd gone to Endovier—she'd *met* fallen rebels in the salt mines. But to have an actual movement growing in the heart of the capital; to have *her* be the one to dispatch them one by one . . . And plans—what plans? What did the rebels know of the king's maneuverings? She shoved the questions down, down, down, until there was no possibility of his reading them on her face.

The king drummed his fingers on the arm of the throne, still playing with Nirall's ring in his other hand. "There are several people on my list of suspected traitors, but I will only give you one name at a time. This castle is crawling with spies."

Chaol stiffened at that, but the king waved his hand and the captain approached her, his face still blank as he extended a piece of paper to Celaena.

She avoided the urge to stare at Chaol's face as he gave her the letter, though his gloved fingers grazed hers before he let go. Keeping her features neutral, she looked at the paper. On it was a single name: *Archer Finn.*

It took every ounce of will and sense of self-preservation to keep her shock from showing. She knew Archer—had known him since she was thirteen and he'd come for lessons at the Assassins' Keep. He'd been several years older, already a highly sought-after courtesan . . . who was in need of some training on how to protect himself from his rather jealous clients. And their husbands.

He'd never minded her ridiculous girlhood crush on him. In fact, he'd let her test out flirting with him, and had usually turned her into a complete giggling mess. Of course, she hadn't seen him for several years—since before she went to Endovier—but she'd never thought him capable of something like this. He'd been handsome and kind and jovial, not a traitor to the crown so dangerous that the king would want him dead.

It was absurd. Whoever was giving the king his information was a damned idiot.

"Just him, or all his clients, too?" Celaena blurted.

The king gave her a slow smile. "You know Archer? I'm not surprised." A taunt—a challenge.

She just stared ahead, willing herself to calm, to breathe. "I used to.

He's an extraordinarily well-guarded man. I'll need time to get past his defenses." So carefully said, so casually phrased. What she really needed time for was to figure out how Archer had gotten tangled up in this mess—and whether the king was telling the truth. If Archer truly were a traitor and a rebel . . . well, she'd figure that out later.

"Then you have one month," the king said. "And if he's not buried by then, perhaps I shall reconsider your position, girl."

She nodded, submissive, yielding, gracious. "Thank you, Your Majesty."

"When you have dispatched Archer, I will give you the next name on the list."

She had avoided the politics of the kingdoms—especially their rebel forces—for so many years, and now she was in the thick of it. Wonderful.

"Be quick," the king warned. "Be discreet. Your payment for Nirall is already in your chambers."

Celaena nodded again and shoved the piece of paper into her pocket.

The king was staring at her. Celaena looked away but forced a corner of her mouth to twitch upward, to make her eyes glitter with the thrill of the hunt. At last, the king lifted his gaze to the ceiling. "Take that head and be gone." He pocketed Nirall's seal ring, and Celaena swallowed her twinge of disgust. A trophy.

She scooped up the head by its dark hair and grabbed the severed hand, stuffing them into the sack. With only a glance at Dorian, whose face had gone pale, she turned on her heel and left.

~

Dorian Havilliard stood in silence as the servants rearranged the chamber, dragging the giant oak table and ornate chairs into the center of the room. They had a council meeting in three minutes. He hardly heard as Chaol took his leave, saying he'd like to debrief Celaena further. His father grunted his approval.

Celaena had killed a man and his wife. And his father had ordered it. Dorian had barely been able to look at either of them. He thought he'd been able to convince his father to reevaluate his brutal policies after the massacre of those rebels in Eyllwe before Yulemas, but it seemed like it hadn't made any difference. And Celaena . . .

As soon as the servants finished arranging the table, Dorian slid into his usual seat at his father's right. The councilmen began trickling in, along with Duke Perrington, who went straight to the king and began murmuring to him, too soft for Dorian to hear.

Dorian didn't bother saying anything to anyone and just stared at the glass pitcher of water before him. Celaena hadn't seemed like herself just now.

Actually, for the two months since she'd been named the King's Champion, she'd been like this. Her lovely dresses and ornate clothes were gone, replaced by an unforgiving, close-cut black tunic and pants, her hair pulled back in a long braid that fell into the folds of that dark cloak she was always wearing. She was a beautiful wraith—and when she looked at him, it was like she didn't even know who he was.

Dorian glanced at the open doorway, through which she had vanished moments before.

If she could kill people like this, then manipulating him into believing she felt something for him would have been all too easy. Making an ally of him—making him *love* her enough to face his father on her behalf, to ensure that she was appointed Champion . . .

Dorian couldn't bring himself to finish the thought. He'd visit her—tomorrow, perhaps. Just to see if there was a chance he was wrong.

But he couldn't help wondering if he'd ever meant anything to Celaena at all.

~

Celaena strode quickly and quietly down hallways and stairwells, taking the now-familiar route to the castle sewer. It was the same waterway that flowed past her secret tunnel, though here it smelled far worse, thanks to the servants depositing refuse almost hourly.

Her steps, then a second pair—Chaol's—echoed in the long subterranean passage. But she didn't say anything until she stopped at the edge of the water, glancing at the several archways that opened on either side of the river. No one was here.

"So," she said without looking behind her, "are you going to say hello, or are you just going to follow me everywhere?" She turned to face him, the sack still dangling from her hand.

"Are you still acting like the King's Champion, or are you back to being Celaena?" In the torchlight, his bronze eyes glittered.

Of course Chaol would notice the difference; he noticed everything. She couldn't tell whether it pleased her or not. Especially when there was a slight bite to his words.

When she didn't reply, he asked, "How was Bellhaven?"

"The same as it always is." She knew precisely what he meant; he wanted to know how her mission had gone.

"He fought you?" He jerked his chin toward the sack in her hand.

She shrugged and turned back to the dark river. "It was nothing I couldn't handle." She tossed the sack into the sewer. They watched in silence as it bobbed, then slowly sank.

Chaol cleared his throat. She knew he hated this. When she'd gone on her first mission—to an estate up the coast in Meah—he'd paced so much before she left that she honestly thought he would ask her not to go. And when she'd returned, severed head in tow and rumors flying about Sir Carlin's murder, it had taken a week for him to even look her in the eye. But what had he expected?

"When will you begin your new mission?" he asked.

"Tomorrow. Or the day after. I need to rest," she added quickly when he frowned. "And besides, it'll only take me a day or two to figure out how guarded Archer is and sort out my approach. Hopefully I won't even need the month the king gave me." And hopefully Archer would have some answers about how he'd gotten on the king's list, and what *plans*, exactly, that the king had alluded to. Then she would figure out what to do with him.

Chaol stepped beside her, still staring at the filthy water, where the sack was undoubtedly now caught in the current and drifting out into the Avery River and the sea beyond. "I'd like to debrief you."

She raised an eyebrow. "Aren't you at least going to take me to dinner first?" His eyes narrowed, and she gave him a pout.

"It's not a joke. I want the details of what happened with Nirall."

She brushed him aside with a grin, wiping her gloves on her pants before heading back up the stairs.

Chaol grabbed her arm. "If Nirall fought back, then there might be witnesses who heard—"

"He didn't make any noise," Celaena snapped, shaking him off as she stormed up the steps. After two weeks of travel, she just wanted to *sleep*. Even the walk up to her rooms felt like a trek. "You don't need to *debrief* me, Chaol."

He stopped her again at a shadowy landing with a firm hand on her shoulder. "When you go away," he said, the distant torchlight illuminating the rugged planes of his face, "I have *no* idea what's happening to you. I don't know if you're hurt or rotting in a gutter somewhere. Yesterday I heard a rumor that they caught the killer responsible for Nirall's death." He brought his face close to hers, his voice hoarse. "Until you arrived today, I thought they meant *you*. I was about to go down there myself to find you."

Well, that would explain why she'd seen Chaol's horse being saddled at the stables when she arrived. She loosed a breath, her face suddenly warm. "Have a little more faith in me than that. I am the King's Champion, after all."

She didn't have time to brace herself as he pulled her against him, his arms wrapping tightly around her.

She didn't hesitate before twining her arms over his shoulders, breathing in the scent of him. He hadn't held her since the day she'd learned she had officially won the competition, though the memory of that embrace often drifted into her thoughts. And as she held him now, the craving for it never to stop roared through her.

His nose grazed the nape of her neck. "Gods above, you smell horrible," he muttered.

She hissed and shoved him, her face burning in earnest now. "Carrying around dead body parts for weeks isn't exactly conducive to smelling nice! And maybe if I'd been given time for a bath instead of being ordered to report *immediately* to the king, I might have—" She stopped herself at the sight of his grin and smacked his shoulder. "Idiot." Celaena linked arms with him, tugging him up the stairs. "Come on. Let's go to my rooms so you can debrief me like a proper gentleman."

Chaol snorted and nudged her with his elbow but didn't let go.

After a joyous Fleetfoot calmed down enough for Celaena to speak without being licked, Chaol squeezed every last detail from her and left her with the promise to return for dinner in a few hours. And after she let Philippa fuss over her in the bath and bemoan the state of her hair and nails, Celaena collapsed onto her bed.

Fleetfoot leapt up beside her, curling in close to her side. Stroking the dog's silky golden coat, Celaena stared at the ceiling, the exhaustion seeping out of her sore muscles.

The king had believed her.

And Chaol hadn't once doubted her story as he inquired about her mission. She couldn't quite decide if that made her feel smug, disappointed, or outright guilty. But the lies had rolled off her tongue. Nirall awoke right before she killed him, she had to slit his wife's throat to keep her from screaming, and the fight was a tad messier than she would have liked. She'd thrown in real details, too: the second-floor hall window, the storm, the servant with the candle . . . The best lies were always mixed with truth.

Celaena clutched the amulet on her chest. The Eye of Elena. She hadn't seen Elena since their last encounter in the tomb; hopefully, now that she was the King's Champion, the ancient queen's ghost would leave her alone. Still, in the months since Elena had given her the amulet for protection, Celaena had come to find its presence reassuring. The metal was always warm, as though it had a life of its own.

She squeezed it hard. If the king knew the truth about what she did—what she'd been doing these past two months . . .

She had embarked on the first mission intending to quickly dispatch the target. She'd prepared herself for the kill, told herself that Sir Carlin was nothing but a stranger and his life meant nothing to her. But when she got to his estate and witnessed the unusual kindness with which he treated his servants, when she saw him playing the lyre with a traveling minstrel he sheltered in his hall, when she realized whose agenda she was aiding . . . she couldn't do it. She tried to bully and coax and bribe herself into doing it. But she couldn't.

Still, she had to produce a murder scene—and a body.

She'd given Lord Nirall the same choice she'd given Sir Carlin: die right then, or fake his own death and flee—flee far, and never use his given name again. So far, of the four men she'd been assigned to dispatch, all had chosen escape.

It wasn't hard to get them to part with their seal rings or other token items. And it was even easier to get them to hand over their nightclothes so she could slash them in accordance with the wounds she would claim to have given them. Bodies were easy to acquire, too.

Sick-houses were always dumping fresh corpses. It was never

hard to find one that looked enough like her target—especially since the locations of the kills had been distant enough to give the flesh time to rot.

She didn't know who the head of Lord Nirall actually belonged to—only that he had similar hair, and when she inflicted a few slashes on his face and let the whole thing decompose a bit, it did the job. The hand had also come from that corpse. And the lady's hand . . . that had come from a young woman barely into her first bleeding, struck dead by a sickness that ten years ago a gifted healer could easily have cured. But with magic gone and those wise healers hanged or burned, people were dying in droves. Dying from stupid, once-curable illnesses. She rolled over to bury her face in Fleetfoot's soft coat.

Archer. How was she going to fake *his* death? He was so popular, and so recognizable. She still couldn't imagine him having a connection to whatever this underground movement was. But if he was on the king's list, then perhaps in the years since she'd seen him Archer had used his talents to become powerful.

Yet what information could the movement possibly have on the king's plans that would make it a true threat? The king had enslaved the entire continent—what more could he do?

There were other continents, of course. Other continents with wealthy kingdoms—like Wendlyn, that faraway land across the sea. It had held out against his naval attacks so far, but she'd heard next to nothing about that war since before she'd gone to Endovier.

And why would a rebel movement care about kingdoms on another continent when they had their own to worry about? So the plans had to be about *this* land, *this* continent.

She didn't want to know. She didn't want to know what the king was doing, what he imagined for the empire. She'd use this month to figure out what to do with Archer and pretend she'd never heard that horrible word: *plans*.

Celaena fought a shudder. She was playing a very, *very* lethal game. And now that her targets were people in Rifthold—now that it was *Archer* . . . She'd have to find a way to play it better. Because if the king ever learned the truth, if he found out what she was doing . . .

He'd destroy her.

DON'T MISS SARAH J. MAAS'S BESTSELLING

COURT OF THORNS AND ROSES SERIES

A COURT OF THORNS AND ROSES
SARAH J. MAAS
#1 NEW YORK TIMES BESTSELLING AUTHOR

A COURT OF MIST AND FURY
SARAH J. MAAS
#1 NEW YORK TIMES BESTSELLING AUTHOR

A COURT OF WINGS AND RUIN
SARAH J. MAAS
#1 NEW YORK TIMES BESTSELLING AUTHOR

SARAHJMAAS.COM